Also by Richard Moran

COLD SEA RISING

DALLAS DOWN

RICHARD MORAN

JOVE BOOKS, NEW YORK

This Jove Book contains the complete
text of the original hardcover edition.
It has been completely reset in a typeface
designed for easy reading, and was printed
from new film.

DALLAS DOWN

A Jove Book / published by arrangement with
Arbor House Publishing Company / William Morrow and Company, Inc.

PRINTING HISTORY
Arbor House edition published 1988
Jove edition / December 1990

ISBN: 0-515-10468-X

Jove Books are published by The Berkley Publishing Group,
200 Madison Avenue, New York, New York 10016.
The name "JOVE" and the "J" logo
are trademarks belonging to Jove Publications, Inc.

PRINTED IN THE UNITED STATES OF AMERICA

10 9 8 7 6 5 4 3 2 1

To Richard Moran, Sr.
This one's for you, Pop.

ACKNOWLEDGMENTS

I would first like to thank Ann Harris who, while she was editor-in-chief at Arbor House, nurtured *Dallas Down* from its conception. A writer cannot be more fortunate than to have Ann Harris as his editor.

I also wish to express my warm appreciation to Allan Mayer, whose astute editorial suggestions did much to hone my manuscript into a book.

Special thanks, too, to Glenna Goulet, the lady who prepares my manuscripts, does instant research, and who over the years has become not just a valued colleague but a dear friend. Thanks for believing, Glenna.

I am deeply grateful to my literary agent, Frederick Hill of San Francisco. Thanks for working so hard, Fred, and thanks for all the times your news was good.

I am indebted to James Curran and to Patrick Curran for their gracious encouragement and support while I wrote *Dallas Down*. I would add that Pat is the best researcher I've ever had the pleasure of working with.

Finally, I wish to thank my wife, Kathleen. Kathy is somehow simultaneously a wife, a mother, and a school-teacher, and is good at all three careers. She is also my first critic. Thanks for climbing all those hills with me, Kathy.

DAY ONE

APRIL 10, 1999

AN HOUR AFTER DAWN

The solitary bull stood sniffing the dry prairie wind at the brow of a long sweep of pasture, motionless but for the quivering of his nostrils and the flick of his tail against the cattle flies that pestered his dark cherry-red hide.

His stance was proprietary, like the lion on his savanna, proud and assured. Deference was his by due, and he expected it from every other living creature in his world.

Prince of Wales IV was the finest bull of his breed on earth, the preeminent scion of the Santa Gertrudis blood-line, an original cattle strain developed in south Texas.

The respect he engendered in humans was palpable to the great bull. He could sense it in the touch of his handlers and the quiet voices of the breeders who came from around the world to hunch over his fence and stare.

An exceptional bull will always excite cattlemen, make orators of laconic, hardscrabble ranchers. Yet Prince of Wales struck an even more universal chord.

He was, it was widely calculated, the most valuable animal on earth.

When the young bull was first put up for bid at the annual Amarillo livestock auction, there had been no question he'd sell high. But not the wildest speculation had approached the winning $16.4 million offer that came in anonymously over an open line from Dallas.

The staggering price and the mysterious reticence of the buyer made Prince of Wales the subject of a front-page story in *The Wall Street Journal* and a one-minute film clip on the *CBS Evening News*.

The animal had proven worthy of all expectations. The first generation he had sired were showing all the best characteristics of the Santa Gertrudis breed: they gained weight quickly on low-cost feed, they were subject to few diseases, and when they were butchered at an average of 1,050 pounds, their meat provided lean, economical cuts.

The value of his lineage established, a long and pampered life stretched ahead of Prince of Wales. He had only one obligation in his royal life, one function that justified his astronomical purchase price, his special pastures and feed, his private barn and doting handlers; he had to produce semen.

Twice a week, two weathered, wary ranch hands would patiently maneuver the highly strung bull into a custom-made squeeze chute where he was electroejaculated.

If Prince of Wales lived an average reproductive life, his semen would inseminate at least 160,000 cows. The stud fees he earned could be expected to triple or even quadruple his buyer's investment.

Left to breed normally, the animal could produce two hundred offspring at best, and there was always the chance that contact with a sick cow could pass disease. The risk was unthinkable. Prince of Wales had never been allowed to mount a female, never permitted to engage in a brief and brutish courtship of his own.

Still, when the hot morning wind brought the spore scent of a cow in season, his nostrils flared and his instinctive excitement was immediate and consuming.

He lowered his great head and snorted twin columns of dust into the arid air, his right front hoof pawing a shallow trench in the baked ground. Suddenly his corded muscles bunched under his loose hide and he shot forward, down the slope toward a herd of languidly grazing Santa Gertrudis cows.

The low-slung bull thundered ahead with a speed that belied his massive bulk. His hooves struck the hardened clay with rhythmic force, and the drought-parched earth vibrated with pile-driver echoes.

His eyes, his senses, were not on the field he crossed but fixed on the herd of cows beyond his fence. The spore scent of the fertile female grew stronger, more compelling, as he cut the distance between them.

The pasture surface before him was blurred beneath shimmering silver heat waves and, even if the charging bull hadn't been maddened by sexual frenzy, he could not have seen the pit that suddenly yawned open at the foot of the slope.

In seconds the mouth of the embryonic sinkhole widened from two to ten and then to twenty feet as the pounding approach of the huge animal's hooves shook loose the crumbling crust of soil at the lip of the abyss.

At the last moment Prince of Wales sighted the black patch directly before him. His front legs stiffened in instinctive terror and his heavy hindquarters thumped down to brake. Too late. Hardly slowing, the great bull slid over the edge of the shaft and smashed head first into the opposite wall.

For one long impossible moment he hung there, his horns embedded in the baked clay. Then, with a terrible primal bellow, the most valuable animal in the world plunged tumbling into the deep black bowels of the earth.

MIDMORNING

The Landsat E earth-mapping satellite passed east across the New Mexico border and began its computer-assigned sweep of a strip of central Texas 545 miles below.

The satellite was operated by the National Aeronautics and Space Administration. It had been sent up in 1997 to monitor the scores of sinkholes that had begun pocking the Texas terrain during the third year of the drought.

On board the Landsat, a cameralike device called a Thermatic Mapper surveyed the planet's upper crust as it passed beneath the probe's flight path. The infrared scanner focused seven simultaneous spectral bands of the earth's electromagnetic field into a single image and then instantly relayed the digital picture to manned ground stations.

Cavities in the crust produce "spectral signatures" that vary recognizably from the surface reflectivity of the surrounding solid ground. The sinkholes dotting Texas showed up on the Thermatic Mapper images like raisins in a tapioca pudding.

Scientists were familiar with the phenomenon of sinkholes appearing in a region during prolonged periods of arid weather. The craters form when the water table drops, draining water from limestone caverns a hundred feet or more underground. Without buttressing reservoirs of virtually incompressible water to equalize pressure against their sides, the caverns inevitably collapse, bringing down the earth above.

A deep stratum of limestone, up to six thousand feet thick in places, lay under Dallas and the surrounding area of east-central Texas. The limestone was formed by the accumulated remains of countless generations of tiny marine animals that lived in the seas that once covered the region.

A geographic area with limestone topography will inevitably have caverns underground because rainwater becomes slightly acidic as it percolates down through the soil. Over the millennia the corrosive water dissolves the calcium carbonate of which limestone is chiefly composed.

The Landsat had been in duty orbit almost twenty-eight months now, and to date it had pinpointed over three hundred sinkholes, either open or forming just below the surface.

What concerned geologists most was not the sinkholes that had already broken through the ground but the hidden pits on the verge of collapse. Dozens of times during the previous two years caverns had suddenly yawned open under buildings and highways, as well as under sewer, water, and electric lines.

The Landsat's infrared eye had picked up most of the forming sinkholes in time for authorities to evacuate inhabited structures and close threatened roads. Yet several smaller cavities had escaped detection until it was too late. In the past few months, two dozen homes and small commercial buildings around Dallas had suddenly disappeared into the honeycombed ground, taking twenty-three men, women, and children down to their dark deaths.

There was a technician on duty twenty-four hours a day at the Landsat ground station in Dallas. At the first indication of a new sinkhole forming in a populated area, an evacuation warning was sent immediately to state officials in the local region where the cavity was detected.

The satellite continued passing steadily east, and the technician monitoring the Landsat data noted that the probe was approaching the city limits west of Dallas. He was jotting figures in the duty log when the green screen before him flickered suddenly and a new, ominous image formed rapidly on the glowing tube.

The technician sucked in his breath and stared dumbfounded at the monitor. "Son of a bitch!"

He whirled toward the videophone and punched in a top-priority emergency number.

NOON

Almost a million people in the greater Dallas area were watching Herb Mueller have a nervous breakdown.

Most of the TV audience who tuned regularly to Channel 7's *News at Noon* took the meteorologist's dispirited delivery as natural—even expected—given the endlessly desolate weather he had to report day after day. Only a handful of viewers, who happened also to be behavioral scientists, recognized the telltale signs of deepening depression, and they kept the knowledge to themselves, assuming Mueller was already being treated.

So far the weatherman had picked up no spoken hints that anyone suspected his aberrant mental state, and he found no skeptical shadows when he searched the eyes of others. Still, he sometimes wondered without caring whether he'd been that good an actor over the past six hellish months.

He coughed and reached for the cigarettes on the cluttered stand in his dressing room. He'd been off the damn coffin nails for fifteen years. Now he needed them, and the pills, and the bottle in the bottom drawer. Without the jacks up and down, he knew the depression would overwhelm him, the hovering panic flood bile up his throat the moment he opened his mouth.

Yet even doubling his intake lately he'd felt the stimulants losing their effect. He couldn't face the cameras much longer.

"You using a new shampoo at home, Herbie?" The woman's voice behind him had a grating nasal tone.

Mueller lifted his eyes to meet the jowly face of the makeup woman pouting at him from the bulb-framed mirror.

"Hell, I don't know, Maxine. I think I've still got the stuff you gave me. I don't remember buying anything else."

Maxine clucked and fluttered a short, fat hand above Mueller's left sideburn. "You've either been using some caustic soap or you're aging alarmingly, Herbie. I did a tint job on you just last week. Tuesday. Already you need a touch-up. Gray hairs all through your temples."

The meteorologist tensed. He hated being called Herbie. Worse was the stolen intimacy, as if Maxine had snaked a hand down his pants and fondled him.

Maxine reached into her kit for the tint. "I'd better start ordering your color by the quart, Herbie."

Mueller felt the burst of heat that came with the sudden rages that seized him with increasing frequency the past few months. His fingers curled nails up painfully into his palms as he fought the near overpowering impulse to kill Maxine, to kill her with his bare hands.

"You goddamned bitch! Get out of my dressing room. *Get out!*"

The makeup woman recoiled at the sight of Mueller's hate-twisted face in the mirror. She realized she'd crossed a line. The "Herbie" bit had been deliberate, a taunt, one of the light lashes she habitually laid against the hides of the male TV personalities she painted each day.

"God, whatever I said, I'm sorry," Maxine said.

Mueller's words squeezed out tightly through his clenched teeth. "Don't ever call me Herbie again, Maxine. Never! Once more and I swear to God I'll rip your miserable head off."

"You got it, Herb," Maxine said, her face a remorseful mask. "Hey, really, I'm sorry."

The paroxysm ebbed in Mueller. He stabbed out his

cigarette in the brimming ashtray, the mound of butts spilling over his trembling fingers. The irrational outburst had frightened him more than it had Maxine. It terrified him that he was losing his grip.

He'd have to be more careful or the damn rumors would start: Mueller's going off the deep end. "Yeah, all right, Maxine. Just forget it. I shouldn't have blown up."

The fat makeup woman began to swab on the tint. "That crack about your gray hair was thoughtless. Hell, you know I'm one of your biggest fans. But I gotta tell you, I'm worried. You've looked kind of frayed around the edges the past few months. You sick or something?"

Mueller leaned forward and examined his teeth in the glass, needing the time to answer. He couldn't tell Maxine the truth, that his nerves were shot, that he was barely able to eat or sleep anymore, that the slightest sudden noise or imagined slight set him off. He couldn't tell Maxine he was falling apart, not unless he wanted the news all over the damn station in thirty minutes. Better a half-truth.

"Bad stomach, Maxine. Digestion's all screwed up. The divorce, I guess. Janet wants everything but the clothes on my back."

Saying it, he knew it was the other way around. His mounting depression had fueled the breakup with Janet. He'd become impossible to live with, ranting at her at the slightest provocation, sitting silent and sullen through meals, locking himself in his den with a bottle every weekend.

"Wives!" The never-married makeup woman snorted in empathy.

Mueller closed his eyes as Maxine raked a wet comb through his hair. It was his job that was the root of his malaise. Each day he found it more agonizing to go on the air and tell people it wasn't going to rain tomorrow, or the day after, or the week after. Probably not for the next month. Maybe not until the seasons changed. Maybe never, the way it'd been going.

Less than ten inches of rain had fallen in the Dallas area since the drought had begun in 1994. It was ironic that the sun that had mercilessly baked the Southwest for the past five years was also the root cause of the prolonged drought.

Meteorologists had known since the early 1980s that solar flares on the surface of the sun profoundly influenced the earth's weather. An area that experienced abnormally high rainfall during heightened solar activity would suffer drought during the following cycle when the surface of the sun was quiet. Conversely, a region thousands of miles away would be parched during solar flare-ups and deluged in rain in times of solar tranquillity.

The drought in the Southwest was all anyone living in Dallas talked about these days. The mercilessly hot, arid weather had withered life, changed everything.

Water had been strictly rationed for the last two years, ever since the emergency decree from Austin in 1997. More and more farms and ranches ceased food production as irrigation and water for livestock were cut to a trickle. In the urban areas, water-intensive manufacturing had been all but strangled, and unemployment was nearing thirty-five percent.

The very look of the land had altered in Texas. What were once green lawns, cultivated fields, and rangelands were now burnt spans of brittle stubble, and everywhere the arboreal skeletons of millions of leafless trees pointed accusingly at the cloudless sky.

What green foliage managed to survive was muted under cloying coats of gray-brown powder. Buildings, fences, cars, trees—anything that protruded above the blowing horizon—were cloaked alike in layers of fine grit.

Of all the drought's trials, the dust was the most maddening. It permeated everything, as pervasive as the very air, blowing through walls and windows into eyes and ears, drawn under the dental plates of the old and into the labored lungs of infants. The grit sifted into penile slits and vaginal recesses. It hurt men to urinate; women, to make love.

Personal water allowances had shrunk to the point where a bath or shower was impossible more than twice a week. Dry, chafed skin made clothes uncomfortable to wear. Tempers hung out raw as cracked dog tongues, and domestic turmoil flared in thousands of stifling homes. On the streets, minor traffic accidents incited murder, and the suicide rate had tripled.

And it fell to Herb Mueller to go before the cameras day after day and tell people their misery was not going to end, that the drought was not about to break.

Behind him, Maxine cleaned up and repacked her kit. The makeup woman formed her usual parting quip, thought better of it, and turned to leave.

"Tomorrow, Herb."

"Tomorrow, Maxine. Thanks."

Mueller reached into the back of the drawer for the vodka bottle the moment the door closed. He managed three quick shots before the assistant producer rapped and called through the frosted glass, "Five minutes to air, Herb."

Mueller lowered his face into his hands and sobbed.

LATE AFTERNOON

Sergeant Manuel Ortega almost fell out of the open door of the Russian half-track, he was laughing so hard at the punchline to Corporal Roca's *yanqui* joke.

Only at the last minute did the driver, Rodriguez, reach across and pull the hefty Ortega back into the cab, still roaring hilariously.

On the two tandem benches behind the command seat, the skinny corporal and five pimply teenage Mexican People's Revolutionary Army privates sprawled equally convulsed, great tears of laughter rolling down to plop on their khaki knees with each bump in the washboard road.

Ethnic jokes with Americans as the butt guaranteed a laugh in Mexico these days, the more derogatory the better. President Wilson performing sex acts with various farm animals was a popular theme. Quite natural, of course, given that the *yanquis* had become, if not yet actually the enemy, certainly a richly hated foe.

Relations between the two countries had plummeted when the Marxists were elected to power in Mexico City back in February 1992. But it wasn't until the drought took hold in 1994—amid bitter mutual accusations of secret water siphoning from the Rio Grande River—that ambassadors were recalled and the first armed skirmish was fought near the bridge at Laredo.

Surprising many, the UN had shown some spine and jumped in with a buffer force before the conflict got beyond the stage of light-arms fire and harassing overflights by military jets.

Things had been quiet for almost five years now. Yet the border remained tense, bristling. The clashes had left a score dead on both sides. Hot hate still burned across the barbed wire from Baja to the Gulf.

If no American bullets had crossed the border for the past year and a half, a great *yanqui* hand did—a hand that gripped Mexico with tightening fingers called economic sanctions.

The U.S. Department of Agriculture abruptly barred the import north of all fruits, vegetables, and cotton. Mexican agriculture, already a shambles after an abortive Marxist attempt at collectivization, virtually collapsed.

It was the small peasant farmers who suffered most. Crops that brought dollars in the States fetched only pennies in the quickly glutted local markets. With no money to buy food during the winter or seed for the spring, hundreds of thousands of poor Mexican families hovered on the brink of starvation.

Six months later Mexican industry was knocked to its knees when Washington barred the import of manufactured goods assembled south of the border. Computers, televisions, communications components, and—despite intense pressure from Japan and Europe—automobiles finished in Mexican plants were all forbidden access to American markets.

The Marxist regime had attempted to strike back with a total oil embargo against the northern imperialists. But it was a fruitless gesture. The advent of hydrogen fuel and the glut of oil on the market in the mid-1990s had drastically shrunk the U.S. demand for imported fossil fuel.

Worse than futile, the embargo had backfired. With no hard cash now coming in from her remaining petroleum customers in the States, Mexico's balance of payments

dipped deep into the red. Wary trading partners abroad
began to demand cash or goods in kind before they would
unload shipments in Mexican ports.

Even the massive Soviet aid program begun three months
after the Marxist takeover had not revived the prone
Mexican economy.

The Russian infusion of training cadres and state-of-
the-art military equipment had been far more effective.
While an American victory was unquestioned should war
break out, any U.S. armed incursion south would now cost
the *yanquis* dearly.

Most galling to Washington was the string of missile pads
stretching across northern Mexico. The Mexicans insisted
the launch sites were strictly antiaircraft defenses, yet as the
Pentagon pointed out, the missile pads were suspiciously
located opposite San Diego, Tucson, Santa Fe, Dallas, and
Houston.

So far U.S. intelligence had failed to uncover any evidence of nuclear warheads in the Mexican silos, but rumors
persisted that Mexican scientists were developing the weapons.

More disturbing, Prime Minister Martí was now negoti-
ating a mutual defense treaty with the Soviet Union. Word
had leaked out of Moscow that one of the provisions Martí
sought was the stationing of Russian missile-targeting
experts in Mexico.

Talk of surgical strikes against the Mexican missile pads
drifted through the Pentagon, but so far the doves had
outflown the hawks.

Sergeant Ortega turned from his joking men and pulled a
regional map from his patrol case. The unit had been
assigned the half-track because they would be crossing open
country today, patrolling a thinly populated stretch of
border along the Rio Bravo del Norte, as the Mexicans
called the Rio Grande. For several weeks, peasants had
been reporting strange noises during the night on the
American side of the river.

Ortega leaned across with the map and pointed out the
turnoff to the driver, Rodriguez. Then he sat back and

daydreamed of the promotion he would get next month. Lieutenant Ortega! His wife, Maria, had been right. It had been a wise career move to join the Communist Party, despite what the priest said.

Forty-five minutes later they reached the featureless map point and Ortega directed the driver out onto the mesquite- and cactus-studded hardpan that rolled north toward the U.S. border.

A mile off the secondary road, the half-track picked up a donkey-cart trail and followed the meandering ruts through the scrub and sandstone outcroppings. At dusk the patrol climbed a rise and paused above the tiny village of Quito. Beyond the settlement of adobe houses and woven mesquite sheep corrals, the Rio Bravo flowed broad with the spring flood, glistening in the late sun like a strip of foil laid across the dun desert.

Ortega waved his men out to stretch and urinate while he swept the village and the riverbanks with his binoculars. Satisfied, he called the patrol back, and the half-track bumped down the rocky slope.

A gaggle of shy, curious children with large black eyes and torn frocks flooded around the army vehicle as it lumbered to a stop beside the town well. Sergeant Ortega told his men to fall out and asked an older boy to take him to the home of the headman.

The toothless village leader shooed several goat kids from his one-room adobe house and offered the sergeant his best bent-willow chair. A moment later, the elder's wife appeared and scuffled over the dirt floor with a cracked gourd of homemade tequila. Ortega's eyes watered at the first taste of the fiery liquor, but he took time to sip the drink slowly and pass polite conversation about the crops and the animals before he began his questions.

Yes, the villagers had heard the strange noises for almost a month now, the headman confirmed. Always at night. Muffled explosions and what sounded like heavy machinery, perhaps earthmovers. Several times the *whop-whop-whop* of a helicopter came from the dark sky. And two women washing clothes in the river late one night reported

seeing lights and hearing *yanqui* voices along the opposite
bank.

The women were called in, and others who'd witnessed
unusual sounds and sights. Ortega listened patiently, gently
probing the timid people. An hour later, the sergeant was
satisfied that whatever the phenomenon across the river, it
was real enough, at least to the villagers.

Ortega assembled the patrol, and one of the women
who'd seen the lights guided the half-track slowly upstream
along the flooded lip of the Bravo. There was no drought in
the distant New Mexico mountains that gave birth to the
river, and the Bravo flowed three times as wide and twice as
deep as the trickle it would become by summer.

A quarter mile beyond the village, the woman signaled a
halt. There, across the water: there was the place the
yanquis were busy in the night.

The sergeant sent the woman back and reported his
position by radio to headquarters in Piedras Negras. Then
he told the men to leave their wallets and personal posses-
sions in the half-track and ordered the patrol down into the
brush along the bank: no smoking, keep quiet, listen.

For over an hour, the only sounds were the crickets and
the birds and the ripple of the river over the stones in its
bed. Then, just before dusk, they heard the clank of metal
against metal and a moment later the muted cough of a
diesel engine being started.

Ortega lifted his glasses. A quarter through his sweep of
the opposite shore he caught a diffused glow of lights
through the gathering darkness. An occasional stick shadow
blinked through the illumination as men passed in front of
the beams. He lowered the binoculars and stared pensively
across the four hundred yards of dark water. What were the
gringo bastards up to? Were they constructing a staging area
for an invasion? A missile emplacement? A tunnel under the
river, perhaps?

The sergeant's eyes narrowed. He meant to find out what
dirty work the *yanquis* did secretly in the night. He formed
his men into a skirmish line and waved the patrol forward
into the shallow river.

The Mexican army patrol had a sovereign right to cross halfway, to the exact borderline bisecting the river. Perhaps, two hundred yards closer, he might hear something, Ortega reasoned, a snatch of conversation, a signature sound that would tell him what kind of machinery was being used.

Twice, as the soldiers moved forward, one of the privates lost his footing on the slippery rock bottom and plunged under the swollen crest of the river. Their splashes sounded loud as cannon shots to Ortega. Both times he froze stock-still, his breath tight in his chest, straining to catch any reaction from the American side.

Were the *yanquis* on guard, listening? Had they heard? Despite the cool breeze running with the river, sweat coursed from the sergeant's pores.

Ten minutes later they reached what he judged to be the river's midpoint, the border. He signaled the skirmish line to halt. The channel here had a sand bottom and the Bravo flowed quickly by them, the current rippling against the chests of the men.

Two hundred yards upstream, four men in black wetsuits stood in the shadows of a cottonwood grove and strapped artificial gills to their backs. The gills were newly developed "hemosponges," polyurethane plastic foam mixed with oxygen-grabbing hemoglobin inside aqualung-size canisters. Like the gills of fish, the hemosponges drew oxygen directly from water, allowing divers to stay down almost indefinitely.

At a signal from their leader, the men crept forward and slipped one by one under the surface of the river.

Ortega's head whipped around at the sound of a barely audible splash somewhere upstream. Were the *yanquis* crossing the water to meet them? The river appeared empty in the fading light. He dismissed the splash and turned to listen for activity on the opposite bank.

As his hearing adjusted, the sounds from the shadowed American shore became more distinct. The diesel engine had a deep, throaty tone. Ortega judged the machine too powerful to be a simple bulldozer. What then?

He raised his binoculars once more. Now he could see

that the glow that had been visible from the Mexican shore came from a line of arc lights strung on high poles. Farther on to the left was a rectangular patch of white that might be a door or window. He could also make out several sets of headlamps stabbing paths through the deepening dark.

The sergeant started as a hand fell on his shoulder. "Do you see anything?" Corporal Roca whispered.

Ortega bent toward Roca's ear to reply. Before his first word, the ear disappeared—down, straight down with the corporal, as if Roca had suddenly been sucked through the river bottom.

Ortega stared dumbfounded at the widening circle of ripples next to him. Then he saw the blood rise to the surface, great frothy bubbles red against the black river.

He spun to his left as a startled cry came from the line of privates, then ended abruptly with a cut-off gurgle. The sergeant's head reeled. There was something in the river! Something was dragging his men down under the water and killing them!

"Fall back!" he screamed, his voice sounding far away in his ears. "Fall back to the bank!"

It was a futile order. Before his words had died away, three more privates disappeared into the river, their shrieks of horror sliced into silence as their heads plunged under the black water. The last three young Mexican soldiers were caught and yanked down before they'd retreated ten feet.

The only one alive now was Sergeant Ortega, and he knew he was about to die. He sensed the presence under the dark river a second before the twelve-inch knife flashed up between his legs, severing his scrotum and burying itself deep in his groin.

His death rattle, like the last gasps of his men, was muffled in the depths of the Rio Bravo del Norte.

DUSK

Black against black, the colony of two hundred thousand bats funneled up out of the jagged cave mouth and swooped into the still velvet of the new Texas night.

For generations the Mexican free-tailed bats had fed nightly on the bountiful suburban fruit trees and small orchards that thrived around Dallas before the drought. The orchards had withered and ceased producing fruit two years past when the ever-dwindling supply of water had forced the Texas Water Resources Board to forbid irrigation beyond the trickle needed to sustain the root systems of the trees.

The bats had adjusted. Now they fed from dumpsters, gorging each night on the spoilt produce of the Safeways and the Pick n' Runs and the loading docks where huge refrigerated trucks from California delivered fruit from the Imperial Valley.

The 7-Eleven chain had successfully driven off the scavengers for a time by hooking up high-voltage electrical lines to the steel bins behind its stores. Sixty thousand bats were electrocuted before the Dallas Humane Society caught wind of the scheme and got an injunction against the slaughter of the animals.

The stores and produce shippers had fought back, insist-

ing the bats were a pestilence, that their bites and droppings
could spread disease among the people of Dallas. For
eighteen months the Humane Society and the fruit vendors
had been tangled up in court. Meanwhile, the bats had
grown dependent on the reliable food source and came
nightly to the dumpsters like small winged pigs to the
trough.

The colony crossed the dark prairie at eight hundred feet,
their tongue-clicking sonar keeping each bat in its precise
place in the mass, then turned fluidly right a hundred yards
off Walton Walker Boulevard and flew soundlessly along-
side the ribbon of road lights.

The bats crossed three off-ramps without pause and then,
as one, wheeled south at the fourth exit and paralleled the
line of speeding cars below toward the sprawling Irving
Mall shopping center.

A formation of eight thousand bats peeled off over the
center and swooped down toward the dumpsters behind the
huge Safeway store, while the bulk of the colony continued
its flight toward other shopping centers to the south.

The smaller flight settled on the Safeway's bulging
dumpsters with squeals and clutching feet, scattering torn
cereal boxes and dented cans over the rim of the bins as they
dug into the garbage for fruit and vegetables.

From the rear door of the Safeway, a teenage boy
watched the feeding frenzy of the bats with morbid interest.
That morning he had palmed several bottles of snail bait
from the garden department and then spent his lunch hour
lacing boxes of spoiled fruit with the poison. He'd tossed
the toxic apples, oranges, and bananas into the dumpsters
before he went back to work.

A week before, he had overheard the store manager and
two executives from the Safeway regional office cursing the
courts for preventing the extermination of the bats. The boy
had seen a chance to become a hero. He'd kill the bats
himself, then bask in the praise of the grown-ups.

The idea of poisoning the bats came to him as he
restocked the garden department shelves. The boy couldn't
know the snail bait was too weak a poison to kill the

animals. Still, the bait was highly toxic, and as he watched, the bats began to gasp and lose their sense of balance.

The bat pups and pregnant females succumbed first, toppling paralyzed into the shifting refuse of the dumpster. The larger males clung tenaciously to the rim of the steel box, fighting the nerve spasms that jerked them like puppets strung from mad hands.

Perhaps a thousand of the animals that had eaten least made it back into the air. But it was a different air. Even the small amount of poison they had ingested was enough to glaze their large eyes and send their sonar haywire. They couldn't orient, couldn't find each other to swarm. In primal terror the bats beat their skin wings and fled up and away from the dumpster.

One after another the lights in the Safeway parking lot began to explode as stricken bats smashed into the bulbs. Others of the animals hurtled head first into storefronts, and the shoppers inside began to scream and cower in the aisles as rivulets of bat blood coursed down the cracked glass.

Only two hundred or so of the bats made it to the highway trail leading to their home cave. Yet their number was enough to wreak havoc on the road below. Dozens of the disoriented animals crashed into car windshields or swooped in through open windows. Within minutes a massive pileup of cars, trucks, and huge semis had completely blocked the Fort Worth highway.

When the toll was taken later that night, four people were dead, thirty injured, and west Dallas was in a state of panic.

EVENING

The President of the United States raced backward, the sweat drops spinning off his forehead and neck as he twisted to one side, then planted his feet and swung his racket viciously at the yellow ball hurtling at him across the net of the floodlit White House tennis court.

The ball careened out of bounds off the rim of his racket, and David J. Wilson cursed under his breath. Set point and he should have had it, would have had it if he'd been in shape. Too many damn state dinners with their rich food and incessant toasts. He resolved once again to have special low-calorie plates served to him from now on, and to have his wineglass filled with mineral water instead of California Chardonnay.

Across the net, Secretary of Defense Peter Beaudry grinned in triumph. "Another set, Mr. President?"

"I believe my ego's bruised enough for today, Peter," Wilson replied, only half in jest. This was something like the sixth time in a row that Beaudry had beaten him on the court, and there were moments in cabinet meetings when Wilson thought he detected a modicum of superiority in the way his defense secretary addressed him.

David Wilson was at the core a decent man, a fair man,

one who was ever ready to listen to another's argument and accept the logic of a contrary point of view.

From the start of his political career as a councilman in the small city of Hayward near San Francisco, Wilson had told the voters the truth, although he softened the edges of some of the harsher realities. His first two political advisers had seen his easy candor as a liability in politics and tried unsuccessfully to imbue in him the doublespeak tactics employed by so many politicians.

His guileless approach had made him a success at his general contracting business before he entered politics, and his up-front style had served him well with the voters. A lifelong Democrat, he'd won six straight elections over the past eighteen years, rising from councilman to state senator in Sacramento, then congressman and U.S. senator, and finally to election as President of the United States in 1996.

The President walked to the sidelines and eased his five-foot-ten 180-pound frame down into a canvas camp chair. The court attendant handed him a towel, and he took off his glasses and swabbed the sweat from his face and hair.

Wilson was the first bearded president since Benjamin Harrison. His brown hair, mustache, and beard were streaked with gray and, after almost three years as president, new facial lines had joined the smile wrinkles around his hazel eyes.

The President put his glasses back on and looked up as an aide opened the wire mesh gate and hurried across the court.

"I'm sorry to interrupt your game, Mr. President," the aide said.

"You're not interrupting, Bob," Wilson said. "Secretary Beaudry just finished beating me again."

"Actually, you beat yourself, Mr. President," Beaudry said, coming around the net post. "You weren't back in time to set your feet properly."

"Thank you for pointing that out, Peter," the President replied. "Perhaps we could arrange for you to give me a lesson or two."

"I'd be happy to, Mr. President." The blond, wispy-haired Beaudry had totally missed the edge of irritation in Wilson's voice.

There was a touch of sanctimony in Beaudry that occasionally irked the President, but the secretary's always-direct criticisms were honest and well-meant, and he was a good balance to the sycophants that surrounded the Oval Office.

Wilson looked at his aide. "What is it, Bob?"

"Kate Levesque is here from NASA, sir. She's brought some photographs from our Landsat in duty orbit over the drought area in the Southwest. We've got a problem, Mr. President. A big problem."

Wilson smiled. "I can't remember any small problems being brought to the Oval Office, Bob."

Five minutes later the President, still in his tennis clothes with a towel around his neck, was sitting behind his large rosewood desk as Kate Levesque was ushered through the Oval Office door.

"Thank you for seeing me on such short notice, Mr. President," she said by way of greeting.

"Not at all, Kate. It's always refreshing to have someone besides a politician, a reporter, or a special-interest advocate walk through that door." The President gestured for her to sit down, then leaned forward to turn on a Tiffany lamp.

"I doubt I shall be as welcome after I give you the news I carry, Mr. President."

"We don't slay the messenger who bears bad tidings anymore, Kate." Wilson smiled. "Although I admit to the temptation at times. What's this problem in the Southwest my aide tells me about?"

"The drought has caused a critical situation in the Dallas area, sir," Levesque said. She snapped open her briefcase, pulled out a folder of eight-by-ten color photographs, and handed them across the desk to Wilson.

"These are from the Landsat monitoring the drought area?"

"Yes, Mr. President. I've numbered them in chronological order. One through five were taken six months ago over Dallas."

Wilson scanned the pictures. The geometric shapes of the buildings and man-made structures of the Texas city were centered in the photographs. Thin lines of highways radiated out from the urban center and were bisected by a web of smaller roads and streets serving the metropolitan area and its suburbs.

The drought-parched earth around the city was pictured in hues of brown ranging from mustard to dark chocolate. Here and there small black spots dotted the landscape.

"May I call your attention to the prairie area around the city, Mr. President?" Levesque said. "Specifically, to the darker blotches. Those black circles are sinkholes that have already opened through the earth. The dark yellow to coffee-colored patches are subterranean caverns now forming in the limestone strata beneath the region."

The President nodded. He was familiar with the escalating problem of the sinkholes around Dallas. Journalists at several of his recent news conferences had peppered him with questions about the federal government's response to the phenomenon. Local congressmen had twice petitioned the White House to declare Dallas a disaster area and make federal relief money available.

Levesque handed the President a second series of photographs. "Shots six through ten were taken approximately a month ago."

Wilson studied the photographs one by one, glancing occasionally at the first series for comparison. "Looks like the number of sinkholes has more than doubled," he said.

"Tripled, Mr. President. And if you'll notice, most of the cavities fringing the city are considerably larger than the sinkholes that first opened six months ago."

"Yes, I can see that."

Levesque hesitated a moment, and Wilson sensed she was steeling herself. Her eyes met the President's, and she handed him the last set of pictures across the large desk. "I received these an hour and a half ago. I believe the Landsat images speak for themselves."

The President's eyebrows knit as he examined the latest photographs from space. Black specks and large dark scars now splattered the prairie area. In several areas, the dusky hues that indicated forming sinkholes had merged into huge chocolate blemishes.

Wilson noticed something else. The sinkholes now surrounded the city of Dallas.

The President laid the photographs on his desk and sank back glumly against his chair. "What's your prognosis, Kate? Is there any chance the ground will stabilize down there?"

"Virtually none, Mr. President. The water table in the Ogallala aquifer continues to drop rapidly beneath central Texas. New sinkholes are opening daily around Dallas and existing pits are merging, forming huge new cavities."

"Then we're facing the threat that sections of the city could collapse, that some of those eighty- and hundred-story skyscrapers may sink into the prairie?"

"It is not merely a threat, it is a certainty. And it's not just scattered sections of the city that are imperiled. Our analysts have gone over the Landsat data a hundred times and their projections remain the same. A monstrous cavity is rapidly forming under the metropolitan area of the city. Dallas must be evacuated as quickly as possible."

Wilson sat stunned. "Evacuated? Good God, Kate, you're talking about a major American city, the hub of commerce, communication, and finance for our entire Southwest. Millions of people would have to be uprooted and moved, Lord knows where."

"We have no choice, Mr. President. None. Our scientists are in unanimous agreement about what's coming. In five days, the ground beneath the city will collapse. Sometime after dawn on April fourteenth, Dallas, Texas, will disappear into the earth."

DAY TWO

APRIL 11, 1999

9:00 P.M.

Major Demyan Turgenev was deep in the wet dream of Ilona that came almost every night when the violent sound of erupting vomit suddenly shattered the dark quiet of his barracks room.

He gasped awake and stiffened under the coarse Russian army blankets, adrenaline and fear surging through him. His disoriented senses probed the night for the threat, straining out like a picket line against the vile terror.

Motionless, a stale breath tight in his chest, the thirty-four-year-old Turgenev listened from his bed in the transient officers quarters at Alkimov Military Airport outside Moscow.

Again, louder now, the obscene sequence built in the hall: a crescendoing retch climaxing in the flat splatter of lumpy liquids on the tile floor.

Turgenev's blue eyes flew fully open as a body slammed heavily against his door and slid slowly down the face. Torn gasps and a terrible stench knifed in through the thin slats.

Turgenev broke out in a cold sweat. He couldn't remember slipping the bolt back in place when he'd returned from the latrine in the night. The door was unlocked. Fat oily drops popped from the pores in his armpits and ran in chill rivulets down his sides to the sheet.

He rose up on his elbows as the drunk sobbed a thick lament against the wood. "No more, no more. I'll kill the sergeant . . . cut off his balls . . . then I'll go home. . . ."

So it was a recruit outside. Probably drunk on antifreeze from one of the tanks. Half the radiators in the Soviet tank divisions were dry these days—and half the enlisted tankers drunk.

He drew his feet from the blankets and sat tautly on the edge of the bunk. Drunken privates had been known to kill. They were driven to it by the brutal Russian military system that punished and dehumanized the lower ranks with harsh discipline, a pittance in pay, and stingy leave.

Men seethed in impotent rage, some just a cross word away from violence, a few just a bottle of vodka from murder. Only last week a drunken recruit had avenged an order to scrub the officers' toilets by decapitating his lieutenant with a fire ax.

Turgenev listened tightly for several minutes as the drunk outside labored to refill his lungs, drawing long wet breaths that hissed in through his lips like sucked soup.

Then a hand slapped high on the door and he heard a belt buckle rasp against the slats as the man pulled himself up. A moment later the *thump-thump* of stumbling steps sounded in the hall, a slow slap of thick army boots fading toward the latrine.

There was a final raucous rise of dry heaves, then silence once more as the iron fire door of the shithouse clanged shut.

Turgenev lay slowly back in bed. As the threat passed, his adrenal glands stopped secreting. His breathing calmed, and his senses eased off from sentry duty.

Yet as the fear ebbed, his anger rose. Anger at the drunk for waking him, for fouling his dream of Ilona with his fetid puking. Anger most of all at the leaden shame he felt. He'd been afraid, terrified of a common drunk in the night. His long-held assessment of himself as a coward had been starkly reaffirmed. There'd never been a time when the slightly built Turgenev had felt himself brave, not since his earliest days as a boy adroitly avoiding the schoolyard fights in which his friends pummeled one another.

An ironic thought crossed his mind. What would the Mexicans think, the consummately macho Mexicans, were they to learn that the vaunted senior Russian missile targeting officer about to be assigned to their Northern Mexico Missile Command headquarters in Chihuahua had never had a fistfight in his life. At 9 A.M. Moscow time he was to be on the daily nonstop Aeroflot flight from Moscow to Mexico City.

He let a long sigh into the night. Mexico. Eight thousand miles from Ilona. Ilona, ever in his thoughts but never in his bed.

Except in the dream. The dream was always the same. It was of the time they had been alone together for two ecstatic days and nights in Ilona's sister's apartment in Odessa.

They'd made love every few hours in the huge antique brass bed her sister bought on the black market. They'd brushed lips and hands and cooed baby talk into each other's ears, their ardor never cooling through the warm days and nights.

He closed his eyes and pictured Ilona on her stomach on the goosedown comforter, her breasts and mound of Venus enticingly demure in the quilted valleys. He'd softly massaged her back and melon hips while she ran her fingers lightly up the underside of his member.

It had been eight months now since Odessa and still he could feel her touch, warm and electric wherever her fingers strayed, capable of bringing him to incredible heights of arousal. He saw her again as she'd turned over on the quilt and he'd bent to bring her nipples erect in his mouth. Then down her stomach to the soft triangle of auburn hair between her legs. How she'd loved his kisses there, and he the taste of her.

Slowly Major Demyan Turgenev felt his fears fall away as he drifted back into the dream of Ilona.

5:30 A.M.

The fingers of Lucia Sanchez were pale talons against the black steering wheel, bloodless and numb from their long relentless grip on the cracked plastic ring. Lucia sat stiffly forward on the tattered seat, driving the tired pickup mechanically, motionless but for the arc of her arms through the turns.

Her high-cheeked, oblong face was strained with fatigue and worry. Dark pouches lay beneath her black eyes, and her full, sensuous lips were pressed together in a hard line of anxiety. Her black hair, which normally hung to her shoulders in a luxuriant fall, was matted with a paste of dirt and sweat.

Lucia was only peripherally conscious of the road, her senses focused instead back over the miles and hours to the place she'd left. She could still picture her brother, Paco, as she'd last seen him almost forty-eight hours before, his ten-year-old face lost in concentration as he peered down into the depths of the sinkhole that had opened in the barren orchard in front of their home.

Sinkholes had begun pitting the Texas prairie when Paco was six, and the boy had become fascinated by these mysterious deep holes in the ground. He'd learned to read quickly, Lucia was convinced, because he so desperately wanted to read the newspaper stories, articles, and books written about sinkholes.

At the age of seven, a serious-faced Paco had announced at the dinner table that he intended to become a speleologist when he grew up. Lucia and their mother, Ana, had solemnly agreed that it was a fine idea, then Lucia went to look up the word in the dictionary. Paco wants to be a cave scientist, an explorer underground, she'd told Ana.

Two days past, Lucia had worriedly watched her brother for a while as he patiently paced off the distance around the rim and then lowered a rock-weighted measuring string into the dark hole. Reluctantly, she'd finally turned away and gone to the chicken shed in back to butcher an old hen for the week's meat. When she came around to the front again twenty minutes later, Paco was gone.

She'd fought back the panic that had risen in her throat. Perhaps the boy had returned to the house early for lunch. Their mother was rolling tortilla shells and humming to herself when Lucia came in. Yes—the flour-flecked Ana had smiled—Paco had come in to get the flashlight. He wanted to see the bottom of the hole.

The look of horror that crossed her daughter's face brought Ana to her feet, her hand clutching her throat. "Mother of God. The hole."

Lucia had raced out across the orchard to the pit, Ana stumbling and weeping along behind her.

"Paco!" Lucia had cried as loud as she could down into the dark abyss. There had been no reply, not to her first call or to the others she screamed until she was hoarse.

She had called the sheriff in the nearby town of Rocksprings, and an hour and a half later the county rescue team arrived in a swirl of sirens and dust.

Two men had descended on ropes, then been winched back an hour later. Paco had not fallen. The walls of the sinkhole funneled inward. They'd found the long scar left by the boy's butt and feet as he'd slid down the steep slope.

His footprints were all over the bottom. He'd been upright, moving about, apparently unhurt.

Vexation had raged in Lucia, but she'd forced her voice to be calm. "Then where is he? Where is my brother?"

Morris Foster, the rescue team leader, had trouble meeting her eyes as he told her. A wide lateral tunnel bisected the bottom of the pit. It was the now-dry course of a subterranean stream. The sinkhole had undoubtedly formed as the drought emptied the channel of water and the ground above collapsed into the empty tunnel below.

The sinkhole was on a direct line with two other pits on the lands of neighbors. Foster was all but certain that the streambed under the Sanchez fields was the north fork of an ancient subterranean river that stretched 450 miles from near Dallas in central Texas to northern Mexico.

Spanish conquistadors had first discovered the underground river in the seventeenth century and named it the Rio Bajo la Tierra, the river under the earth. In millennia past, the Rio Bajo had coursed with trillions of gallons of sweet water. But over the centuries the flow had steadily decreased as the climate of the Southwest became semi-arid. It had finally ceased altogether during the current drought.

The riverbed forked repeatedly into separate channels, some cutting far below the main stream, others a mile or more to the sides.

Foster had followed Paco's tracks almost a mile into the tunnel leading northeast before losing the boy's trail on a stretch of rock floor. The cave divided into three tunnels just beyond. Paco could be anywhere in a labyrinth of hundreds of miles of underground tunnels and shafts.

More searchers had been summoned from town, and for the next two interminable days team after team had descended into the pit. They'd brought in bloodhounds, lowering the whimpering dogs in harnesses. But the dust stirred by the searchers had clogged the animals' noses and the handler finally gave up.

Except for a few hours' sleep, Lucia kept a constant vigil at the sinkhole. Shortly after three in the morning on the third day, she'd overheard a dispirited volunteer talking to Foster.

"Morris, without the dogs we ain't got a prayer of finding

that kid alive. Not without Heff. We gotta get Heff over here."

Foster had shaken his head. "Heff doesn't cave anymore, Billy. You know that as well as me. Not after what happened in Spanish Cavern."

"Maybe he'd come—you know, it being a kid an' all."

"Forget it," Foster had said. "I've talked to him twice since his partner got killed. Whatever happened that day in Spanish Cavern, it changed Heff. He told me he'll never go down again, and I believe him."

"Goddamned shame. . . ." Billy's voice had trailed off.

Lucia had confronted Foster a few minutes later. "Who is this Heff? Could he really help?"

"Jedediah Heffernan, miss. He used to be the best damn spelunker in the Southwest. Maybe the best cave-rescue man in the country. Heff's found people lost underground where fifty men with dogs before him tried and failed."

"Then send for him, Mr. Foster."

"Wouldn't do any good. Like I said to Billy, Heff doesn't cave anymore. As far as I know, he hasn't been down once in the past four or five years. Not since his partner got killed on their last descent."

"I'll ask his help myself. I'll beg if I have to. Do you know how I can reach him?"

"He has a ranch outside a little town called Hondo over in New Mexico. You can call him, but I'm telling you all you're going to get for your trouble is a phone hung up in your ear. I've asked Heff's help twice since that accident in Spanish Cavern. He's turned me down flat both times."

"I won't make it so easy for him to say no, Mr. Foster. I'm going to ask him face to face to save my brother. How long will it take me to get to Hondo?"

Twenty minutes later, Lucia was on her way.

Now, after two hours on the road, she barely noticed the town names as they flashed past in the dark: Senora, Ozona, Sheffield.

Every few miles her mind would flit from the scene at the sinkhole to her coming confrontation with Jedediah Heffernan. She wondered whether he was old or young,

pleasant or nasty. Would he be a redneck racist who'd
refuse out of hand to search for a Mexican-American boy,
or a sexist who'd talk down to her as he leered at her body?

Twice Heffernan had turned down Foster's calls for help.
He could not be moved by the mere issue of a life at stake.
What then? Money? How much could she raise? Their
three-room adobe home was little more than a hovel. Yet
the house was surrounded by 140 acres of farmland. The
fields were baked bare now, the orchards withered in the
grip of the drought. Still, when the rains returned the land
would once again bloom with fruit trees. Twice the wealthy
rancher who owned the huge neighboring spread had tried
to buy them out. His first bid had been $80,000, his second
$100,000.

She could offer Jedediah Heffernan $100,000 to find
Paco. Was the money enough? What if he wanted something more to search for her brother? What if he wanted her?

At twenty-six, Lucia Sanchez had never come close to
marrying. Her father had bled to death after a harvester
chewed off his arms in a cornfield when she was sixteen.
There had been no insurance, and government assistance
provided only a pittance for Lucia, her Spanish-speaking
mother, Ana, and her newly born brother, Paco.

It had fallen to Lucia to provide. Her straight-A marks
allowed her to skip a grade and graduate a year early from
high school. She'd gone to work in the Rocksprings hospital
as a night orderly. During the day she attended nursing
school, and two years later she was an RN.

Lucia had never forgotten that her father had died
because there was no medical care near enough their rural
farm. After completing her training, she'd volunteered to
work in a small medical clinic serving mostly sick and
injured Chicano field workers outside Rocksprings.

She'd enrolled in university courses at night while she
worked at the clinic, determined to go on and become a
doctor serving the neglected farmers of rural Texas.

Then the drought struck, farms and orchards withered,
workers and farmers drifted away, the clinic closed, and
Lucia lost her job. She continued to study at night,

squeaking through on scholarships and dishwashing jobs that kept her on her feet until midnight in the student union.

Men were drawn to Lucia, and she dated occasionally, when she wasn't studying, or working, or just too bone-tired. Most of the men she went out with she found immature, either all macho and little mind or all mind and little macho: boys anxious to prove their strength or seeking the shelter of hers.

Lucia had formed relationships with two men, one the doctor who took her virginity and left for California six months later, and the other a Mexican field foreman with a good face and gentle eyes whom she'd taught to read and who taught her passion in return.

Lucia glanced at her watch in the dim glow of the dashboard lights. Two and a half more hours. She would arrive at the ranch of Jedediah Heffernan early in the morning.

DAWN

The richest man in America banked his sleek Lear jet against a dawn parade field of pink cirrocumulus clouds and began his descent toward the sprawling complex of buildings, silos, and corrals that comprised the headquarters of the Ralt ranch on the still-shadowed prairie below.

The obscene wealth of Otto Ralt was mirrored in his toys. He collected gold-plated guns and diamond-studded daggers. He owned planes and helicopters, antique cars, teak-decked yachts, and palatial playhouses on four continents.

Yet of all he owned, the possession he most valued was his great Santa Gertrudis bull, Prince of Wales IV. He'd purchased the bull at auction three years before, and it wasn't long before he'd come to see in Prince of Wales the animal replica of himself.

Ralt found the parallels mystic: where he was the wealthiest human in the country, Prince of Wales was the most valuable animal; where his presence engendered timid deference in others, the bull's majestic bearing inspired awe; where the man spent his seed in women all over the world, the animal's issue was implanted in cows on every continent.

Ralt saw the great bull as he saw himself, a ruler in his

own world, immutable and immortal, and he could no more consider the death of the animal than he could admit the possibility of his own end.

The news that Prince of Wales had perished in the depths of a sudden sinkhole had reached Ralt at a business meeting in Riyadh, Saudi Arabia. The death of his great bull had struck at Ralt's very core, shocked him as had no other event since the traumatic realization of his family's poverty during his boyhood.

He'd been so obviously stunned that several business associates had urged him not to fly back to Dallas immediately. Otto Ralt rarely took advice, and he shunned it this time. He'd chartered a long-range jet and flown to Miami International Airport, then picked up the plane he'd left there and rushed back to Texas.

The plane lowered on its glide path. At five thousand feet Ralt's handsome colonnaded house took shape and behind it a hodgepodge of barns, shops, bunkhouses, and outbuildings.

He came in fast, too fast, the fury raging in him over the loss of Prince of Wales fueling recklessness, and the jet set down hard onto the concrete runway and drifted dangerously from side to side.

A cold rancor settled over Ralt as he fought to regain control of the swaying aircraft. If, before, he'd harbored the slightest inclination to spare Madero, his keeper of the bulls, that shadow of mercy dissipated along with the smoke pouring off the jet's screaming tires.

Ralt taxied to the tarmac lip of the runway and shut down the engines in front of a cavernous hangar that housed his private fleet of aircraft. Before the whine of the Pratt & Whitney turbines had died away, a motorized boarding ramp was wheeled up against the plane and an open jeep gunned across the concrete and pulled to a stop at the foot of the metal stairs.

Ralt ignored the ground crew as he thundered down the steps two at a time and hefted his 220 pounds into the front passenger seat of the jeep.

"Welcome home, Mr. Ralt," ranch foreman Bill Edwards said from behind the steering wheel.

For a moment Ralt stared wordlessly through the dusty windshield, a sheen of sweat glazing the hairless dome of his large head and trickling in rivulets down his jowly face. Then he turned his hard hazel eyes to Edwards. "Where's Madero?" he said without preamble, his thick lips tight against his teeth.

Edwards wanted to say something in defense of his friend Madero. It had been a mistake, a terrible, fatal mistake, to let Prince of Wales out into his enclosure when there were cows in season pastured in the near field. Even if the sinkhole had not opened to swallow the great bull, the animal would surely have injured himself against the fence in his frenzy to get at the sexually ripe females.

Yet Madero swore he hadn't been told that a herd of cows had been moved into the abutting field at dawn. He'd fed the bull just after first light, hand-mixing the special feeds as usual, then brought Prince of Wales into his wide pen for his morning exercise and sun. Standing inside the barn, Madero had neither seen nor heard the cows grazing four hundred yards away down the slope.

Edwards believed him. He wanted to plead with Ralt to remember the long and faithful service Madero had given. From the day Ralt had bought the bull three years ago and assigned Madero as guardian, the faithful keeper had devoted himself mind and soul to the well-being of his charge.

Madero had seen to the needs of the bull day and night, sacrificing evenings and weekends with his family to attend to the animal, twice moving into the barn when Prince of Wales went off his feed and showed signs of illness.

Edwards wanted to say all this, but he didn't. His dark eyes flashed behind his glasses but he kept his own counsel, just as he'd bitten his tongue a dozen times past when he'd witnessed the injustice of Otto Ralt. He stayed quiet because he was nearing forty and had three children under ten at home and no skill save running a ranch, and in these drought years there just weren't a hell of a lot of jobs out there for guys like him. Sometimes a man had to eat shit to feed his kids.

"He's in the bull pasture, Mr. Ralt," Edwards said instead. "He's been sitting at the edge of that sinkhole all day and all night, crying and calling down to the Prince. I left a man with him to make sure he didn't throw himself in."

"No, that would be too easy, too quick," Ralt said.

"Beg your pardon?"

"I called Naturalization from the plane. Their people will be here within the hour. I want you to give them Madero."

Disbelief twisted Edwards's range-weathered face. "Mr. Ralt, Demetrio's got his whole family up here. Seven kids, his parents, his wife's grandfather, a couple of nieces. None of them has papers. The INS will send the whole family back."

Ralt continued to stare through the windshield. "Take me to the command center."

A sick dread welled up in Edwards's gut. Just this once, for Demetrio, he would shed the cloak of caution. "You know what will happen to them down there, Mr. Ralt. Every little town in Mexico's got its Marxist fanatics, its informants. When they find out who Demetrio worked for up here, they're going to make it rough on him and his family. Real rough."

Ralt turned wordlessly, and Edwards saw in his eyes the finality of Madero's fate. The foreman's shoulders drooped. He threw the jeep in gear and started across the runway.

The powerful will that stilled Bill Edwards had propelled Otto Ralt from the poverty of a west Texas farm to the boardrooms and salons of the super rich. It was the poverty of his father that drove him.

Jacob Ralt had been a singularly inept farmer who'd never been able to earn more than six or seven thousand dollars a year from his eighty dusty acres northeast of Lubbock. There'd been years when drought or hail or insects had wiped out entire plantings and the Ralts had been forced to accept charity from relatives, neighbors, or, most debasing of all, county welfare.

Ralt took his family's poverty as a personal disgrace, a stigma that separated him from his schoolmates with successful fathers. Boys who came from money had barber haircuts and baseballs with all the stitches and wore clothes no one had worn before. Girls with rich daddies nibbled at crustless white-bread sandwiches at lunch and had big bubbly laughs, not like the shy, short giggles poor girls tittered behind their hands.

Oil was the fountainhead of wealth in west Texas when Otto Ralt was growing up in the late 1950s. Oil was what bought new baseballs and gave girls radiant laughs. From the day the why of things first dawned on him in the third grade, Otto Ralt set his course on the star that hung over the oil business.

The jeep passed the turnoff to the Santa Gertrudis barn, and Edwards stole a glance at his billionaire boss. Ralt stared hard toward the barn for a moment, but he said nothing and the foreman never slowed the jeep.

Ralt took every college entrance course he could in school, studied hard, and won a scholarship to Texas A&M. Three years later he graduated at the top of his class with a degree in petroleum geology.

A week out of college he accepted a job with Texas Oil, the largest privately owned energy-producing company in the country. Ralt then began an unrelenting procession of eighty-hour weeks, and a steady rise to the top. By the age of twenty-six he was a vice-president of Texas Oil. Yet still his pace upward was not rapid enough for Ralt. He saw a faster way to the top, and he took it. He married Rebecca Wainscott.

Rebecca Wainscott excited neither love nor lust in the young Otto Ralt. Her Calvinist upbringing was reflected in her humorless face, and her unblinking eyes saw only black and white in a world she gazed upon with disapproval. She'd grown up graceless, a tall gawking weed amid the cheerleader flowers that bloomed around her. Before Otto Ralt began his pursuit of her hand, she'd never been kissed beyond the pecks of her parents and relatives on her worry-furrowed forehead.

Yet if Rebecca Wainscott was bereft of loveliness, she was surfeit with lineage. The Wainscotts were a pioneer

Texas family, socially solid, and—of greatest moment to Otto Ralt—her father, Rupert, was chairman and majority stockholder of Texas Oil.

Two years after his marriage to Rebecca, Ralt was president and chief operating officer of Texas Oil. When his father-in-law died six years later, Otto Ralt, now thirty-four, took control of a company with a net worth of almost four billion dollars.

The first thing Ralt did when he took over was to start moving Texas Oil out of the oil business. Far before most of his fellow oilmen, he had seen the handwriting that had begun to appear on the wall in the early 1980s.

With the mushrooming development of industry in the Third World, particularly Asia and South America, an ever-mounting tonnage of carbon dioxide and particulate matter was being spewed into the atmosphere each year from the burning of fossil fuels.

Over the past century, the volume of carbon dioxide in the air had increased almost 20 percent, and the level was rising steadily year after year. Authorities around the world were reporting the first indications of the "greenhouse effect."

A cellular telephone on the dashboard of the jeep began to beep insistently, and Edwards reached for the receiver. "It's the command center, Mr. Ralt."

"Tell them I'll be there in five minutes. I want that report on the incident with the Mexican patrol ready when I come down."

"Yes, sir," Edwards said, and repeated the message into the phone.

The gases in the upper atmosphere of the earth—especially carbon dioxide—act like the glass roof of a greenhouse, allowing light from the sun to pass through the layers of ozone, carbon dioxide, water vapor, and clouds but trapping much of the heat that builds up as a result, which would otherwise radiate outward.

The more carbon dioxide released into the atmosphere, such as by the use of combustible fuels, the more heat the "glass" of the greenhouse traps, and the warmer the earth becomes. In the three years between 1990 and 1993, average temperatures around the world had risen over 2 full degrees, twice the increase recorded during the entire previous century.

Glaciologists saw a dire scenario ahead for the earth. A rise in mean temperatures of just 2½ to 3 degrees more, the scientists warned, could bring on a meltdown of the world's glaciers and polar ice. Inevitably, the oceans would rise and flood the coasts.

America, Europe, Japan, and China were imposing ever stricter, ever more expensive emission controls on their industries and automobile manufacturers, only to see the planet's atmosphere grow dirtier year after year as Third World nations, unable to afford expensive pollution controls, flooded the air with wastes from their burgeoning factories.

What the world desperately needed was a cheap, environmentally benign source of energy. Otto Ralt saw the answer in hydrogen fuel.

Hydrogen is lightweight, nonpolluting, and obtainable from water. The gas burns more efficiently than fossil fuels and by weight contains almost three times more energy.

Scientists had long been able to extract hydrogen from water by a process called electrolysis. Like a car battery, the system employs both a positive and negative electrode immersed in water that has been made conductive by the addition of salts, acids, or other electrolytes. When an electric current passes between the terminals, water molecules are split into their component hydrogen and oxygen.

The drawback to producing hydrogen fuel by electrolysis had always been economic. The cost of the fossil fuel that had to be burned to generate the necessary electric current was far above the value of the hydrogen fuel that was produced.

Water could also be split into hydrogen and oxygen by beaming light directly onto the system in a process termed photolysis. But the light-to-hydrogen conversion efficiency had traditionally been so low that photolysis had simply not been commercially viable during the early years of experimentation.

The first breakthroughs came in the early 1980s when scientists fabricated photolysis systems using single-crystal semiconductors as electrodes. When the newly developed electrodes were immersed in dilute sulfuric acid, a small external electrical charge applied, and light then beamed on the system, hydrogen and oxygen were produced abundantly.

Although the conversion rates of the early light-to-hydrogen systems were only in the 10- to 15-percent range, Otto Ralt had seen great promise in the emerging hydrogen fuel technology. What mattered more, Ralt was willing to risk everything he had that he was right.

The jeep approached two dust-cloaked ranch hands replacing fence posts along the road. The men spotted Ralt's distinctive huge bald head through the windshield and stood with their hats in their hands in sullen respect as the jeep passed.

Ralt began construction of his first hydrogen refinery on the northern fringe of Dallas in 1990. He poured almost $400 million into the building of a plant that was technologically state-of-the-art both in its physical production facilities and in its research and development laboratories.

He staffed his laboratory with scientists he hired away from universities and research centers with promises of fat salaries and unlimited funds to pursue development. Conversion rates rose steadily, and within two years Ralt was producing hydrogen fuel he could sell at a profit.

Against a chorus of howls from his board of Texas Oil, Ralt gambled $2.5 billion more on the construction of another three plants in a huge industrial park on the southwest fringe of Dallas.

The bet began to pay off almost immediately. Assured a steady supply of hydrogen from Texas Oil, light industries throughout the Southwest began to convert their power plants to burn the cheap pollution-free fuel. Within eighteen months Ralt's refineries were shipping hydrogen to heavy industries as well.

Four years from the day Otto Ralt produced his first liter
of hydrogen, he was worth almost $6 billion on paper and
had a virtual monopoly over the commercial production of
hydrogen fuel.

Then the drought struck the Southwest. For decades man
had been siphoning up an ever-increasing volume of water
from the Ogallala aquifer, an ancient subterranean stratum
of permeable rock and sand that stretched like a huge
underground lake from Texas north through Kansas and
Nebraska. Now, with no rain to supplement the surface
needs for water, wells were drilled ever deeper and the level
of groundwater in the aquifer lowered ominously.

The Texas Water Resources Board responded with increasingly stringent restrictions on the use of the state's
rapidly dwindling water reserves.

Personal human consumption was given the first priority,
agricultural needs were slotted second, and industrial demand for water was assigned third. The first restrictions that
were imposed limited Ralt's hydrogen refineries to 75
percent of their normal water use.

As the drought wore on through 1998, the allotment of
water to Ralt's refineries was slashed a second and a third
time, until his plants were operating at barely 30 percent of
capacity. With less and less hydrogen to sell, and the debt
service he incurred to build his refineries steadily draining
away cash, Texas Oil skidded from a financially robust
energy producer to a company on the brink of bankruptcy.

Otto Ralt acted. He hired the foremost hydrologists in the
country to search the subterranean strata below the Dallas
area for an alternative source of water. There was always
the chance of finding an uncharted underground river or
perhaps a smaller aquifer below the steadily shrinking
Ogallala. The test wells were drilled in secret because every
gallon that Ralt found and diverted to his hydrogen fuel
plants would have to be stolen surreptitiously from the
people of Dallas.

Bill Edwards squeezed the jeep to the right as a pickup
truck crammed with ranch hands passed the other way.
Light laughter floated from the truck bed, and Edwards

marveled again at the capacity of the Mexican-Americans to find mirth in the midst of lives of enduring toil and poverty.

Exploratory borings by Ralt's hydrologists at six separate sites around Dallas not only failed to find new water sources, they turned up evidence of a subterranean threat far more ominous than a shrinking aquifer.

Dallas sits on a limestone formation. Such strata are commonly honeycombed with subterranean caverns hollowed out of the soft rock by acidic groundwater that percolates down through the porous rock over millions of years and dissolves the calcium carbonate in the soft stone.

Caves had been forming under Dallas for countless millennia, yet there had never been any danger that the surface cap of rock and soil would collapse because the groundwater that collected in the cavities buttressed the sides and kept the pits from falling in upon themselves. The rock walls vaulting between the caverns served as immense arches supporting the earth ceiling above.

But by 1998, after decades of heedless pumping by man and four years of relentless drought, the water table beneath Dallas had dropped so sharply that the walls of the rapidly emptying limestone caverns were crumbling and caving in upon themselves.

As the rock partitions between them collapsed, caves were merging, Ralt's hydrologists discovered. In some areas test bores had drilled down into open spaces of dead air thousands of yards in diameter.

The conclusion reached by Ralt's scientists was chilling. A monstrous sinkhole was forming under Dallas, stretching from the community of Richardson on the northern fringe of the city to Lancaster in the south, from Mesquite in the east to Arlington in the west. At the rate the water table was dropping, the limestone cap beneath Dallas would collapse en masse into the growing cavity below within twelve months.

Unless the aquifer beneath the city were somehow miraculously replenished, Dallas would go down within a year.

The incredible verdict of his hydrologists seized Otto Ralt

by the throat. It was not the loss of the homes, workplaces, the very way of life for millions of people that concerned him. There would be monumental disruptions, of course, but almost all of the city's houses and businesses were insured and there would be money to build a new city somewhere on the near prairie.

Insurance would rebuild his refineries as well. Yet no matter how fast the new plants went up, it would be too late. With no product to sell, the billions in short-term debt with which he'd saddled Texas Oil in order to build his refineries would be impossible to repay.

Even if he sold off company assets to service the debt, by the time his new plants were back on stream he'd have lost his vital lead in the field of hydrogen production and his customers and potential customers would have signed long-term contracts with rival producers now waiting in the wings.

The top of a grain silo appeared above a low slope to the right of the road ahead, and Ralt shifted his eyes from the windshield to stare at the jutting tower.

The hydrologists offered only one hope of saving Dallas from plunging into the bowels of the prairie. Water must be pumped back into the honeycombed limestone strata beneath the city. Trillions of gallons of water would be needed—from what source, the hydrologists could not say.

Could seawater be piped in from the Gulf of Mexico? Ralt wondered. The hydrologists shook their heads; the salt water would inevitably seep out from the sinkholes under Dallas and pollute the Ogallala aquifer. Well water would be rendered unfit for human consumption and crop irrigation for hundreds of thousands of years.

What Otto Ralt needed was a limitless supply of sweet water, and there were but three possible sources conceivable in the central United States: the Great Lakes, the Mississippi River, and the Rio Grande River when it was at flood stage each spring.

A plan to pipe water from Lake Huron to the Southwest had been on the drawing boards as early as the 1960s. Fed by countless rivers and streams in Canada and the United

States, Lake Huron could be tapped for trillions of gallons annually without appreciably lowering its water level. Yet for thirty years an agreement on the sharing of water from the Great Lakes had eluded negotiators; there was little prospect such a treaty could be hammered out and a pipeline built in the year remaining before Dallas went down.

Siphoning water west from the Mississippi was also ruled out by Ralt's engineers. The pipeline would have to run through huge tracts of suburban homes and highly industrialized areas, and the cost and length of legal battles over easements would be patently prohibitive.

It came down to the Rio Grande. The 1,885-mile-long river rose in the San Juan Mountains of southwest Colorado, cut through the middle of New Mexico, then wandered generally southeast, forming the border between Texas and Mexico.

Most of the year, the Rio Grande was little more than a wide, shallow stream. But it was a bitter irony of the drought that the winter rains that normally fell over Texas now came down as snow in the mountains of Colorado where the headwaters of the Rio formed.

Each spring, the snowpack melted and the river swelled to flood stage all the way to its mouth at Brownsville on the Gulf of Mexico.

At its closest, the Rio was 350 miles from Dallas. With nothing but largely open prairie between the city and the river, a pipeline could conceivably be built in less than a year. Yet there was an obstacle to the project even more formidable than the difficulties of drawing water from the Great Lakes or the Mississippi.

The United States and Mexico had signed a treaty evenly dividing the waters of the Rio Grande. Mexico had suffered as severely as the American Southwest during the drought, and hundreds of thousands of subsistence farmers in northern Mexico needed every gallon of the river water to which they were entitled.

Given the present state of hostilities between the two countries, there wasn't the remotest chance Mexico would agree to relinquish any of her share of Rio Grande water, certainly not to save Dallas, a city the Communist government in Mexico City considered a racist bastion of capitalism.

There seemed no answer, no salvation for Dallas, until, unable to sleep the week after he dismissed his hydrologists, Ralt rose in the middle of the night and began leafing through a history of early Texas in his library.

There, suddenly crystal clear before him, in a chapter detailing the discoveries of the conquistadors, he found a way to save Dallas.

The next morning Otto Ralt set in motion a plan to steal the Rio Grande River.

7:00 A.M.

The head groundskeeper at Texas Stadium brought his heel down hard against the surface of the artificial turf that covered the field between the ten-yard line and the west end zone.

Thump-ump!

Sam Welch's brow furrowed at the faint dull reverberation he felt through the thin soles of his tennis shoes. The ground sounded almost hollow, as if the stadium's playing surface were the taut head of a huge drum.

For almost a week now he'd had the vague sense that something was wrong with the earth under the football field.

Again he stomped down on the turf. The resonant vibrations that answered were far too subtle to be picked up by any of the other people busy on the field: the line chalkers, the NFL advance team, and the TV crew laying camera cable.

But to Welch the low reverberations were as clear as a near clap of thunder.

For several minutes he stood staring down at the field. Could the damn drought have sucked the subsurface hard enough to account for the strange resonance?

He had a sudden thought. Several large subterranean

conduits carrying water, waste, and electrical wires crossed beneath the stadium floor. One of the pipes had been pulled up last year to weld a break.

If the dirt had not been packed tightly enough when the trench was refilled, it was possible a cavity had formed as the soil dried out and crumbled.

Did the line cross near the west end zone? He couldn't remember. He was about to call the stadium engineer on the mobile phone in his electric cart when the public address system suddenly blared to life.

"Down on the field there. You, Welch. Get up here."

Welch's stomach tightened at the voice of the Cowboys' owner, Max Frankenhoff. He was certain Frankenhoff had been watching him through the powerful binoculars mounted before the plate glass window in his luxury skybox high above the fifty-yard line.

Reluctantly Welch climbed into his cart and started across to the nearest field exit. What did the bastard want now?

Frankenhoff directed the Cowboy organization with a fascist hand. An employee summoned before the team owner could expect a rapid-fire inquisition. Frankenhoff knew every job in the stadium, and he was unforgiving of mistakes. Welch pressed the elevator button for the second tier.

What the hell was it this time? Had the owner spotted a wavy chalk line, a two-inch rip in the turf fabric, bird shit in the end zone?

Whatever Frankenhoff wanted done, Welch knew the task would eat into the few hours he had left to prepare the stadium before the exhibition game with the Forty-Niners this afternoon. The unusual spring contest was being played to raise funds for drought relief, but the worthy cause did little to alleviate the special problems posed by staging a game so early in the off-season.

He wouldn't have time today to check out his vague suspicion that there was something wrong with the field's subsurface.

He'd have to wait until Monday to find out why the floor of Texas Stadium sounded so hollow.

7:30 A.M.

Bill Edwards braked the dusty jeep in front of a huge concrete grain silo that towered 150 feet above the ranch of Otto Ralt. He turned off the ignition and glanced uneasily at the three nondescript wood-frame buildings that surrounded the silo in a rough circle.

The layout of the satellite structures was purposeful. In each a laser cannon faced inward from behind a camouflaged port so that the silo was the center of a clear field of fire.

"Go back to the Santa Gertrudis barn and make sure Immigration gets Madero," Ralt ordered, climbing from the jeep. "Hand over his family too. All of them."

"Surely you could have someone else handle this for you, Mr. Ralt," Edwards said dispiritedly. "Madero's a friend of mine."

"How good a friend is he, Bill?" Ralt said, then turned and walked toward the tower, leaving the unspoken threat hanging like a noose around Edwards's neck.

For a moment the ranch foreman stared after Ralt; then he started the jeep and drove away, his heart a stone in his chest.

Ralt crossed to a steel door at the base of the tower and

pressed his fingertips against a foot-square pane of milk glass set into the door at chest height.

Photoelectric cells in the glass scanned the arrangement of lines and circles surfacing the skin of Ralt's fingertips and compared the pattern to print records stored in the memory of a computer within the silo.

The computer made a match and the door clicked open. Ralt stepped into the cool, dim interior of the concrete tube.

Not so much as a kernel of corn or a grain of wheat had ever been stored in the silo. Instead, the tower's gleaming interior housed elevator machinery, generators, communications equipment, air-conditioning units, fat electrical conduits, and a tangle of water and waste pipes.

Ralt paused a moment to allow his eyes to adjust to the dim light, then walked to a pneumatic elevator that rose through the silo floor in a ten-foot-wide stainless steel cylinder. He pressed a call button and a moment later the elevator doors opened soundlessly. The car took only six seconds to descend the 240 feet to the subterranean command center Ralt had constructed under his ranch.

The shaft beneath the tower had been sunk by Colorado Mine and Mineral, a subsidiary of Texas Oil and a company wholly owned by Otto Ralt. Ralt had hand-picked the superintendent, engineers, and laborers who worked on the project. He'd chosen the men not for their construction prowess but for their politics; each was a trusted member of the Posse Comitatus.

The Posse was an extreme right-wing movement that preached a twisted fundamentalist religion advocating violence against intrusive government as well as Jews and other racial minorities.

The Posse was spawned during the American farm crisis of the 1970s and 1980s, years in which tens of thousands of farmers and ranchers lost their way of life as a combination of low crop prices, heavy debt, and plummeting land values dispossessed families throughout the nation's agricultural areas.

Farmers thrown off their lands were ripe for the Posse doctrine that a national conspiracy of Jews, bankers, and

Communist infiltrators in Washington was responsible for the theft of their livelihood and the shattering of their families' futures.

The movement was financed by Otto Ralt and a handful of other wealthy ultraconservatives and given moral credence by several television evangelists, who preached fiery, thinly veiled racist rhetoric from flag-draped pulpits.

The Communist takeover in Mexico in 1992 had been a windfall for the Posse Comitatus. Here was the godless red wolf at the door, and hundreds of thousands of alarmed Americans, particularly in the Southwest and West, joined the movement.

The elevator reached the bottom and the car doors opened. The command center Ralt entered was a thirty- by sixty-foot rectangular room. Its stainless steel walls were broken only by the entrance to the elevator and a door leading to the tunnel complex that would soon stretch from Dallas to the Rio Grande.

In the middle of the room, a bank of computers, electronic monitors, and communications equipment stretched almost thirty feet down the length of the rectangle. A control engineer sat at a command console midway along the line of machines, overseeing an array of computer screens and digital readouts.

The engineer looked up as Ralt approached from the elevator. Like the three colleagues with whom he shared eight-hour shifts as duty officer in the subterranean complex, Mason Sneed was a fiercely loyal member of the Posse Comitatus. Sneed saw his work beneath the Texas prairie not as a well-paid job but as the duty of a soldier. The enemy was the Communist horde coiled to strike from Mexico, and the front line was the border of his beloved Texas.

"Good morning, Mr. Ralt," Sneed said.

Ralt nodded curtly, his eyes sweeping the computer screens behind Sneed. The machines were monitoring the progress of a tunnel the crews from Colorado Mining were boring under the prairie to the south.

The completed tunnel would link the vast sinkholes

forming under Dallas with the now-dry channel of the Rio
Bajo la Tierra, the ancient subterranean river that began
twenty-eight miles south of Dallas and ended sixty miles
below the Mexican border.

That sleepless night in his library, Otto Ralt had recognized the Rio Bajo for what it was, a natural subterranean
pipeline that could carry water north from the Rio Grande
River to the hollowed bowels of the earth beneath Dallas.

With trillions of gallons of virtually incompressible water
restored to the Ogallala aquifer, the walls of the limestone
galleries under Dallas would once again be buttressed
against collapse. The city would be spared destruction by
the immense sinkhole forming beneath it, and the Texas Oil
refineries would continue to produce hydrogen fuel—and a
fortune for Otto Ralt.

The scheme required three separate crews. While the first
bored a tunnel from the southern fringe of Dallas twenty-
eight miles to the northern terminus of the Rio Bajo, a
second crew blasted down cave ceilings to plug the side
channels of the subterranean river so that all the stolen water
would flow directly north through the main tunnel.

The third crew labored beneath the Texas-Mexico border,
raising a shaft from the Rio Bajo toward the bed of the
Rio Grande River above. When the shaft reached a point
twenty feet beneath the bedrock bottom of the surface
river, nitroglycerine charges would be set. When all was
ready, the explosives would be detonated and the spring-
flood-swollen waters of the Rio Grande would cascade
down into the main channel of the subterranean river. Huge
pumps would then send the entire flow north beneath the
prairie to empty into the titanic sinkhole forming under
Dallas.

Ralt relished the thought of the consternation in Mexico
City when the Rio Grande suddenly disappeared into the
depths of the earth. The cream of Mexico's scientists and
engineers had fled the country during the first years after the
Communist takeover, and there were few experts the
Marxist government could call on to investigate the phenomenon.

The red bastards would, of course, suspect that the *yanquis* were somehow behind the disaster. But Mexico had no Landsat satellite that could trace the course of the stolen water under the earth, and excavations south of the Rio Grande would tell the Communists nothing.

True, the communities on the Texas side of the border, from Eagle Pass southeast to the mouth of the Rio Grande at Brownsville, would suffer the loss of their river water as well. Americans along this stretch of the border would no doubt scream as loudly as their Mexican neighbors.

But the Rio Grande would have to be dammed upstream from Quito, and the vertical shaft explored, before the experts could be sure what had happened, and no such dam could be built without an agreement between the United States and Mexico. Given the present state of hostilities, Ralt was confident an accord was not even remotely conceivable.

Ralt eased his heavy body down into a small chair in front of a computer screen and called up a progress report on the mining crews busy under the prairie to the south. The monitor flickered momentarily, then lines of cryptic words and statistics appeared on the screen. For several minutes Ralt digested the data before him, occasionally making notes on a small pad.

The crew digging the tunnel south from Dallas was ahead of schedule. The huge boring machine they were using was now within five hundred feet of the southern wall of the sinkhole under Dallas. The ninety-ton "mole," as the miners dubbed it, should take its last bites of earth and reach the forming cavity within six to eight hours.

Ralt's eyes strayed to the door leading to the tunnel complex beyond the command center. A monorail car waited in the passage, the single steel track before it running down the dark bore ahead all the way to the workface of the Dallas tunnel. For a moment, Ralt was tempted to board the monorail and inspect the tunneling progress personally. Then he realized he didn't have the time, and he began scanning a second report.

The foreman of the crew plugging the side channels of

the Rio Bajo reported all the subterranean exits from the main tunnel had now been sealed. Ralt turned on a television monitor to his left. There were twelve side passages feeding into the underground river, and Ralt had ordered TV cameras mounted high on the wall of each exit before it was plugged.

Many of the passages led to caves and sinkholes feeding down from the surface, and there was always the chance an intruder might wander into the cavern system of the Rio Bajo. If any of the dams were discovered and reported to authorities, Ralt's entire scheme would be jeopardized.

As insurance, he had ordered explosive charges set at strategic tunnel junctions throughout the labyrinth of passages that fed the main tunnel. If his plans were uncovered and the main tunnel blocked, Ralt could simply blow the tunnel downstream and rechannel the flow of the Rio Grande around the barrier through one of the dozen side passages paralleling the main tunnel.

The only really vulnerable point was the main pump station where the many passages of the Rio Bajo merged and met the tunnel being bored south from Dallas. Yet the pump station was six hundred feet underground, and there were no passages leading to the surface within fifty miles. Ralt was confident the main pump was safe from discovery.

He flicked quickly from one camera to another. As each camera was activated, an infrared floodlight, invisible to the human eye, turned on simultaneously. All was quiet. Ralt shut off the television.

"Get me Stroesser on the scrambler phone," he ordered Sneed. Karl Stroesser was the Posse Comitatus's chief of security on the tunnel project, commanding a paramilitary force of eighty ex-paratroopers and Green Berets who'd joined the Posse after leaving the army.

Ralt had no illusions about Stroesser and his men. They were mercenaries, men of shallow intellect and morals who'd joined the Posse out of a twisted need for the authority of uniforms, weapons, and a strong leader, however perverse he might be. Stroesser was the worst of the lot, Ralt knew, a psychotic killer, as he'd proved again the night before when he'd led a knife-wielding attack on a Mexican army patrol in the middle of the dark Rio Grande.

Stroesser's coded message reporting the interception of the Mexican patrol had reached Ralt in flight back across the Atlantic. He'd seethed in rage over the murders of the Mexicans. It was not the deaths of the eight peasant soldiers that infuriated him, but the chance that the disappearance of the patrol would set off an intense search of the border area by the Mexican army.

The subterranean shaft being raised toward the bottom of the Rio Grande was impervious to discovery, but the air ducts to the first pump station below could easily be spotted by searchers combing the desert on the American side of the border.

"I've got Stroesser," Sneed said, handing Ralt the scrambler phone.

"What's the situation down there, Karl?" Ralt asked without preamble.

"Quiet, Mr. Ralt. I've got three men watching the Mexican side. There hasn't been a sign of life over there all day. Just that patrol's half-track baking in the sun."

"The Mexicans are bound to send a search column out, probably within the next few hours. You got everything screwed down tight on our side?"

"Yes, sir. All our surface equipment was brought down into the pump station during the night, and the air ducts and vehicle ramp entrance have been camouflaged."

"What'd you do with the bodies?"

"We bulldozed them under the desert about ten miles north, Mr. Ralt. No one but the scorpions and rattlers will ever know those Mexicans are there."

"I want sentries sent out along the border five miles on each side of our position there, Karl. They're to report back the minute the Mexican search column is sighted. If their troops cross the river, don't interfere. As long as they don't uncover anything that gives away our operation, just let them roam where they will."

"I got a problem with letting them wetback bastards cross the Rio Grande, Mr. Ralt. The air duct openings are well hidden, mesquite piled around them and on top. But if those Mexican soldiers were to stumble on a duct—hell, they'd be bound to spot the grille. What do I do if that happens?"

"You kill them, Karl," Ralt said before he hung up. "You kill them all."

8:00 A.M.

The solar-powered flying wing banked into a steep, tight dive and the co-pilot yelped his elation into the cool rushing wind, as the hybrid glider nosed at 180 miles an hour toward the earth below. The Irish setter had loved the air since he'd first flown as a puppy.

The small earphones strapped to the dog's head crackled to life. "How was that, Sam?"

Sam barked enthusiastically into the speaker mike set into the bulkhead before him.

In the forward cockpit, Jedediah Heffernan laughed, laughed as he only laughed in the air. Flying had become his one guiltless passion, his single release during the past five long years.

Heffernan pulled the stick back and brought the flying wing out of the dive. "Time to go home, Sam," he said, putting the glider on a heading for the small, dusty airstrip he'd leveled on the rim of the box canyon that enclosed his ninety-acre ranch.

God, how he loved this hour of pure freedom he shared with the dog each day! Sam would nudge him awake at dawn and together they would cross the shadowed canyon floor to the cliff face three hundred yards from the house. At the foot of the rock wall they would climb into the small wooden lift Heffernan had built, and he'd hand-winch them up the side of the cliff. The pulleys and counterweights Heffernan had designed made the winching relatively easy, yet there was still enough resistance against the ropes to give him a good workout each morning.

At the top, at the head of a ramp that inclined twenty degrees toward the edge of the palisade, the flying wing waited. The aircraft, which Heffernan had modified from a Lockheed design, had a 130-foot wingspan. The large spread of wing provided both the lift necessary to carry the glider to great heights and the surface area for the solar cells that powered the craft's fifteen-horsepower engine. High-tech batteries on board stored electricity for flights during cloudy weather and at night.

On most clear mornings, the rising sun would quickly warm the air that had settled into the cold cup of the canyon the night before, and soon the sight of red-tailed hawks and bald eagles circling skyward on still wings would signal that thermal currents were rising up the cliffs.

Heffernan would lift Sam into the front seat, then climb into the rear cockpit and release the brake. It took only a few seconds for the glider to slide down the ramp and dip into the warm, ascending air. Once out over the canyon, the soarer would spiral up on the lift of the thermal currents, circling with the hawks and eagles until the features of the rugged New Mexico countryside softened to an indistinct blur thousands of feet below.

As the glider climbed against the sun, man and dog would exult alike in their warm, soundless envelope of peace. Five years ago it had been Heffernan's best friend, Alex, in the front cockpit. Each clear morning they weren't working, they'd go up to meet the day at five thousand feet. They'd shared a passion for gliders, as they'd shared so much of life.

Gliding down toward the rim of the canyon, Heffernan thought of Alex, and the vise jaws that relaxed only when he was in the air clamped tight again against his spirit. Alex. His partner, his best friend for twenty-five years.

Dead now. Dead at his partner's hands. Horribly dead in a black pit in Spanish Cavern.

He and Alex had met as ten-year-old explorers in a wind-sculptured cave near their rural hometown in northwest New Mexico.

While other boys their age were playing ball, he and Alex were worming their way through the dark reaches of every cavern and old mine shaft within hitchhiking distance of the small community of Hondo.

By their mid-teens they'd become competent enough spelunkers to join the county Cave Rescue Unit. Within a year the team of Heff and Alex brought five missing people back from the depth of caverns; twice they'd handed children lost in mine shafts back to their rejoicing mothers.

They became known to spelunkers all over the Southwest as the New Mexico Mounties because they never came back to the surface without their man. By their senior year they were leading rescues as far away as Wyoming and Texas.

That year they brought a squad of six boy scouts out alive after the youngsters had been given up for dead in the half-flooded Whiskey Sluice Silver Mine north of Albuquerque.

One of the city's newspaper reporters interviewed them, learned neither could afford college, and began a drive to raise full scholarships.

Donations poured in from across the Southwest, enough, if they worked part time, to see them both through four years of tuition and board. They enrolled together to study geology at the University of New Mexico at Albuquerque.

For four years they shared a tough curriculum of engineering courses and rebelled with gliders, drinking bashes, and pliant coeds. College for Heff and Alex had been a blur of cramming, flying, drinking, and chasing women.

The day they graduated they formed a partnership as geologists specializing in mine and cavern surveys. They made enough money that first year for Heff to marry Margo, a gushing sorority girl he'd given a ring to in their senior year.

Eighteen months later he and Margo bought the canyon

ranch. Alex came with them, turning the hayloft of the
ramshackle barn into a skylit bachelor apartment and tiny
office.

For three years Heff had taken Margo to bed while Alex
fell asleep with geological charts strewn across the covers.
Margo was an only child, pampered and sheltered, and as
Heff's passion cooled he gradually came to see her as a
shallow, grasping woman.

The seclusion of the ranch soured Margo. She com-
plained of the loneliness of the desert, the bother of the
crude plumbing and the coal stove and the leaky roof of the
old ranch house. Even the bright new home Heff and Alex
hauled logs and split rocks to build didn't placate her.

Margo grew shrewish, her sexual favors abstemious and
then withdrawn entirely. She began going home to visit her
parents for long stretches; then, five years after she'd
married Heff, she went back to Daddy for good.

Heff shook off the past and pressed his throat mike.
"Time to set her down, Sam," he said as they closed on the
dusty strip along the top of the cliffs. The glider was a
hundred yards from the end of the runway when he spotted
an old pickup turning off the highway and starting down the
road to his ranch.

Heff set the plane down smoothly, then taxied to the head
of the ramp and braked the soarer in takeoff position on the
incline. He unstrapped Sam from the front seat, and the two
descended in the small lift and crossed the canyon floor
toward the pickup. The driver had gotten out of the truck as
they were coming down the cliff face, but it wasn't until
they were close that Heff realized it was a woman.

For the first time in three days, Lucia Sanchez smiled as
the big Irish setter ambled up and stuck out his paw to
shake. She obliged, bending to pet the dog, then straightened as the man approached. "Mr. Heffernan? Jedediah
Heffernan?"

He stopped six feet away and returned her smile. "Heff
will do." He nodded at the dog. "My friend's name is
Sam."

Lucia felt disconcerted. The man before her looked

nothing like what she'd pictured. When Foster told her that Heffernan had twice refused his pleas for help in cave rescues, she'd envisioned a heartless ogre, pinch-faced, with dull eyes and passionless features.

Instead, the man before her had friendly dark blue eyes with laugh wrinkles fanning toward gray-brown temples. His face radiated warmth and strength, and the smile beneath his bushy brown mustache was spontaneous and open. She guessed him to be a shade over six feet tall, lean but with a broad chest and arms muscled from decades spent hauling himself up and down the depths of caves.

"I'm Lucia Sanchez." She stroked the dog's neck. "I'll bet he's a good friend."

"Also a hell of a co-pilot."

"So that was you up in that plane I saw when I drove in."

"It's a glider."

She grinned. "That's pretty rare, isn't it? A flying dog."

"You've got it backwards. Sam's a dog that flies, among his many other interests."

"He must be a terribly intelligent dog." She laughed.

Heffernan rolled his eyes. "Sam has genius beyond plumbing. Would you like some coffee?"

She let out the deep sigh of a night on the road. "God, I'd love some."

"You look like you could use a little breakfast too. C'mon."

She stole a sideways glance at him as they walked. He was going to cook her breakfast without even asking her why she'd suddenly appeared on his ranch. He was telling her that he could wait to know, that in his scheme of things hospitality came first.

Sam led them across the wide dusty yard to the ranch house. The rustic structure was built with rough planks milled from the aspen trees that abounded in stands through the canyon.

There was no question as she entered that this was a man's home. The two long facing walls were paneled, though there weren't many spots where the wood showed. Most of the space was covered with floor-to-ceiling bookshelves crammed with thousands of titles, including several reference sets.

To one side was a long serving counter with a small kitchen behind. Two doors stood open to the left of the kitchen. Through one she could see a toilet and tub, the other framed a rumpled bed.

It was the fourth wall, though, that dominated the large living room. It was built of native stone its entire width, encasing two wooden windows set on either side of a massive fireplace. There were more books piled on the thick hewn plank that served as a mantel.

Heffernan's home was stark, the oak furniture scarred by boots and tools, and the smell of leather wafted from two huge tanned-hide armchairs in front of the the fireplace. Yet there was warm comfort too, and lightness in the gingham curtains and Indian throw rugs and the rainbow colors of the thousand book spines that crowded the walls.

"I like your home," she said, meaning it, surprised at how safe she felt even though she was totally alone with a man she'd just met.

"Thank you. A friend and I built it a few years back."

"Does your friend live here with you?"

"No."

He almost added that Alex didn't live anywhere anymore. Instead he offered her a choice of the two leather chairs facing the stone hearth. She sank into one as he bent to light the fire against the high-country chill that had settled into the canyon during the night.

When the kindling was crackling he turned, rubbing his hands. "How do you like your bacon?"

"Crisp," she said.

He started for the kitchen. "Eggs over easy?"

"Yes, thank you, Jedediah."

He stopped in his tracks, his back to her. Of all the people he knew, only Alex had called him Jedediah. To everyone else, he was Heff. "Like I said, you can call me Heff. Most do."

"Heff" was the dull-eyed, passionless man she'd thought she'd find. To Lucia, the easy, smiling man about to cook her breakfast would always be Jedediah.

"I prefer your given name, Jedediah. If that's all right with you."

"Suit yourself," he said, and started again for the kitchen. A few minutes later there was the sound of fat spattering in a frying pan.

"Do you mind if I look at your books?" she called.

"Go ahead. Borrow any of them you want."

Almost half the first bookshelf held volumes on geology. Below these were reference works on archaeology and anthropology, and along the bottom row large ring-bound sets of satellite ground-survey charts leaned against each other.

The neighboring shelves were crammed with literature, biographies, political treatises, histories, and novels. Heffernan read Voltaire, Dostoyevski, Brontë, Shaw, Twain, Saroyan, le Carré.

The smell of bacon and eggs wafted from the kitchen, and a moment later he called her to breakfast. She'd hardly eaten in the three days since Paco disappeared into the earth, and now, the hard knot in her gut gone for the first time, it was all she could do not to wolf down the meal.

On the floor Sam gnawed on a thick rind from the slab bacon.

Breakfast was fun. Jedediah held forth on Sam's prowess as a flyer, a judge of human nature, an alto soprano howling canine opera against the stage of the full moon. He was direct, open, candid in his opinions, and she liked his habit of tilting his chin up when he spoke and throwing his head back when he laughed.

She realized as she listened to Jedediah that he was something of a renaissance man. He had written two books on speleology and had designed and hand-built both the solar wing and a hydrogen-powered combination plane and hovercraft he called a hoverjet. He had used the hoverjet, named Caverunner, for both surface and subterranean exploration.

He had even built his own house. "I like working with my hands," he said. "I like the feel of tools, and the smell of fresh wood, and the house coming to life around me."

Lucia glanced at the thick collar around the dog's neck.

The leather ring was studded with odd-shaped clips and metal flanges.

"What are all those things on Sam's collar?" she asked.

"Slip rings to attach hardware," he said. "That large flange on top is for a light, the one on the left is for a compass. The other two take a small radio finder and a battery pack." He looked back into her quizzical eyes. "Spelunking gear," he explained in a flat tone. "Sam and I used to spend a lot of time underground in caves and mines."

"Used to? Then you don't cave anymore?"

"Nope. Not for the past five years. Sam's too old now, and I'm strictly a surface geologist."

"Where do you work?"

"California to the Mississippi, Mexican border north to Wyoming and Montana. I freelance, mostly for the energy companies."

"A freelance geologist? Do you go around finding new oil fields or something?"

He shook his head. "Most of my work is routine enough. I interpret satellite surveys for the drillers, then overfly the formations they're interested in with my hoverjet. Usually they just want independent confirmation of their own findings. Sometimes I turn up a surprise."

"I thought the need for oil was passing. I mean with all the factories changing over to hydrogen fuel. Even my gas station has a hydrogen pump now."

Heffernan leaned back against the cane chair. "Yeah, oil's on the way out as a fuel. The refineries are closing left and right. But petroleum is still used in plastics, chemicals, lubricants, paints. When Mexico turned off the tap, a whole new crop of wildcatters sprang up."

"Your work must bring you satisfaction," she offered. "The excitement of exploring, of finding something new."

His voice sounded far away, as if he'd left the room. "As much as anything can."

He rose to clear the table. "More coffee?"

She shook her head no. It was time to tell him about Paco.

"I understand you're the best cave rescue man in the Southwest, Jedediah, perhaps the country," she said.

His back was to her as he stacked the dishes on the kitchen counter, and she saw the muscles in his shoulders stiffen under his shirt.

He turned toward her. "I assume whoever told you that spoke in the past tense. As I said, I haven't been underground in five years. I don't cave anymore."

She looked at him a moment. "Are you a compassionate man, Jedediah?"

"I hope compassion is one of my instincts."

"I pray to God that's true," she said, then she told him why she was there, the words tumbling out of her. "My brother Paco is lost somewhere down a sinkhole near our home in Texas. He's wandered into the north fork of the Rio Bajo la Tierra. That's an underground river near—"

"I know the river," he said. "My partner and I charted about thirty miles of channels on a state survey about eight years ago. The north fork branches off from the main tunnel system ten or twelve miles from a little town we stayed in down there. Rock something."

"Rocksprings," she said. "That's where I live."

He studied her. "How long has your brother been down?"

There was a hairline crack in her voice. "This is the third day. He's only ten, Jedediah. He's never been away from his mother and me for more than a few hours before."

"How about his clothes? What was he wearing?"

Lucia searched her memory. It had been cool the morning Paco disappeared and the boy had been dressed warmly. "He had on a long-sleeved wool shirt and a quilted vest. The thermal kind. Jeans and sneakers. And a baseball cap, I think."

"Did he have a light?"

"Yes, he took a large flashlight from the house."

Heffernan was silent a moment. "Three days is a long stretch to be down, especially a boy alone," he said finally. "Still, if your brother hasn't panicked, the odds are on his side."

She clutched at the straw. "Do you think so? Then you believe Paco's still alive?"

"The greatest dangers in a cave are hypothermia from the damp cold and falls in the dark. Your brother has both warm clothes and a light. Who's conducting the search?"

"The rescue team leader's name is Foster. Morris Foster."

Heffernan nodded. "I've worked cave searches with Foster. He's organized, competent, always knows where his teams are underground. He's a good caver."

"But you're better, Jedediah, even Foster conceded that. One of the searchers said that without you it was hopeless, they'd never bring Paco out alive. Please, I implore you, come back to Rocksprings with me and find my brother."

He went to the window, his back to her as he gazed out into the canyon. "I wish to God I could, Lucia," he said miserably. "I wish to God I had the power to give your brother back to you. But I don't. You have no idea what you're asking of me. I don't cave anymore." He turned to face her. "I can't."

"For God's sake, why?" There was desperation in her voice now. "Why can't you search for my brother?"

He stared at her, the pain coming over his face like the tide over a beach. "The last time I went down I killed a man. My best friend, Alex. He was my partner for twenty-five years, the man who helped me build this house. There was no corner of my life he didn't share. When I triumphed, he was the one ready with the laurel wreath. When I tumbled into crap pits, he was the one with the shovel to dig me out. And I killed him. He's still lying in the bottom of a black shaft where I left him five years ago."

Heffernan's voice had that far off echo in it again.

"Every cave is his tomb now. I can't go down into Alex's grave. I can't go down into the Rio Bajo after Paco, not if he were my own brother."

Lucia's heart sank at the vehemence in his voice. She couldn't move him, certainly not while he sat in this house, the house Alex had helped him build, twisting in the agony of his best friend's death. If she could just get him to Rocksprings.

"I understand," she said after a moment. "I won't ask you again to go down into the Rio Bajo. But surely you could still help. Come back with me and direct the rescue operation. You could lead the searchers to Paco from the surface."

His face twisted scornfully. "Send people down into miles of dangerous tunnels while I warm my ass safely in the fresh air above? I couldn't run a rescue that way, Lucia. When I send men down, I go with them. I don't assign risks I can't accept myself."

"Then leave Foster the leader," she pleaded. "You could be an adviser, Jedediah, a second source of ideas. Even your presence at the sinkhole might encourage the searchers."

He shook his head. "How do I get you to understand, Lucia? If I were there, I'd have to go down. And that I can't do. If you want someone to give Foster a hand, I can recommend two or three good men."

In one impassioned movement she was on her feet, her voice almost a scream. "Two or three good men? There are thirty good men searching for Paco now and they haven't found him. My brother is beyond finding by good men. It will take the best caver in the country to bring him out of that black pit. The best. You. But you won't help. You won't even try."

She burst into tears, the one thing she'd promised herself she wouldn't do.

"My God, you're abandoning a ten-year-old boy to die alone and terrified in some cold dark tunnel. How can you live with that? Tell me. Tell me how you will live with that."

She turned and, with her shoulders heaving, fled to the fireplace.

He stared across the room at her for a moment, then walked to the door and went out onto the plank porch. Sam followed slowly. Heff sat on the top porch step and gazed out into the canyon, the dog nuzzling his lap.

He had given up trying to live with himself five years ago. The day he'd killed Alex. Only at dawn when he and

Sam flew free for an hour did Jedediah Heffernan know any vestige of peace.

He and Alex had gone down into Spanish Cavern on a job for the Texas Water Resources Board, a routine check of the water level in a great subterranean reservoir that had collected over the millennia six hundred feet down in the cave.

They'd chosen the fastest route to the reservoir, a plunging, narrow descent spelunkers eschewed because of its dangerous drops. The worst of these was a 135-foot cylindrical shaft called the Drainpipe.

Perhaps he hadn't been careful enough where he'd hammered in the piton that would anchor them as they rappeled one after the other into the deep black well. Later he could only guess that he'd missed some critical weakness in the rock-face crevasse he'd spiked.

By some forever inexplicable quirk of fate, the anchor held when he'd strapped his cave light beam down on his back and rappeled safely to the floor of the pit.

Two minutes later, when Alex started down, the same piton failed. Heff had watched mesmerized, rooted where he stood, as his partner plummeted toward him.

Alex's body scraped the side of the shaft as he fell, loosing a rockslide behind him. The last thing he remembered was Alex coming at him in slow motion, a canopy of boulders and stones floating down behind him.

When he came to he was racked with pain from head to foot and the pit was as black and soundless as a tomb. He tried to move and couldn't. He could feel with his knees and shoulders that he was lying lengthwise in a narrow fissure in the floor of the shaft, with loose rocks wedged around him.

There was a weak groan from somewhere near his ear, and he suddenly realized that the bulk pressing down painfully on him from above was his partner's body.

"Alex, can you hear me? Alex."

Silence. He felt the panic rise. "Alex!" His shouts had echoed unanswered between the rock walls of the shaft. Echoes. He had shouted into the open! That meant his head was free of the debris of the slide. It took only a moment for his elation to cool. He was still pinned in the crevasse from the shoulders down. Trapped by his partner's body.

Only his right hand was out of the rock coffin of the fissure, and it was wedged between sharp rocks and the crevasse edge. It took him twenty minutes of agony before he worked his hand free at last, bloody and scraped to the bone. He found the emergency flashlight on his belt and flicked it on.

Alex's glazed eyes stared back at him from two inches away.

He gasped, then reached up to feel his friend's face. It was cold. He pulled his hand back convulsively as the death rattle built in Alex's chest, and a moment later he tasted Alex's last soft breath as his partner exhaled into Heff's own mouth.

He turned off the light and lay torn and shaking in the blackness. He knew he had just one way to escape, and the bile rose into his throat at the abhorrent act he faced. For almost an hour he shivered violently and fought against what he had to do. Finally, he felt himself growing drowsy and knew he was slipping into hypothermia and death.

At the threshold, something in him opted for life. He'd slammed his raw hand deliberately against the edge of the crevasse, and the wave of excruciating pain that coursed through his body tore away the stuporous fingers of hypothermia that would soon mean death.

When the pain subsided, he slid his five-inch knife from its sheath and fingered the edge in the dark. The blade felt like a razor against his skin. He turned on the light and saw where he'd make the first cut.

Then he began to butcher Alex.

First the ribs that were pressing against his mid-body. He cut away Alex's coat and shirt, then sliced the flesh from his friend's chest in long strips. Blood, cold now, flowed down to soak him. He snapped off the thin rib bones with his hands, then crushed the sternum with a rock.

Alex's foot came next. It was wedged bone to bone against his hip. He reached down and laboriously hacked off the foot at the ankle joint.

Last, most unbearable, was the head. Rigor mortis had
stiffened Alex's neck, and his head was pressing against
Heff's shoulder, immobilizing his left upper arm. He
needed two hands free to dig himself out.

He snaked the knife up and began sawing across the spine
at the base of Alex's neck. It took over an hour and all that
time Alex's eyes watched him from bobbing sockets.

Finally, it was done. He could move. Heff dragged
himself forward inch by inch along the crevasse until at last
he pulled his feet free of the slide.

Heff's body folded back in agony when he tried to rise.
Blinding pains shot from his back and hips and forced him
into a grotesque crouch. He ran his hand up under his shirt
and felt the muscles bunched into knotted ribbons after
hours pressed against the cold, damp rock.

He couldn't straighten. Dumbly he watched his curled,
blood-encrusted fingers swing slowly back and forth below
his knees, like the Neanderthal hands of some primordial
murderer.

He struggled back into the debris-filled crevasse and
brought out Alex's head. Sobbing, bent half over in agony,
he closed his friend's eyes and put the head on a ledge high
above the shaft's flood line.

Then he began the torturous climb out, the corded
muscles in his back screaming every foot he pulled himself
up. Finally, five hours after he'd started up the drainpipe, he
stumbled out into the light at the mouth of Spanish Cavern.

The Water Board superintendent who met him outside
had retched and fallen back in horror at the sight of him bent
over like an ape, his blood-caked face twisted in pain, his
flaming eyes staring madly into the light.

Three weeks of heat therapy and muscle relaxants
straightened his back, and he checked out of the hospital.
All the hours he had lain in bed he'd been planning a
solitary descent into Spanish Cavern to bring out Alex's
remains.

But the morning he went back he'd stopped dead in his
tracks at the cavern's mouth, feeling Alex's presence near
and overpowering.

He'd gathered himself and shone his light into the cave, then stiffened in a silent scream as the glow illuminated Alex's head suspended in the blackness, his friend's lifeless eyes staring back accusingly into his own.

He'd fled Spanish Cavern, but he'd never been able to flee what had happened that day in the depths of the earth.

Behind him, Heff heard Lucia compose herself and start for the door. He rose as she stepped onto the porch.

"Lucia, I'm sorry. You must believe me, if I could go down into the Rio Bajo, I would. I would search for your brother on my knees if I had to." There was desperation in his eyes now. "But I can't. I can't."

She stared back at him. "What a cruel paradox. Both my brother and you are trapped in an underground hell. And because you cannot escape yours, Paco will never escape his. Good-bye, Jedediah."

He stood on the porch and watched the old pickup grow small down the ranch road, Sam loping along in escort to the gate. She was right. His hell was underground, blazing from the eyes of Alex's severed head. He couldn't face those eyes again. Never. Never.

9:00 A.M.

The rumor that the killer bats that had terrorized the Irving Mall had been drugged by Mexican provocateurs was first heard in Dallas sometime after midnight. By 9 A.M. the monstrous lie had spread through most of the city and its suburbs.

There had been a racist climate in the American Southwest since the first Anglo-American settlers migrated to the area in the early 1800s and began displacing the indigenous Mexicans and Indians. For decades the whites had treated the browns with condescension and brutality.

Although great strides toward equality had been made through the 1970s and 1980s, the social progress and acceptance of the Latino population had suffered a grievous blow in 1992 when the Marxists took power in Mexico City. Like the Japanese-American population in California at the outbreak of World War II, Mexican-Americans were suddenly faced with suspicion, and often open animosity, by a small but vociferous segment of Texas society.

The report that the bats had been poisoned by terrorists among the Mexican fruit workers rekindled the flames of hatred that had long simmered in racist souls. Throughout the next morning, incensed Texans armed themselves. The

78

enemy was among them; the Communist agents must be hunted down and dealt with.

At 10 A.M., a short-order cook from Tijuana was gunned down as he cored apples behind the restaurant where he worked in Garland. On the Stemmons Freeway, a man in a speeding car tossed a stick of dynamite into the fruit-laden pickup of a Mexican-American farm family, killing a mother, father, and two children.

Latinos employed in the wholesale produce market were attacked with knives and clubs, and two road workers were beaten to death. Despite pleas for restraint and reason from law enforcement agencies and city and state officials, the racist rampage against the Spanish-speaking citizenry of Dallas continued unabated throughout the day.

Violence fed on violence. By midmorning sixteen Latinos were dead and the Mexican-American citizens of Dallas went into hiding.

10:30 A.M.

Ten-year-old Paco Sanchez trudged along wearily, following the beam of his flashlight through the dusty tunnel of the Rio Bajo la Tierra. He was in the lower channel of the subterranean river's north fork, 120 feet beneath the burnt Texas prairie, and now almost eleven miles from the sinkhole where he'd entered the underground maze.

He was hungry, scared, tired, and lost. His one spark of hope had come a day past when he'd found a small pool of water that had survived the drought in a rock depression in the cavern floor. He'd drunk his fill and moved on.

The optimism and strength of youth fueled his steps, but he was nearing exhaustion, and he knew it. From time to time the dark thought of his own death would creep like a shadow over his mind and an overwhelming panic would well in his chest. At these moments the stoicism of his people would sustain him. In his genes he carried the courage of uncounted generations of Indians who had survived lives of deprivation, looming famine, and the myriad hardships of a primitive existence. It was not in the blood of Paco Sanchez to surrender his life without a fight.

For an hour the boy continued on down the tunnel, the beam of his flashlight reflecting off cave walls smoothed by millennia of swiftly flowing water. The glow caught only empty blackness ahead, and his numbed mind had come to expect nothing more.

Then, suddenly, the beam shone on a jumble of rocks ahead. He stopped in his tracks and swung the flashlight from one side of the tunnel to the other. The passage before him was blocked from side to side by a cave-in. The boy stumbled forward and collapsed at the foot of the mass of boulders.

For the first time in his ordeal, great sobs racked his body and tears washed channels down his dirt-smeared face. Then gradually Paco quieted and fell into an exhausted sleep.

Almost four hours after the boy closed his eyes, a small television camera set in a niche high above the tunnel floor hummed automatically to life and began a slow pan of the rockslide and the near tunnel. The camera reached the form of the boy and abruptly stopped its sweep.

Almost imperceptibly, the lens rotated, focusing on the sleeping face of Paco Sanchez.

11:00 A.M.

Lamar Jackson raced down the sideline of Texas Stadium a half step behind the pass receiver he was covering and at the very last possible moment reached up and knocked the football from the near grasp of his opponent.

Despite the fact that this was just a light workout to limber up two hours before the exhibition game with San Francisco, he felt elated at breaking up the play.

There were many reasons why Lamar Jackson was a great free safety, a $2-million-a-year, once-in-a-decade free safety. He was extraordinarily fast, he could turn on a dime, and he had long arms at the ends of which extended huge hands.

Yet his greatest single athletic asset was not physical but metaphysical. Lamar Jackson could look into an opponent's eyes on the playing field and read the man's next thought.

It wasn't just the other player's coming move he could see. There were many good safeties who could tell from their adversaries' eyes the very moment the football was coming in. No, what made Lamar Jackson different, special, was that he could see so much more.

Most of the time, the man opposite him was thinking about the play he'd carried back to the line from the huddle. If it were a pass to him, the receiver would be worried about which shoulder the ball would come over, would he be too close to the sideline, could he trick Lamar off him by cutting, curling, slowing down, accelerating in a sudden burst?

Occasionally, searching the eyes of his opponents, Jackson would be disconcerted by a receiver who wasn't thinking about the play. Sometimes he read thoughts that upset and even scared him. He'd stolen insights into other men's marital woes and money problems. He'd read thoughts of love and thoughts of murder.

Usually during these light pregame workouts, Jackson saw only optimism in the eyes of his Dallas Cowboy teammates. Almost every player, starter or second-string, was fired up with the secret thought that today he would make the starring play, the winning play of the game.

This Sunday, though, there was little of this excited anticipation. The whole team was subdued. When Jackson glanced into his teammates' eyes, he read only uneasiness and, in some, foreboding.

He had that same cloying sense of depression himself. The feeling seemed to extend to the stadium vendors and the light crowd of early fans. Usually you'd hear beer and ice cream being hawked and people shouting down encouragement to their favorite players. Not today. Fans sat quietly in their seats while food and souvenir spielers worked the aisles with listless calls.

Perhaps it was the strange coolness on the field that was unsettling everyone. Driving to the stadium that morning, Jackson had heard the radio weatherman announce the 9 A.M. Dallas temperature as eighty-seven degrees. Yet the thermometer behind the players' bench read a mere sixty-nine.

One of the coaches said that a pocket of cool air must have drifted down through the open roof during the night and become trapped in the semi-enclosed bowl of the stadium by a layer of warm air above.

That might explain the temperature, Jackson thought, but what about the smell? It was a wafting, almost ethereal smell that he caught only occasionally, and for a long time he was preoccupied trying to remember where he'd encountered the subtle odor before.

Then, backing up to cover a pass play, it came to him. Those summers on his grandmother's Arkansas farm. Even on the hottest day, there'd always been a cool place to go: his grandmother's root cellar.

The playing field of Texas Stadium smelled like his grandmother's root cellar.

NOON

The first thing Ignacio Baptista thought when he looked into the ten-thousand-year-old face in the sinkhole was that just at the moment of her death the ancient Indian woman must have been told the sweetest of secrets.

Even now, a hundred centuries after the day she was mummified, the woman's perfectly preserved face radiated an expression of pure—thousands would later insist blessed—serenity.

The farmer Baptista had been mucking out the corral behind his barn when he felt the ground tremble beneath his crusted rubber boots. A moment later a deep rumble rose from the west and a roiling cloud suddenly shot into the air above his distant fruit field.

Baptista had crossed himself and then walked slowly across the burnt ground toward the place where the dust billowed skyward. He knew what had happened, yet he prayed every step that it hadn't.

The ragged edges of the sinkhole were still breaking off in large root-veined chunks when he reached the field. An acre of his best farmland, a table of rich topsoil on which he'd raised succulent melons and strawberries before the drought, had disappeared down a yawning sinkhole ninety feet deep.

For several minutes Baptista stared numbly into the swirling bowl of dust. Then the air in the pit began to clear and for the first time he saw the human figure embedded to its shoulders in the bottom.

Baptista tore his eyes away and fled to his house.

Twenty minutes later he was back with his ashen-faced wife, Alicia, and several long lengths of rope. While Alicia wrung her hands and begged him to call the sheriff, Baptista drove a stake into the hard ground thirty feet back from the lip of the crater. Then, as Alicia knelt and wailed entreaties to God, he let himself gingerly over the rim and slid backward in an awkward half crouch down the thirty-degree slope of the sinkhole.

He reached the bottom and paused to gather himself, fighting to shut out the courage-sapping lament of his wife above, then timidly approached the soil-gripped corpse.

Like all men who raise animals on the land, Baptista was intimate with the sickly-sweet smell of death, and he expected it now. Instead, an almost imperceptible odor of ancient dust wafted from the exposed head and shoulders.

He forced his hand forward and with trembling fingers began to brush the residue of dirt from the head of the mummified figure. The hair emerged as black and shiny as obsidian. Below, the skin of the forehead was brown, with the look of softly creased leather.

He cleaned out the empty eye sockets with a pocket knife, then gently scraped off the broad straight nose and high cheeks. Finally, he picked the soil from the tender furrow of the woman's mouth and scrubbed clean the hardened jaw, neck, and shoulders.

As his hands worked along the collarbone, his fingers brushed a small convex surface tight against the woman's chest. In a moment he had dug away the dirt to expose the small mummified head of a newborn infant, after ten thousand years its tiny mouth still suckling at the dry breast of its mother.

Baptista stepped back and felt a transporting peace wash over him as he gazed at the vision still tender in death of the ancient mother nursing her ancient baby.

"It is the Madonna," he whispered.

He might have stared raptly at the narcotic image of the Madonna for hours had the beseeching moans of Alicia not shattered his trance. With a great effort, he tore his eyes away and pulled himself back up the rope.

Baptista collapsed wordlessly into the dust next to his kneeling wife, oblivious to her pleas to leave this place. The sight of the tears streaming from her husband's eyes finally quieted Alicia and she took his hand. "Why do you weep, Ignacio? Are you so afraid?"

He shook his head almost imperceptibly, his eyes riveted on the mummified woman and infant in the crater. "It is the Madonna, Alicia. And she is Indian. She is one of us."

EARLY AFTERNOON

The studio in New York cut to a commercial eight minutes
into the second quarter of the Cowboy–Forty-Niner game,
and in the CBS Sports broadcast booth high under the eaves
of Texas Stadium, play-by-play man Keith Henning ripped
off his headset and turned to color commentator Jack
Francis.

"What the hell is wrong down there? There are twenty-
two players on that field, and I don't think a single one of
them gives a shit who wins this game," he said in
exasperation. "I've covered football for thirty-two years,
and this is the most spiritless performance I've ever seen.
For God's sake, even the coaches are standing around with
their hands in their pockets."

Francis pulled his earphones down around his neck and
shook his head. "It's not just the teams, Keith. Have you
noticed how quiet the fans are? No screaming, no banner
waving, no drunks jumping around in those huge cowboy
hats. The whole stadium's like a morgue."

On the field below, Dallas free safety Lamar Jackson
swallowed a last gulp of Gatorade as the referee blew his
whistle for play to resume and the water boys and trainers
finished their ministrations and scurried for the sidelines.

So far the first half had been a cakewalk for Jackson.

During an ordinary game, he would have been bathed in
sweat by now, pumped up with adrenaline, a spring coiled
to release the instant the ball was snapped. Forty-Niner
quarterback Will Shaffer had one of the best arms in the
National Football League, and he'd burned Jackson more
than once with his deadly accurate passing.

But nothing was as it should be today. Shaffer's timing
was off and his passes had been long, short, low, wide.
Jackson had covered seven Forty-Niner series of downs and
his jersey was barely damp with perspiration.

San Francisco hadn't been able to get beyond their own
thirty-yard line since the opening kickoff. Not that Dallas
had done any better. The Cowboys had had one fluke run
that got them to the forty-two, but the offense had fumbled
on the next play and the monotonous exchange of punts had
continued.

There was something terribly wrong in Texas Stadium,
something that was distracting the players, disrupting their
timing, sapping their will to win. A maddeningly vague
dread hung in the air, a cloying malevolence that had settled
like a thick cloak over the collective spirit of athletes and
spectators.

Lamar Jackson focused on the Forty-Niner quarterback as
Shaffer stepped into position behind his center and began
the count in a low monotone. The ball was snapped and
Jackson heard the dull thud of helmets and bodies at the line
as Shaffer took three quick paces back and set himself to
pass.

Jackson drifted along behind his lineman, then broke to
his right as Forty-Niner tight end Manny Oprotkowitz cut
across tackle and curled toward the sideline downfield.

Oprotkowitz was fast, one of the swiftest ends in the
league, but today he seemed to lope more than run and
Jackson had no trouble staying by his side. As always,
Jackson watched his opponent's eyes, trying to read the
receiver's·next move. He caught anticipation in Oprotkowitz's widening pupils and knew the ball would be coming in
any second now.

Then suddenly a great communal gasp, a hiccup of

horror, rose from fifty thousand throats in the stands and at the same moment the anticipation vanished from the receiver's eyes. Instead, Jackson saw terror there, gaping terror, as the Forty-Niner tight end stopped dead in his tracks.

Jackson reined in and followed Oprotkowitz's mesmerized stare back toward the line of scrimmage. Only there wasn't any line of scrimmage. Where the two opposing teams had battled each other across the Astroturf there was now a gaping hole in the floor of Texas Stadium, a black pit that stretched from the end zone out to the Forty-Niner thirty-yard line.

While Jackson had been watching the eyes of Manny Oprotkowitz, the earth had swallowed up the linemen on both teams and the entire San Francisco backfield.

The din in the stands rose to a hysterical roar as the lip of the sinkhole widened suddenly, advancing toward the players' benches on both sidelines. Jackson watched, rooted where he stood, as the pit continued to grow and players, coaches, VIPs, and television technicians hurtled themselves over the rails at the fringe of the stands and clawed their way toward the safety of the seats.

Jackson broke out of his spell and with Oprotkowitz beside him fled for the players' tunnel behind them. There was already a throng at the entrance as everyone still alive on the field jammed into the narrow corridor.

Behind them, panic swept like a wave through the stands as fifty thousand people erupted in flight for the exits. In less than a minute almost two hundred spectators were trampled to death in the aisles and stairwells.

Sporadic pistol shots added to the tumult as men tried to shoot their way through the mobbed escapeways. Children were torn from the grasp of their screaming parents and crushed underfoot, and dozens of spectators were pushed over railings in the upper tiers to plummet to their deaths on the concrete below.

In the CBS booth above, Keith Henning stared down at the bottomless field and the spectacle of dying people below him. "Ladies and gentlemen, there's been a terrible . . . oh, my

God, oh, my dear God," he managed hoarsely before his throat constricted and he tore off his headset.

The huge nationwide television audience watching the Cowboy–Forty-Niner game needed no verbal description of what had happened before their eyes. For months the sinkholes plaguing Texas had been a peripheral phenomenon to the rest of the country. No longer. From Maine to California, forty million viewers understood that what they had seen was the beginning of the end of a great western city.

Through the eye of television, America witnessed the death rattle of Dallas.

EARLY AFTERNOON

The three huge Russian transport helicopters came in low over the dun hills to the south and hovered in a ring over the Mexican border village of Quito. One minute it was quiet and peaceful in the tiny hamlet, the next there was terror everywhere.

Most of the simple herders and farmers below had never seen such machines before, and the terrified peasants ran through the narrow adobe alleys snatching up screaming children and cowering piglets and goat kids.

Slowly, the heavy helicopters settled to the earth, each stirring up its own whirlwind of dust. The doors burst open while the blades above still turned, and the 160 men of Company C, Che Guevara Division, Mexican People's Revolutionary Army fanned out from their aircraft to join in a skirmish line around Quito.

The empty transports lifted off as soon as the last soldier had leapt out onto the desert, and for a moment after the aircraft noise had died away over the hills there was an eerie silence. Then a baby cried out in one of the huts and its tiny shriek was answered by the bark of officers' orders. A twenty-man squad ran forward in a half crouch toward the village.

The soldiers hugged the adobe walls as they advanced to

the well that was the center of Quito. The lieutenant in charge motioned to one of his men for the battery-powered loudspeaker. "This is Lieutenant Pablo Rua of the People's Revolutionary Army. I wish to speak to the headman of Quito."

Heads poked out of curtained doorways at the words in Spanish. So it was not the American army after all. The soldiers were theirs. Mexicans.

An old man tottered up to Rua, his worry-webbed face sculpted with the deep creases of time and the desert. "I am Raphael García," he said, his frayed sombrero twirling in his bony hands. "I am the headman here in Quito."

Lieutenant Rua softened at the fear he saw in the old man's eyes. "Señor García, two days ago a patrol of the People's Revolutionary Army was sent to Quito to look into a report from your village, a report of strange noises at night across the river. The patrol has not returned to our head-quarters. Have you seen these soldiers?"

"Yes, they were here. Sergeant Ortega and his men."

"Do you know where they went?"

"The sergeant asked for a guide, then at dusk they went up the river."

"That's the last time you saw our soldiers?"

"That is the last time anyone will see them, lieutenant. They are all dead. The *yanquis* killed them."

Rua stared at the headman. "How do you know this, Señor García? Was there a battle with the *yanquis*?"

"We saw no battle."

The officer knitted his eyebrows. "Then you heard something—rifle fire, artillery—up the river?"

"No." The headman shook his head. "We heard noth-ing."

The lieutenant was becoming exasperated. "Señor Gar-cía, you saw no battle, you heard no gunfire, yet you tell me our soldiers are dead."

The old man turned and yelled to his wife in their adobe, "Consuelo, bring the sergeant's hat."

García's little round wife appeared, a mound of shawls

from which peered a wizened, toothless face. Timidly she handed the military cap to the officer.

"One of the women doing wash found it in the brush along the river," García said. "Yesterday at dawn."

Lieutenant Rua looked at the hat impatiently. This was the old man's evidence that eight men were dead?

"Turn it over," the headman said quietly.

Rua flipped the cap and gasped. "*¡Madre mia!*" The underside of the visor and the cotton liner were soaked with thickly clotted, dark-red gore. It looked as if the hat had been dropped straight down into a vat of human blood.

Rua spun to a sergeant with him. "Tell Capitán Santos to bring up the company."

Captain Santos had been awarded his commission through political contacts, and he'd spent most of his eight months in the People's Revolutionary Army behind a desk in Guadalajara. He blanched when Rua showed him the hat.

"We must call the colonel at once," Santos said, turning the hat over nervously in his hands. "We need the entire division up here. Perhaps artillery support as well."

Lieutenant Rua lowered his voice below the earshot of the soldiers and villagers. "With all respect, *capitán,* what are we to report, a bloody hat? We came here to find Sergeant Ortega and his men. The headman says the patrol went up the river. May I suggest we at least mount a reconnaissance before we call in reinforcements?"

The captain's eyes flitted to the American side of the river. "What if the *yanquis* are waiting for us? An ambush?"

"That is always possible, *capitán.* Yet it is equally conceivable the patrol is trapped, pinned down by guns across the river. They may need our relief. Now, not tomorrow morning when the division gets here."

The way Rua put it, Santos could hardly disregard the lieutenant's advice. Not without appearing a coward.

"Yes, of course, a reconnaissance," the captain said unhappily.

"If it is your wish, *capitán,* I will take two squads, forty men, and mount the reconnaissance while you hold the village with the balance of the company."

"Yes, yes, an excellent plan, lieutenant." Santos brightened, his shoulders straightening as the risk of personal combat receded. "I will be ready to lead the company to your side at once should you meet the *yanquis*."

Rua didn't bother to grace the lie with acknowledgment. "With your permission, sir, I will pick my men and get started."

He turned to the headman. "How far up the river did your guide take our soldiers?"

"Not far," the old man said. "A kilometer at most."

Five minutes later Lieutenant Pablo Rua led forty men on foot up the sheep trail fringing the Mexican side of the Rio Bravo del Norte. The twin ribbons of track treads left by Sergeant Ortega's personnel carrier were still visible, stretching ahead over the sandy ground.

The soldiers snaked around a bend and left the small village behind. Rua sent two men ahead to take the point, then loosened his tunic to let the climbing sun warm his neck. Out of sight of their martinet captain, the men ambled more than marched, their rifles slung over their shoulders to serve as yokes to hold their hands.

But for the waffled treads of the half-track to remind them they were soldiers on a mission, the men might have been on a holiday hike through the countryside. The river rippled peacefully by on their right and desert birds called to each other from their perches amid the towering saguaro cacti.

The reconnaissance patrol had gone three-quarters of a kilometer up the river when Rua saw the point men trotting back through the shimmering heat waves. The soldiers arrived out of breath, flushed from their run and the news they brought. They'd found the half-track ahead. It was near the river.

Rua pulled back into his soldier shell and split his men into two squads. He sent twenty men into the desert to approach the half-track from the south while he led the second squad on a direct route up the river.

The lieutenant could sense the fear kindling in the men

double-timing up the trail behind him. The spark of a
yanqui bullet would ignite them, whether in flames of
courage or cowardice he did not know. He didn't even know
about himself. Three minutes later the squad rounded a rock
outcropping and Rua saw the half-track.

He signaled the men into a skirmish line and swept the
personnel carrier and the near ground with his binoculars.
There were no soldiers in sight, either Mexican or American. Something moved on the front of the half-track. He
adjusted the glasses. It was a rattlesnake. The reptile had
climbed the treads at dawn and was sunning itself on the flat
metal deck. But for the snake, there was no sign of life.

Rua waited until he saw the second squad fan into
position to the south. Then he waved his pistol in the air and
the reconnaissance patrol closed on the abandoned half-
track.

Fifty yards from the vehicle, there was a sudden explosion of electrified voice and forty men dropped to the desert
as one. There was a moment of silence, then the voice came
again, punctured by static this time, and Rua realized the
transmission was coming from the half-track's radio. He
slashed his pistol forward and the Mexicans again advanced.

Rua halted the patrol five paces from the vehicle. The
rattlesnake was a problem. He didn't dare shoot the snake.
If there were *yanquis* across the river, gunfire on the
Mexican side could bring a fusillade against his men.

"This is Lieutenant Pablo Rua of the Che Guevara
Division. Is there anyone in the half-track?"

The rattlesnake brought its head up at the sound of Rua's
voice, then slowly coiled as its forked tongue sensed the
massed body heat of the nearby humans.

There was no reply to Rua's call, and he turned his
attention back to the snake. The reptile obviously meant to
stand its ground on the warm steel deck, and the door was
well within striking distance.

Rua picked up a rock and threw it at the snake. The stone
clanged noisily off the metal plates several feet from the

hissing reptile. He was about to throw another rock when Private Largo stepped forward.

Largo had been the best knife fighter in La Prienta, Mexico City's jungle of a slum, when the army drafted him. It was said he could put a knife in a man at fifty paces. Largo grinned insolently at his lieutenant, then took a step forward, his eyes riveted on the snake.

For a moment Largo stood motionless. Then, in a movement Rua saw only as a blur, he fell to one knee, whipped a knife from his boot and flicked it forward with a sharp snap of his wrist.

The double-edged blade entered the snake's neck horizontally, severing the head. The force of the throw carried the head and the knife out into the desert beyond the half-track, and the reptile's lifeless body flopped onto the steel deck. Largo glanced back in triumph at the officer, then went to retrieve his blade.

Rua crossed to the troop carrier and opened the thick steel door. The passenger compartment was empty, in regular order. There were no empty shell casings strewn about, no ammunition boxes hastily opened, no blood. Whatever had happened to the patrol of Sergeant Ortega, it had not happened in the half-track.

As Rua's eyes adjusted to the dim cabin, he noticed small squares on the shadowed seats: wallets, some with watches stretched around them. Why would the missing men . . . ? The obvious answer hit him. The soldiers had left their wallets in the half-track to keep the papers and pictures inside from getting wet.

Rua straightened and searched the surrounding sand. The footprints of the patrol were clearly visible leading north toward the Rio Bravo. He sent ten men to reconnoiter the riverbank for a kilometer to the east and west while he used the half-track's radio to report in to Captain Santos.

Half an hour later the search party was back. The missing men had entered the water but there was no sign they had come back out. Lieutenant Rua stared at the shimmering ribbon of the river and made his decision. They would search the American side.

He ordered his men into a skirmish line, and forty
soldiers of Company C of the Che Guevara Division waded
into the waters of the Rio Bravo del Norte.

In a camouflaged observation post across the river, Karl
Stroesser lowered his binoculars and fingered the oiled
trigger of an AK-47 assault rifle.

MIDAFTERNOON

General Hugo Santamaría stared down at the horizonless white ice fields of northern Greenland 35,000 feet beneath the Aeroflot jetliner and felt himself transported by the consummate peace that seemed almost to radiate up from the pristine glaciers.

The vast frozen land passing below offered no climate to nurture civilization, no soil to farm, no rivers to fish, no forest to shelter, nothing to attract the avarice of man. No human had ever set foot in the trackless wilderness, and, because man had never come to this place, peace had never left it.

Peace. Santamaría pinched the fatigue from the bridge of his Roman nose and ran his fingertips through the angry cloud of white hair rising from his great leonine head. Had there ever been a day on this earth since Cain slew Abel that humankind had known peace? History set dates for the ends of wars but they were only route numbers on a highway that ran on and on.

Santamiaría had been a soldier on that road for forty of his sixty-four years. A Communist soldier. His ancestors must be spinning in their graves at how he'd turned out.

The Santamarías were patricians who traced their roots to the conquistadors. Since the seventeenth century, the family

99

had been sending its sons to Europe to study, and after
private schools and tutors, Hugo Santamaría had found
himself at the University of Madrid at the age of sixteen.

Four years of school in Spain were followed by two
graduate years at the Sorbonne in Paris. He was supposed to
be studying business to prepare him to run the family estates
in the Yucatán. Instead, for the first time in his life, he
learned what was really happening in his country.

From the French and the European press he discovered
that six and a half million Indians had starved to death in the
Yucatán peninsula alone over the past ten years. He learned
of the devastating mortality rate among infants in rural
Mexico, the appropriation of peasant farms by large land-
owners, the Swiss bank accounts of those in power in
Mexico City.

Hugo Santamaría had looked back in revulsion on his
own life of ease, ashamed of his family's theft of the
peasants' labor, of the degradation of so many lives.
Vowing to make it up to his people, he joined the Communist guerrillas operating out of northern Guatemala in the
early sixties. He'd long since lost track of the number of
battles he fought over the next thirty years.

His tall thin body and age-lined face bore the scars of
eighteen bullet and shrapnel wounds, and his thick curly
hair and broad mustache were white. He had fought not for
personal glory but for his people, his country; he felt
himself at the core a man of peace.

The purity and tranquillity of the glaciers of Greenland
mocked the contents of the briefcase on the seat next to
Santamaría. He was carrying home to Mexico the final draft
of the mutual defense treaty he'd just negotiated in Moscow
on behalf of his country.

The Soviet-Mexican Mutual Defense Treaty should have
been the ultimate triumph of his career as a revolutionary
soldier diplomat. The pact was being hailed in Moscow and
Mexico City as a bulwark against the threat of an American
invasion of his homeland, an invasion his Marxist government had feared since its first day in power.

Yet Santamaría was haunted with misgivings that the

treaty would spawn not peace but war. The Americans were certain to be incensed when they learned of the alliance. The Pentagon was already apoplectic over the missile pads in northern Mexico. The defense treaty would send new believers stampeding to the side of those hawks in Washington who argued for preemptive military action against Mexico.

Santamaría closed his eyes against the sun that reflected off the white ice fields below, filling the airliner with harsh bright light. The treaty could lead to dangerous miscalculations on the Mexican side as well. He was returning home with a piece of paper, a hundred-thousand-word promise, but he knew that in the minds of Mexico's jingoistic junta he was bringing back Russian divisions, Russian nuclear missiles, Russian power.

There would be laurel wreaths heaped upon him at home, Santamaría knew. He would be greeted as a hero. But if the definition of betray was "to lead astray, to seduce, to deliver to any enemy by treachery," then perhaps he was a traitor, for the treaty he had signed would, he feared, ultimately ill serve his beloved country.

The week-long negotiations in Moscow had drained him, and he longed more than anything for rest. He pulled down the small window shade against the glacial light and fought for a sleep that wouldn't come.

In the regular passenger compartment twelve rows behind the Mexican general, Major Demyan Turgenev put down the dry technical manual detailing missile thrust and glanced down at the ice fields.

The endless expanse of white snow reminded him of the Russian steppes in winter. Kiev was on the steppes, and Ilona was in Kiev. He wondered once more if he'd ever see her again, hold her again, make love to her again.

He hadn't been able to shake the fear that had settled in his bones when the drunken recruit had crashed through his dream the night before. It was not the remembered menace of the drunk that plagued him. That had passed, a fleeting symptom of his innate cowardice. He was afraid of failing as a man in Mexico. His assignment would be tough, and he saw himself as soft.

All his life there had been the breast of the motherland state to succor him, to assuage his frail image of himself. He'd thrived in the Young Pioneers, in the Communist Youth League, in Kiev Technical Institute, in Officers Training School. His courage, he knew, was the courage of orders, of doctrine, of official stamps and official conduct. In uniform he was courageous; naked, a coward.

He'd read every book on Mexico he could get his hands on in the six months since he'd learned of his possible assignment. The common thread running through all the accounts was the consuming machismo of Mexican men, their penchant for fighting with knives and guns over the smallest imagined slight to their honor, their patriotism, their manhood.

A shudder shook Turgenev at the mental image of a bandoliered, mustachioed Mexican taking umbrage at some slip of his tongue and facing off against him with a ten-inch knife. Despite the fact that he was a soldier, Turgenev hated weapons. Perhaps, he reflected, that was the real reason he'd chosen the Soviet missile service as a career rather than the infantry or artillery where he could gain rank quicker. Missiles were abstract, impersonal weapons. To fire a rifle or a cannon, a soldier had to become physically intimate with the gun, the bullets, the shells, the smell of cordite, and the small shock of detonation. To fire a missile, a man merely had to sit in a comfortable chair in a sterile control room and punch a code into a quiet computer.

Turgenev chewed at the inside of his mouth. It was possible his assignment to Mexico could force on him that moment of inescapable personal conflict he had feared all his life.

Only he possessed the codes and the programming knowledge to convert the Mexican missiles from their defensive antiaircraft mode to offensive weapons able to reach distant North American cities.

Of course, without nuclear warheads, the missiles could only deliver a payload of conventional explosives. One rocket would inflict about the same damage as a single load of bombs dropped from a plane.

Still, if the Mexican missiles were reprogrammed, there remained only the addition of a nuclear tip to change the entire strategic equation between Mexico and the North American behemoth across her northern border.

The great Soviet fear was that the volatile Latinos might answer a U.S. provocation with a barrage of missiles that would involve the Soviet Union in a war with the United States. Thus, despite fervent Mexican pleas during the treaty negotiations, Moscow refused to give the missile targeting codes and programs directly to the Mexican military.

As a concession, they agreed to send a Russian missile officer to Mexico with the programs. The codes would not leave the officer's possession. The officer would be under direct orders not to retarget any Mexican missile without both voice and code authorization from the Kremlin.

Turgenev stared down at the sweeping glaciers and wondered what he would do if in a time of tumult the Mexicans came to him with a demand for the firing code. Would his uniform be buttress enough against furious pressure, perhaps even beatings and torture? Could he suddenly become a man when all his life he had been a boy?

The barren ice fields below offered no answer, and Turgenev sank into his seat and searched for thoughts of Ilona.

MIDAFTERNOON

The hoverjet circled lazily 3,500 feet above the Sanchez farm and then began a slow wide spiral down toward the sinkhole-pocked prairie.

Jedediah Heffernan banked the delta-winged craft, and one after another of the cave searchers, newsmen, and spectators gathered below craned their necks to look up as the shadow of the strange plane crossed the sinkhole.

Lucia recognized the hoverjet from Jedediah's description at the breakfast table and steepled her hands in an instinctive gesture of thanksgiving prayer. He had come after all. Thank God, he had come.

Heff descended to five hundred feet, then throttled back and gradually angled the thrust ports downward so that the jets were directed below instead of behind the aircraft.

A roiling ring of dust shot out from beneath the aircraft as it settled down fifty yards from the crowd around the sinkhole. Lucia abruptly broke off her conversation with Morris Foster and ran toward the hoverjet as Heff shut down the engine.

"I knew you would come. I knew it," she said, barely resisting the impulse to hug Jedediah as he climbed out.

"Then you're clairvoyant, Lucia, because I only made up my mind a few hours ago."

"No, Jedediah. Within yourself, you knew you had to come from the moment you learned a ten-year-old boy was lost in the Rio Bajo. I saw it in your face as I told you about Paco."

He looked at her for a long moment. "Maybe you're right, maybe you're not," he said finally. "My thought processes are not something I care to have second-guessed."

"I merely meant that your conscience gave you no choice. You're here because that's the kind of man you are. Why deny it?"

"Don't be so dammed ready to mark me out a hero, Lucia. I'm here, but I'm giving no guarantees."

"You'll find Paco," she said.

"I don't mean Paco. I'm telling you I don't know if I'll be able to pull this off. I could come unglued. If Alex is waiting for me down there . . ." He let his voice trail off.

She was stunned by the anguish she saw in his eyes. In the small Mexican church in Rocksprings there was a wall fresco of the Crucifixion, and the pain the artist had put in the stares of the disciples looking up at the cross was mirrored now in Jedediah's eyes.

She reached a hand to grasp his arm above the elbow. "You won't be caving by yourself this time. I'm going with you."

He shook his head. "Thanks, but I work alone."

"You'll need me down there."

The determination came back to his face. "Look, Lucia, I appreciate your offer. And I'm sure there'll be times when I could use some help, assuming I get past the damn entrance. But moving through caves isn't like strolling down a country lane. It's dangerous. You could get hurt or killed down there, and I can't split my attention between searching for Paco and shepherding you."

She bristled. "There'll be no need for you to shepherd me. I've managed to take care of myself for the past twenty-six years without your help."

"Lucia, you have to understand that a cave is not just a tunnel. Deep pits can suddenly open under your feet,

stalactites jutting down from the roof can gouge out an eye.
There are deceptive passages you can squeeze into but not
out of, and there's always the danger of a rockslide or a
cave-in. The Rio Bajo is no place for a novice spelunker."

Before she could argue her case further, Heff turned and
hoisted himself to the cabin rim of the hoverjet. He reached
toward a toggle switch on the control panel.

"What are you doing?" Lucia asked, intrigued by the
strange aircraft despite her angry frustration.

"Retracting the wings," Heff said. He flipped the switch,
and simultaneously an electric motor hummed and the delta
wings slipped into the body of the craft and stored themselves away in hollow slots beneath the cockpit.

"So this is the Caverunner you invented," Lucia said.

"Actually, I modified a design that's been around since
the fifties," Heff said. "It's based on the original VTOL
concept, vertical takeoff and landing, first developed by the
British."

"But why do you need a craft that's both a plane and a
hovercraft?" Lucia asked.

"I use her as a plane when I'm overflying geological
formations on the surface. And if I were entering the usual
cave system with small tunnels, tight passages, sumps and
crawl spaces, I'd go in on foot. But in a large labyrinth like
the Rio Bajo la Tierra, with hundreds of miles of large
tunnels and caverns, I'll use the Caverunner. She never
touches the ground so she can travel over the roughest cave
floor and the deepest crevasse."

He climbed into the cockpit and reached down a hand to
Lucia. "C'mon. I'll give you a ride over to the edge."

Lucia squeezed into the co-pilot's seat and Heff lowered
the bubble of plexiglass. A moment later he began flicking
switches, and then there was the building sound of the
hoverjet's motor starting beneath them.

Dust flew out from beneath the craft and Lucia felt an
almost imperceptible lift as the Caverunner rose inches
above the prairie on its cushion of air.

"What's that strange contraption out on the front there?"
she asked as they moved slowly toward the sinkhole.

"That's a laser cannon. It's for boring into rock formations and cave walls for subsurface ore samples."

A knot of searchers and media people surrounded the hoverjet as Heff shut off the motor and helped Lucia down thirty feet from the lip of the huge pit.

For several minutes Heff answered the shouted questions of the reporters. Yes, he was Jedediah Heffernan, one of the two "New Mexico Mounties." No, his partner was not with him. His partner was dead.

Heff explained the Caverunner, then, Lucia in tow, brushed past the clutching reporters and threaded his way through the throng to where rescue leader Morris Foster stood.

"I'm glad you've come, Heff," Foster said. "To tell you the truth, I didn't think you would."

"Neither did I, Morry," Heff said. "Any sign of the boy?"

"I tracked him about a mile and a quarter down the north fork, then lost the trail on a stretch of rock floor. We haven't found a single damn sign since."

"Let's take a look at a map," Heff said. "I want to know where you've had your search parties."

The two men pored over the map for twenty minutes. "Call your people up, will you, Morry?" Heff said when they'd finished. "I'm going to take the Caverunner down and I don't want anyone under the jets."

"Sure, Heff," Foster agreed, moving to the lip of the sinkhole with a walkie-talkie.

Heff turned to Lucia. "I'm going down on foot first to see what kind of bottom I'll have beneath the jets. I'll be back in a few minutes."

Lucia put her hand on his elbow. "May I go with you?"

"You may not," he said, seeing in her eyes that she knew the real reason he was going down alone.

Lucia walked Heff to the edge of the pit, then watched him climb down a rope ladder as Foster's men climbed up another ladder on the other side. He wasn't going down to test the bottom, Lucia told herself. He was going down to test himself.

Heff reached the floor of the sinkhole and pretended to examine the dusty surface as the last of the searchers climbed out. Then he gathered himself and walked slowly into the black tunnel leading northeast.

The light from the sinkhole behind faded rapidly as he moved into the cave until, fifty yards down the tunnel, he rounded a bend and inky blackness surrounded him.

The darkness felt close, encasing, and the sound of his own labored breathing echoed back thickly off the near walls. Then, almost imperceptibly at first, he felt the presence near him. Alex. Heff strained his senses into the blackness, searching. Far down the tunnel, two red specks appeared and began to move in tandem through the dark. Slowly the specks came closer. They grew to marble size and began to glow before him like red-hot coals. But they weren't coals. They were eyes. Alex's blood-glazed eyes.

He suddenly heard his name called through the darkness. "Jedediah. Jedediah." Only Alex called him Jedediah. Terror paralyzed him as he waited for his friend's bloody face to materialize around the eyes. He could smell his own fear in the sickly sweet sweat coursing through his open pores. Then he felt a hand on his shoulder and screamed.

Heff tore away from the hand, falling backward against the near wall of the cave. His head smashed into the limestone and he collapsed dazed onto the dirt floor.

He was dimly aware of a sudden light, then a voice, a voice that was not Alex's voice. "Jedediah. Jedediah, are you all right?"

Heff's senses slowly oriented as he stared up into the face of Lucia Sanchez kneeling beside him, her olive skin looking eerily pale in the white glow of her flashlight.

Lucia. It had been her hand on his shoulder. Groggily, he pushed himself up into a sitting position against the cave wall, relief and anger coursing through him together. "What the hell are you doing down here? Dammit, don't you know better than to sneak up on a man that way?"

"I didn't sneak up on you. I called your name. Twice."

"You must have whispered because I didn't hear—" Then he remembered. Lucia, as well as Alex, called him Jedediah. "I thought I told you to stay above," he grumbled.

"You may be used to giving orders to women, Jedediah, but I'm not used to taking them from men. I thought you might need me."

"Oh, you did, did you? Did you think that after five years I'd forgotten how to cave?"

"No, Jedediah. I came because I didn't think you'd forgotten. I didn't think you'd forgotten anything."

He got ready to bluster at her, then let a long breath ease from his tight chest. "You were right. Alex was here."

"Alex was in your head, Jedediah. He's always been in your head. You haven't told me everything that happened that day in Spanish Cavern. I don't think you've told anyone. You'll never be free of Alex, never exorcise your guilt over his death, not until you share what happened with another. I want you to share that day with me."

He stared into the blackness of the cave. "Maybe someday, Lucia, but not yet. I'm not ready to talk about Alex's death yet. At least not now."

She saw a thin rivulet of blood trickle down from his hairline. "You're hurt, Jedediah."

He felt the wetness and brought his hand up to the top of his forehead. "Small cut. Lucky. I hit that wall like a truck."

Lucia tore a swatch of cloth from the hem of her blouse and dabbed at the wound. "I'm going with you, Jedediah. You needed me once, you'll need me again."

Heff remained silent a moment. "You have no idea what you'd be letting yourself in for. There are a hundred ways to die down here. And it's not just the physical danger to worry about. Caves do funny things to people. You could find yourself suddenly seized by depression, paranoia, claustrophobia. What would you do if we're ten miles in and you suddenly feel like the walls are closing in on you?"

"I'd ask you to help me, as I will help you. I'm not brave, Jedediah. I know I'll be afraid. I don't want to die. But even more, I don't want my brother to die. I can't find him alone, and I don't believe you can either. But together we can. You must take me with you."

Heff looked into Lucia's imploring eyes. Hell, she was right. He needed her as much as she needed him. With Lucia along, perhaps Alex would leave him in peace.

"Let's get the Caverunner down here," he said, rising away from her dabbing hand.

Lucia stood with the light. "Then you'll take me?"

"We'll take each other."

Ten minutes later they were sitting in the cockpit of the Caverunner. Heff exchanged some final words with Foster, then lowered the plexiglass canopy and started the motor. The hum of the turbo built steadily beneath them.

Heff turned to face Lucia. "There's one last thing before we go down. While we're in the cave, you will do what I tell you, when I tell you. I'm the boss."

Lucia bristled. "You say 'jump,' I ask 'how far?'—is that what you have in mind?"

"Look, Lucia, we can get into trouble real fast down there. If there's a sudden rockslide or cave-in, I won't have time to explain why you must take a certain action. If you don't move quickly, without questions, you may not ever move again. That's the way it's going to be. Now you either understand that or you bail out now. Make up your mind."

"I've already made up my mind, Jedediah. Whatever it takes to bring Paco out alive, that's what I'll do. You're the boss."

"I hope you mean that," he said, and turned back to the controls.

The drone of the motor rose in pitch and the Caverunner lifted eighteen inches above the baked prairie. Heff eased the stick forward, and the hoverjet moved slowly toward the lip of the sinkhole. As they crossed the rim, he turned once more to Lucia. "You're sure you want to do this?"

She looked down into the depths of the sinkhole where the tunnel of the Rio Bajo led off into the deep black bowels of the earth. She wasn't sure. She was scared. He'd never know how scared.

She took a deep breath and looked at Heff. "My brother's down there, Jedediah. Let's go."

Heff turned around and the Caverunner slowly lowered into the sinkhole on the farm of Lucia Sanchez.

MIDAFTERNOON

Rebecca Wainscott Ralt was in her sitting room hand-addressing invitations to the annual convention of the Daughters of the Texas Revolution when she heard her husband's jeep coming up the semicircular gravel drive of the Ralt mansion.

She rose from the exquisite Louis Quatorze desk that had been a wedding gift from her father and walked through the French doors and out onto the broad balcony overlooking the front grounds.

Her lips compressed at the sight of her husband in the right-hand seat of the jeep. She seldom allowed herself to remember that she'd loved him once, that once she'd broken through the timid caution that fenced her life and given herself heart, mind, and soul to another.

Otto Ralt had opened his sack wide and taken. Taken and taken without ever giving back until he'd sucked her dry of love, of caring, of any tender emotion. She hated him now, hated what he'd done to her, what he'd done to others.

Over the years she'd come to savor her hate, to hoard it like money in a jar under the bed. The day would come when her husband finally made a mistake, a day when he left himself vulnerable, and that would be the day she would spend her hate to destroy him.

The jeep disappeared under the columned portico below, and she turned and walked back through her sitting room and down the wide hall that bisected the second floor of the house.

Oil paintings of family ancestors hung the length of the hall, all but two of them Wainscotts. As always, Rebecca deliberately averted her eyes when she passed the portraits of her husband's mother and father. When they were alive, she'd considered her in-laws crude, uneducated dirt farmers, and in death her estimation of them had fallen even more. They had raised the boy, planted the seeds, and the blame for the twisted man her husband had become must be heavily theirs.

Her suite was at one end of the forty-room house; her husband's bedroom study was at the other. They had not shared a bed in twenty-three years, not since the eighth month of their marriage when she'd miscarried their first child and the doctors had told them she'd never have another. Otto had wanted a son, and when she couldn't give him that, he wanted nothing more of her body.

She'd known all along, of course, why Otto Ralt wanted to marry her, why a young dynamic man of twenty-six would want to marry a drab, horse-faced, socially awkward woman of thirty-five. She knew he wanted her money, and the power that flowed from her father.

Still, during their honeymoon and for the first months of her pregnancy, for the only time in her life, she'd allowed herself a fantasy. It was a dream that in time he'd come to love her, that as the years passed the money wouldn't matter anymore. The dream died with her baby.

Rebecca reached the top of the broad marble staircase sweeping down to the entry hall and stood watching as Gabriel, the ebony butler who'd been with the Wainscott family for sixty-two of his seventy-four years, opened the door to her husband.

"Welcome home, Mr. Ralt." Gabriel smiled, his three gold teeth gleaming.

"Get my bags out of the jeep, Gabriel," Ralt said. "Bring the two briefcases to the library."

"Yes, sir," Gabriel said, and shuffled wearily through the door.

Ralt started across the marble foyer toward the double doors of his library, then stopped as he caught sight of Rebecca on the balcony above. For several seconds the two stared wordlessly at each other.

"Gabriel is an old man, Otto," she said at last. "Too old to be dragging your heavy luggage around. In future, I wish you'd ask one of the other servants to do that sort of thing."

"You're right, Rebecca, Gabriel is old. Old and increasingly useless. I want to get rid of him," Ralt said.

She stiffened. "Gabriel's been with my family for over sixty years. He's not some faceless employee you can dismiss with a snap of your fingers."

"That's always been one of your family's failings, Rebecca, believing that an employee owns his job rather than earns it. You value the old over the efficient."

"We value character, Otto. But that's something you know nothing about. I'm going to send one of the gardeners around to carry your bags," Rebecca said, then turned and walked toward her suite before he could answer.

Ralt continued to stare up at the empty balcony for a moment longer, then strode on to the library. He shut and locked the doors behind him and crossed the Qom rug to his large oak desk facing the fireplace.

He had inherited the library, along with the house, from his late father-in-law, and the old man's books still inhabited the shelves. In the sixteen years since the room became his domain, Ralt had read no more than a handful of the library's 3,100 volumes.

He left the books there for effect, like paneling, and only occasionally when mulling over a decision would he absentmindedly leaf through one of the works.

The videophone rang as he lowered himself into his chair. Ralt flipped on the trans-receiver, and the face of Mason Sneed appeared on the screen.

"We've got an intruder in the north fork of the Rio Bajo, Mr. Ralt," Sneed said. "The TV camera at the dam site picked him up about five minutes after you left."

"One man?"

"One boy. Mexican kid about ten."

"Do you have him on the screen now?"

"Yes, sir."

"What's he doing?"

"Sleeping."

"Sleeping?"

"That's right, Mr. Ralt. At first I thought the kid was dead, lying there so still and all. Then I panned the camera in for a close-up and I could see his chest was moving. I think he's just lost and wore out."

"If the kid's lost, there'll be searchers down in the tunnels looking for him. Keep that camera on, Mason. If you monitor anyone else at that plug, I want to know about it fast."

"Yes, sir," Sneed said as an insistent buzz sounded behind him. The engineer turned and looked at a flashing button on the communications console. "It's the line from the tunnel head, Mr. Ralt."

"Switch the call to me," Ralt ordered.

"Yes, sir," Sneed said, and vanished from the screen. An instant later the face of Ralt's chief tunnel engineer appeared.

"Bill Lancione, Mr. Ralt. The mole broke through into dead air about ten minutes ago. We pulled the bore back and fired some cannon flares in there. Nothing, but nothing. No sign of walls or bottom. We've reached the sinkhole under Dallas."

Ralt tensed. "Any doubt it's the main pit?"

"No, sir. I checked our position with the survey the seismic team did last week, and the numbers match. We're there."

Ralt brought himself forward in his chair. "Get your men out, Bill. Now."

"What about the mole, Mr. Ralt? I got eighteen million dollars' worth of tunneling machinery down here."

"We don't have time to bring it out. Run the mole into the sinkhole and clear the tunnel. Call me when you reach the surface."

Ralt turned off the videophone, his mind on the next step, the final step. Everything was in place. The passages pocking the sides of the Rio Bajo had all been plugged, and Stroesser's men had finished placing the charges of plastic explosive beneath the bed of the Rio Grande. Now, at last, the tunnel linking the underground river with the sinkhole under Dallas was finally finished.

An arrogant thought caressed Otto Ralt's ego. He was about to reorder his corner of the universe, to mutate the grand design of the earth itself, to capture a river flowing south on the surface and with great pumps force its water north beneath the prairie.

When it was over, when the vast sinkhole under Dallas was filled with the spring flood of the Rio Grande and the earth beneath the city was safely buttressed against collapse, he would let the world know what he had done.

They would raise statues to him, to Otto Ralt, to the man who had defied nature and saved Dallas.

LATE AFTERNOON

Lucia Sanchez stared up at the headlamp-lit ceiling of the Rio Bajo la Tierra as the Caverunner moved steadily down the thirty-foot-wide north fork of the dry subterranean river. It was almost three hours since they'd lowered into the sinkhole, and she'd slowly become less afraid as the time passed.

"How did the rock get like that, Jedediah?" she asked, her eyes on the parallel lines of ridges and grooves that ran along the course of the roof. "The ceiling looks like the back of a gray whale."

"The whale's back and the rock are fluted for the same reason, water passing along a surface," he said. "For hundreds of thousands of years the entire four-hundred-mile length of the Rio Bajo was filled floor to roof with swift-flowing water. The abrasion of limestone deposits in the water eventually wore those channels."

Heff slowed the Caverunner as the hoverjet approached a fork in the tunnel ahead. He flipped a toggle switch on the control panel, and a row of lights flickered on around the rim of the oblong vehicle.

It was suddenly bright as day in the cave and Heff opened the canopy and climbed down to search the tunnel floor for tracks. "It looks like Attila the Hun marched his horde through here," he said in disgust. "There must have been fifty of Foster's men tramping around."

He straightened and took a lamp hat from the Caverunner's equipment locker. "I'll be back in a few minutes," he said, then disappeared into the smaller feeder tunnel. He returned ten minutes later, waved at her, then plunged into the blackness of the main bore. A quarter hour later he was back.

"The searchers split up here. Half went each way. I didn't find any trace of Paco's tracks, but then Foster's men could have obliterated them."

Lucia looked at him in despair as he climbed back into the Caverunner and lowered the canopy. "Then we don't know which way Paco went, which tunnel to search."

Heff was silent a moment, staring at the juncture of tunnels. "Paco went straight ahead, down the main bore," he said finally.

"What makes you think that?"

"The feeder tunnel's smaller. I was about the same age as Paco, nine, when I first caved, and those tight tunnels scared me. I was afraid the walls would close in and squeeze the juice out of me or something. Paco kept to the large tunnel."

Heff flicked off the rim lights and started the hoverjet again down the course of the Rio Bajo. In the next two hours he rejected three more side tunnels after searching the feeder caves for tracks.

"This is as far as Foster's men got," he said when he'd probed the final feeder system. "The last two searchers turned around here and went back."

"Why did only two come this far?" Lucia asked.

"The rest split off into those side passages. The more branches in a cave system, the thinner the search parties get."

"Do you still think Paco came this way?"

"We'll know if I'm right soon enough," he said. "There won't be any tracks in the dust now but Paco's. As long as the tunnel floor is rock, I'm still going on intuition. But if we get a stretch of five or six feet of sand, I'll know for sure. One way or the other."

Forty-five minutes later the Caverunner's headlamp illuminated a shallow sand-filled depression in the tunnel floor ahead, and Heff stopped the hoverjet and opened the canopy. Lucia shut her eyes and said a silent prayer as he walked down the tunnel ahead.

Heff reached the fringe of the sand and craned his neck. Slowly he moved forward, his eyes searching the gritty floor. A moment later he suddenly stopped and bent, his back to Lucia. When he straightened and turned he was smiling.

"Paco's been here," Heff said as he climbed back into the Caverunner. "He's still ahead of us."

Lucia's eyes misted over at this first tangible sign that her brother was still alive, still moving. She reached across and put a hand on his arm. "You've been right all along. You did know how Paco would think."

Heff grinned. "Just proves there's more boy in me than most. If I get a sudden urge to ride a pony, give me a kick in the ass and snap me out of it, will you?"

She smiled softly. "A lot of men would be afraid to show the boy inside."

Heff started the Caverunner. "I was almost thirty before I was comfortable with that part of me, with the rest of what makes me what I am."

"What happened when you reached thirty?"

Heff increased the thrust and started the Caverunner forward. "Some men start shedding hair about that age. I started shedding guilts. It penetrated my thick skull that I'd been seeing myself as others saw me. My parents, my teachers, my friends, my ex-wife—everybody held up a mirror and I accepted the image that came back. Well, it finally dawned on me that my reflection in others' eyes was the truth once removed. I turned to my own mirror, the one inside."

"What did you see, Jedediah?" Lucia asked quietly.

"An imperfect man, a man with his share of warts and scars, but on balance, I think, a guy with the right instincts.

I've learned to trust those instincts before I trust opinions, others' opinions. My tribunal of judges is down to one. Me."

"You've found peace within yourself, then?"

"No, Lucia, not entirely. I won't know peace until I've come to terms with Alex's death, with what happened that morning in Spanish Cavern. For now I'm wrestling with understanding myself. I know that if there's charity in my heart, there's a seam of larceny too. Most of the time I'm a decent guy, but I can be a bastard when I lose my temper. Still, I'm not such easy prey to self-delusion anymore."

"Do you care what others think, Jedediah?"

"Sure, to a point. I'd rather be respected than not. But people will buy you at your own price, Lucia. If you have a sense of worth, a faith in your own morality, if you know where you're going and have the purpose to get there, people will sense that strength in you. If you sell yourself short, so will everyone else."

"Do you know where you're going, Jedediah?"

"The direction, not always the road."

"Have I detoured you, bringing you to the Rio Bajo to search for Paco? Bringing you back to caves?"

Heff turned and looked at her. "The truth is the opposite, Lucia. I was stuck, mired in self-pity over Alex's death, until you came along. My work is down in these caves. There's a whole world under the earth, a frontier as vital as the depths of the sea or the reaches of space. And far less known than either. The crust holds caches of minerals and huge reservoirs of million-year-old virgin water. All over the planet there are places where geothermal energy is near enough the surface to be tapped. The world desperately needs those minerals and clean water and nonpolluting energy. I'm a caver, a damn good caver, with the tools to help open up the subterranean world. Down here is where I belong."

The tunnel ahead doglegged sharply left and Heff brought the Caverunner smoothly through the turn. "I've got to keep the speed down through here," he said. "The drought's weakened the tunnel walls. The force of the air jets could bring down a cave-in." He noticed Lucia yawn. "I have a feeling it will be a while before we find Paco. Why don't you close your eyes for a couple of hours? Foster said you hadn't slept in days."

For the first time since her brother disappeared down the sinkhole, Lucia felt the tight tension ease inside. "Before we find Paco," he'd said. It was no longer whether they'd find her brother, but when. A drowsy peace washed over her. He was right. She needed sleep. Desperately. "You promise you'll wake me if you think we're near?"

"I promise." He reached into a compartment in front of her and pulled out a blanket, then pressed a button in the side of her seat. The seat snapped back and Lucia thumped down onto the makeshift bed.

"You might have warned me," she said, pulling the blanket off her head.

"I like surprises."

"You have a warped sense of humor, Jedediah."

"Go to sleep."

Lucia spread the blanket over her. "I'll just close my eyes for a little while."

"You do that."

The strangeness of the situation worked on her as she closed her eyes. She was miles underground in a strange craft, about to go to sleep next to a man she'd just met. She should have been nervous, ill at ease, at least a little afraid. Instead, she felt warm and secure. She sneaked a look at the back of Jedediah's neck. Such a funny man, she thought.

Then, deep in the black bowels of the earth with millions of tons of rock over her head, Lucia Sanchez fell into a deep, peaceful sleep.

AN HOUR BEFORE DARK

Karl Stroesser shot too soon. He hadn't meant to fire. One of the Mexican soldiers searching the American side of the Rio Grande for the missing patrol of Sergeant Ortega had paused at a pile of mesquite camouflaging an air vent, and Stroesser's finger had tightened reflexively against the hair trigger of his AK-47 assault rifle.

In the last instant before the AK barked, Stroesser had seen the man's hands go to his groin and he'd realized the soldier had merely stopped to take a piss. But by then it was too late. By then twenty 7.65 millimeter bullets had ripped across the desert and the soldier was dead still standing.

There was a skipped heartbeat of thick silence after the rifle spoke; then the quiet of the desert burst like a ripe fruit in the sun. Stroesser's mercenaries took his first shot as the signal to open up, and they poured automatic fire on the Mexicans from their hidden foxholes.

The order to cease fire formed on Stroesser's lips. Then he realized the die was cast, and he turned and made his way toward the rear.

"Fall back on me," Lieutenant Rua shouted to his men as he ran in a crouch toward the cover of a small rise facing the *yanqui* positions.

Four of Rua's raw recruits panicked in their first heat of

battle and turned to flee toward the river. They were mowed down by the withering American fire before they got ten paces.

The lieutenant cursed and gestured violently with his pistol. "Down, get down."

His order was answered by the distinctive hollow *thru-ump* of a *yanqui* mortar, and a moment later the sand exploded with a roar twenty yards to his left.

Rua's first sergeant crawled up and pointed with his rifle barrel at the riddled tops of the saguaro cacti around them. "They're using fragmentation shells, lieutenant," Sergeant Manuel Copala shouted above the battle din.

"I know it," Rua said, risking a look over the rise as more of his men snaked in from the desert and began returning the *yanqui* fire. He counted thirty, perhaps thirty-five muzzle flashes before a burst of American bullets ripped up the slope before him and he pulled his head down.

There was another *thru-ump* from across the desert and a second shell whizzed toward them, exploding ten yards closer this time.

Rua rolled toward his first sergeant. "We'll have to fall back to the riverbank before they walk those shells in on us. You take the first squad. I'll cover you with the second squad until you reach the bank. Then you cover me."

"Yes, lieutenant," Sergeant Copala said, and began to crawl along the slope of the rise gathering his men.

Rua waved his radioman over. "Get through to Captain Santos at battalion."

Private Jimenez put on his headset and made the connection. A moment later his face twisted in disbelief at the reply to his request for the Mexican commander. "The *capitán* is taking a siesta, sir. They want to know if they should wake him."

Rua swore and grabbed the mike. "We are under attack by American troops. I repeat, we are under attack. Get the *capitán* at once."

As Rua fumed, twenty men in black wetsuits emerged silently from the depths of the Rio Grande. Quickly they removed the hemosponge canisters from their backs and slipped their weapons from their waterproof tubes.

The ex–Green Beret master sergeant in charge fanned his men out facing the Mexican rear. For several moments the sergeant stared at his watch. Then he sliced the air with a sharp downward cut of his hand and instantly the American position erupted in automatic rifle fire.

Sergeant Copala crawled quickly back. "The *yanquis* are behind us, lieutenant!"

"Position half your men facing the rear," Rua ordered, then spun back to the radio. Before he could speak, a burst of American bullets ripped through the young signalman's chest and Private Jimenez pitched forward wordlessly into the sand.

Rua yanked the headset off the lifeless corpse. "Where is Captain Santos?" he screamed into the mike. "Where is he?"

"Calm yourself, lieutenant, I'm here," Captain Santos answered irritably.

"We are surrounded, *capitán*. The *yanquis* have cut us off from the river. They're working us over with automatic fire and mortars."

"The Americans have invaded?" Santos asked incredulously.

"We're on the *yanqui* side."

Santos sputtered. "You've crossed the border? Are you insane? I gave you no such orders. You'll bring a war down on us, Rua."

"My orders were to search for our missing patrol. The search led across the river. We can discuss my actions later, *capitán*; right now we need reinforcements."

"How many enemy do you estimate?" Santos asked warily.

"Thirty or forty facing us, perhaps as many along the river."

A mortar round exploded close to the top of the rise and Rua instinctively rolled away from the impact. He looked down the line as the smoke cleared. One of his privates had been firing from the crest of the slope. He was dead in the sand, the top of his head gone.

"Their mortars have our range, *capitán*. I need help up here."

Captain Santos was shaken by the sounds of battle he heard through his earphones. "You say there are perhaps eighty *yanquis* against you, Rua. Where there are that many American soldiers, there are bound to be more. This could be a trick. They may plan to ambush the battalion when we come to your relief."

"They didn't know we were going to cross the river, *capitán*. Shit, *I* didn't know. How could it be a trick?"

"You underestimate the Americans, lieutenant. It's best to be prudent. I'm going to radio for the rest of the division. They could be here in a few hours."

"Tomorrow morning, *capitán*. No sooner. And you know it."

"Don't be insolent, lieutenant. When I explain we're under attack, headquarters will get the division off at once."

A rain of sand fell on Rua as a mortar shell tore up the desert twenty yards away. "Will you reinforce me before the division gets here?" Rua pleaded.

"No, lieutenant. The risk of ambush is too great. You got yourself in that position. Now you'll just have to hold on until the division arrives."

"You're a goddamned coward, Santos. A lousy, stinking coward," Rua screamed into the mike. He slammed the headset into the sand and crawled toward Sergeant Copala. "We're on our own for a while. Have the men dig slit trenches. Tell them to maintain a steady fire without exposing themselves more than necessary."

In a communications van hidden behind a large rock outcropping two hundred yards away, Karl Stroesser took off a set of earphones. One of the things they'd taught him in Green Beret training was the value of searching out an enemy's radio frequency during battle.

Stroesser spoke only broken Spanish, but he understood the language well and his interception of Lieutenant Rua's call had told him all he needed to know. He punched a number code into the long-distance scrambler phone and put through a call to the Ralt ranch in Dallas.

"There's a shitload of greasers coming my way, Mr. Ralt," Stroesser said when the billionaire came on the line. He told Ralt about the Mexican patrol he had pinned down on the American side of the river and about the radio call for reinforcements he'd intercepted.

"How long do you estimate before that Mexican division gets there?" Ralt asked coolly.

"According to their radio parley, not before tomorrow morning."

"That should be more than enough time."

"Time for what, Mr. Ralt?"

"Time to arrange a trip to Dallas for our Mexican friends," Ralt answered. "I'll let you know when everything is ready. Meanwhile, set up a television camera with a telescopic lens focused on the river there. I want camera control and live pictures direct here to the ranch. And keep the enemy as close to the river as possible. Good-bye, Karl."

Stroesser stared at the phone in frustration. What the hell did Ralt mean, "a trip to Dallas"? Then it hit him. Suddenly he knew why Ralt wanted the Mexicans kept close to the river. The tunnel up north must be ready, and Ralt was getting set to blow the plastic explosives under the bed of the Rio Grande. When the surface river plunged into the depths of the Rio Bajo below, the near banks would collapse into the void as well.

Five thousand Mexican soldiers would be sucked into the tunnel of the Rio Bajo and pumped north under the prairie to Dallas.

DUSK

The news of the unearthing of the Madonna of Dallas spread within hours through the barrios of the city, and by dusk on September 12 legions of Mexican-American faithful had gathered at the shrine on the farm of Ignacio Baptista.

Almost fifteen thousand people now surrounded the sinkhole, and still they came, streaming in across the prairie in cars and trucks, on motorcycles and bicycles, a dozen on horses and mules, thousands on foot.

Sets of rickety wooden stairs were hammered together down each side of the sinkhole, and people descended to bask in the radiance of the beatific smile of the Madonna. Each emerged from the shrine with the deep conviction that the Madonna had been sent by God to sustain the Mexican-American people of Texas in this their time of greatest troubles.

As the sun set, a team of anthropologists, geologists, and archaeologists from the University of Texas arrived and descended into the sinkhole. Using soft whiskbrooms and instruments like dental picks, the scientists probed the earth surrounding the Madonna.

They found the ashes of cooking fires, charred bones of bison and mammoths, and stone weapons used during ancient hunts. The sinkhole floor had once been the campsite of paleo-Indians, the scientists declared, and the pit represented a rare prehistoric habitat that must be studied carefully.

As to how the Indian woman and child had come to be mummified, the geologists offered an incredible explanation. The phenomenon, they insisted, was the result of a stupendous earthquake and volcanic eruption ten thousand years past.

On the day the Indians perished, the scientists surmised, a monstrous volcanic eruption had spewed a violent discharge of volcanic gases into the upper atmosphere.

The gases were shot far up to the fringes of space, where they were chilled to incredibly low temperatures, then drawn in a spiral toward the pole. As the planet spun through space, the volcanic vapors hurtled at incalculable speed back down through the atmosphere.

One of these subfreezing blasts had struck the Texas plains ten thousand years ago near the present site of Dallas, descending on the unsuspecting Indian woman with such unimaginable cold that she and her child were frozen solid where they sat in less than a second.

Volcanic debris drawn along in the wake of the killer wind then encapsulated the corpses in layers of fine dust, mummifying the bodies more perfectly than the pharaoh wrappings of ancient Egypt.

Thus, the scientists explained, did the Indian woman and child come to be preserved in the earth under the farm of Ignacio Baptista.

To the fervent Mexican-Americans gathered at the sinkhole, the anthropologists' clinical explanation was no more relevant to the fact of the Madonna's appearance than the details of esoteric and far-off weather patterns were to the dawning of a beautiful day.

The only thing that mattered to them was that now, when they most needed inspiration and faith, their Madonna had come. When the anthropologists insisted that the mummies should be taken at once to the university for study, a great ground swell of furious indignation swept the thousands ringing the sinkhole.

The Anglo scientists viewed the ever-growing throng with jaundiced eyes. To them, the sinkhole was not a place of miracles but an invaluable anthropological site that was in danger of being destroyed by trampling mobs of Latinos.

An hour after the anthropologists had examined the Madonna, a sympathetic judge issued an order at the behest of the University of Texas declaring the sinkhole a state archaeological site, henceforth closed to the public. Forty-five minutes later, ninety Texas Rangers arrived in a convoy of raucous sirens and flashing lights to enforce the decree.

The Anglos were met before the shrine by Ignacio Baptista and the young priest from San Juan parish, Father Quinn. The captain in charge of the Rangers read the judge's order, then told the priest that the crowds must disperse and leave the area at once.

"Your order is no good here," Father Quinn said quietly.

The Ranger captain straightened. "I beg your pardon, father."

"This is a holy place now, a church. Man's laws do not apply here, captain, only the law of God."

"Father, I'm sorry, you people can believe what you want, but that sinkhole and all that's in it are now under the jurisdiction of the state. I want everybody out of here."

Ignacio Baptista stepped in front of the captain. "No. This is my farm and these are my people. It is you who must go."

"Are you refusing a lawful order of the state of Texas?"

"The Madonna belongs to us, captain, not the state of Texas."

The officer turned to the sergeant at his elbow. "Arrest this man."

The crowd, which had been listening quietly to the exchange, closed in angrily as the Ranger sergeant went to handcuff Baptista. No one could be sure where the knife came from, but suddenly the sergeant sucked in a sharp rasping breath and jerked straight upward. Then he rolled his eyes to the night sky and pitched forward dead into the front rank of his horrified comrades.

There was a moment of stunned silence. Then the police

went for their weapons and the crowd surrounding the trapped company of Rangers surged forward with a roar.

In the battle that followed, 206 Mexican-Americans were killed and 23 Rangers were beaten or stabbed to death. In the end it was the police who retreated, dead and wounded draping the fenders and guns blazing from the windows of their cars.

MIDEVENING

An expression of shocked disbelief crept across the face of Texas Governor Lynn Duecker as he sat behind his desk in Austin listening to the President of the United States on the phone.

"Mr. President, I find it difficult to believe what you're telling me, sir," the fifty-four-year-old ex-oilman said when the President was finished. "Surely you mean *parts* of Dallas will have to be evacuated, not the whole city."

"Every living soul, Lynn," President Wilson said soberly. "The scientists tell me that what happened at Texas Stadium a few hours ago is just a prelude to what's coming. The limestone stratum under Dallas is weakening by the hour. I think you'll grasp the urgency of the situation better when you've seen the satellite photographs and the projections of the geologists. You're facing an inevitable natural disaster down there, Lynn, and unless you evacuate Dallas within the next forty-eight hours, three million people are going to be buried alive."

Duecker came forward in his chair. "What in God's name do I do with all those people, Mr. President? How do I house them, feed them? What do I do with hospital patients and the handicapped and the old?"

"I've ordered our military bases in Texas geared up to

help. Reception centers for the refugees are being organized at Fort Hood, Fort Sam Houston, and Bergstrom Air Force Base. The military will provide food, bunks, sanitary facilities, and emergency medical care. As soon as possible, the refugees will have to be dispersed to the remaining urban areas of Texas and the rest of the country. Any city with housing and jobs."

Governor Duecker sank wearily against the back of his large leather chair and ran a hand through his wavy gray hair. His jowly face was heavy with strain and there were dark pockets of fatigue under his red-rimmed eyes. "Mr. President, no matter how well we plan, we both know there are going to be some horrendous problems getting those folks out of Dallas. I wonder if you understand, sir, what the drought has done to these people psychologically."

"I know it's been rough down there, Lynn. On my last visit to Dallas, the motorcade passed a line of people stretching four deep around the block. At first I thought they were there to watch the President go by. But they didn't wave, didn't pay the slightest attention. When I pointed them out to the mayor, he said it was a welfare line. If ever I've seen beaten people, it was in that line."

"Beaten into the dust of the drought, Mr. President. The severe water rationing in the Dallas area has cost over four hundred thousand jobs. Five years ago these were a successful, swashbuckling people with the world by the balls. Now half a million families are on welfare, and everywhere you go in the city there's a sense of dejection, hopelessness. People feel betrayed; by nature, by society. They rage at the weather, they rage at those closest to them. The statistics on wife-beating and divorce have gone through the roof. Churchgoing grandmothers get into brawls in supermarkets. The media are full of stories of suicides and murders."

Duecker paused and slowly shook his head.

"And now we have to tell these poor suffering bastards that they're about to lose the last thing many of them have, their homes. These people are going to take two things with them on the roads out of Dallas, Mr. President. They're going to take their anger, and they're going to take their guns. Traffic accidents, the heat—it could be a very bloody evacuation."

President Wilson was silent a moment. "I have an even greater fear than a bloody evacuation, Lynn. Our relations with Mexico have reached the flash point. God knows what Prime Minister Martí's reaction will be to the slaughter of two hundred Chicano worshipers at that religious shrine. If this incident sets him off, I don't have to tell you what that could mean."

Duecker paled. No, the President didn't have to tell him about the Mexican missiles seventy miles south of the Texas border.

"I've sent the National Guard in to keep the rednecks, the Rangers, and every other trigger-happy bastard away from that shrine, Mr. President. I'll be leaving for Dallas myself in a few minutes to take charge of the situation personally."

"I have full faith you'll do your best, Lynn," the President said. "Let me know if you need any help from Washington. Good-bye. And good luck."

Governor Duecker hung up the phone and dragged his fingers down his tired face. The President was counting on him to do his best. But how good was his best? Good enough to get three million people safely out of Dallas in under forty-eight hours?

Duecker swiveled his chair and stared out the windows facing south, facing Mexico.

Was his best good enough to prevent a war?

LATE EVENING

Aeroflot Flight 605 nonstop from Moscow lowered its
wheels and, with landing lights blazing, descended into the
fulvous haze that each year grew thicker over Mexico City.

The capital of Mexico was the largest city in the world in
1999. Its steel skyscrapers, adobe churches, and tarpaper
hovels teemed with an estimated 36 million people. Yet had
he tried, man could not have chosen a worse geographic
location for the earth's major population center.

The city sat on the drained bed of an ancient lake
surrounded by high peaks. The bowl of encircling mountains blocked out cleansing winds and trapped a layer of
pollution-laden air over the urban sprawl below.

The inhabitants of the capital had seen neither the yellow
of the sun nor the blue of the sky for almost a decade now.
Instead, each day was a long shadowless twilight, eerily
absent of vivid color or contrast.

The Soviet jet set down heavily and followed directional
lights through the dun gloom to the government VIP
terminal.

General Hugo Santamaría rose wearily from his seat as
the plane rolled to a stop. The ten-hour flight had left him
stiff and sore, and he longed more than anything for a hot
bath and a drowsy glass of wine at home.

The stewardess flipped back the curtain between the VIP section and the regular passenger compartment, and Santamaría glanced through at a young Russian officer buttoning his tunic in the aisle. The Soviet soldier wore the insignia of his country's elite missile force. Santamaría paused to stare. So this was the officer with the targeting codes.

Santamaría had felt humiliated that the Soviets would not trust Mexico with the computer programs necessary to retarget the missiles across northern Mexico. As senior Mexican military representative at the treaty negotiations, it had been one of Santamaría's prime objectives to obtain this concession, along with increased Russian logistical support.

The Soviets had agreed only to send a Russian missile officer to Mexico with the codes. If war came, the Mexican rockets could be reprogrammed quickly, but only after approval from the Kremlin.

Perhaps, Santamaría reflected, because his heart did not embrace his country's position, he had not argued hard enough at the treaty table. Targeting the missiles on American cities was, to his way of thinking, another dangerous step toward total war, and he had seen enough of the suffering of war.

Santamaría was uncomfortable with missiles in any case. He was an infantry general and an administrator. He was in his element dealing with people, not computerized rockets. Santamaría had been assigned to head the Northern Mexico Missile Command for the simple reason that, among the prime minister's senior commanders, Martí considered him the most reflective and stable.

As Martí had put it, if tensions along the border rose, Santamaría was not likely to become a Pancho Villa and attack the United States on his own volition.

The Russian felt Santamaría's stare and for a moment their eyes met. Then the major turned away and busied himself collecting his belongings. So young and so unsure of himself, Santamaría thought.

The door opened into the accordion tube of the boarding tunnel, and Santamaría took his bulging briefcase from the overhead compartment and left the aircraft. An aide met him as he entered the terminal.

"Welcome home, General Santamaría. May I take your case?"

"Thank you, captain."

"Sir, we've had a call from the palace. Prime Minister Martí wishes to see you immediately."

Santamaría sighed. There went his bath. "Very well, captain."

"Will you follow me, sir?"

The captain led the way to a locked door halfway down the concourse. He inserted a plastic card into a slot next to the door and led Santamaría down a set of stairs to a waiting ten-year-old Chrysler New Yorker.

Three minutes later the large black car cleared the checkpoint at the airport perimeter and headed onto the highway into Mexico City. Santamaría sank into the soft leather of the back seat and closed his eyes. Despite his aching fatigue, it was good to be home.

He had spent so many years during the long struggle in foreign lands—in Nicaragua, Belize, Cuba, the Soviet Union. No more. He would retire next month, and he looked forward to returning to quiet anonymity in his native Yucatán in southeastern Mexico.

Things were different in Yucatán since the Revolution. Before the Communist takeover, most of the large Indian and peasant population worked as *campesinos*, agricultural workers, earning an average $190 a year. Peasant families lived in miserable hovels without electricity or plumbing. They suffered digestive ailments from fouled water and contracted respiratory illnesses from their poorly ventilated dirt-floor huts. Almost all the *campesinos* were malnourished.

For a time back in the 1970s, the people had believed that the discovery of the great Mixteca oil field off the Gulf coast of southeastern Mexico would relieve the ages-old poverty of their country. Mexico had rapidly become the world's fourth largest oil producer, and tens of billions of pesos flowed into Pemex, the state-owned oil monopoly.

Yet the enormous oil wealth dissipated long before any money could trickle down to the voiceless peasants of rural Mexico. *La mordida,* the bite, was a way of life in the country, and hundreds of millions of pesos stuck to the corrupt hands of Pemex officials, union leaders, bureaucrats, and government ministers.

What revenues did reach the Mexican treasury went toward the payment of the country's huge foreign debt. The PRI, the Institutional Revolutionary Party that had been in power for most of the century, had borrowed billions of dollars abroad, mostly from U.S. banks, and when the bottom fell out of the oil market in the mid-1980s, Mexico was hard put to pay even the interest on its loans.

The collapse of petroleum prices doomed the PRI version of democracy in Mexico. The severe austerity programs forced on the people undercut support for the government and sent thousands fleeing to the banner of the Communists.

Some claimed that the death of Mexican democracy could be traced to a specific day. On September 19, 1985, a great earthquake struck Mexico City, gutting hundreds of buildings and leaving twenty thousand people dead in the rubble. The cost of rebuilding added almost $2 billion a year to Mexico's borrowing requirements and broke the back of the country's already strained economy.

Hugo Santamaría remembered the exact date of the great quake for a different reason. It was the day life was given back to him. A week before, an informer had betrayed the safe house where he was staying in Mexico City and plainclothes detectives from the Federal Security Directorate had broken down the door in the middle of the night and seized the Communist insurgents inside.

He had been under torture for seven days when the earth shuddered suddenly and the shoddily built Procuraduria de Justicia jail collapsed in upon itself. Most of the police and the other prisoners had been killed. But Santamaría was being held in a basement interrogation cell where the screams of prisoners under torture were muffled from pedestrians on the street above, and the thick foundations around him saved his life.

When rescuers dug Santamaría out three days later, he
had a broken arm and collarbone, his body was dehydrated,
and he was badly bruised from head to foot. Despite his
injuries, he'd stunned Red Cross workers by declining an
ambulance trip to the hospital. Instead, he'd hobbled off and
disappeared into the tattered crowds of homeless refugees
wandering aimlessly around their shattered neighborhoods.

He'd fled south to recuperate in his native Yucatán.
He would not return to Mexico City until March 1,1992, the
day the Mexican People's Revolutionary Army entered
the capital and seized control of the government from the
defeated PRI.

The Chrysler swept onto the Paseo de la Reforma, the
broad main boulevard of the capital, and Santamaría remembered what it had been like the day the Communist
brigades marched in triumph down the crowd-lined thoroughfare. His countrymen had cheered and wept ecstati-
cally, and the way was strewn with flowers. The Paseo de
la Reforma had been vibrant with flags and joy and
kaleidoscopic hopes.

Santamaría stared out the window at the grimy tableau
the boulevard had become. Most of the expensive shops,
restaurants, and business offices were closed now, victims
of the country's soaring inflation and unemployment.

Starvation had returned to rural Mexico, and in the cities
and towns deprivation sucked incessantly at the physical
and mental stamina of the people. The young suffered most.
Meat and milk were only sporadically available to the poor,
and an entire generation born since the Revolution would
grow up with flawed bodies and stunted minds, susceptible
to every disease, doomed to old age by thirty and death by
forty.

The car passed a government food store, and Santamaría
was torn by the sight of the ragged line of people stretching
for a block down the Paseo de la Reforma. Lines. That was
all one saw in Mexico City these days. It was the same in
Chihuahua, Torreón, Monterrey, Durango, Guadalajara.

The government blamed the United States and the unforgiving weather for the country's plight, but the ideological

missteps of the Marxists had done at least as much damage. A four-year attempt at collectivization of Mexico's farms had ended in an ignoble debacle that almost wiped out the nation's agriculture. Nationalization of industry had served only to leave Mexico with a plethora of idle, obsolescent manufacturing plants and empty warehouses.

Mexico was a mess, a cheerless festering mess, Santamaría admitted to himself. As conditions worsened, Prime Minister Teodoro Luis Martí and his fellow high-ranking party officials increasingly shunned political rallies where criticism and questions could be voiced.

Instead, the Mexican people were weaned to five-minute film capsules that showed the prime minister steadfastly conducting the business of state: signing decrees, dedicating buildings and bridges, receiving foreign dignitaries, or being received in Moscow, Havana, or Ho Chi Minh City.

The Chrysler turned off the Paseo de la Reforma onto the Boulevard Juarez, and several minutes later the snow-white facade of the Palacio National came into sight. Usually cars entering the palace grounds were given a desultory inspection at the gate by sleepy-eyed guards. Today there were crack paratroopers on duty, and both the Chrysler and the documents of the officers inside were checked thoroughly by the soldiers.

The car continued up the drive to the porticoed main entrance to the palace. Santamaría told his aide to wait with the driver and climbed the broad steps to the main entrance.

His credentials were checked again inside the entrance. Santamaría wondered why the unusual precautions today. Had there been a bomb threat, a rumor of discontent in the city?

He took back his papers and started across the grand foyer, pausing halfway to stare up at the magnificent crystal chandelier that had graced the marble entry since the reign of Emperor Maximilian. His mouth turned down at the sight of the huge Mexican hammer-and-sickle flag that had been draped from the lowest tier of the fixture.

He had fought for that flag, and he would willingly die for the socialist cause it represented, but the forced union of the banner and the chandelier muted the glory intrinsic in each, and Santamaría turned for the stairs in disgust.

Several senior military officers and high-ranking party members nodded curtly as they hurried past him down the stairs, their faces set in worried frowns. Midway up he recognized the shrapnel-sculpted face of Demetrio Batiz, an old comrade from the early days of the Revolution. They'd both been wounded at the battle of Mérida and convalesced together at a small evacuation hospital in the Yucatán jungle. Batiz commanded the Che Guevara Division now.

The two men embraced. "I just spoke with Martí," Batiz said, stepping back. "He told me the treaty was done and signed."

"Yes, late last night, finally," Santamaría said.

"You look exhausted, my friend."

"The negotiations were hard, and I couldn't sleep on the plane back. We only landed forty-five minutes ago."

"I know you, Hugo, you can run on adrenaline, like me," Batiz said. He gripped his old friend above the elbows. "I want you to know that when I take my men across the Bravo del Norte, I shall do so with a boldness born of knowing your missiles stand behind our army. Viva Mexico!"

Batiz pulled away and started again down the stairs.

"Demetrio, what are you talking about?"

Batiz half turned. "Good luck up there. He's in one of his 'total-leader' moods." Then the division commander was gone down the stairs.

Santamaría shrugged wearily and climbed to the second floor. The wide hall of government offices above was crowded with soldiers and civilians, and it took several minutes for him to negotiate his way down the corridor to the open cathedral doors of the prime minister's suite.

There were always government functionaries, foreign diplomats, and various supplicants milling about Martí's anteroom, but the crush today was the worst he could remember. What the hell was going on, and what had Batiz meant about taking his troops across the Bravo?

He threaded his way to the receptionist desk guarding the

private office of the prime minister. The young captain on duty came to his feet as Santamaría approached.

"General Santamaría, the prime minister has ordered that you be brought in as soon as you arrive. Will you follow me, please, sir?"

The captain cleared a path to the closed doors, rapped twice, then disappeared inside. A moment later the doors opened and the captain emerged, followed by the minister of propaganda and two of his assistants.

"Please go in, general," the captain said.

Prime Minister Teodoro Luis Martí rose behind his ornate mahogany desk as Santamaría entered his office. No matter how many times he saw Martí in person, Santamaría was always unsettled anew by how small a man the prime minister was. The leader of the Revolution was the physical antithesis of his heroic reputation.

Martí was barely five foot two and weighed no more than 120 pounds. Incongruously, although most of his fifty-five years had been spent in a violent struggle for survival and power, his face was unlined with the furrows of grief, worry, and thought that most men wore at his age. His hair had grayed, but his skin was a smooth pinkish-brown and, except when he was in one of his rages, Teodoro Martí looked more than anything like a prepubescent boy with a paste-on mustache.

As all who knew the leader would attest, the frail husk concealed a steel center. He had joined the Pancho Villa movement twenty-two years before, after his small farm was seized by the local PRI-backed landlord. He had climbed a ladder of gutted rivals on his rise to the chairmanship of the party, and he'd ruled Mexico with a totalitarian hand since the Marxists took power. Teodoro Martí was anything but the mild child he appeared.

Martí gestured Santamaría to a chair before his desk. "Our ambassador cabled me of your work during the treaty negotiations, General Santamaría," Martí said. "All Mexico is in your debt. You have served your country well."

"Thank you, Comrade Prime Minister. The negotiations were long and tiring, and it's good to be home."

"You deserve a long rest, general. Unfortunately, now is not the time. Until the U.S. provocation is answered, every Mexican patriot must be at his post."

"You'll forgive me, Prime Minister, I'm just off the plane from Moscow. We were under radio silence during the flight. What crisis do you speak of?"

Martí came forward in his chair. "The *yanquis* have attacked along the Bravo del Norte. They wiped out one of our reconnaissance patrols, and at the moment they have an infantry company of the Che Guevara Division pinned down under heavy fire. I've sent the full division north to the border in relief."

Santamaría sat stricken. "Why would the United States attack, Prime Minister? Why now?"

"Our mutual defense treaty with the Soviets goes into effect when I fly to Moscow for the formal signing," Martí said. "That gives the *yanquis* a window to take military action against Mexico without facing a mandatory Soviet response."

"But what could they possibly hope to gain?" Santamaría asked. "Our only treasure is our oil, and if they were after the Pemex fields they would have landed their marines along the Gulf coast of Yucatán."

"You're wrong, Santamaría. Mexico possesses one treasure the *yanquis* value more than our oil. The great drought has hammered industry to its knees in the American Southwest. Huge defense plants have been shut down in Texas, and the idle pools of skilled labor and capital are steadily leeching away into the consumer economy. The American military-industry complex cannot allow this decimation of their critical defense contractors." Martí paused, his small black eyes sparkling angrily. "It is our water they are after, Santamaría. The *yanquis* mean to seize the Rio Bravo del Norte."

"It is difficult to believe." Santamaría slowly shook his head. "Surely they must know we would have to react to such a provocation, regardless of whether the Russians back us."

"You don't understand how they see us. Time and again

through history the United States has defeated us on the battlefield. We have been the soft stone from which they've carved their military icons, their Alamos and their Halls of Montezuma. They have no respect, no fear. To the *yanquis*, Mexico is a cheap whore their armies can screw any time they want to."

Santamaría's bones ached with the exhaustion of the past weeks of negotiations and the long sleepless flight from Moscow. He had no will to argue American motives with Martí. Tomorrow, perhaps, things would have sorted themselves out at the border and he could make his own judgments. "What is it you wish of me, Prime Minister?" he asked.

"The *yanqui* attack came midway along our border with Texas," Martí said. "Our nearest rocket installation is at Nueva Rosita. Two hours ago, on my personal order, the missile there was armed with a nuclear warhead."

Santamaría sat appalled. So it was true, the rumor that Mexico had developed nuclear weapons. There had been speculation among his fellow officers for years, but until now the work of the Cuban physicists in the closely guarded laboratories in Mexico City had remained the secret of Martí and his top ministers.

"I want you to fly north and take command of the base," Martí continued. "The missile is to be fully fueled, the pad prepared for launch, every man at his post."

Santamaría never thought he'd think it, but at that moment he was profoundly thankful for the Soviet treaty restrictions. "I can prepare to launch, Prime Minister, but I cannot target the missiles without reprogramming the on-board computers. You approved the treaty provisions personally. Surely you're aware that only the Russian missile officer to be attached to my command possesses the necessary computer codes."

"I was forced to accept that restriction or the Soviets would not have agreed to the treaty," Martí said with distaste. "Because I was coerced, I do not consider that provision binding on Mexico."

"Binding or not, we do not possess the codes."

"Don't we, Santamaría?" Martí leaned back in his chair. "Under the agreement with the Russians, they've assigned a major"—Martí picked up a paper from his desk—"a Major Demyan Turgenev. I believe he was on the flight back with you."

"Yes, I saw him on the plane." Santamaría's stomach churned. He knew where Martí was leading.

"I want Major Turgenev brought to our missile installation at Nuevo Rosita immediately," Martí said.

"He will not relinquish the codes," Santamaría warned. "Not without authorization from Moscow."

"A team from the political police section will interview the major at the base. The codes will not be a problem," Martí said smoothly.

It was the truth, Santamaría knew. With the new mind drugs, a man could be made to reveal anything—the murder of a rabbit when he was eight, the intimacies of his marriage, or, perhaps easiest of all, the secrets of his country.

Santamaría stared across the desk at Martí. "You could start a nuclear world war," he said hoarsely. "I beg you to—"

He was interrupted by a crescendo of enraged voices and shouts of indignation coming from the anteroom. There were two sharp raps on the tall gilt doors and Martí's agitated secretary burst into the room and crossed rapidly to the prime minister's desk.

"What's going on out there?" Martí demanded.

"We've just picked up a news bulletin from Dallas," the secretary stammered. "The Texas Rangers fired into a large gathering of our people at a religious shrine. Two hundred and six Mexicans are dead, Prime Minister, slaughtered by the Rangers."

Martí came slowly to his feet, his boy face transformed by rage to a savage mask. "Ready that missile, Santamaría," he said, his voice low and guttural. "Ready it to launch against Dallas."

DAY THREE

APRIL 12, 1999

MIDNIGHT

The noise started like the sound of hail on the roof, and Lucia Sanchez dreamed she was home in bed listening under the quilt as a storm rolled over the farm in the night.

Then, suddenly, the sound began to feed on itself, building in seconds to a cacophony of sharp metallic claps that shattered Lucia's sleep and brought her shooting up from the prone co-pilot's seat in the hoverjet.

"Cave-in," Heff shouted beside her, his hand flashing forward to the thrust-reverse switch on the control panel. The hoverjet bucked, then began to move slowly backward as a rain of earth and stones pelted the plexiglass cockpit bubble. Heff jammed the throttle forward and the Caverunner shot back down the tunnel they had traveled moments before.

Two hundred yards from the cave-in, Heff shut off the engine. He looked across at Lucia as the lights went to battery power and dimmed. She was sitting motionless, staring out desperately into the thick brown dust that swirled around the hoverjet.

"You all right?" he asked.

There was a terrible fear in her eyes when she turned to him. "Paco? Do you think . . . ?"

"No, I don't think. Cave-ins are almost always localized.

Ten or twenty yards of ceiling collapse, leaving the tunnel on both sides clear. Paco's well beyond the cave-in."

"Thank God," Lucia breathed.

"While you're thanking him, ask him what the hell we do next," Heff said.

"Don't be blasphemous."

"If you've got a better idea than praying right now, I'd like to hear it. I think you're under the illusion I can solve any problem we run into down here. I can't."

"You found Paco's tracks when no one else could," she reminded him. "When everyone thought it was impossible."

"That makes me a good tracker. That is not a skill that will help me move the several million tons of earth that now block the tunnel between us and your brother."

"You said there was a labyrinth of passageways and caverns down here, Jedediah. Surely there's a way around the cave-in."

Heff reached forward and slapped the release button on the map compartment. "Probably. But we're not talking about a little detour in the road here," he said, spreading a chart. "We've passed a dozen side tunnels, each of which divides and then divides again into forks and side passages. Labyrinth is the right word. We could wander around down here for weeks."

"We don't have weeks to find Paco," she said. "We have hours."

"Thank you for pointing that out. That was very helpful. Now if you don't have any other succinct observations for a minute or two, perhaps you'll let me read the map."

"Is that a map of the Rio Bajo tunnel system?"

"There is no such thing. Only scattered sections of the system are charted. Alex and I surveyed about twenty miles of tunnels around Rocksprings, and I doubt if we covered more than a fiftieth of the passageways down here."

"If that is not a map of the Rio Bajo, may I ask what it is?"

"It's a geological chart of the ground features above us."

"What will a map of the surface tell you?"

"I'm looking for riverbeds, depressions, limestone out-croppings. The topography of an area can give you a pretty fair idea if there are any caves below."

"Well, what does it look like? Have you found anything?"

"No, but then it's a trifle hard to concentrate with you chattering in my ear."

"Chattering?"

"Quiet!"

Lucia folded her arms across her chest and sank back against the seat.

Heff pored over the map for several minutes, then took a calipers from the map compartment and made some mea-surements. Finally he looked at Lucia. "I can't guarantee I'm right, I can't guarantee anything at the moment," he said. "But I'd say our best bet is the second side tunnel to the west about a mile and a quarter back."

"Do you think that tunnel will reconnect with the main passage?"

Heff folded the map. "I don't think we'll be that lucky. I'm hoping the tunnel will run north. Once we're beyond the cave-in, we'll look for passageways east back to the main bore."

"I guess there's nothing else to do." The days of frustration and disappointment erupted in Lucia, and she slammed a small fist against the plexiglass. "We were so close, Jedediah, so close to Paco."

"Yeah, for a while there I thought—"

The dull roar of a second avalanche ahead drowned out Heff's words and a boiling cloud of dust suddenly shot down the tunnel, swallowing up the Caverunner.

Lucia recoiled in horror from the brown blanket pressing against the clear plastic above her. She felt the panic rise, and for an instant she forgot her brother. She felt as if she were closed in a tomb, suffocating, and she suddenly wanted to flee this place, to gulp fresh air at the surface and feel the infinite sky above her.

"We'll never get out of here," she whispered hoarsely, the blood draining in a rush from her face. "We're trapped."

Heff gripped her arm. "You're going through what every first-time caver experiences: claustrophobia. You've got to fight the feeling, Lucia, push it back down, swallow it like a big lump of oatmeal. If you don't, you'll go to pieces and our search for Paco will end here."

"No!" she screamed at him, then screwed her eyes shut and slowly, deliberately, forced herself to be calm. "Let's go," she said after a while. "I'll be all right."

"You sure?"

"Go, just go, will you?"

Heff looked at her a moment longer, then turned to the controls and restarted the engines. He threw a switch and gingerly increased the thrust. Slowly the Caverunner rotated on its axis, the lights at its oblong ends barely clearing the rock walls on each side.

"Is any of this any use?" she asked dejectedly as the hoverjet retreated down the dust-filled tunnel. "Tell me the truth, Jedediah. Will we ever find Paco?"

"You're a big girl, Lucia. You ought to know by now that you don't always win on the first roll. You want to quit, fine. I'll take you back to the sinkhole. But that will cost hours I could use finding your brother. Make up your mind."

"Damn you, Jedediah, you know the answer. I won't quit. And I'm a woman, not a girl."

"A matter of semantics."

"It's not semantics. Calling a woman a girl is demeaning."

"Wonderful. This is just what I needed on this trip, a raving feminist for a co-pilot."

"Feminists do not rave. You wouldn't feel so threatened if you weren't such a sexist."

"Sexist?"

They stared at each other a moment, then suddenly Lucia was laughing and crying at the same time. "Do you realize how absurd this all is, to be having this argument in a choking cave five miles under the earth?"

Heff grinned. "It is a tad ridiculous, now that you mention it."

She smiled back. "Shall we get on with finding Paco?"

"As long as it wouldn't offend your feminism being chauffeured around by a sexist like myself."

"Under the circumstances, I don't think I have any choice."

Heff increased the forward thrust. "At least you're a pragmatic feminist."

"Besides, down here who will ever know?"

He laughed. "You're wily, Lucia, like all women."

"All women?"

Slowly the Caverunner picked up speed and plowed through the thinning dust ahead.

TWO HOURS BEFORE DAWN

Texas Governor Lynn Duecker stared through the plexiglass bubble of the National Guard helicopter at the lights of Dallas blinking on the horizon thirty miles away. From five thousand feet he could see to the fringes of the metropolitan area, where the last of the city's lights dimmed into the dark sea of the surrounding prairie.

To the east, west, and north, glowing red ribbons wound out into the night, the taillights of thousands of cars fleeing Dallas with evacuees. To the south, toward his position, the roads were eerily dark, save for the occasional sweep of police car searchlights probing the empty highways.

As Duecker watched, tiny bursts of orange-white sparks erupted from below and red tracer bullets stitched the night beneath the chopper.

Duecker cursed and turned angrily to the pilot. "Get me that National Guard commander down there. What the hell's his name—Walters, Watkins?"

"Major General Wilkerson, sir," the pilot said.

"Get him on that radio, lieutenant."

"Right away, governor."

Duecker watched the tracer fire below and fumed while the pilot put the radio call through. Finally, the pilot handed him a headset. "I have General Wilkerson, sir."

"General, this is Governor Duecker," he bellowed into the throat mike. "I ordered your troops to cease fire. Why am I seeing tracer rounds down there?"

"Your orders were not to fire unless fired upon, governor," Wilkerson replied. "We're taking sniper rounds. Three of my men have been wounded in the last hour."

"Unprovoked fire, general?"

"Entirely unprovoked, sir. The men were on a routine reconnaissance patrol on the perimeter."

"Your routine patrol is a provocation to the Chicanos. Keep your people within your own lines, general. Do you understand?"

"If I don't send out reconnaissance, I won't know what the enemy's intentions are, governor. They could mount an assault and be within our lines before we know it."

"They're not the enemy, general. You're facing several thousand scared men, women, and children who were peacefully worshiping at a shrine when the Rangers waded in with their guns blazing. The Chicanos didn't start this confrontation, and I think it's ridiculous to assume they'll attack your troops. I'll be at your position in five minutes. And I don't want to see any more tracers."

Duecker handed the headset back to the pilot without waiting for a reply from the Guard commander. "You heard, lieutenant. Put her down."

"Yes, sir," the pilot said, banking the chopper for the local grammar school where the National Guard units had established their command post.

Several minutes later the helicopter descended slowly onto a playing field behind the school, its landing lights all but obscured by a thick vortex of dust drawn up from the baked ground by the whirling blades above.

Duecker unstrapped himself. "Wait here," he ordered the pilot. "I'll need you again shortly."

"I'll be ready, governor."

Duecker popped the door and trotted in a half crouch to where a knot of Guard officers waited. The officers came to attention and saluted as Duecker came up.

A guardsman with two stars on each flap of his fatigue

collar stepped forward and extended his hand. "General Wilkerson, governor. I'd like you to meet my staff."

Duecker ignored the three field grade officers preening behind their general. Half the National Guard officers were politicians or businessmen on the make, and the thought of the inevitable small talk as he shook each hand sickened Duecker.

"This isn't a reception at the officers' club, general. The only people I want to meet at the moment are the leaders of those Chicanos you've got bottled up. Do you know who they are?"

General Wilkerson stiffened at the rebuke. "I was merely extending a courtesy, sir," he said coolly. "As far as we know, the rebellion is being led by a man named Ignacio Baptista."

"Is he a barrio leader?"

Wilkerson scowled. "He's a goddamned farmer. That mummy or statue or goddess or whatever the hell they think they're fighting over is on his land. He's got an adviser, a priest named Quinn. He's the local padre."

"Have you talked to Baptista?"

"Briefly, about two hours ago. He asked for a truce long enough to pass wounded out to a hospital. Two of theirs and a Ranger with a cracked skull. I went in with the ambulances."

"What was your conversation with Baptista?"

"I ordered him to surrender, governor."

"His reply?"

"He claimed it was the Texas Rangers who provoked the battle. He said the Rangers had come onto his land and attempted to seize their Madonna by force. Then the priest piped up that the sinkhole was a holy shrine and that their people didn't recognize civilian authority there. I tried for another ten minutes to talk them into disarming. Neither one would budge. I finally gave up and came back out with the wounded."

"I want to talk to those people, General Wilkerson. Take me forward."

"I don't advise that, governor. My entire line is under sporadic sniper fire."

"Let's go, general."

Wilkerson hesitated a moment, not used to being bull-dozed, then threw Duecker a hard salute. "Yes, *sir*," he said formally, then spun on his heel and led the way to a caravan of two jeeps and an armored half-track.

Five minutes later the small convoy arrived at the National Guard front line four hundred yards from the sinkhole shrine of the Madonna. Two huge Abrams tanks blocked the intersection, facing a Chicano roadblock of lumber, couches, and overturned cars a hundred yards down the boulevard.

A knot of Guard infantrymen was clustered behind the tanks, and Duecker could see occasional muzzle flashes from the line of riflemen strung out into the fields on both sides of the road. A major turned and saluted as the command party ran in a half crouch from the jeeps to the cover of the huge tanks.

"What's the situation, major?" General Wilkerson asked as the party came up.

"Sporadic rifle and pistol fire, general. No sustained volleys for several hours. I think they're low on ammunition. They haven't fired any tear gas since around dusk. They may be out of shells."

Duecker stared at the major. "Where the hell did they get tear gas?"

"From the trunks of the Ranger squad cars they captured, governor. Same place they got the rifles and pistols they're firing."

"You mean the Chicanos were unarmed when the Rangers went in?" Duecker asked.

"Hardly unarmed, governor," General Wilkerson said. "They had sufficient knives and clubs to kill twenty-three police officers and wound half the survivors."

Duecker shook his head disgustedly. "Knives and clubs against automatic weapons and tanks. Your little war here seems rather lopsided, general."

Wilkerson bristled. "There's another part of that equation, governor. We're facing religious fanatics more than willing to be martyred for their Madonna. My boys aren't quite that ready to die, not over a dirty statue in a sinkhole in some Mexican's backyard."

"There's been enough dying on both sides, general. Order your men to cease fire," Duecker said.

Wilkerson hesitated a moment, then wheeled on his aide. "Send runners down the line, major. Cease fire."

"Yes, sir." The officer saluted and was gone into the darkness of the fields. Within minutes the guns of the guardsmen had quieted. There was no fire from the Chicano barricades, and an eerie silence descended on the prairie battlefield.

"You have a megaphone around here, general?" Governor Duecker asked.

"In my jeep," Wilkerson replied. He sent an enlisted man after the megaphone. The private returned and handed Duecker the instrument.

"Have one of these tanks throw a spotlight on the road out front," Duecker ordered.

"Illuminate our position?" Wilkerson sputtered.

"What's the problem, general? You don't think the Mexicans know you have a couple of tanks down here?"

The general stared deliberately at Duecker. "You insist on baiting me, don't you, governor."

"Not baiting, general, prodding. Get a light out there."

"Do we return fire if the Chicanos open up on us?"

"You do not," Duecker said.

Wilkerson wheeled and strode angrily to the back deck of the first tank. "Sergeant Fuller."

The noncom popped his head through the hatch. "Yes, sir?"

"Throw your turret searchlight on the road."

"You want me to light up the area, sir?" the sergeant asked incredulously.

"The governor wants you to light up the area, sergeant. Do it."

"Yes, sir." Sergeant Fuller disappeared into the tank, and a moment later the turret light flashed on. Immediately a rifle barked behind the Chicano lines and a bullet ricocheted off the far side of the tank.

There was a sudden loud rebuke in Spanish in the dark distance, and the firing stopped.

"Whoever opened up is getting his ass chewed," Duecker observed. "I hope his friends were listening. Keep your men under cover just in case, general." He tied a white handkerchief to the megaphone and stepped from behind the tank into the open road between the battle lines.

General Wilkerson blanched. "God almighty, governor, you're going to get picked off out there."

Duecker ignored the warning and brought the megaphone up to his mouth. Despite the bravado, he was scared, his body braced for a half-expected bullet out of the night. He willed his voice not to quake and pressed the talk button.

"This is Governor Lynn Duecker speaking," he began. The volume of his electrified voice startled him momentarily and he cleared his throat. "I'm here to end this senseless bloodshed. I've ordered the National Guard to cease fire. I want to talk with your leaders."

There was an excited babble of Spanish voices from behind the Chicano barricade, then an answer hurled back in English. "We recognize your cease-fire, governor. Walk forward to our lines. Alone."

"You'll be putting yourself in a hostage situation, governor," General Wilkerson warned from the corner of the tank.

"You don't break a stalemate by playing it safe, general. The highways south have got to be opened." Duecker tossed the megaphone to Wilkerson and walked purposefully toward the Chicano position. He reached the barricade and two sets of brown arms helped him through the jumble of crates and old cars.

Duecker found himself facing a graying Mexican-American in his mid-fifties wearing faded jeans, a collarless work shirt, and dusty boots. Gentle, intelligent eyes appraised Duecker evenly from a weathered, mustachioed face.

"I am Ignacio Baptista. It is my honor to meet you,

governor," the man said. He turned as a priest came up to join them.

"Father Quinn from San Juan parish," the priest introduced himself.

Duecker looked at the two. In their faces he saw bewilderment, pain, and pride, but no hostility. How had such innocents found their way to violence? How had prayer turned to war?

"Señor Baptista, Father Quinn, I wonder if you realize what this fight over your Madonna has come to? Those are National Guard soldiers your people are firing on. As far as the government is concerned, you and your people are in open rebellion against the United States of America. Each and every one of you could be tried for sedition."

"That's a ludicrous charge," Father Quinn said in agitation, his eyes flashing behind his rimless glasses. "My people are only protecting a religious shrine that is sacred to them. There is nothing political about this. Surely, Governor Duecker, you know I speak the truth."

"I know you are armed with stolen police weapons and you refuse to surrender to government authority. That's called insurrection."

"It is the Madonna we refuse to surrender, governor," Ignacio Baptista said quietly. "As for myself, the others who've used weapons, we're willing to answer for what we've done. We understand the law, and we've always obeyed it. But your authority is over the temporal. The Madonna is of our souls. We will die before we allow you to desecrate Our Lady's shrine."

"That is what provoked this violence, governor," the priest said. "The Rangers wanted to take the Madonna away in a truck to be locked away in some university warehouse. They tried to take the Madonna by force. There is a question of sanctuary they choose to ignore."

The governor held up his hands. "I am not here to assess guilt or innocence on either side. What circumstances brought on the situation is immaterial at the moment. Good God, don't you people know what's happening to Dallas?"

"There are portable radios and televisions among the

faithful," Father Quinn said. "We know about the sinkhole and the evacuation of the city."

Duecker turned and pointed toward a line of blacked-out light poles silhouetted against the dark-gray horizon. "Highway Forty-five over there is one of the main arteries out of Dallas. Thousands of cars should be passing us right now, taking people to safety out in the countryside. Instead, those cars, those people, are backed up into south Dallas. They're trapped in traffic jams on roads that could collapse into the earth without warning. We cannot open that road and let those trapped people through with a gun battle going on fifty yards off the highway."

"What is it you propose, governor?" Baptista asked.

"An armistice. I want you to surrender your arms, take down the barricades, and return to the peaceful, lawful practice of your religion. In return, I'll pull back the National Guard."

"What of the Madonna?" the priest asked.

"The Madonna remains with your people, father. I recognize the sanctuary of your shrine."

"If we give up our weapons, we are defenseless," Baptista said. "What assurances do you offer that we will not be attacked by armed civilians? Chicanos are fair game these days."

"You have my word as governor that the State of Texas will do all in its power to protect not only your people gathered here but every other Chicano resident of Texas, regardless of citizenship. I want it clear that an armistice is not a pardon. You two, and undoubtedly others of your people, can expect civil charges and arrest when this is all over. But for now, the state is offering to leave you in peace. What is your answer?"

The farmer and the priest looked at each other and silently agreed. "We accept the terms of your armistice, Governor Duecker," Baptista said. "Our weapons will be passed forward and piled in the road."

"Gentlemen, we have just saved a lot of lives," Duecker said. "A Dios gracias." The priest and Baptista crossed themselves.

"Hurry," Duecker said. "There isn't much time." The governor turned, maneuvered back through the barricade, and strode back to the National Guard lines.

"We have an armistice, general," he told a stony-faced Wilkerson. "The Chicanos have agreed to surrender their weapons. When you've collected their arms, I want you to withdraw your troops."

"You don't intend to intern those rebels, Governor Duecker?"

"They'll face justice later, general. They know that, and they accept it. The most important thing now is to get that highway open. Leave an infantry company to run off any rednecks and get your men the hell out of here. I need your troops to help with the evacuation of Dallas." Duecker turned before the general could protest further and strode toward the waiting jeeps. "Get me back to my chopper."

Seven minutes later he was strapped in his seat with the sixteen-foot aluminum props whirling above. "Return to headquarters," he ordered the pilot.

The helicopter lifted off and rose quickly above the darkened prairie. Duecker looked at his watch in the glow from the cockpit instruments: 4:36.

If the computations of the geologists were right, in two days' time the limestone cap beneath Dallas would collapse and the city would plunge into the depths of the huge sinkhole forming under the prairie.

At four thousand feet the radio suddenly crackled to life. "National Guard One, this is Dallas Operations. I have a request for a patch-through from the U.S. Geological Survey to Governor Duecker. Is the governor on board?"

Duecker turned on his throat mike. "This is Governor Duecker. Put the Survey call through."

There was a moment of static, then the connection was made. "Ed Mullins from the Survey office in Dallas, governor. I thought you ought to know right away."

"Know what, Mr. Mullins?"

"Our laser tiltmeters have detected significant crustal sag in between Lawnview Avenue and the Thornton Freeway.

We're looking at the imminent collapse of two, maybe three square miles."

"What's on that land?" Duecker demanded. "Homes? Hospitals? Roads?"

The voice over the radio took on an odd, abstract tone. "Nothing like that. Most of the land belongs to Grove Hill Memorial Cemetery. Kind of macabre, isn't it, governor? The dead are going down first."

DAWN

National Reconnaissance Office deputy director Joanne Hauser lowered her red-rimmed eyes from the television monitor she'd sat glued to for the past three hours and suddenly noticed she was wearing two different shoes. It didn't surprise her, given the fact that she'd gotten dressed in her darkened Arlington, Virginia, bedroom in something under three minutes.

The call from the duty officer at the Mexican desk had come at 3:45 A.M. There had been a "development." The information from CHICO was unsettling. Could the deputy director come in as soon as possible?

There were times lately, especially when CHICO summoned her in the middle of the night or on a weekend, that Hauser felt she'd lost control of her life, that she'd become little more than the extension of a machine.

CHICO was an acronym for Close Hovering Intelligence Camera Orbiting, an NRO television surveillance satellite that had been sent into geostationary orbit over northern Mexico in February 1997. It was CHICO's incredible television camera that so often drew Hauser back to her analyst's seat before the TV monitor. The Israeli-developed camera was capable of perspectives ranging from a satellite-height

162

view from space to an extreme close-up of the gold in the teeth of a man on the ground.

And CHICO was live television.

Twenty-four hours a day, the satellite's cameras supplied the American intelligence community with information on virtually every facet of Mexican life. Did the National Security Council want to know how much steel was being produced in a new Soviet-built mill outside Chihuahua? CHICO obligingly zeroed in on the mill's shipping yard, and analysts counted every I-beam that left the plant. Was the Pentagon nervous about what Russian arms were being unloaded from a Bulgarian freighter docked at Tampico? CHICO watched the stevedores empty the vessel. Troop movements, factory shipping, crop plantings, road construction, even the faces of individual Mexican leaders leaving their offices—nothing in northern Mexico escaped CHICO's gaze.

Yet it wasn't the satellite's live television eye that had sounded the alarm this early morning, but a sister infrared camera on board. CHICO's temperature probe had detected the heat signatures of two suspiciously long strings of vehicles moving up separate Mexican highways toward Texas.

In normal civilian traffic, cars and trucks tend to leapfrog each other at random speeds. The vehicles CHICO had spotted were spaced evenly apart in one lane and moved in tandem down the highway. There was no question these were convoys, almost certainly military, one heading directly north from Monterrey, the second traveling northeast out of Torreón.

Hauser looked at the clock above the monitor. It was 6:35 A.M. in Mexico. The sun would be rising in a few minutes.

"Let's go to television," she said to video engineer Mike Pennessi sitting at the console next to her. Pennessi had become an expert on Soviet military hardware after several hundred hours before CHICO's monitor.

"Which convoy do you want to see first?" Pennessi asked.

"Let's have a look at that bunch out of Monterrey," Hauser said.

"One sunrise over Mexico coming up," Pennessi said cheerfully, programming the switch to live coverage into CHICO's computer brain. "I'll start with an overview of the area and move the camera in as the light gets better."

"Sounds good," Hauser said, then sat back and watched as the infrared blips and digital highway grid disappeared from the screen to be replaced by a live television shot of a desert landscape still shrouded in shades of predawn gray.

Pennessi centered the camera on a long sinuous valley with a white string of highway meandering down its center. At the left side of the screen, the sun began to tinge the highest crags of the Sierra Madre Mountains, and gradually the deep shadows ebbed out of the valley. In another minute they could see tiny black rectangles moving along the white pencil line of the road.

"Is it light enough for a close-up?" Hauser asked.

"Yes, I think so," Pennessi said. He moved a mouse across the video screen until it was centered on the far convoy. Then he keyed an instruction into the computer and the monitor was suddenly filled with passing trucks. The camera angle made it appear they were looking down on the road from a high overpass.

Hauser came forward in her chair. "Iveska heavy troop transports. Look at the size of the damn things."

"Biggest transports in the Mexican ground fleet," Pennessi said. "Capable of carrying thirty-five to forty troops each, depending on equipment."

"How many trucks, Mike?" Hauser asked.

Pennessi posed the question to CHICO's computer. "One hundred and twenty-six. Down two from the last infrared count."

"Probably a couple of mechanical breakdowns along the way," Hauser guessed. "Let's have a look at that convoy out of Torreón."

Pennessi typed in the code he had assigned the second convoy during the infrared tracking, and the screen changed to a low-altitude shot of a long line of trucks moving down a straight, cactus-fringed highway.

Like the troop transports, the trucks were Russian made. But they were bigger, huge twenty-wheelers, and on the back of each loomed a large canvas-covered bulk.

"Tank carriers," Hauser said.

"By the shape, I'd say those were Soviet T-Seventy-twos under those tarps," Pennessi said.

"There must be twenty-five or thirty of them," Hauser said.

Pennessi keyed the computer. "Thirty-six," he read from the screen.

"That's an entire armored division," Hauser said. She sat back and thought for a minute. "Assuming both convoys maintain their present headings and speeds, where will they converge? And when?"

Pennessi queried the computer. "If we extrapolate their routes out four hours, the convoys will join somewhere around Piedras Negras on the Texas border a little after nine this morning local time."

"What the hell's going on in Piedras Negras?" Hauser wondered out loud.

"Want to have a look?" Pennessi asked.

"Yes, I do," Hauser said. "Overview from two thousand feet."

Pennessi programmed the code for the Mexican city into CHICO's computer and a moment later the screen changed to a live shot of Piedras Negras as it would be seen from the top of a nearby hill.

"I'll move in slowly," the engineer said.

Hauser nodded silently and watched the monitor. She could see from one end of the city to the other and beyond, to the waters of the Rio Grande glinting gold in the rising sun.

Oblivious to the television eye watching them from the edge of space, the citizens of Piedras Negras were beginning an ordinary day. As the camera moved in, early shoppers took shape wending their way through the sleepy streets toward the already bustling marketplace. Elsewhere, women swept twig brooms across their thresholds and concrete trucks lumbered toward distant building sites.

"If there's something going on in Piedras Negras, nobody told Piedras Negras about it," Pennessi said.

"Certainly nothing to interest a Mexican mechanized division," Hauser said. "Still, those convoys are headed this way. Pan northwest along the Rio, will you, Mike? Maybe there's a staging area upriver."

Pennessi programmed CHICO, and for the next five minutes the satellite camera followed the upstream course of the Rio Grande as it cut through the desert. The camera passed over several small towns and villages perched on the Mexican riverbank. All looked quiet. The monitor was showing yet another tiny settlement when Hauser abruptly came forward in her seat again.

"Hold it, Mike. In that field next to the village. Those look like helicopters."

Pennessi brought the camera in. "About a dozen Mi-Thirty-two troop transports," he said.

"Let's have a look in the village," Hauser said.

Pennessi panned the camera. Knots of Mexican soldiers were visible eating their breakfasts around the fountain in the town square, their weapons stacked carelessly against the nearest adobe wall. A Mexican flag hung from the balcony of the largest house and two guards flanked the door below.

"Looks like a rear area headquarters," Pennessi volunteered.

"That's my guess, Mike," Hauser said. "But if those are rearguard troops, where's the front line?"

Pennessi pointed to the top center of the screen. The tiny figures of a half dozen soldiers were visible strung in from the river in a rough line. "Sentries," he said. "They're guarding that track coming down along the river. I'd say the action's upstream."

"Continue the pan along the river, Mike," Hauser said. "We'll know soon enough."

Pennessi saw the half-track first. "There's an armored personnel carrier on the Mexican side ahead." He zoomed in on the vehicle. "The doors are wide open. I don't see anybody around. It looks deserted."

Hauser pointed to a swath of disturbed sand leading down to the water. "Whoever was in that carrier went into the river. Can you see where they came out?"

Pennessi panned the camera up and down the near banks. "They didn't," he said finally. "At least not on the Mexican side."

Hauser stared intently at the screen. "Pan across the river, Mike. Slowly."

The broad expanse of the Rio Grande was placid, empty of soldiers, and CHICO's camera was beginning its search of the American bank when Hauser suddenly jabbed her finger into the upper left corner of the screen.

"Did you see that?"

"What?" Pennessi asked.

"A burst of flashes against the base of that rock outcropping. Automatic rifle fire, I'm sure of it."

"There's someone lying in the sand in the foreground," Pennessi said. "I'm going in for a close-up."

Slowly the camera moved in to a head-and-shoulders shot of a teenage Mexican soldier lying on his back with his eyes wide and his mouth gaping open as if in astonishment. The picture's resolution was so fine they could see every detail of the youngster's face. He had shiny black hair, large brown eyes, a wispy adolescent mustache, and slightly crooked teeth. There was a crucifix and chain visible in the V of his fatigue shirt.

"It's almost as if he can see us," Hauser said quietly. "Like he's staring back up at us in surprise."

"I don't think he—" Pennessi began, then stopped in midword, horrified, revolted by the picture on the screen. He gagged, lurched for the wastepaper basket, and began to vomit.

Hauser's body shrank back involuntarily from the loathsome scene on the monitor, yet she was incapable of tearing her eyes away. Mesmerized, her gaze fused to the screen, she watched a scorpion crawl out of the boy's mouth and down his still cheek to the sand.

The young Mexican soldier wasn't looking at anything. He was dead in Texas.

AN HOUR AFTER DAWN

"Looks like a crevasse in the passage floor ahead," Jedediah Heffernan said to Lucia Sanchez in the cabin of the Caverunner.

For the past seven hours, they had been following the meandering course of the side tunnel feeding the north fork of the Rio Bajo. Heff had used the time to teach Lucia to pilot the hoverjet.

Lucia worked the thrust throttle, and the Caverunner passed over the dark defile below them. She had a deft touch at the controls, Heff admitted to himself. Even in tight tunnel necks where the walls pinched in to within inches of the craft's oblong fuselage, Lucia had managed to pilot through without so much as scraping the paint.

Beyond the fracture, the bow lights showed the passage running as round and true as a drainpipe on into the distant dark. The crevasse had been the only challenge to their progress for the past hour, and Heff resumed the game of "Capitals" they had been playing to relieve the tedium of the long, straight stretches of featureless tunnel.

"As I recall, it's my turn to name the country," Heff said. "Outer Mongolia. Child's play, I know, but then these gifts to you just reflect the sweet guy I am."

"I would never use the word 'sweet' in any description of

you, Jedediah. Never. Besides which, Outer Mongolia happens to be a part of the Soviet Union. It is not an independent country; therefore, it does not belong in this game."

"It's in the United Nations."

"Yes, but that's one of those old East-West political things. The United States allowed Outer Mongolia a UN seat, and the Soviets recognized one of our allies."

"I dare say the people of Outer Mongolia will be enthralled to hear this astounding theory of yours that they're not living in a real country. They'll probably want to interview you on the local news and find out just exactly what the hell happened since the last time they ran their flag up."

"You'll hound me until I give you your little victory, won't you, Jedediah."

"Hound is a strong word, Lucia."

She laughed. "All right, all right, what *is* the damned capital of Outer Mongolia?"

He grinned. "Ulan Bator."

"Thank you for sharing that, Jedediah. You know what a thrill it is for me to join the isolated handful of people worldwide who know that Ulan Bator is the capital of Outer Mongolia."

"That makes it fourteen to nothing," Heff said happily. "And I go again. Corsica."

"I'm not playing anymore unless we stick to countries."

"C'mon, Corsica's easy. The birthplace of Napoleon, harbor for the jet set, right out in the middle of the Mediterranean where everybody can see it."

"Countries. I'm only going to guess countries."

"I don't usually do this," he said expansively. "But I'll give you a hint. The capital starts with an—" Heff stopped in midsentence, his eyes drawn suddenly to the illuminated tunnel ahead. After numbing hours of sameness, endless miles of staring at the close curving walls of the Rio Bajo, a vast shadowed chamber opened suddenly before them.

Heff flicked on the Caverunner's exterior floodlights and they stared wordlessly around them as the hoverjet nosed into a soaring subterranean hall four hundred feet high and over fifteen hundred feet across. The far end of the immense cavern was lost somewhere in the dark beyond the reach of the lights.

Limestone pillars six feet thick rose through the dim heights to support a stalactite-studded ceiling 410 feet above the cavern floor. Other columns had toppled over and lay broken in the primordial sand, their shattered sections lying end to end like great links of dusty sausage.

"Let me take the controls," Heff said. "I want you to enjoy all of this."

Lucia drew in a breath. "It looks like Greece," she whispered. "Like ancient Greece."

Heff looked at her strangely. "That's exactly the thought that struck me the first time I was in a columned hall," he said quietly. "I imagined I had rediscovered the ruins of the Parthenon after an earthquake had swallowed the Acropolis."

"There can't be other places like this," Lucia said, awestruck.

"But there are, Lucia," Heff replied as the hoverjet cruised slowly past the first majestic pillars. "There are vistas under the earth undreamed of by men above. I've entered huge chambers that looked like amphitheaters in imperial Rome. There's a cave in New Mexico where rock formations rise from the floor like the stumps of giant felled oaks, and a cavern in Kentucky where twin sets of stone pilings lead out into the dark like a plankless pier into a lake."

Heff was silent a moment, staring out into the dark depths of the cavern. "There were times, Lucia, when I didn't think it possible that nature was the architect of what I saw, and times when I thought there could be no other."

For several moments they said nothing, each absorbed in the pristine netherworld emerging into the lights of the Caverunner.

"How did the columns form, Jedediah?" Lucia asked finally. "Did the rock erode around them?"

"Just the opposite. The columns grew in place long after water hollowed out the chamber."

"Grew? How does stone grow?"

Heff craned his neck and played a searchlight across the vaulted ceiling high above them. "There, do you see that conical-shaped rock hanging down?"

Lucia stared up. "That one that looks like a big icicle?"

"Yes. That's a stalactite. It formed from the limestone deposits in tiny drops of water that evaporated against the ceiling. Over the centuries, billions of drops evaporated, leaving their dissolved minerals behind in tiny rings, one building on another so that year after year the stalactite grew longer and thicker."

Heff sliced the floodlight beam straight down through the dark to the tip of a formation sprouting from the cave floor like a giant canine tooth.

"That's a stalagmite," he said, playing the light over the rough face of the rock cone. "You often find them directly beneath a stalactite because at times the waterdrops on the ceiling become so heavy that they fall to the cave floor before they can evaporate. The lime in the water is deposited on the floor, and gradually a stalagmite grows up toward its sister stalactite advancing down from above. Eventually the two spires meet and the formation thickens into a column."

The Caverunner moved through an avenue of columns. "It's as if we were entering Athens in a chariot two thousand years ago," Lucia said quietly.

For several minutes they stared out silently at the passing pillars, then Lucia started and came forward suddenly in her seat. "Jedediah, look, behind that last column on the left. There's a huge orange curtain hanging from the ceiling."

Heff smiled. "A stone curtain. We call those formations draperies. When water flows down only one side of a stalactite, the limestone forms a thin blade that gets wider without getting thicker. The water meanders slightly from side to side as it courses down the stalactites over the centuries, and slowly the formation takes on the appearance of a drapery with graceful curves and folds."

"What gives it that orange color?" Lucia asked.

"Impurities in the water stained thin strips of calcium carbonate in the stone. The stream that fed this particular drapery was obviously rich in iron, thus the rusty orange color."

Heff suddenly caught sight of a radically different formation in a grotto behind the free-hanging foot of the drapery. He reached across and put a hand over Lucia's eyes.

"Jedediah, what are you doing?"

"I have a surprise for you, Lucia. Don't look until I tell you."

"The first time in six hours there's been anything but tunnel walls to see and you don't want me to look."

"Quit squawking," he said, maneuvering a floodlight so the beam lit the interior of the small stone cove ahead. He stopped the Caverunner fifty feet away and killed all the lights but the lone flood. Then he took his hand from Lucia's eyes.

Lucia blinked and stared at the most beautiful apparition she had ever seen. The small grotto before her was filled with flowers, flowers with crystal petals, flowers of stone blooming in the dark bowels of the earth.

She looked at him questioningly, her eyes wide.

"They're gypsum flowers," he said. "Cave flowers, some call them."

"They look like they've just opened," she said softly. "As if all through time they've waited down here in the dark for this one moment they could blossom for us."

Heff looked across the darkened cabin at Lucia's profile against the floodlit grotto. She had never been in a cave before their descent into the sinkhole eighteen hours ago, yet she was as passionate about the beauty of the subterranean world as was he. Where most would have seen only stalagmites and gypsum clusters, Lucia saw Greek temples and blooming flowers.

"Part of me wants to know how the cave flowers form," she said, "and part of me doesn't. Part of me wants to believe the flowers are magic, that they grew from stone seeds planted by a race of gentle giants living under the earth."

"We can leave it at that. Magic."

"No," she said. "Someday I'll tell my children about this place, and when they ask me how these flowers came to be, I want to be able to tell them."

"The flowers form when aragonite—that's a carbonate mineral found in sedimentary rocks—builds up slowly along a fine crack in the stone. Over time, a cluster of long slender crystals grows around the center. Other clusters form behind the first until slowly crystal petals grow into an open flower."

They gazed into the grotto for several minutes more, pointing out to each other bouquets blooming from the ceiling and single blossoms peeping from hidden niches. Finally, Heff pushed the throttle forward and they started again down the length of the vaulted hall.

Twenty minutes later, the hoverjet neared the far end of the chamber and they both strained their eyes toward the shadowed wall ahead, searching the rock face for a way out of the cavern.

"I don't see any tunnels, Jedediah," Lucia said, the wonder gone from her voice. "We've come to a dead end."

"Tunnels don't often meet like highways flowing into each other," he said. "They enter and leave large halls like this at different levels, and they're not necessarily opposite each other."

Lucia looked out into the dark. "The cavern's huge. It will take us forever to find the way out."

"It will take us exactly seventy-two seconds." Heff leaned forward and punched a command code into the control computer. The antenna of the onboard Gravprobe began a slow radarlike sweep of the surrounding cavern walls.

"Why exactly seventy-two seconds?" Lucia asked.

"The Gravprobe can scan five degrees of arc per second. A full circle of three hundred and sixty degrees takes seventy-two seconds."

"What's a Gravprobe?"

"It's a microgravimeter," Heff explained. "It pulses sound waves through the rock and measures the echoes that return. A cavity will have a recognizable gravity signature quite different from the surrounding solid stone."

As the antenna turned, the cockpit computer interpreted the returning signals, and a three-dimensional digital map of the cliff appeared on the soft green screen of the command monitor before them.

Lucia watched the screen fascinated as the computer traced a jagged tear in the cliffs fifty feet above the cavern floor.

"Jedediah, look. Isn't that an opening?"

Heff studied the numbers superimposed on the screen. "It's a small vertical lead," he said. "Only a couple of hundred feet deep. Not what we're looking for."

The Gravprobe continued its deliberate circle. Several times the microgravimeter picked up the signature of a cavity in the dark walls. Each time Heff ruled out the opening as too small, a dead end, or a cut-around that looped behind the cliffs and reentered the chamber farther along the walls.

The Gravprobe had surveyed 315 degrees of cavern before Lucia pointed to a large black semicircle being etched onto the monitor map. "It's the biggest opening yet," she said hopefully.

Heff nodded. "I think that's it. The dimensions are close to the tunnel we left."

"Why didn't we see it as we passed through the chamber?" she asked.

"We came in along the western side," Heff said. "The mouth of the exit passage is high on the eastern wall."

Heff brought the Caverunner around on a heading for the tunnel leading out of the chamber. He guided the hoverjet slowly over the stalagmite-studded floor of the cavern, maneuvering deftly past the shattered trunks of topless columns and over the rubble of the million years of building and tearing down that had passed in the huge cave.

He slowed the Caverunner as they neared the Gravprobe compass fix. "The tunnel mouth is about eighty feet above us," he said, reading the graph numbers on the monitor. "There must have been one hell of a waterfall through here a couple of hundred thousand years ago."

A gently arching rock formation suddenly loomed in the hoverjet's headlights and Lucia let out a little gasp. "Jedediah, the waterfall. The waterfall is still there. It's turned to stone."

Heff had seen formations like this before, but never one remotely near the size and beauty of the arching rock before them. From its tip three feet off the cavern floor, the thin, multicolored tongue of stone rose in a graceful bow to the black tunnel mouth eighty feet above them.

"It's flowstone," he said.

"Flowstone? You mean the stone actually flows, like lava from a volcano?"

"No, flowstone formation is a far slower, far more gradual process. Streams in limestone caves are often saturated with calcium carbonate that settles to the streambed as lime. Over the centuries, the limestone sediment forms a smooth coating on the river floor that can grow several feet thick."

"But this flowstone isn't following a streambed, Jedediah. It's flowing through the air."

"You're looking at a stone mirror of the waterfall that once fell here," Heff said. "One day, maybe half a million years ago, the first microscopic deposit of lime settled below the lip of the falls up here. From that infinitesimal toehold, the flowstone grew downward, drop by drop, century by century, following the arc of the falls to the cavern floor."

"The way you describe it, I can almost hear the water breaking on the rocks," Lucia said.

"Yeah," Heff said, his voice barely audible. "Almost." For several moments they stared up silently at the glistening stone waterfall towering up through the glow of the Caverunner's lights.

"Well, we won't find Paco sitting here admiring the scenery," Heff said finally. He leaned forward and flipped a switch on the control console. "Ready? We're going up."

He increased the thrust to the jet ports below, and slowly the Caverunner began to rise. The hoverjet was ten feet over the cavern floor when a raucous shriek of tearing metal came from the cluster of jet ports below. The Caverunner teetered in the air, then the engine quit and the hoverjet dropped heavily to the cavern floor.

The metallic echoes of the crash boomed madly over the walls of the huge cavern as Heff turned anxiously to Lucia. "You OK?"

"Yes," she said, lifting herself gingerly in her seat. "But I think I'm going to have a sore bottom for a while."

"Lucky we weren't higher," Heff said. "If we'd been near the top of the falls, padded seats wouldn't have helped."

"What happened?"

"I don't know yet," Heff said, popping the plexiglass bubble of the Caverunner. He took a flashlight from the equipment drawer and heaved himself over the side of the hoverjet. His head disappeared and Lucia heard him probing around below. A moment later he was back, his face grim.

"There's a bad gash in one of the main thrust ports. A rock must have ricocheted up under there during the cave-in."

"But we've come miles since the cave-in. Why did it break now?"

"The rock probably scored the metal deeply but didn't tear it. So long as we cruised along slowly, the damagéd port section could withstand the pressure. But the moment I increased the thrust, the creased metal gave way and tore."

"Can you fix it?"

"Not without an arc welder."

Lucia climbed out of the Caverunner. "What do we do now?"

"*We* do not do anything. You stay here while I search for your brother on foot."

"You're out of your mind if you think you're leaving me behind, Jedediah."

"I was out of my mind to take you in the first place. I

should have known the time would come when I'd have to go on alone, and when that time came you'd argue with me."

Heff went to the rear cargo door and began rummaging through assorted cave gloves, ropes, thermal vests, knee crawlers, and several battery-lit miner's hard hats.

"I'm going, Jedediah," Lucia said quietly. "If I have to, I'll follow behind, but I'm going."

Heff whirled on her furiously. "Goddamn it, Lucia, the cruise is over. From here on it gets rough. You're not an experienced caver. You could get hurt. You could get killed."

"I'm willing to take that risk."

"Will you feel that way after you've duckwalked through two miles of low cave and can't straighten your back, after you've crawled over sharp rock spurs until your elbows and knees are bleeding? Will you tell me that when you're hanging over a hundred-and-fifty-foot pit by your finger-nails and your light goes out?"

"Paco is my brother, my blood," she said quietly. "There is nothing I would not do for him."

Heff threw up his hands. "I don't know why the hell I'm arguing with you. You'll never get twenty feet off the ground."

She looked at him suspiciously. "What do you mean 'off the ground'?"

"The tunnel mouth is up there," he said, pointing toward the black hole at the fringe of the Caverunner's lights eighty feet above them. "You want to follow me, fine. I'm going up the waterfall."

Heff turned back to the cargo space and strapped on a hat light. Then he took out an aluminum crossbow, a coil of nylon cave rope, and a three-pronged grappling iron with a long thin shaft.

He tied one end of the line to a needle eye in the end of the shaft and dropped the rest of the rope still coiled to the ground. Then he pulled the bowstring back to the trigger catch and fitted the shaft of the grappling iron into a thin slot along the top of the bow stock.

"What are you going to do with that?" Lucia asked, taking out a hat light for herself.

"Get a line to the top of the falls," Heff said. "That is if I can still aim this thing. It's been five years."

Heff sighted the crossbow on the tunnel entrance above and pulled the trigger. The bowstring snapped forward, and the grappling hook flew up the arc of the falls. Well below the lip, the iron bounced off the flowstone and started back down through the lights.

Heff yelled and lunged for Lucia, dragging her out of the way a second before the three-pronged hook slammed down into the sand where she'd been standing.

Lucia straightened her hat light. "Remind me not to take you to any turkey shoots, Jedediah. You missed the entrance by twenty feet."

"Five years, I'm a little rusty," he grumbled, tightening the tension on the bowstring.

"Where do you think it will come down this time?"

Heff refitted the grappling iron shaft into the bow, aimed, and shot again. The hook sailed straight up the face of the walls and angled into the black cave mouth above. They could hear the iron clang against a rock wall, then fall to the passage floor.

"Right where it should." Heff grinned in triumph. He caught the rope dangling down from the hook and slowly eased the line back. He drew down three feet of rope before the hook caught in a crevasse in the tunnel floor above and the nylon came taut in his hands. He yanked twice, then swung his weight up onto the line. The rope held.

Heff got down and went to the cargo hold and pulled out a cave pack. He began stowing away a flashlight, water canteen, emergency rations, an extra pair of socks, a first-aid kit, and four packages. Two of the foil-wrapped boxes were brick-shaped, and two were the size of cigarette packs.

When he had everything packed, he turned to Lucia and handed her a flashlight. "There's plenty of food and water in the Caverunner. You'll be fine until I get back."

In answer, Lucia marched over to the Caverunner and

shut off the large spotlights. Now only their hat lights and flashlights shone on the face of the falls. "I'm going."

"You'll never get up that rope."

"If you can get up that waterfall, Jedediah, I can."

Heff shrugged. "Have it your way. But when your arms get tired, and they will, and you get scared of the height, and you will, just close your eyes and hold on tight. I'll lower you."

"There'll be no need to lower me, Jedediah." Lucia tightened the chin strap on her hat light. "Just go ahead and climb. I'll take care of myself."

Heff looked at the defiant young woman for a moment, then turned and started up the rope. His shoulder and arm muscles were still in shape from his outdoor work around the ranch, and he found his rock-climbing technique came back to him easily. In three minutes he'd reached the top of the waterfall.

Heff shone his flashlight down the falls and watched beneath him as Lucia grabbed the rope and pulled herself up with all her strength. The way she held the line, her body was deadweight and she struggled to gain barely five feet.

"Don't be stubborn, Lucia," he called down. "This isn't for you."

"You're used to deciding things for women, aren't you, Jedediah," she shouted up through clenched teeth. "Well, I make my own decisions. I'm not giving up."

Despite her bravado, Lucia was scared to death. Suppose her arms gave out halfway up? She shuddered at the thought of plunging through the dark to the cavern floor.

She heard Jedediah curse above. "You're a pain in the ass, do you know that? A pain in the ass."

Lucia closed her eyes, searching for the strength to go on. Then she heard Heff pounding in a piton. A moment later she saw his hat light arc out away from the face of the falls as he rappeled back down.

"If you're going to get to the top, you'll have to follow every move I make," Heff said, landing next to Lucia. "I want you to do exactly as I say. Understood?"

"Of course."

"I don't like the way you said that."

"You're the boss. Honestly."

"Sure, this time will be different," he muttered, then turned and braced his boot tips against a tiny smooth ledge in the stone face. "You've got to use your feet as well as your arms when you climb. Now watch." He bent his knees, pushed against the small protrusion with his boot tips, and simultaneously pulled himself several feet up the rope. "Got it?"

"I think so," Lucia said. "I can try."

"Good. If you get tired, wrap the rope around one leg, then coil it over your boot and rest your weight. And whatever you do, don't look down."

"Don't worry, Jedediah, looking down is the last thing I intend to do."

Hesitantly at first, but with growing confidence and skill, Lucia followed Heff up the face of the subterranean waterfall, their hat lights bobbing in the cavern gloom like fireflies in a darkened barn.

Slowly the Caverunner became smaller against the cavern floor, and finally their last contact with the surface world faded into the dark far beneath them.

9:00 A.M.

Bill Edwards stood in the entry hall of the Ralt mansion watching Rebecca Ralt descend the sweeping stairs. Even though he'd worked for the Ralts for the past eight years, he'd never really come to know her.

She was almost always correct with him, a mistress to an underling, a lady pale and removed under a mannequin's calm. Yet there were times, wistful fleeting moments when they were alone on the prairie, when something would remind her of her childhood on the ranch and she'd offer a timid intimacy, like a hummingbird landing on his finger.

"Good morning, Bill," Rebecca said as she reached the landing.

"Good morning, Missus Ralt."

"Bill, do you know what this is all about? My husband would only tell me he had a surprise to show me and that you'd take me there."

"Mr. Ralt's orders were to drive you over to his command center, ma'am. He didn't tell me why."

"Command center? Is that some sort of office he has tucked away?"

"I believe Mr. Ralt would prefer to explain the command center to you himself, ma'am."

"Of course, Bill. My husband is unmatched at explaining

181

the things he does. Have you ever met such a man for explaining black into white?"

Rebecca hadn't meant to say that and she bit her lip in annoyance. Otto's attack on old Gabriel yesterday had hit a nerve. Gabriel was family, her last living link to her parents and the way it had been, and now Otto wanted to take even that from her.

Their eyes met for a moment and Edwards read the desperation in them and, not for the first time, the hate. "The jeep's outside, Missus Ralt," he said. "Shall we go?"

"Do we have a choice?" she asked, and strode toward the front door.

They drove in silence across the ranch to the large concrete grain silo Rebecca had half noticed being built last year. She turned to Edwards in disbelief as he brought the jeep to a stop before the tower.

"A grain silo, Bill? My husband has his office in a grain silo?"

"Not in, Missus Ralt, under," Edwards said, climbing out of the jeep. He helped her down, then led the way to a small handleless door set flush into the side of the tower. He stopped three feet from the entrance and stood there wordlessly.

"Aren't you going to knock or something?" Rebecca asked.

"That's not necessary," the foreman replied without looking at her. "Mr. Ralt knows we're here."

Rebecca noticed the surveillance camera mounted on the silo wall at the same moment the door clicked open. Edwards held out his hand for her to enter and she stepped inside, then stopped dumbfounded at the array of bright machinery and pneumatic tubes that rose from the stainless steel floor up into the dim reaches of the tower.

"What is all this, Bill?" she asked, awed by the gleaming spectacle before her.

"You'll know soon enough, my dear," Otto Ralt's voice answered from a speaker somewhere in the shadows. "Please join me."

Twin doors slid apart in the face of the large tube in the

middle of the room. Rebecca started uncertainly toward the pneumatic elevator, then stopped when she realized that Edwards hadn't moved. She turned and looked at the foreman. "Aren't you coming, Bill?"

"The help always stays in the kitchen, Missus Ralt. I'm not cleared for the command center. This is as far as I go."

"Cleared?"

"Come along, Rebecca," Ralt's voice urged from the hidden speaker. "Bill will wait there and drive you home when you come back up."

Rebecca half turned to the elevator, now suddenly uneasy. What was this command center that not even the ranch foreman was "cleared" to enter? And why was it so deep in the earth that an elevator was needed to reach it?

In the shadows thirty feet above the silo floor, a camera lens rotated slowly, focusing on Rebecca's anxious face. "Perhaps this was a mistake, my dear," Ralt's voice goaded from the speaker. "Shall I have Bill take you back?"

He touched her button, as she knew he intended, yet her response to his challenge was reflexive. "And ruin my surprise, Otto? I wouldn't think of it."

She entered the elevator and the doors closed. A humming sound built in the tube and Rebecca suddenly felt her stomach lift as the car began its descent into the earth at forty feet per second. She closed her eyes, feeling suddenly naked and afraid. The ranch above was terra cognito, open to the air and the sun. Safe. She was descending into Otto's world, a hidden, sunless world, dark and dangerous like the man himself.

The car took just six seconds to reach the bottom of the shaft 240 feet beneath the prairie. Before Rebecca could collect herself, the doors opened to reveal an Otto Ralt she had glimpsed only once before. Her husband's habitually preoccupied and dour visage was at this moment transported and glowing, his hard features blurred into his softened face.

The single other time her husband had looked this radiant was the day Prince of Wales arrived at the ranch. Rebecca had stood to one side, mesmerized by the change that came over her husband's face as he gazed at the great bull. She'd realized finally that Otto had been taken over by an all but sexual rapture, a bliss born of the triumph of possessing the majestic animal.

Rebecca stared at her husband and wondered what great victory had inspired his transcendent look today.

"Welcome, Rebecca. Thank you for coming."

"My curiosity compelled me, Otto, as you knew it would," she said, looking past him at the long line of computers, monitors, digital readouts, and communications equipment jamming the control console in the middle of the rectangular room.

Ralt turned to the technician on duty before the console monitors. "Go on up and get some air, Mason. I'll watch the board."

"Yes, Mr. Ralt," Mason Sneed said, avoiding Rebecca's eyes as he rose and crossed the room to the elevator. In a moment they were alone.

"Bill called this your command center, Otto. What do you 'command' down here?" Rebecca asked.

"All manner of things, my dear," he said, taking her arm and guiding her toward the console. "Tunnel drilling equipment, pumps, generators, conveyors, subterranean and surface communications; the list is rather long."

"And you did it all under my nose, with me none the wiser. I underestimated you, Otto. You're even more devious than I credited you with being."

He ignored the barb. "I've been tempted to tell you about all this for some time, Rebecca. But in the end I decided to wait until everything was ready."

"May I ask what exactly you are getting ready for, Otto?" she said, accepting the cushioned armchair he offered her before the console.

Ralt made a production of sitting himself, stretching out and savoring the moment. Here was the payoff for all the humble pie stuffed down his throat by the Wainwright family since the first day he'd courted Rebecca. Today he, Otto Ralt, the usurper, the scion of white trash, the bought husband, stood at the threshold of a triumph that would make the previous success of the Wainwright family pale into insignificance.

Ralt leaned forward, his eyes riveting Rebecca as he told her. "I've been preparing to save the city of Dallas, Rebecca. And to save Texas Oil in the process."

She stared at him. "I've learned never to underestimate you, Otto," she said at last. "But surely saving Dallas is beyond even you. The television is full of pictures of new sinkholes opening. Every five minutes another house or stretch of road plummets into the earth. A geologist on the news this morning showed a chart of the main pit under the city and said the crust beneath downtown Dallas was on the verge of collapse."

"That is the scenario of nature, my dear, a plan the earth set in motion millions of years ago when the first limestone deposits formed. On the geological clock, it is one second to midnight in Dallas. Very shortly I shall stop the hands on that clock. Then I shall turn them back in time."

"How, Otto, how? If I understand what the geologists are saying, the only way to save Dallas would be to refill the Ogallala aquifer, and that would take hundreds of years of steady rains."

"So it would, Rebecca. However, I don't intend to replenish the entire aquifer. Only the reservoir that lies beneath the city and the near prairie."

Rebecca shook her head dubiously. "Still, Otto, you are talking about an immense infusion of water."

"Perhaps eight hundred million acre feet to fill the primary sinkhole under the downtown area," Ralt said.

"Where is this water to come from, Otto? Tell me that. Where will you get trillions of gallons of water when there is not a drop to spare in all of Texas?"

"Ah, but there is water to be had, my dear, a river brimming with water, and it is at our doorstep," Ralt said, leaning forward to flip on a live television monitor set into the console.

Rebecca turned to the screen and watched silently as her husband worked a dial, focusing a faraway camera on the scene before its long-range lens. In a moment a river took shape, flowing languidly through a landscape of sand, cacti, and jagged rock outcroppings. There was no question in her mind which river it was.

"The Rio Grande, Otto? You intend to get your water from the Rio Grande?"

"Precisely, my dear. The waters of the Rio Grande will begin filling the sinkhole beneath Dallas within twenty-four hours."

"But the Rio is over three hundred miles from Dallas," Rebecca protested. "And it flows away southeast to the Gulf."

"So it does, so it has for uncounted millennia," Ralt said. He glanced at a digital clock on the console. "In slightly under eleven minutes I intend to alter that course ninety degrees, Rebecca. At my command, the Rio Grande will no longer flow southeast to the Gulf but northeast, northeast to Dallas."

Rebecca stared at her husband incredulously. "How will you work this miracle, Otto? How will you send a great river north across more than three hundred miles of hills, gorges, canyons, and baking prairie?"

"Not across, but under," Ralt said, his eyes blazing now with fervor at what was at hand. He leaned his face two feet from hers. "I have found a way, Rebecca, a glorious natural tunnel under the earth. It is an ancient dry river called the Rio Bajo la Tierra."

Excitedly, Ralt told her of his late-night discovery of the great subterranean river stretching from near Dallas to below the Mexican border. She sat stunned as he recounted the year-long secret work of his engineers and hydrologists readying the vast cavern system to carry the waters of the Rio Grande north.

Halfway through, he keyed a program into the center's computer and a map of the Rio Bajo appeared on a console screen. Ralt pointed out the site sketches and calculations with which his hydrologists had annotated the map as they emplaced huge pumps and dammed side passages beneath the earth.

He finished finally and settled back complacently into his

chair. "Do you see now how I shall do it, Rebecca? Have I left anything out?"

"I understand the engineering, Otto," Rebecca said quietly. "And, knowing your thoroughness, I have no doubt your scheme will work."

Ralt beamed.

"But you have left something out, Otto, the same something you leave out of every equation you calculate. People. The Rio Grande doesn't flow through a vacuum. Along both sides of the border and for hundreds of miles around, the river is the lifeblood of millions of people, Americans and Mexicans alike. What is to become of these people if you steal the water from their farms, their shops, their homes?"

Ralt's eyes narrowed suddenly. "I am faced with an inflexible choice: life for Dallas, a rich and vital U.S. metropolis, the hub of commerce and population in the Southwest—and, I might point out, the repository of every penny we have—or the perpetuation of a string of small seedy cities and hand-to-mouth farming communities. The survival of the fittest is a basic tenet of nature, Rebecca, and it applies no less to cities than to people."

"Who gave you the right to choose, Otto?" she challenged him. "You are assuming powers never given to any man."

Ralt stood, his face flushed with anger now. "How do you think your father started Texas Oil, Rebecca? He talked illiterate farmers into signing leases that left them on the edge of poverty while millions in oil was siphoned out of their land. Your father made men and towns, and he broke them too. He did what he had to do to build Texas Oil and to give you the soft life you've wallowed in since you were born. For all he did, you marked him a hero, and when he died you added his portrait to that gallery of Wainwright heroes lining the hall to your rooms."

Ralt spun in fury to the computer terminal and stabbed the print button. There was a soft *click* and a copy of the map of the Rio Bajo fed out of the printer chute. He snatched the paper from the machine and flung it at Rebecca.

"Hang this in your gallery. It's always been your proudest boast that the Wainwrights helped build Dallas. Well, damn you, here is a picture more heroic than all the portraits of your ancestors strung together. Here is a picture of the salvation of the city."

A buzzer sounded suddenly from the command console, and Ralt turned to flip on the speaker phone.

"Karl Stroesser, Mr. Ralt." The voice of the Posse Comitatus leader sounded tinny after emerging from the scrambler. "I got company."

"That Mexican division arrive?" Ralt asked, forcing himself to be calm.

"Yes, sir. If you'll turn on your monitor there, I've got that television camera you requested focused on the main force."

Ralt flicked on the set tuned to the long-range signal from the border. Beside him, Rebecca stared at the sight of the Rio Grande River black with Mexican infantry, artillery, and tanks. The leading elements had almost crossed to the U.S. side.

"When the bastards reach my position, they'll overrun us in five minutes, Mr. Ralt."

"Are the explosive charges in place beneath the river?" Ralt asked.

"Yes, sir. The gelignite's set for remote detonation from your command center there."

"Good, now listen to me carefully. I want you to open up with everything you've got the moment the first Mexican soldier reaches the Texas bank. Keep them pinned down in the river for a couple of minutes. Then pull your men back fast. Get your people loaded into trucks and head inland as fast as you can."

"How much time have I got, Mr. Ralt?"

Ralt glanced at the countdown clock on the console. "You have nine minutes, Carl. In nine minutes I pull the plug."

He flipped off the phone and turned back to Rebecca. His

wife was staring at him in horror. "Otto, what are you going to do?"

"I believe it's time for you to leave, my dear."

"You cannot kill those soldiers. It's murder. Nothing is worth that, not Dallas, not the money."

Ralt depressed a button on the console, and the elevator doors hummed open. "I really must ask you to excuse me, Rebecca. I have much to do."

Rebecca came slowly to her feet. "I will stop you, Otto," she said, her voice shaking. "I will find a way and I will stop you."

"Good-bye, Rebecca."

For a long moment Rebecca glared at the monster she had married; then she turned and strode quickly to the elevator. The doors closed behind her and she rose in a white heat toward the silo above.

Just before the car reached ground level, Rebecca realized she was still clutching the map of the Rio Bajo that Otto had thrown at her. When the doors opened a moment later, she knew she had found a way.

Otto Ralt had finally made a mistake.

9:25 A.M.

Lieutenant Pablo Rua scoured the *yanqui* lines with his field glasses, wary of the sudden cease-fire from the U.S. positions. Why had their guns abruptly fallen quiet?

He caught a distant flash of reflected sunlight near the top of a ridge three hundred yards to the north and quickly adjusted the focus. The reflection was coming from the mirror of a troop carrier heading away from the river. As he watched, a second, then a third truck climbed the slope and disappeared over the top toward the north.

Were the *yanquis* retreating? It seemed likely, given the sudden appearance of the five thousand heavily armed troops of Che Guevara Division. Rua turned over painfully, the shrapnel wounds in his legs and chest oozing blood as he moved, and trained his glasses on the Mexican forces crossing the Bravo del Norte.

A few minutes later the point company reached Rua's position and the captain in command knelt by his side. The officer stared at Rua's blood-soaked uniform, then his eyes swept along the line of what was left of his patrol. "They chewed you up pretty bad, lieutenant."

"The bastards used fragmentation shells on us, captain. I crossed the river with forty men. There are three of us left."

The captain rose and shouted toward the troops advancing from the river. "Corpsmen! Corpsmen up here!"

A moment later a corporal and two young privates with Red Cross emblems on their helmets trotted up and dropped into the sand to bandage the wounded.

"I want these men evacuated at once," the colonel ordered.

"Yes, sir," the corporal said, and reached for the field radio in his pack.

Several minutes later Rua heard the *whop-whop-whop* of the descending medevac helicopter. The sand swirled around him, then he and his two fellow survivors were lifted onto stretchers. The litters were strapped on a mesh platform beneath the chopper cabin, and the aircraft rose slowly into the hot air.

Rua turned his head on the litter as the helicopter began to gain altitude. A third of the division was on the U.S. bank now, with almost fifteen hundred more troops wading north across the river. The chopper continued to rise, sweeping south across the Mexican shore, and at twenty-five hundred feet the soldiers began to blur into the land and water below. The pain came back, and Rua turned away and closed his eyes.

At that moment, 340 miles to the north, Otto Ralt sat rigidly before the television monitor in his command center watching the Mexican division cross the river. Ten seconds now. A bead of sweat broke out on his upper lip. He was about to kill.

Ralt felt an adrenal wave surge through him, and a thin red haze swam before his eyes. He wondered if this was how a stalking predator felt before the last step toward his unsuspecting prey. For this one moment in time, he was the lion tensed to spring through the bush onto the back of the wildebeest, the snake coiled to take the mouse, the falcon diving on the sparrow.

Five seconds now. Four seconds. Ralt stared at his finger hovering an inch above the button. Three seconds. His lips parted. Two seconds. An animal groan rushed from deep in

his chest. One second. Otto Ralt stabbed his finger into the
button and watched five thousand men die.

The immense explosion from below sent a towering
shock wave of water and debris mushrooming into the dry,
roasting air above the Rio Grande. The edge of the blast
caught the Mexican medevac chopper broadside, shoving
the aircraft violently out over the desert to the south.

Rua's hands shot out instinctively to grip the sides of the
stretcher as the helicopter swooped up drunkenly in the grip
of the maddened wind. Then, as suddenly as it came, the
shock wave passed and the chopper leveled off.

He watched in disbelief as the huge roiling umbrella
cloud reached its apex and collapsed back on itself in a
torrential deluge of water and debris. Rua forced against the
straps of his litter, straining to see through the tempest
below. For several seconds more the shrinking maelstrom
hid the river. Then the dust began to settle and Rua gasped.

Where only moments before long lines of troops had been
fording the Rio Grande, now there was nothing but a huge
black hole in the desert. The 5,200 men of the Che Guevara
Division had ceased to exist, their bodies blown into
fragments of gore that rained down to earth within the cloud
of debris.

For a quarter mile along the river, the banks had
disappeared into the looming void. So great had been the
force of the explosion that the river waters had been pushed
several hundred yards back upstream.

For an impossibly long moment, the towering wall of
water hung above its bed. Then gravity prevailed and Rua
watched mesmerized as the severed river suddenly surged
forward down the empty channel before it.

In seconds the frenzied waters reached the rim of the
huge pit pocking the riverbed. Even with the chopper blades
whirling above, Rua could hear the great roar build below
as the waters of the Bravo del Norte plunged foaming into
the black abyss.

Rua felt himself going mad. Could it have happened
before his eyes? Where moments before the Che Guevara

Division had been crossing the flood-swollen river, now a mighty waterfall cascaded into the depths of a two-thousand-foot-wide shaft.

At the base of the falls, the fragmented bodies of five thousand young Mexican men bobbed armless, legless, faceless in the tossing backwash from the foam-flecked river. Then the current took them, and the human flotsam began to drift north with the flow, north under the earth toward Dallas.

10:10 A.M.

Soviet Major Demyan Turgenev stepped from the Mexican air force transport plane into the blast furnace of a Mexican spring heatwave. Before he'd reached the bottom of the ramp, his heavy Russian khaki uniform was already sticking to his back and legs.

An air force lieutenant was waiting on the tarmac to escort him the fifteen miles to the Nueva Rosita Missile Base. The ride in the open jeep took almost half an hour, and when he arrived at the Mexican base there was hardly a square inch of his uniform that was not dark with sweat.

Turgenev had a moment of panic when he learned he would not have time to change before his appointment with the Mexican commander. To appear before a Soviet general officer in such a uniform would have been unthinkable, and Turgenev began to stammer an apology as the door to General Santamaría's office closed behind him.

The courtly officer waved a deprecating hand and bade Turgenev sit down. "My dear major, you are not in Mexico twenty-four hours and our air force bunglers put you on a flight in the middle of the day. Your system needs time to acclimate to our weather."

"You are most kind, General Santamaría," Turgenev

ventured in his heavily Russian-accented Spanish, astounded at the Mexican officer's solicitousness.

"Really, you've been twice disserved." Santamaría smiled sympathetically. "Once by our air force, again by your military outfitters. Your summer uniform is the weight of our winter issue. Perhaps you'll allow me a suggestion."

"Of course, General Santamaría."

"The missile silo where you'll be spending most of your duty hours is hot at best and a roasting oven most of the time. The air conditioners are American, and we haven't been able to obtain spare parts for several years. You'll swelter in those heavy khakis of yours. Please allow me to outfit you with a wardrobe of our summer uniforms."

Turgenev was taken aback. "I am most grateful for your offer, sir, but I am a serving Soviet officer. To put on the uniform of another country would be . . ."—he searched, embarrassed, for the words—"would be highly irregular."

"Come, come, major, I am not suggesting you wear Mexican badges. The color of our cottons is almost the same as your khakis. There is nothing sacrosanct about the material a soldier wears. Pin on your Soviet insignia and it's all the same. However, I leave your comfort up to you."

Turgenev wavered. He didn't want to offend his high-ranking host. Besides, once past the shock of Santamaría's suggestion, the offer made eminent sense. "Thank you, General Santamaría. I shall be glad to have the cottons."

"Splendid." Santamaría rose behind his desk. "The missile team stationed here has assembled at the silo to meet you. We'll stop first at supply and get you properly outfitted."

On their way through Santamaría's outer office, the general's aide approached. "Sir, that political police plane you were expecting has just landed at the air base. You asked to be notified."

"There's a radio in the jeep we sent?"

"Yes, sir."

"Contact the driver. Tell him to bring our interrogator friends out here by way of Sabinas."

"But, sir, the trip is at least an hour by that route," the captain pointed out.

"So it is." Santamaría smiled enigmatically. "But the ride is far more picturesque, and they are, after all, first-time visitors. I'll be in the missile tube with Major Turgenev."

The moment Turgenev stepped from the elevator onto the command level of the silo, he was glad he'd accepted Santamaría's offer. The tube was stifling. Staring up, the reason was easy to see. The silo was roofed with huge semicircular steel doors that were kept tightly shut except during the bimonthly launch drills. The heavy metal plates above turned the ninety-foot-deep tube into exactly what Santamaría had described: a roasting oven.

The Mexican missile team received him with a quick camaraderie that left Turgenev as pleasantly nonplussed as had their general's kindness; things were very much different in the Mexican army. General Santamaría stood to one side observing while Turgenev answered questions in his thick accent.

Forty minutes later Santamaría dismissed the missile officers. "Gentlemen, I wish a few moments alone with Major Turgenev. You will please excuse us."

The elevator ascended, and Santamaría gestured toward the two duty-officer chairs before the launch board. "What do you think, Major Turgenev? Do my people have a grasp of all this computer gadgetry you Russians have sent us?"

Turgenev nodded. "I believe your officers are well grounded in the technology, general. Of course, it takes some months of instruction before individuals mesh into a missile team that can run through a launch drill smoothly and quickly."

"I am interested in right now, Major Turgenev. Assuming my people had the launch codes, could they target and fire the missile today?"

"Not a drill, you mean actually launch the missile?" Turgenev asked uncomfortably.

"Actually launch."

"The targeting would be the most difficult part, depending on distance. Atmospheric conditions, topography, even the tilt of the earth must be computed in. Still, your two senior officers each spent an eighteen-month tour at our launch center at Baikonur. I believe they could target ground zero, or very close."

Santamaría let out a long, weary sigh. "I was afraid so."

"I beg your pardon, general?"

"You must forgive me, Turgenev. I am a leader of men, not a launcher of missiles. I command Mexico's northern missile forces, yet I have neither background nor training in any of this supersonic wizardry of yours. I am here because it is a most sensitive military position, and Prime Minister Martí needed an old soldier he could trust."

"I'm afraid I don't understand, General Santamaría. Why should you fear the competency of your own officers?"

"Because Mexico is at the brink of war with the United States, Major Turgenev. One misstep on either side, and the border will erupt in flames from the Gulf of Mexico to Baja, California," Santamaría said slowly. "Martí has already told me that if the fighting goes badly, he will launch a missile strike against Texas. After that, it will not be just the valley of the Rio Grande that is turned to ash. It may be the world as well."

Turgenev gave a short, hollow laugh, like a man who's just been told a loved one is dead and snorts in reflexive disbelief. "Surely you are being alarmist, general. Conventional hostilities may be impossible to prevent. But your cruise missiles—without nuclear warheads and retargeting programs—are no more lethal than so many bombers."

"Both these prerequisites are present in this silo, major."

Turgenev stared at the general. "I beg your pardon?"

Santamaría nodded toward the solid-fuel rocket twenty yards away. "That missile over there is nuclear armed. I believe it is the only nuclear warhead Mexico possesses, but then one is all it takes to start a global conflagration."

Turgenev turned and looked at the missile. "It could be armed with fifty nuclear warheads. What's the difference?

The missile cannot be launched without the programming codes."

"Which you possess."

"Which I am under penalty of death to hold close, until and unless the General Secretary himself authorizes me to reprogram those computers."

"The codes are in your head, major?"

"Yes, of course, memorized. I would never have been permitted to board the plane in Moscow with such information on paper."

"Tell me, Major Turgenev, is your mind so strong a vault that its doors may not be sprung? Not with torture? Not with drugs?"

"What are you suggesting?" Turgenev asked, his face pale.

"That police team that landed as we left my office, they are here for you. Prime Minister Martí has given orders that the interrogators are to obtain the retargeting program. At whatever price to you."

The room swam before Turgenev's eyes. Suddenly, like a knife thrown from the dark, here was the nightmare of his soul. It was worse than the blackest scenario his self-doubt had ever scripted. Before, at least, he'd always imagined that if his dreaded call to bravery came, he'd answer arm in arm with strong comrades, Russian bugles urging on the charge. Instead, the moment had trapped him alone in a strange and faraway land, not even the uniform on his back his own.

"When will they arrive?" Turgenev asked tonelessly, the utter hopelessness of his situation rendering him an almost dispassionate observer of his own fate.

Santamaría glanced at his watch. "Not for another twenty minutes or so. Time enough to get us sealed up in the silo."

"Sealed up?"

"I don't intend to give up either you or that nuclear warhead without a fight," Santamaría said. "I have served my country all my life, and I hold the honor of Mexico more sacred than my own. Yet, no matter how galling the *yanqui* provocation, to answer back by launching our missiles against the United States would be an act of national suicide. I cannot allow the pride of a megalomaniac in Mexico City to destroy my country, and perhaps the world."

Turgenev's eyes lifted to the elevator shaft and the steel doors over the silo. "One well-placed charge of plastic explosives, and your political police could peel the steel off this silo like the lid off a can," he said dubiously.

Santamaría shook his head. "They won't use explosives. There's too big a risk that the shrapnel ricocheting around in here would kill you or knock out the computers. Maybe even set off the missile fuel. No, Major Turgenev, their only option will be to cut their way in with torches. The doors and blast shield above are fabricated of titanium-alloy steel two feet thick. It will take the political police at least twelve hours to penetrate the silo."

"And when they do?"

"Before that happens, I hope to have convinced my fellow officers on the General Staff that we must pull Martí's finger off the nuclear trigger. Now let's get this place buttoned up."

They spent the next ten minutes shutting surface air vents, filling the silo's water reservoir, and making sure the emergency generator was fueled. One by one, they checked the circuits controlling the huge launch doors, lights, elevator, and entry alarms. Finally, Santamaría led the way back to the duty desk.

"I'll start calling the General Staff now. If I can bring enough of my old comrades to see the tragedy ahead for Mexico, perhaps I can unite the military against Martí and stay his hand."

The phone rang, and Santamaría turned to pick up the receiver. A moment later he stiffened, the blood draining from his lined face. "Repeat that, please. Did you say the entire division?"

For several more seconds Santamaría held the phone tightly to his ear; then slowly he lowered the receiver to its cradle. "Mother of God, five thousand men! Five thousand dead, and they are only the first."

Turgenev stared at the Mexican's stricken face. "What is it, General Santamaría? What's happened?"

For a moment Santamaría sat in rigid silence, his fists clenching and unclenching. "The *yanquis* have annihilated an entire Mexican army division," he began brokenly. "They lured one of our patrols across the border and then, as the Che Guevara Division was fording the river in relief, they blew up the bed of the Rio Grande with some sort of huge mine."

Turgenev shook his head. "The Americans must be insane."

Santamaría nodded slowly. "And their madness will be answered with madness. After this, Martí will be a man possessed. This means war, Turgenev. War with the United States."

AN HOUR BEFORE NOON

Lucia Sanchez stumbled ahead through the tunnel of the Rio Bajo, each step a battle between will and exhaustion. The climb up the flowstone waterfall had sapped her strength, and the two-hour trek through the tunnel at the top had all but finished her off.

Ahead, Jedediah Heffernan's light bobbed in the dark. He seemed indefatigable, continually checking out side tunnels or spurting forward to see what was around the next bend. He'd been patient with her slowing progress, restraining his own pace and offering rest breaks that, were he alone, she knew he'd not have taken.

Lucia's right foot caught suddenly on a ripple of rock and she pitched to the side. She gave a small, involuntary cry as her head struck the cave wall. Then her world went blank.

Lucia's mind floated under the balm of unconsciousness, the pain and the exhaustion blissfully gone from her body. From far away she heard Jedediah call out. Then he was lifting her, stretching her out on the soft sand, easing his jacket under her head.

She could feel his face close now, and his hands gently pushing back the hair at her temple. His touch made her warm. Such a gentle, nurturing touch from such rough, calloused hands.

A sudden stab of pain pierced the swirling mist around her, and Lucia groaned and opened her eyes. Jedediah was kneeling above her, worry etched in his face as he dabbed at the side of her head with a reddening cotton swab.

"Lucia, are you all right?"

She winced as full consciousness returned, bringing with it a wave of pain. "What happened?" she asked, bringing her hand up to the wound Jedediah had been tending at her temple.

He caught her fingertips. "Careful. You've got a nasty bruise near the hairline."

She forced herself up on one elbow. "It's just a bump on the head. I'm fine."

"Bump on the head, my ass. You knocked yourself cold."

"Don't be ridiculous. I was merely a bit woozy."

"Woozy is your normal state. You were unconscious. Look in my eyes."

Despite her throbbing head, he looked so serious she couldn't resist. "Why, Jedediah, whatever have you in mind?" she drawled in her thickest Texas belle accent.

"In your case, a frontal lobotomy." He grinned. "For the moment I'll content myself with checking if your pupils are dilated. You may have a concussion."

"Well, do I?" she asked as he brought his face close.

"No, I don't think so," he said, lowering the light.

"Good. Now as soon as that tapping sound in my ears goes away, we can get started again."

Heff took a gauze square and a roll of adhesive tape from the first-aid kit and bandaged her wound. "Tapping sound in your ears, huh? Anyone else gets smacked in the head, they hear a ringing. Not you, though. You hear—"

Heff stopped abruptly, the grin fading on his face. He heard it too, an irregular tapping. He sprang to his feet. It was the sound of rock striking rock.

For a moment Heff stood stock-still, straining to hear out into the dark.

Lucia rose beside him. "You hear it too?"

"Yeah, quiet."

Then the sound suddenly stopped. Still, the tapping had

lasted long enough for Heff to be certain the sound was coming from the unexplored tunnel ahead.

Lucia brought her hand to her mouth. "Do you think it's Paco?" she asked, hope back in her voice for the first time in hours.

"It's sure as hell someone. Rocks don't bang themselves together," Heff said. "Can you walk?"

"Yes, yes. Oh, Jedediah, let's hurry."

Eighty yards ahead, their lights suddenly played into the blackness of a broad bisecting tunnel. The tunnel was easily twice the diameter of the passage they'd been traveling. Heff shone his light one way, then the other.

"It's the same tunnel we were following before the cave-in," he said.

A gurgle caught in Lucia's throat. "Look, look," she stammered, her light playing across a single small footprint in a patch of sand.

Heff knelt and examined the track. The imprint showed a waffle sole and a low heel with a nick in the rim. It was the same track he'd spotted back near the sinkhole.

Heff rose. "It's Paco."

His words were hardly out before the tapping started again. It was louder now. "He's close," Heff said. "C'mon."

Three minutes later they rounded a bend and Lucia let out a joyous scream.

There, a barely glowing flashlight in one hand and a football-sized rock in the other, Paco Sanchez stood pounding at the face of a massive rockslide.

Lucia shot forward and enveloped her brother in her arms. "Paco, oh, Paco, you're alive, you're alive, you're alive!"

The ten-year-old let his sister smother him a moment, then his pubescent bravado returned and he eased back, out of the vise of her arms. "'Course I'm alive. What'd you think, I don't know how to take care of myself in a cave?" He suddenly noticed her bandaged temple. "Hey, what happened to your head?"

All of a sudden Lucia was laughing and crying at the

same time, the tears streaming down her face. "What happened to my head? I'll tell you what happened to my head. I bumped it looking for a little boy I thought I'd never . . . oh, never mind what happened to my head. You. You know what you've put me through. And Momma. Wait until I get you home." She clutched Paco to her again, rocking him back and forth. "You just wait."

Paco grinned. "You always say that." Then for the first time he noticed Heff. "Hey, I know you. You're Jedediah Heffernan, one of the New Mexico Mounties. I saw your picture in my speleology field manual."

"How do you feel, son?" Heff asked, reaching for the boy's wrist.

"I'm fine. Kind of a little hungry. You're checking my pulse, aren't you? I bet it's regular."

Heff smiled. "Pretty close," he said, cupping the back of the boy's neck with his hands.

"You're worried about hypothermia, aren't you?" Paco said.

"You know about hypothermia, do you, Paco?"

"Yes, sir. Hypothermia is the biggest danger if you're in a cave a long time. You get really cold and then you get sleepy and pretty soon you die. But see, I wore my heavy clothes and thermal vest and I slept in a ball just like in the field manual."

"You've got a pretty remarkable brother," Heff said to Lucia. "He's taken good care of himself down here. I'm sure he's lost weight, and he'll ache for a week from sleeping on the rocks, but I'd say Paco is going to be just fine."

"You see, Lucia?" The boy grinned. "You didn't have to worry."

"You may have studied the survival part of that manual, Paco," Heff said. "But it seems to me there's one section you didn't get around to."

Paco lowered his eyes sheepishly. "Yeah, I know. The part about knowing your limits and not going in too far."

"That's the part."

"I was going to start back as soon as I dug through that

slide and got some water," Paco said, tossing the rock in his
hand toward the mound of debris behind them.

"You would have been digging a long time, Paco," Heff
said. "The river channels of the Rio Bajo la Tierra have
been bone dry for hundreds of thousands of years."

"Well, if it isn't water running behind those rocks, it sure
sounds like it. A few hours ago I heard this roaring sound
back there, and then I could hear water gurgling."

Heff straightened and played his light over the jumbled
rockfall that climbed up away from them into the dark. For
the first time, they could see the cave-in completely blocked
the tunnel ahead.

Heff picked his way over the rubble on the floor, then
stopped and listened intently at the foot of the slide. There
was a barely audible rushing sound coming from behind the
boulders. It could just be an errant wind blowing through
the tunnel beyond from a surface entrance miles away, he
warned himself. Wind plays funny tricks in caves.

Heff shucked his pack and climbed the steep slope.
Halfway up two large boulders had wedged together to form
a narrow V-shaped shaft that pierced fifteen or twenty feet
back into the mound. Heff crawled in as far as he could and
listened again. This time there was no doubt. There was
water rushing past beyond the rock barrier. A river of water,
to judge by the power of the sound and the vibrations he
could feel in the rocks.

Heff had backed almost all the way out when his light
picked up the long inch-wide groove furrowing the face of
the rock slab to his left. It was the scar of a bore hole drilled
for explosives. The rockslide wasn't natural. Someone had
blown down the ceiling and walls, sealing off the river on
the other side.

He climbed back down, his adrenaline flowing. "You
were right, Paco, there *is* water flowing behind there. A lot
of water." Heff reached for the packet of maps in his
backpack.

"Where could the water be coming from?" Lucia asked.
"There isn't a river in Texas that's flowed the past five

years, except the Rio Grande. And that's sixty or seventy miles from here."

Heff looked up from a map. "I'm all but certain we're at the junction where the north fork of the Rio Bajo joins the main tunnel," he said. "The main channel runs south all the way into Mexico, and it passes beneath the bed of the Rio Grande. It's possible that the floor of the Rio Grande fractured and let part of the river water down into the Rio Bajo."

"What difference does it make where the water came from, Jedediah?" Lucia said dejectedly. "All that matters is the tunnel ahead is blocked. And with the Caverunner broken down, it's too far to go back the way we came."

"Too far by foot," Heff said, kneeling to open his pack. "But not too far by boat."

Lucia and the boy exchanged puzzled looks. "What boat?" Paco asked for both.

"I'll explain later," Heff said, taking out the two six-by-twelve-inch packages he'd stowed in his backpack when they abandoned the hoverjet.

"That's plastic explosive, isn't it?" Paco said excitedly.

Lucia's eyes widened. "Jedediah, what are you going to do?"

"Get us out of here, I hope," Heff said, pulling the timers from a side pocket. "Now go on, get moving. I'll catch up."

Lucia hesitated. "You won't be long?"

"Ten minutes. No more."

"Please be careful," Lucia said. She looked at Heff a moment longer, then took Paco's hand, and the two turned and disappeared into the dark tunnel behind.

Heff set his first charge at the base of the slide, then climbed the jagged slope again and shoved the second brick far back into the wedge-shaped shaft piercing the mound.

He calculated they were roughly two hours' walk from the Caverunner. He allowed an hour's safety margin and set the timers to detonate in three hours.

A sinister sense of being watched came over Heff as he climbed back down the slide, and he shone his light into the tunnel ahead. There was nothing there, but at the upper fringe of the circle of light he caught the glint of glass near the ceiling.

Still facing down the tunnel, Heff slowly lifted his eyes up to the side. There was just enough light to make out the camera watching him. He swung the light carelessly back along the other side of the cave, then shouldered his pack and set off after Lucia and Paco.

Hidden in a niche near the tunnel ceiling, the small television camera swiveled noiselessly on its mount, its electronic eye following Heff until he disappeared around the first bend.

Then the camera swung back and two infrared lights bracketing the lens switched on. For several minutes the TV eye searched the jumbled pile of rocks. Then the camera found the first explosive charge and abruptly stopped its sweep.

Slowly, very slowly, the lens rotated, focusing in on the timer ticking away in the dark.

MIDAFTERNOON

Mexican Prime Minister Teodoro Luis Martí stared through the arched window of his office at the crowds swelling by the thousands across the palace grounds below.

Sunk in a profound political apathy born of a decade of broken promises and deepening despair, the Mexican masses could no longer be stirred by the nationalistic harangues of their Marxist leaders. Yet if the hammer and sickle now failed to stir Mexico's blood, the icons of the church still called forth primal passions.

The attack on the Madonna of Dallas by the Texas Rangers, and the massacre of Chicanos defending the shrine, had rent the Mexican soul. Through the tear poured all the crushed hopes and dormant emotions of a people too long denied.

By the tens of thousands, the faithful had abandoned the tin and cardboard hovels of the capital and streamed to the presidential palace, there to beseech their leader for relief from the intolerable blasphemy that had been committed against the Madonna and child in Texas.

It was the mark of Martí's understanding of his people that when he appeared on the balcony outside his office it was to speak of a crusade. He had sent the Che Guevara

Division north not to answer the border provocation but on a mission to save the Madonna of Dallas.

He made no mention of the conciliatory U.S. answer to his telexed demands of the night before. The assault on the shrine by the heavily armed Rangers had been without official sanction, the governor of Texas insisted. He had taken steps, and the Texas National Guard was no longer attacking but protecting the shrine and the Mexican-Americans worshiping there. Such a revelation would not have suited Martí's purposes.

He turned from his musing by the window at a knock on the ornate doors of his office and stiffened instinctively as his aide hurried crestfallen across the marble floor.

The aide stopped several feet from the prime minister, unable, for the moment, to find his voice.

"What is it?" Martí demanded.

"Comrade Prime Minister," the aide began brokenly. "I must tell you . . . I must tell you that Mexico has suffered a terrible defeat."

Martí listened in disbelief and mounting fury as his aide told him of the titanic explosion that had ripped open the bed of the Rio Bravo del Norte and swallowed up the five thousand soldiers of the Che Guevara Division.

"There is something else, Comrade Prime Minister," the aide continued in trepidation. "It is not just the brigade that is gone. The river itself has disappeared."

"What are you talking about?"

"At the site of the explosion, there is now a gaping hole in the riverbed. The Bravo del Norte disappears into the pit in a huge waterfall."

"The river does not resurface downstream?"

"Nowhere, Prime Minister. From the small village of Quito south to the Gulf of Mexico, the Rio Bravo del Norte has ceased to exist."

For a long moment, Martí stood still as a stone, the blood drained from his face. So he'd been right all along. It was the river, the precious waters of the Rio Bravo del Norte, that the *yanquis* were after. Obviously they had tunneled

under the river and diverted the flow north somewhere into
Texas.

"Get me General Santamaría at Nueva Rosita," Martí
erupted, barely in control. "At once, do you hear me? At
once!"

Martí began furiously pacing his office as his aide picked
up the phone. A minute passed, two. Finally the aide got
through to Nueva Rosita.

"Prime Minister Martí calling for General Santamaría. . . ." The aide's face paled as he listened to the
operator, then slowly put down the phone. "General Santamaría has locked himself in the missile silo at Nueva
Rosita. Apparently he's been making phone calls out to the
other members of the general staff."

Martí stopped his pacing, his back to the aide. "Is there
anyone in the silo with Santamaría?"

"Yes, Comrade Prime Minister. He's got that Soviet
missile targeting officer, Turgenev, in there with him."

For a moment, Martí stared at the marble floor. "I sent a
police interrogation team to Nueva Rosita. Get me their
commanding officer immediately."

A minute later the aide handed Martí the receiver. "I have
the commander, sir. Colonel Vargas."

Martí strode across and took the phone. "Colonel, I want
to know your situation there."

"I've positioned a T-Seventy-two tank before the silo
door," the colonel said hopefully. "It should take no more
than one or two armor-piercing shells to smash our way in."

"No, you fool," Martí sputtered. "You could damage the
missile or kill Major Turgenev. We need them both intact."

"Then I must cut through the door with torches," the
colonel replied. "It will take some time, Prime Minister."

"How long?"

"The entrance is fabricated of twenty-four-inch-thick
titanium-alloy plates. I shall need ten, perhaps twelve hours
to cut through them."

"Get those torches to work immediately," Martí ordered.
"I shall expect reports every hour."

Martí slammed down the receiver and began pacing again

in impotent rage. Damn Santamaría. Damn him through eternity. He had locked Mexico's nuclear sword in its scabbard. With the nation's northern defenses decimated by the loss of the Che Guevara Division, there was little to throw at the *yanquis*.

The tumult from the impassioned throngs below made it all but impossible for him to think. Would the people blame their leader for allowing the Che Guevara Division to fall into the *yanqui* trap? Would the blood of five thousand martyred soldiers be seen to drip from his hands?

Martyrs. Martí stopped in his tracks. Martyrs. He spun toward his aide. "There is a large religious tapestry on the wall outside the chapel. I want it brought up here at once and hung from the balcony outside."

"The tapestry of the Virgin and Child, Prime Minister?"

"Yes. Bring it at once."

Martí waited for several minutes after the tapestry had unfurled over the crowds, letting the fervor build below. Then he stepped out onto the balcony, to be met by a frenzied chorus that broke over him like waves against a beach.

He allowed the crowds to vent their passion, then raised his arms for quiet. "People of Mexico," Teodoro Martí began, "the Madonna of Dallas calls. Do you hear her? Do you hear Our Lady wailing over our comrades fallen at her feet? Do you hear her pleas for deliverance from under the guns of the *yanquis?* Answer me, people of Mexico, do you hear the Madonna call?"

Martí shrank back involuntarily at the sheer physical force of the voices that rose in a deafening crescendo against the balcony. Yes, two hundred thousand throats screamed as one; yes, we hear the call of the Madonna!

Martí swelled with the fever of the moment. I shall send a human wall against the *yanquis*, he thundered inside himself. For an hour more he harangued the fervent faithful below.

The Che Guevara Division has fallen, he told them. Was the crusade to save the Madonna to be washed away with

the blood of our soldiers dead in the torn depths of the Rio
Bravo del Norte?

"No, no," the anguished answer reverberated back.

"North, then," Martí screamed at the last. "North to save
the Madonna!"

Almost as one, the impassioned multitudes turned from
the palace and spilled into the broad avenues leading out of
the city. Along the way, groups splintered off to comman-
deer buses, trucks, cars, motor scooters, anything that could
carry passengers.

By the time the leading cars in the ever-longer convoy
reached the outskirts of Mexico City, a hundred thousand
peasants had jammed themselves onto vehicles, with triple
that number still scouring the urban streets for transportation.

North the convoy rolled, its banners countless portraits of
the Virgin and Child hung from bus windows and whipping
from radio antennas.

North to Texas and the Madonna of Dallas.

LATE AFTERNOON

Texas Governor Lynn Duecker watched mesmerized as the CHICO satellite tape of the Rio Grande catastrophe six hours before was replayed in the taut silence of the governor's emergency headquarters outside Mineral Wells, seventy miles west of Dallas.

Duecker and his staff stared in spellbound horror as the screen showed the river black with Mexican troops suddenly erupting in a towering geyser of vaporized water, shattered rock, and torn men.

For several moments longer, Duecker watched footage of the roaring waterfall now cascading into the depths of the desert. Then he signaled his secretary to stop the tape.

"Lord God almighty!" Duecker shook his head. "There must have been several thousand men on that river."

"Over five thousand, governor," Major General James Wilkerson replied. "The satellite intelligence boys at the Pentagon identify the unit as the Che Guevara Division, normal strength fifty-two hundred and fifty men."

"Was the division one of their border outfits?" Duecker asked the Texas National Guard commander.

"No, sir. The Che Guevara Division was the best-trained, best-armed fighting force in the Mexican army, their version of our marines. Over the past couple of years they'd

213

been supplied with the latest tanks, artillery, and shoulder-fired antiaircraft rockets. The loss of those troops will just about cripple the Mexican forces facing Texas."

"Why was the division crossing the border?"

Wilkerson threw up his hands. "Who the hell knows what the bastards were up to? There are no military objectives on our side along that stretch of river. Shit, it's nothing but cactus and sand down there."

"And the explosion, the collapse of the riverbed, what caused that, general?"

"My guess is the bottom of the river was mined."

"Mined? By who?"

"American S[ ]ial Forces, maybe the SEALS, those navy underwater commandos."

Duecker stared at his National Guard commander in disbelief. "Are you suggesting the Pentagon had the balls to mine the border of Texas without telling the governor of the damn state?"

Wilkerson shrugged. "You got a better guess?"

As Duecker fumed, the portable videophone behind his desk began to ring. An aide took the call, then turned quickly to the governor. "It's the President calling from Camp David, sir."

Duecker rose and walked to the phone as the screen blinked and the President of the United States appeared on the monitor. Duecker recognized the room behind him as the Aspen Lodge at Camp David.

"Good afternoon, Lynn," President David Wilson said. "You look exhausted."

"Good afternoon, Mr. President. To be frank, sir, I'm more disturbed than tired. I want to know what's going on along the Mexican border."

"That's why I'm calling. I've just finished a conference call with the Joint Chiefs of Staff. The Pentagon is as perplexed as you are."

"Are you telling me our military was not involved in any way? That it was not a U.S. minefield that blew up under those Mexican troops?"

"You have my word on that, Lynn."

"I don't understand any of this, Mr. President. Mexico suddenly decides to invade Texas, and just as suddenly their invasion force gets blown to smithereens. And we have nothing to do with any of it?"

"Let me tell you what our intelligence analysts have put together so far," the President offered. "Our satellite surveillance picked up the Che Guevara Division moving north toward a staging area near Piedras Negras. Shortly thereafter the satellite spotted dead Mexican soldiers on our side of the river."

"When was this, sir?"

"Around dawn your time this morning. At that point I ordered a general mobilization of our armed forces throughout the Southwest. Advance elements from Fort Hood were on the way in by helicopter when the Rio Grande blew apart."

"You ordered a general mobilization in Texas without notifying me, Mr. President? I must object in the strongest possible terms." Duecker glared at the videophone.

"Calm down, Lynn. I had my reasons, not the least of which is we're simply not sure of anything. The Che Guevara Division was the only large Mexican unit anywhere near the border, so it doesn't appear Mexico's planning any imminent invasion. Anyway, I really want your energies directed toward the evacuation of Dallas."

"I'll accept that for the moment, but that doesn't tell me who annihilated those five thousand Mexican soldiers."

"We've only formed a hypothesis so far. The evidence is far from conclusive."

"I'll settle for supposition right now, Mr. President."

"We believe the Posse Comitatus is involved."

"Those right-wing fanatics?"

"It's beginning to shape up that way. The FBI's been keeping pretty close tabs on the Posse for some time now. A dozen or more of their more rabid members have been spotted shopping in small towns in the region over the past few months. The bureau figured they were down there for their usual blustering with guns-across-the-border bullshit. Looks like we underestimated them."

"But how the hell did they manage to goad the Che Guevara Division into crossing the Rio Grande?" Duecker asked.

"My intelligence people believe the Posse either surprised a Mexican patrol on our side of the border, and wiped them out, or raided a Mexican outpost across the river and dragged the bodies back like trophies. However those first soldiers died, it was enough to provoke Mexico City into sending the Che Guevara Division north across the Rio. Right into a Posse Comitatus trap."

"Mr. President, not twelve hours ago I sent a message of reconciliation to Prime Minister Martí assuring him of the safety of his citizens within the state of Texas. Now five thousand of his best troops are dead on my doorstep. Martí will never believe a catastrophe of this magnitude is the work of right-wing extremists. He'll pin this on the Pentagon."

"I know that, Lynn. This couldn't have come at a worse time. Once the Soviet-Mexican Mutual Defense Treaty is signed, Prime Minister Martí will be uncomfortably close to being able to retarget those Soviet missiles pointed at us across the border."

"I'd hate to imagine what's going through Martí's mind, Mr. President. His finest fighting force is obliterated, and at the same time the river supplying water to the entire northern tier of his country disappears into the earth."

"The Rio Grande hasn't disappeared, it's changed its course. Our Landsat earth mapping satellite picked up the river now flowing several hundred feet below the prairie. Flowing north into Texas."

Duecker was stunned. "Into Texas?"

"Infrared scanning by the Landsat indicates the headwaters are already almost a hundred miles northeast of the border. Geologists from the Army Corps of Engineers tell me the water is flowing through a long-dry subterranean river system called the Rio Bajo la Tierra."

"How far north does this subterranean river system run?" Duecker asked.

"The geologists are vague on that. The scant information

we have on the Rio Bajo comes largely from ancient accounts found in the journals of the Spanish conquistadors. There've been some preliminary Landsat surveys, but most of the tunnels are too deep to show up as more than vague tracings."

"You realize, Mr. President, that when Prime Minister Martí finds out the Rio Grande has been diverted north into Texas, he'll be convinced it was by our design and not some natural occurrence of a subterranean river system."

"I'm aware of the realities, Lynn. Somehow we've got to block the arteries of the Rio Bajo and return the Rio Grande to its bed along the border."

"Can't the Corps of Engineers excavate from the surface?" Duecker asked. "Sink a shaft and collapse the river channel with explosives?"

"Unfortunately, it's not that simple," the President said. "The Rio Bajo is a labyrinth. The geologists tell me that even if we blocked one channel, the river would probably back up and find a bypass tunnel. The Corps of Engineers insists the only certain way to contain the flow north is to locate a bottleneck where all the tunnels converge and the Rio Bajo can be dammed with one explosive charge."

"Is there such a bottleneck?"

"The geologists don't know. Most of the tunnel system is too deep for the Landsat to tell us much, and echo sounding from the surface would take months. Our only alternative is to send a team of geologists down into the caves of the Rio Bajo."

"You called the river system a labyrinth, Mr. President," Duecker said. "Are there any maps at all to go by?"

President Wilson picked up a sheet of paper from his desk. "Apparently there's one, drawn by a freelance geologist named Heffernan. Jedediah Heffernan. The Corps of Engineers insists he's the best man, the only man, to lead the exploration team."

"Have your people contacted Heffernan?"

"We haven't been able to find him. He left his ranch in New Mexico two days ago on a cave rescue mission. From notes found in his house, we believe he's in Texas, somewhere around Rocksprings. I need your help in tracking him down."

"I'll get the Rangers on it immediately, Mr. President."

"I don't have to tell you what's hanging in the balance," the President said. "The longer the Rio Grande continues to flow north, the closer we come to war with Mexico. We've got to dam the Rio Bajo, Lynn. We've got to find Jedediah Heffernan."

DUSK

Jedediah Heffernan looked at his watch for the fifth time in the past five minutes, then turned and cast a worried eye back down the tunnel to where the lights of Lucia Sanchez and her brother approached slowly through the dark.

He calculated they were still half an hour from the huge subterranean amphitheater where the Caverunner waited at the foot of the frozen falls. Half an hour, maybe more. Yet in less than forty-five minutes the explosives he'd set against the dam face would go off, and a raging torrent would sweep out over them from the black tunnel behind.

He berated himself for cutting the time so close. Lucia had seemed to rebound with new strength when they'd found Paco. Yet, he realized now, it had only been the euphoria of the moment. The flash of adrenal energy had burned itself out in Lucia before they'd gained a mile on their trek back to the Caverunner.

It wasn't Lucia's fault, it was his. His five-year hiatus from caving had dulled his perception of limits beneath the earth. The chill struggle of caving sapped the strength of the most experienced spelunker, and he'd been dangerously remiss to ignore what Lucia had been through.

Heff walked back toward the woman and the boy. He'd

219

have to tell them time was running out. "How are you two holding up?" he asked, keeping his voice light.

"Fine, Jedediah, fine," Paco bubbled. To the ten-year-old, it was all a wonderful adventure. "Except I think Lucia's a little tired."

Heff met Lucia's eyes. "More than a little, I'd say."

"I just need ten minutes' rest," Lucia insisted, all but swaying on her feet.

"I can't give you ten minutes, Lucia," Heff said. "I can't give you any time at all. Those explosive charges I set will go off in a little under three-quarters of an hour. It will take us nearly that long to reach the Caverunner."

Lucia looked from Heff to the boy, then back. "I'm the slowpoke here. Look, you two go on ahead and get the Caverunner ready. That'll save time. I'll follow along as fast as I can."

Heff shook his head. "No way, Lucia. I'm not leaving you behind."

"Paco, would you go on down the tunnel," Lucia said. "I want to speak to Jedediah alone."

"Uh-oh, when she wants to talk to you alone, it means you're in trouble." The boy grinned under his headlamp. "Watch out, Jedediah."

Heff smiled. "I believe I know what you mean."

Lucia made a grab for Paco. "Why, you little traitor."

The boy laughed and skipped away down the tunnel. "I'll hear you anyway, Lucia, as loud as you yell," he called over his shoulder as he padded away into the dark.

"I can't keep up, Jedediah," Lucia said when the boy was gone. "I don't think I can take another step. Please, you've got to take Paco and go on ahead. I won't have your deaths on my hands."

"I don't have time to argue with you, Lucia. The three of us make it, or none of us make it. I'm going to carry you."

"Don't be ridiculous. I'm too heavy and it's too far."

"I've carried packs that weighed more than you," Heff said.

"But you weren't racing against a clock when you did it,

were you, Jedediah. No, I won't let you carry me and that's final."

"Stop being so selfish," he snapped.

"Selfish?"

"Yes, selfish. Do you think Paco wants to make it without you? Do you think I do?" In one movement, Heff swooped her into his arms.

Lucia flailed against his chest. "You're a Neanderthal, do you know that? A ridge-browed, gape-jawed throwback. No wonder you're so at home in caves. You were probably born in one."

"I'm glad you got that off your chest. You might as well accept that I'm not going to put you down, Lucia. Your thrashing around is only burning up energy we'll both need to get out of here."

She tried a new tack. "All right, then, I'll let you carry me for ten minutes. That's all the rest I need. Then you put me down and I'll walk the rest of the way on my own. Agreed?"

"Forget it."

"I'm not going to beg, Jedediah. Damn you, you're being unreasonable."

"*I'm* unreasonable? That's rich coming from the stubbornest, most contrary, most exasperating woman I've ever met. I'm not putting you down. Period. Not until we reach the falls. Now stop squirming."

After all she'd been through, the resolve in Jedediah's voice and arms was a challenge beyond her strength to meet. Exhausted, Lucia finally let go and sagged against his chest, one last reflexive joust on her lips as she closed her eyes. "Remember," she murmured, falling asleep. "Ten minutes. Just carry me for . . ."

Heff looked down at her sleeping face in the lamplight. Her dirty, tired, stone-bruised face. A wave of caring flooded through him, a surge of emotion that all but took his breath away.

The sudden intensity of what he felt surprised and then scared him. By God, he wasn't going down that road again. He tore his eyes away and stared down the cave ahead.

Looking at Margo used to take his breath away. It was like that right through the honeymoon. Then Margo changed. One hundred and eighty degrees.

Heff wore fifteen years of scabs over the wounds Margo left, but still the healing was only on the surface. They'd been lonely years. There'd been long nights when he'd tossed until dawn aching for a woman. A lover in his bed but, more than that, he yearned for a kindred spirit, a woman to laugh with, to share with. A woman to accept him as he was. To accept all that was in him to give.

No, the wanting still burned. It was the trusting he despaired of ever knowing again.

"Paco," Heff called ahead to the boy. "Give a yell when the tunnel starts to pinch in. There's a narrow stretch before the falls."

"I will, Jedediah," Paco shouted back. "I'll yell as loud as I can."

"And Paco, no disappearing acts. Stay within sight of my light."

"All right." The disappointed answer floated back.

For almost a mile down the rock-strewn tunnel, Heff fought the magnet that was Lucia's sleeping face. Then he said a resigned "damn" into the dark and looked down again. Her nose twitched in sleep. Like a rabbit's. The notion amused him. Lucia would bristle at the analogy. She thought herself a tigress, and given the fierce courage she'd shown searching for her brother, he could not disagree.

Lucia's head nodded back at an uncomfortable angle, and he gently eased her cheek back against his chest. For the first time he noticed how long her eyelashes were. Something else about her to like in secret. Damned if he'd ever tell her, but he even liked the feistiness, the tigress part.

Heff curled Lucia's shoulders toward him and glanced at the illuminated watch on his wrist. A little under thirty-two minutes left. It was going to be close. The first forays of guilt and fear assailed him. Why had he shaved the time so close? How could he have handed their fate over to a timer, a pitiless machine that was now remorselessly devouring perhaps the last moments of their lives in precisely spaced gulps?

If they were even one moment, one fraction of a second late sealing themselves into the cabin of the Caverunner, they would drown, their bodies lost forever in the deep, dark arteries of the Rio Bajo la Tierra.

DUSK

Otto Ralt paced the sixty-foot length of his subterranean command center, a man consumed. Strangers had penetrated the secret reaches of the Rio Bajo. Who were they, and why had they placed explosive charges against the dam at the junction of the north fork and the main channel near Rocksprings?

The dynamite would go off in under an hour. There was no time to get a Posse Comitatus team underground before the timer Ralt's TV surveillance had spotted set off the charge.

He had already sent an electronic command from his headquarters to the robotic pump station ten miles south of Rocksprings. The moment the dam blew and the water pressure slackened ahead, the station's computer would close huge steel sluice gates and send the waters of the Rio Grande north through a bypass tunnel.

Ralt calculated he would lose perhaps a quarter of the water already in the tunnel system of the Rio Bajo. In the scheme of things, it would be a relatively minor setback that didn't overly concern him. No, what worried Otto Ralt was not the lost water but the identity of the man who had placed the explosives.

When Ralt's TV camera first spotted the lost boy, he'd

estimated confidently that searchers would take weeks to find the youngster—or, rather, to find his body. Yet the intruder and the woman with him were at the dam site within hours.

The ground above was a stretch of low, serried hills, and Ralt knew from his geological surveys that the nearest possible sinkhole entrance to the Rio Bajo system had to be out on the prairie, at least ten miles away.

Given the distance and the labyrinth of tunnels in between, how had the intruder found the boy so quickly? The feat suggested a knowledge of the Rio Bajo and a caving expertise far beyond the skills of some local cave rescue volunteer.

Ralt broke off his pacing and wheeled toward the command console where Mason Sneed was scrutinizing a videotape from the TV camera at the dam site. The technician had frozen a single frame from the tape, a close-up of the intruder's face as he'd risen from placing the explosives.

"Have you identified him yet?" Ralt demanded impatiently.

"It's in the computer, Mr. Ralt," Sneed answered.

If the man on the screen had had his picture in the newspapers or on television anytime during the past ten years, the computer would make a match through its media photo-memory program.

A chime toned softly and a crawl of words began across the intruder's picture on the screen.

Ralt studied the monitor. The man was Jedediah Heffernan. He was credited with several dozen cave rescues from the 1970s to the early 1990s, although he'd apparently been inactive the past five years. Until now, Ralt thought bitterly. But it was the final part of Heffernan's biography that made Ralt suddenly start as if slapped.

The speleologist was considered the nation's best subterranean cartographer, having mapped previously unexplored cave systems from California to Florida. Among the maps he'd drawn, one detailed a section of the Rio Bajo la Tierra.

Ralt's mind turned as the biography ended. When Hef-

fernan reached the surface, there would no longer be any
doubt where the missing Rio Grande had gone. Ralt could
expect the authorities to take action as soon as the news
reached them.

There wasn't much they could do to stop the underground
flow of the Rio Bajo, not unless they blocked all the bypass
tunnels. That would take months, even if this Jedediah
Heffernan found and blew every dam Ralt had had constructed.

The one vulnerable part of the entire system was the main
pump station where the passages of the Rio Bajo met the
tunnel Ralt's men had bored north the final twenty-eight
miles to Dallas. Was it possible this man Heffernan could
find his way north under the earth to the head of the Rio
Bajo?

He reread the biography on the screen. Heffernan was
good, damn good, the best subterranean explorer in the
country. There was no doubt in Ralt's mind: Jedediah
Heffernan represented the first real threat to his plan to save
Dallas.

"Get me Karl Stroesser on the scrambler," he ordered the
technician at the command console.

Ralt resumed his pacing as Mason Sneed put through a
call to the Posse Comitatus leader.

"I have Stroesser, Mr. Ralt," Sneed said.

Ralt grabbed the receiver from the technician's hand.
"Karl, I want you to get up here on the double. As soon as
you arrive, we'll take the monorail north to the main pump
station."

"We got trouble, Mr. Ralt?"

"The Rio Bajo has been penetrated."

"How many men will we be up against?"

"One, Karl. And if we don't destroy him, he will destroy
us."

AN HOUR AFTER DARK

The sudden shouts of Paco Sanchez echoed back through the dark tunnel of the Rio Bajo. "Jedediah, Jedediah, the tunnel's getting narrower up here!"

Lucia Sanchez stirred in the arms of Jedediah Heffernan as her brother's voice pierced her exhausted sleep. "Paco. Was that Paco?" Her eyes flew open. "Is he all right? Paco!"

"Easy," Heff calmed her. "Paco's fine. We're almost to the waterfall."

He put Lucia down, steadying her while her disoriented senses cleared.

"How long have I been asleep?" Lucia asked groggily.

Heff glanced at his watch. "About half an hour," he said, not adding that they had less than nine minutes left to descend the falls and close themselves into the Caverunner before the dam behind them blew and the tunnel flooded with water.

A moment later their hat lights picked up Paco standing in a neck of tunnel ahead. Beyond, the corridor flared out into a black void. They'd reached the huge cavern where the Caverunner waited.

The grappling iron was still on the floor of the tunnel mouth, and Heff reeled up the cave rope dangling into the black cavern below. He tied a loop in one end. "I'll let you down first, Lucia. When you reach the bottom, turn on the Caverunner's lights."

Lucia felt the fear fingers tighten around her throat as she backed over the lip of the falls.

"I'll play the rope out slowly," Heff reassured her. "Try not to swing out away from the rock or you'll get twisted up. Ready?"

"Ready as I'll ever be," Lucia said with a bravado she didn't feel.

Heff eased Lucia over the lip of the stone falls and she began to descend the face of the frozen cascade.

"Keep your light on her, Paco," Heff said to the boy as Lucia lowered into the cavern depths.

Lucia fought back panic as she descended alone into the black womb of the immense cavern, her hands tight on the nylon umbilical cord stretching up to the grasp of Jedediah above.

Halfway down her confidence flowed back, and she began to worry instead about how little time they had left. "Faster, Jedediah," she called up toward the head of the falls. "Let me down faster."

Above, Heff eased his grip on the rope, letting the nylon slip through his fingers in increments of yards instead of feet. "Start looking over your shoulder," he shouted down.

Lucia craned her neck, and a moment later the cavern floor emerged through the murky darkness twenty-five feet below. Twenty feet, ten, five, she was down.

"Send Paco down," she yelled up at the two dots of yellow light far above. "I'm there."

Lucia's light found the Caverunner twenty yards away in the darkness, and she ran for the side of the hoverjet. Behind her she heard the rope brush against the stone face of the falls as Jedediah retrieved the line.

She climbed into the cabin and searched the control console. Quickly she found the light switch and flicked the toggle. The Caverunner's large exterior spotlights came on, shining up the arc of the falls in the same position as Jedediah had left them hours before.

Lucia hurried back to the foot of the falls and watched with her heart in her mouth as her young brother was lowered toward her through the hoverjet's lights. Three minutes later, Paco reached the cavern floor.

"He's down, Jedediah," Lucia shouted.

Heff hammered in a piton, tied off the rope, and quickly rappeled down the smooth stone face. He reached the bottom and looked at his watch. "We've got a minute and a half. Let's get in the Caverunner."

The three climbed into the cabin and Heff lowered the plexiglass bubble above. He shut all exterior air vents and snapped down the safety catches that rimmed the flange of the glass. Then he started the motor. A steady hum built beneath them.

"I don't understand, Jedediah," Lucia said. "I thought the thrusters were broken."

"The lift jets are out, Lucia. But there's nothing wrong with the propulsion ports behind. We may not be able to rise, but, given buoyancy, we can control the Caverunner's forward motion."

Paco's face lit up. "Buoyancy. That's why you wanted to blow up that rock dam and flood the tunnel. You're going to turn the hoverjet into a boat."

"I've used the Caverunner on a dozen or more subterranean river explorations," Heff said. "Afloat, she handles like a jetboat. As soon as—"

The sound of a muffled explosion came suddenly from the tunnel mouth above, and a moment later a plume of sand and dust shot out of the opening and roiled in the hoverjet's overhead lights.

"Get your seat belts on," Heff shouted above the building roar of water from the top of the falls.

The booming rumble of the torrent coming at them echoed and re-echoed off the far walls of the huge cavern, reverberating through the black depths like thunder trapped in a jug. The crescendo grew, threatening, deafening, inexorable.

A rain of spray descended suddenly over the hoverjet, a frothy advance scout for the deluge behind.

"Hang on," Heff shouted above the calamitous din.

At that instant, the flood emerged from the tunnel mouth above, and for the first time in two hundred thousand years the great falls of the Rio Bajo la Tierra roared to life.

Thirty thousand gallons a second poured madly down the frozen arc and smashed into the primordial dust of the cavern floor. A tower of spray and sand erupted toward the rock ceiling four hundred feet above, and a wall of water raced out into the black bowels of the cavern.

The Caverunner lifted on the crest of the deluge, rocking madly as the frenzied wave carried the hoverjet forward through the dark. For a terrifying moment, it felt to the three inside as though the craft would turn turtle in the tossing waters. Then the Caverunner righted itself and Heff jammed the throttle forward.

The Caverunner shot ahead with the surging waters, their visibility cut to a few yards by the dust-blackened spray streaming back from the crest of the wave before them. Lucia screamed as a huge stalagmite loomed suddenly in the foam-muted glow of their lights. Heff gunned the starboard jet behind and the Caverunner heeled violently to the left, missing the rock column by inches.

Behind them, almost two million gallons of water a minute poured over the falls and down into the fifteen-hundred-foot-wide, three-mile-long cavern. Like a huge bathtub filling from a stone faucet, a tossing subterranean lake rose slowly against the rock walls.

Waves thrown back by islands of columns washed over the bow of the Caverunner as Heff throttled back in the middle of the lake and flipped on the echo sounder. The green monitor in the cabin glowed with a three-dimensional computer map as the Gravprobe's antenna swept the rock walls ahead.

The Gravprobe picked up four cavities in the cliffs before them. Two were high on the rock face, and Heff ruled these out. The tunnel mouth from which they'd entered the huge cavern was at ground level, and he studied the remaining possibilities.

Lucia sensed his indecision. "Look, Jedediah, near the

left tunnel. Isn't that the Greek temple we saw when we came in?"

Heff looked at the screen. Lucia was right. The stand of stalagmites was the same columned formation they'd seen on first entering the chamber. The left tunnel was the way home.

Heff turned the Caverunner toward the passage mouth, and the hoverjet left a luminous wake behind as it skimmed across the growing subterranean lake. The three in the cabin stared ahead, their eyes straining to see beyond the arc of light racing before the hoverjet.

Paco saw the opening first. "There, Jedediah, there's the tunnel. Behind those last rock columns."

Heff slowed the Caverunner as they neared, maneuvering to center on the black hole in the cliff. A hundred yards out they felt a current build under the hoverjet as the lake waters rushed forward toward the drain.

Fifty yards away, Heff circled the Caverunner, positioning for the final run through the cliff. He looked over at Lucia and Paco. "This is the worst part. We've got to hit that tunnel entrance dead center, or we'll be thrown against the rocks and smashed to pieces. Keep as still as you can. Even a small shift in weight could make a difference."

He brought the nose of the hoverjet around, letting the Caverunner align with the current. Twenty yards now. A wave sloshed back off a near stalagmite, pushing the craft to the side. Heff quickly compensated with a thrust to the port jet, and the Caverunner centered again in the flow.

Ten yards, five. The rock walls loomed close enough to touch, and the deafening roar of the water through the narrow neck filled the cabin.

Then, suddenly, they were through the mouth, racing on the current down the spray-filled tube beyond, the rock walls passing in a brown blur. For miles through the flooded tunnel, the current hardly slowed. Heff fought continuously to keep the Caverunner in the middle of the stream while Lucia manned the Gravprobe beside him.

Three times Lucia spotted forks in the tunnel ahead and Heff maneuvered the Caverunner to stay in the main flow.

Once he miscalculated, and before he could bring the craft back on course the raucous sound of metal scraping against rock screeched through the cabin.

"Check for leaks," Heff shouted above the roar of the river.

Lucia and Paco searched the cabin interior for signs of water coming in. They could find none.

"Lucky," Heff yelled. "Damn lucky."

Slowly the force and speed of the current eased as water was drawn off into side passages and their distance from the subterranean lake behind increased. The raging torrent was now more a swiftly flowing river, and for the first time Heff eased back against his seat.

"We're going to make it." He let out a long breath. "By God, we're going to make it."

"I knew it, I knew we'd get out," Lucia cried, whirling to hug her brother and then Jedediah, in turn.

Heff grinned. "I wish you'd told me. A few times there, I wasn't real sure."

Lucia laughed. "How long before we reach the sink-hole?"

"That half-hour ride we just took must have carried us a good quarter of the way back," Jedediah said. "The way the current's running, I'd say we'll be under your farm in five or six hours."

"Oh, to see the sun again," Lucia said dreamily, leaning back and closing her eyes. "I never thought I'd miss it so."

Five hours and forty-five minutes later, Lucia saw the dawn sun. Its reflection came first, glinting off the river ahead of the Caverunner. Heff switched off the hoverjet's lights as they approached, each staring in silent wonder at the warm glow of natural light ahead.

Heff popped the plexiglass bubble and a moment later they heard the first shouting from the surface. Then they were through the wall of the sinkhole and a loud cheer rose from above as the rescue team on the prairie welcomed the Caverunner back from the depths of the earth.

Heff reversed engines and kept the hoverjet steady in the

river as ropes were tossed down from the sinkhole lip. Paco caught a line and with Lucia's help pulled the craft in to the steep bank.

For several minutes they stood encircled by the exuberant crowd of rescuers, spectators, and reporters, congratulations and questions flying at them from all sides.

Then two uniformed men pushed through the dusty throng. The taller of the two flashed a badge at Heff.

"Jedediah Heffernan?"

"Yes?"

"Texas Rangers, Mr. Heffernan," the shorter one said. "The governor of Texas is looking for you."

DAY FOUR

APRIL 13, 1999

DAWN

Like vultures over a field of carrion, helicopters hired by news media from around the world circled lazily over downtown Dallas, their camera eyes recording the final spasms of a city about to die.

There were no humans left below, save those who were dead. The evacuation of Dallas' almost three million inhabitants had begun as an orderly neighborhood-by-neighborhood withdrawal, but it had swiftly degenerated into an every-man-for-himself stampede out of the doomed city.

The two main evacuation centers, set up in the communities of University Park and Cockrell Hill, were mobbed with twice the number of people who could be taken out on the available evacuation buses and National Guard transports.

Those left behind surged out into the surrounding suburbs in a frenzied search for transportation. Over two thousand cars were stolen, many at gunpoint, and a maddened rampage of looting and wanton destruction left thousands of houses gutted and burned.

At both Love Field and Dallas–Fort Worth International Airport, mobs commandeered incoming and departing flights, forcing the regular passengers off. With guns at their heads, pilots were ordered to take off with three times the normal passenger load crammed into aisles, lavatories, even cargo holds.

Those who could find no transportation began an exodus from the city on foot. Secondary roads and eight-lane highways alike were soon jammed with columns of slogging refugees. Several hundred pedestrians were run down and crushed as cars, buses, and trucks forced their way through the bottlenecks of foot traffic.

Only about two-thirds of the evacuees found their way to the federal refugee reception centers set up at Bergstrom Air Force Base and at forts Hood and Sam Houston. The remaining third scattered to the towns and small cities on the surrounding prairie, sparking confrontations with the local inhabitants.

In Sulphur Springs northeast of Dallas, four men and a teenage girl were killed in a pitched gun battle over the water from a garden hose. In Waxahachie to the south, a vigilante group sprang up to defend the town from marauding refugees, and a half-dozen car thieves from Dallas were hanged from telephone poles before the National Guard moved in.

Local and state police struggled in vain to maintain law and order amid the human tide of refugees. For almost the entire thirty-six hours of the evacuation, the staccato sound of gunfire, police and civilian, could be heard in Dallas and on the roads out of the stricken city.

There had not been time for an official body count yet, but estimates of the number of Dallasites killed in the evacuation ranged from three to six thousand. From the news helicopters, live television cameras followed a final lone Red Cross ambulance driving slowly along Commerce Street, packed with so many bodies that corpses were stacked on the roof and tied to the sides, like deer slain for sport.

Elsewhere, abandoned cars and buses lined the streets, and the sidewalks were littered with suitcases, files of paper, odd pieces of furniture, and personal memorabilia discarded as panicked inhabitants fled to the safety of the surrounding prairie.

At City Hall Plaza, the ground had settled and a sagging water main had burst. A column of water jetted into the air from the broken pipe, the runoff draining into a latticework of ever-widening fissures below. The fountain would continue to erupt to the end, for there was no one left at the utility district headquarters to shut off the flow.

Sinkholes had begun swallowing land and buildings all over the city, precursors to the titanic pit eating its way up into the guts of Dallas. Ownby Stadium at Southern Methodist University had vanished during the night, along with much of the surrounding campus.

In scattered locations, several large skyscrapers had gone down, and Routes 75, 45, and 30 were segmented, with stretches of concrete missing near the city center.

Occasionally, one of the media helicopters swooped down low, searching for the odd bit of poignant trivia that would lend a human touch to the vista of concrete, steel, and glass the cameras watched.

A close-up of a little girl's doll lying in a gutter brought tears to the eyes of millions of viewers; a shot of dozens of stray cats streaming out of a delicatessen, their mouths crammed with salmon and roast beef, occasioned thousands of calls to the network from around the country demanding the animals be rescued.

The switchboard operators issued perfunctory promises that everything possible would be done to save the cats, but the vow was as hollow as the earth beneath the city. The realists watching knew the truth: no human lives would be risked in the cause of animals.

The beasts had inherited the vacant streets. Let them feast, for they were doomed to die with Dallas.

MIDMORNING

The Texas National Guard headquarters outside Mineral Wells was a madhouse of ringing phones and frenzied aides as Jedediah Heffernan was shown through to the office of Governor Lynn Duecker.

Duecker put down the phone and rose behind his desk as Heff entered with the National Guard commander. "Mr. Heffernan, half the state of Texas has been looking for you," the governor said, extending his hand.

"So General Wilkerson has been telling me," Heff said. "Where I've been, you weren't likely to find me."

"No, I don't believe we would have, not in the Rio Bajo. Please sit down," Duecker said. "The boy you went in to rescue—how is he?"

"Tired and sore, and a few pounds lighter," Heff said. "Otherwise fine. I left him with his sister and mother at their farm."

"I take it General Wilkerson briefed you on the way in," Duecker said.

Heff nodded. "As a geologist, I'm not surprised at the Landsat evidence of the sinkhole under Dallas. Given the limestone formation beneath the city and the depletion of the Ogallala aquifer, the collapse was almost inevitable."

"I'm afraid that the disappearance of Dallas is not the

only catastrophe we face, Mr. Heffernan," the governor
said. "Unless we stop the flow of the Rio Grande north
through those tunnels you just left, war with Mexico is all
but certain."

"Damming the Rio Bajo is going to take time, sir. There
are parallel tunnels along much of the river's length, in
places up to a dozen passages side by side."

"So I understand from the U.S. Geological Survey,"
Duecker said. "The Survey geologists insist we have to find
a bottleneck, a stretch where those tunnels funnel into one
or two main river channels."

"Assuming such a conflux exists," Heff said. "There's
something else, governor. General Wilkerson tells me you
believe the Posse Comitatus blew the bed of the Rio
Grande."

"Yes. Apparently the bastards mined the river as part of
an attack on Mexican troops along the border," Duecker
said disgustedly. "Only that mine did more than kill
Mexicans. It tore open the riverbed and let the Rio Grande
down into the subterranean system of the Rio Bajo."

"I think it was the other way around, governor. I believe
the Posse knew the Rio Bajo passed beneath the Rio Grande
at that point. I believe they meant to divert the river north
into Texas, and when those Mexican troops stumbled on the
preparations—well, their deaths were a nice bonus."

Duecker came forward in his chair. "Why do you say
that?"

Heff told the governor of the evidence of blasting at the
dam site and the TV camera he'd spotted watching him.

"The Posse Comitatus?" Duecker said incredulously.
"But why? Why would they go to all that trouble to divert
the Rio Grande north?"

"I can answer that, Lynn," said a woman's voice from
the doorway behind them.

The men turned and looked at Rebecca Ralt as one of the
governor's aides rushed in beside her.

"I'm sorry, governor," the aide apologized. "I told Mrs.
Ralt you were busy."

Duecker rose from his chair. Not only was Rebecca Ralt

the wife of the richest man in America, she had contributed generously to the governor's last three political campaigns. He crossed the room and dismissed the aide.

"Rebecca, what on earth are you doing here?"

"My husband has stolen the Rio Grande River, Lynn," she said expressionlessly. "I'm here to give it back."

For the next twenty minutes, Heff and the governor sat listening incredulously as Rebecca Ralt told them of her husband's scheme to fill the huge sinkhole under Dallas with the stolen waters of the Rio Grande.

"I believe this may help you stop Otto," she said, taking out the map Ralt had thrown at her in fury in his command center.

Heff spread the chart out on the governor's desk. For several minutes he pored over the details: the dam sites, the pump stations, the final twenty-eight-mile-long tunnel Ralt's engineers had bored north to Dallas.

He straightened finally. "How much time have we got?"

Governor Duecker stared fixedly at Heff. "We are on the brink of open hostilities with Mexico, Mr. Heffernan. Every minute the Rio Grande continues to flow into Texas is a minute closer to war."

"Then we have no choice," Heff said. "We'll have to hit the tunnel system where it's most vulnerable—at the main pump station where the bore south from Dallas joins the Rio Bajo."

"Can we reach it from the surface?" Duecker asked.

"That pump station's six hundred feet underground, governor. We'd need at least two, maybe three days to get heavy equipment in there and sink a shaft. No, the only way is for me to go in through the tunnel from Dallas. I should be able to reach the station in six to eight hours."

"What will you need?" Duecker asked.

"My hoverjet's damaged. I'll need a repair crew of welders and turbojet mechanics, and a cargo chopper to ferry the hoverjet up here."

"You're going to be up against the Posse Comitatus. I'll order a company of National Guard troops to go in with you."

"I'm afraid foot soldiers couldn't keep up with my Caverunner, governor. In any case, they'd only be in the way. Those passages are narrow enough for one well-armed man to hold off a hundred against him."

"The repair crews will be waiting when your hoverjet arrives, Mr. Heffernan," the governor said. He stepped forward and put out his hand. "Good luck. Texas and the entire nation will be praying for your safe return."

"Thank you, governor," Heff said, and turned to leave.

Rebecca Ralt stepped forward. "Kill him. I want you to kill my husband."

Heff paused, struck by the vehement hate in the woman's voice. "My job is to dam the Rio Bajo, Mrs. Ralt. If your husband tries to stop me, then what will be will be. But I don't intend to hunt him."

Heff nodded to the governor and opened the door.

"I warn you, Mr. Heffernan." Rebecca Ralt's words followed him out. "Otto will be hunting you."

NOON

The temperature inside the Mexican missile silo at Nueva Rosita had reached 115 degrees Fahrenheit, and Major Demyan Turgenev found it increasingly hard to breathe in the still, stale air of the tube.

General Hugo Santamaría regarded the Russian's sweat-bathed face sympathetically. "You must try to think of something cool, major. When I was in Moscow, I took a walk in Gorky Park with our ambassador to your country. I remember we passed an ice-skating rink, the skaters whirling about in mittens and earmuffs. The image does much to alleviate the heat."

"You apparently have more control over your mental processes than I, general," Turgenev said, his eyes raised toward the huge metal doors capping the silo tube above. "I can think of only one thing at the moment."

Santamaría followed the Russian's gaze. For almost ten hours now the political police had been up there, cutting through the titanium-steel plates with their torches. They were slicing open a square, eighteen inches on each side, just large enough for a man to drop through.

The scorched fissure that marked the track of the torches was within an inch of the last corner. The square was almost complete.

"The political police will be coming very soon now," Santamaría said.

Turgenev lowered his eyes and returned the old general's stare. "I know."

Santamaría swiveled his chair to the duty desk behind him, unlocked a drawer, and took out two nine millimeter MaKarov pistols. "Have you ever killed a man, major?"

Turgenev flinched. "No."

Santamaría handed him a pistol. "Then today you will draw blood for the first time."

"I've never even been in a fistfight," the Russian blurted out. "Never in my life. Always I've found a reason not to fight, a reason to back away. I'm a coward."

"Do you think I've never backed away?" Santamaría said. "One doesn't reach my age and position by being an oak but by being a willow. Only the brute or the fool seeks the vindication of his manhood in combat. No man of intellect fights merely for the sake of it, for love of the blows."

Turgenev could see the jagged scar ridges of old battle wounds through Santamaría's clinging, sweat-soaked shirt. "But when there was no other way, you stood and fought. You've never run, have you?"

"Have you?" Santamaría challenged. "Or have you simply avoided the moment when you would have to make that decision? Have you proved yourself a coward, Major Turgenev, or do you merely expect it of yourself? Don't you know that all men in the face of battle expect the same?"

Santamaría stabbed his pistol barrel toward the silo cap above. "When they come, my fear will be as deep as yours, my self-doubt as choking. But fear is a door. A man either walks through it or turns away and remembers for the rest of his life that he did. You have tortured yourself at the threshold long enough, major. Now is the moment you must choose."

The sudden scream of tearing metal came from the ceiling of the silo, and they looked up to see the square of steel plate dangling by a thin, twisted ribbon. For a moment, the plug dangled impossibly from the metal cord.

Then the ribbon parted and the steel square plunged into the silo.

An earsplitting clang of metal against metal reverberated through the tube as the plug struck the steel floor ten feet from the foot of the Mexican missile aimed at Dallas. The din had hardly died away before a rope dropped through the square of sunlight above and uncoiled to the bottom.

Santamaría put out his hand. "So, the moment has come for both of us. Shall we walk through the door together?"

Turgenev clasped the old revolutionary's hand. "Together."

A shaft of shadow fell across Turgenev's face from the square of sun above and a moment later a foot-long cylindrical canister dropped toward the silo floor.

"Gas!" Santamaría lunged for a storage box set into the console. He jabbed at a button above and the box front slid open. He reached in and grabbed the two gas masks inside.

The canister reached bottom and split open. A thick cloud of gray-green smoke billowed toward them as they pushed the masks over their faces.

"They'll drop down through the gas, one after another in a string," Santamaría shouted, his voice eerily muted through the filtered breathing port. "I'll go to the other side of the missile and we'll have them in a cross-fire."

Turgenev stared at the thick gas roiling up around the rope, like cotton candy spinning around a stick. "How will I see them in the gas?"

"Fire at their shadows as they come through the light," Santamaría said. "Do you understand?"

Turgenev took comfort from the calm courage of the old man. "I understand."

Santamaría put his hands on the shoulders of the Russian, and for a moment they stared wordlessly into each other's eyes through the glass of their goggles. Then the general turned, darted across the silo floor, and disappeared into the smoke.

Turgenev watched him go, then looked up toward the square of light above. The gas had almost reached the apex of the silo now. Suddenly, two legs straddled the top of the dangling rope, then the trunk of a body filled the square.

From somewhere across the silo, Santamaría's gun barked twice and the man on the rope screamed and dropped into the gas cloud, his mask-muffled shrieks following his body to the silo floor. There was a sickening thud that Turgenev could feel through his feet.

A shadowed form momentarily blocked the light, then was gone into the gas. Another blurred body followed the first down, then another, and another. Across the tube, he heard the sharp reports of Santamaría's gun firing. Screams came again, from more than one throat this time, and Turgenev heard the crash of bodies against the silo floor.

He raised his pistol toward the light above. A shadow appeared in his sights. He couldn't fire. If he sent death out into the gas, death would come back at him. Fear wasn't a door, it was a wall. He heard Santamaría fire again. An anguished cry tore out from the root of Turgenev's being and he threw himself against the fear and pulled the trigger.

No sound came from the shadowed form above. He'd missed. Another blurred body appeared. This time Turgenev gulped a deep breath first, aimed deliberately, and fired. The ghost man screamed and dropped into the gas-filled silo.

But they were coming one after the other now. Between the pistol shots Turgenev could hear the rasping whistle of rope sliding through hands, and the grunt of men as they hit the floor and rolled away into the smoke.

The political police were down in the tube with them. Somewhere. Santamaría had stopped firing. Why? Was he out of ammunition? The silence stretched into a minute. Two. The sounds of men struggling came suddenly from across the silo.

A last shot came from Santamaría's gun, the orange tongue from the barrel licking out into the gas. Then the sounds of the struggle abruptly ceased, and Turgenev heard an order shouted in muffled Spanish. Whatever the political police had done to Santamaría, the old general was no longer fighting.

Turgenev was alone now. All the accoutrements of his courage, the badges of army, party, nation, were gone. He faced death naked, yet for the first time in his life Demyan Turgenev was not afraid.

He stared into the billowing gas, straining for the shadows of the men he knew were coming. An electrified voice suddenly cut through the smoke.

"Major Turgenev. This is Colonel Vargas of the political police. I order you to lay down your weapon and surrender."

Turgenev answered with a shot in the direction of the voice.

"Your resistance is futile. Give up, major."

Turgenev wondered how many bullets he had left: three, four?

"You are only prolonging your ordeal," the colonel taunted.

Turgenev fired again, twice. A shadow rose from the vapors and lunged toward him. He shot at point-blank range. The form toppled. Before the body hit the floor, another soldier came at him from the other side. He spun to meet the new threat. His finger was tightening on the trigger when he felt the arms grab him from behind and the needle plunge into his back.

Major Demyan Turgenev's first and last fight was over. He had won the battle with himself, but the drugs that coursed through his blood would give the war to the madmen.

Within the hour, the computer codes to fire the nuclear warhead against Dallas would be in the hands of Prime Minister Teodoro Martí.

MIDAFTERNOON

At Governor Duecker's emergency headquarters near Mineral Wells, several heads turned at the sound of Jedediah Heffeman yelling at Lucia Sanchez.

"We've had this argument five thousand damn times," he exploded, slamming his hand down on the outer shell of the Caverunner.

The welders had just finished cutting away the damaged lift port a few feet below and the metal skin was still hot from the torches. Heff jerked his hand away in pain. "Damn it all to hell, now look what you made me do."

Lucia grinned. "*I* made you do? It serves you right for losing your temper."

"Do you realize you are the only person on the face of the earth that can make me blow up like that?" Heff said, shaking his burned hand in the air. "I used to be a rational man, an even-tempered, mellow guy. Then I met you."

"Nonsense, you were born with that terrible temper," Lucia said, taking Heff's reddened hand in hers. "I'd better put some salve on your fingers."

"Never mind that. You're just trying to ingratiate yourself again, worm your little butt back into the Caverunner. Forget it."

Lucia put her arm through his and began marching Heff

toward the small four-story office building being used as emergency headquarters by the governor.

"C'mon, Jedediah. There must be a nurse's station somewhere in the building."

Heff shook his head and sighed as he was urged along. "Doesn't anything get through to you?"

"Yes, Jedediah, a blistered hand makes an impression. But instead of ranting and raving, I, in my quiet way, prefer simply to tend the burn."

Halfway to the building, they passed the field machine shop set up by the National Guard to work on the Caverunner's lift port. Heff dug in his heels and pulled them to a stop.

"How long before I can take her up again, sergeant?" he asked the NCO in charge of the repair crew.

"Parts won't be ready for another couple of hours," the sergeant said. "Figure an hour to install them. I'd say you'll be able to take off in about three hours, sir."

"The swelling on your hand should be down by then," Lucia said brightly, urging him forward again.

Heff quit resisting. "Wonderful. I'm going to spend the next three hours watching my blisters shrink."

Lucia asked directions from the guard at the building entrance, and five minutes later they found the Red Cross–emblazoned door to the nurse's station toward the rear of the building's second floor.

Lucia inserted the key the guard had given her and unlocked the door. The room inside was a windowless fifteen- by fifteen-foot cubicle. In one corner was a portable X-ray machine, and next to it an array of oxygen administering equipment. To the right was a stainless steel sink, its drainboard topped with jars of cotton balls, tongue depressors, and gauze bandages.

A large leather couch was set against the left wall as they entered, and in the middle of the room was a white-sheeted examination table. The sound of the lock automatically clicking closed as the door shut behind them made them both acutely aware of how alone they were.

Lucia found a towel in the cupboard under the sink and

handed it to Heff. "Spread your fingers out on this on the table," she said, turning to search for the salve among the neatly ordered medicines in the sink-side cabinet.

Heff sighed. "How the hell did you get the National Guard to bring you up here?"

Lucia found the ointment and began gently dabbing on the medicine with a cotton swab. "I told them I was your co-pilot. They were happy to give me a ride in the cargo helicopter that ferried the Caverunner."

"My co-pilot, huh? May I ask who bestowed that title on you?"

"Stop wiggling your thumb," she said. "Now, Jedediah, you know perfectly well that I piloted the Caverunner for hours while we were searching for Paco. You said yourself I had a deft touch at the controls."

"One trip through the Rio Bajo does not make you my co-pilot, Lucia. There's more to caving than taking the controls of a hoverjet."

"Is it experience that makes a caver, or is it how you feel when you're down there? When I went into the Rio Bajo with you I was afraid, terrified of the closeness of the walls and the black pits and the stalactites hanging down like daggers. But something happened to me when we entered that great chamber with the Greek ruins and the cave flowers and the stone waterfall."

Heff watched the passion work in her face.

"I'll never forget what you said at that moment. 'There are vistas under the earth undreamed of by men above.' Well, I've been there with you. Remember? I've seen the beauty, the mystery of unexplored caverns, the awesome stonework sculpted by water and time. It's not just your world anymore, Jedediah. It's my world now, too."

Heff let out a long breath. "You're the most exasperating woman I've ever met. One minute I want to wring your neck, the next I want . . ." He left the thought unfinished.

Lucia raised her eyes from his hand. "You want to what?"

"What I want and what is possible are two different

things, Lucia. I have a difficult job ahead. I can't allow myself the luxury of personal feelings right now."

"How about my help, Jedediah. Is that another luxury you can't allow yourself? I've heard the soldiers talking. The Posse Comitatus is waiting for you in that tunnel."

Heff kept his voice light. "All right, so there'll be a handful of rednecks down there. They'll be the ones at a disadvantage, not me. They'll be guarding the approaches from the Rio Bajo side. I'm going in from the Dallas entrance. I should be able to take them by surprise, blow their main pump station, and be out of there before the Posse can turn around."

"You think you can do it all alone? Pilot the Caverunner, set the explosives, and fight off the Posse all at the same time?"

"Lucia, listen to me—"

"No, you listen to me, Jedediah. You wouldn't leave me in the Rio Bajo when I couldn't walk another step. You said I was being selfish to ask you to go on without me. Well, now you're being selfish. If you go into that tunnel alone, you'll never come out. You think I could live with that? Knowing you needed me and I wasn't there to help?"

"You have a family, Lucia. Paco and your mother. I'm alone."

"Do you really believe you're still alone? I think you've got the same problem with your heart that you have with your hand; you got burned. Margo left you with ashes in your mouth, and now you're afraid to feel again, to trust again. Well, I'm not Margo, and it's time you realized that."

"First my co-pilot, now a psychoanalyst. You're a real jack-of-all-trades, aren't you?"

"Stop trying to dance away, Jedediah. I mean as much to you as you do to me."

Heff pushed his face an inch from Lucia's small nose. "You think you know all there is to know about me, don't you, Miss Smart-ass. Well, I happen to be an old-fashioned sort of guy. I like to speak for myself. Whom I care for is my business. Until and unless I make it someone else's. Got it?"

Lucia put her cheek next to his. "I don't want to change you. I don't want to own you. Only to be there for you, as you've been there for me. When we searched for Paco we were the two halves of a whole. Don't cut us apart, not now. Please take me with you."

Heff pulled back and looked at Lucia wordlessly for a moment. He knew she was right. He needed her. She handled the Caverunner like a pro, and she knew the systems. But it was far more than that. He needed her in his life. Suddenly, the dam broke in him. Their lips met, and then their tongues. Slowly, savoring the moment, they explored each other's mouths and passions.

"You said we were two halves of a whole, Lucia," Heff whispered against her ear. "Did you mean that? Friends, partners, lovers? No secrets, no end?"

"All those things, Jedediah," Lucia said, her eyes holding his. "All those things and more."

For another long moment they kissed, their bodies pressed tightly against each other. Then, without a word between them, they walked hand in hand to the couch.

They made love unhurriedly, bringing each other to heights of arousal neither had known before, until they could hold back no longer and they climaxed together.

For a long time afterward, they lay side by side, their hands entwined and their faces inches apart, talking lovers' talk and telling lovers' secrets.

Three hours after they entered the Red Cross station, they walked hand in hand back to the Caverunner to find the National Guard crew packing the explosives Heff had ordered into the hold.

"She's ready to go up, sir," the sergeant in charge said, wiping his hands on a grease rag.

Heff inspected the repaired lift port. "You did a hell of a job, sergeant," he said. "Please thank your men for me."

"I will, sir," the NCO said.

Heff and Lucia climbed into the cabin and went through a systems check as the last plastic explosives were stowed aboard. Then Heff lowered the plexiglass bubble and started the motors.

Gradually, he increased the thrust and the Caverunner rose slowly into the hot Texas afternoon, its exhaust ports sending small dust devils whirling off to the sides.

The news of the Caverunner's mission had spread through the governor's emergency headquarters, and the sound of the jets brought people streaming out of buildings and tents to watch them leave.

Below, the repair crew of welders and mechanics unfurled a banner reading, GOOD LUCK CAVERUNNER. For several moments there was an eerie silence as the three thousand National Guardsmen, Texas Rangers, and evacuation workers assembled beneath them. Then a cheer began to build among the crowd, the hurrahs and shouts of encouragement rising in a crescendo around the hoverjet.

Heff rolled the oblong craft from side to side in acknowledgment, then leveled off at five hundred feet and set a course toward Dallas.

"Ready to take over?" he asked Lucia.

"Any time," Lucia said.

"She's all yours," Heff said, reaching for Rebecca Ralt's map as Lucia took the controls. The chart showed that the tunnel Ralt's engineers had bored north from the Rio Bajo emptied into the sinkhole under Dallas from the southwest.

"It looks like the tunnel entrance is somewhere under Fair Park," Heff said. "We'll have to find a sinkhole in the area that feeds down into the main pit."

He put an overlay of the downtown area on the Ralt map and made some calculations with a caliper. "Bring her around to a hundred and forty degrees south-southeast."

Lucia turned the hoverjet, and they cruised steadily toward the dying city ahead. The sinkholes grew more numerous beneath them as they neared Dallas.

The pattern of devastation below was random. Here a block of houses stood undisturbed, while the next was pocked with a black void that had swallowed the surrounding homes and streets. Everywhere were scenes of panicked evacuation; cars left in the middle of roads, suitcases abandoned on sidewalks, house doors swinging in the arid ground breeze.

Twenty minutes later they were over the outskirts of the

city. Here the destruction was much greater. The immense pit gnawing its way up into the guts of Dallas had already claimed vast tracts of the metropolitan complex. Several skyscrapers had gone down under their own massive weight, taking with them the smaller buildings around. Whole blocks had disappeared into the earth, and in several places they could see the shadowed depression of ground about to collapse.

Heff studied the map. "I think our best bet is to go in along Commerce Street. Bring her down to two hundred feet."

Lucia lowered the Caverunner toward the forest of glass and steel towers. "Some of the buildings along Commerce Street are forty and fifty stories," she said. "The upper floors will be above us."

"Try to keep us centered on the street," Heff said.

The hoverjet crossed Fort Worth Avenue and neared the first of the tall buildings downtown. Heff pointed across the Dallas floodway ahead. "There's Commerce. Take our speed down to ten knots."

Lucia slowed the Caverunner and swung the nose around to intersect the thoroughfare below. Three minutes later they entered the canyon of tall buildings leading into downtown Dallas.

Heff brought out a pair of binoculars and peered into the empty offices twenty stories above the street. He could see half-typed letters standing in hastily abandoned typewriters. Computer printouts and files lay on vacant desks, and cardboard boxes filled with framed pictures and small plants were strewn across tables and floors, the personal belongings of office workers who'd fled in panic.

Heff swung the binoculars to the left and started suddenly. In a corner office, a heavyset man was slumped forward, dead at his desk of a heart attack, a vial of nitroglycerine tablets spilled open next to his lifeless hand.

Something was moving on the back and neck of the body, and Heff brought the glasses into sharper focus. A second later, he yanked the binoculars away in revulsion. Hordes of cockroaches, sensing the collapse of the earth below, had climbed from the sewers up the elevator shafts and were gorging on the corpse.

"Fair Park dead ahead," Lucia said, and Heff turned his attention gratefully from the sight of the ravaging insects.

Moments later the Caverunner crossed over the line of trees and shrubs bordering the park. The hoverjet's engine startled a pack of dogs hunting squirrels and rats among the trees, and the animals stared up, their marbled eyes wide in terror at the strange craft above them.

Lucia jabbed a hand down toward the right. "There, isn't that a sinkhole on the other side of those pine trees?"

Heff looked down. "You're right," he said, turning to the map. "From the location, I'd say it empties into the main pit about two miles from the mouth of Ralt's tunnel. Let's go down."

Lucia hit the wing retraction switch, and the delta wings slipped smoothly into their storage slots under the cabin. Then she angled the thrust nozzles downward and the Caverunner moved toward the sinkhole below. A minute later they were over the dark abyss, the jets beneath them stirring up dust from the rim of the crater.

"Careful easing through the mouth," Heff warned. "The Caverunner's fifteen feet bow to stern. That opening can't be more than twenty feet across."

Cautiously, Lucia centered the hoverjet over the sinkhole. Then she eased back the thrust throttle, and the Caverunner lowered into the cavity beneath them. The cabin came even with the ground; then the sides of the sinkhole closed in a circle around them and they descended into the earth at a foot a second.

Ten feet down, the roots of the near trees reached out from the surrounding soil, their forking tentacles sending an eerie brushing sound through the cabin as the Caverunner passed through the fibrous collar.

Fifty feet below, the sides of the sinkhole began to slope back, forming an inverted funnel. Soon, the walls had angled away out of range of the lights. All around them now, a black vacuum stretched away into the depths beneath Dallas.

The altimeter on the console before them showed they were 110 feet below the park. "We're in the main pit under the city," Heff said, punching an order into the onboard computer. "We'll navigate with the Gravprobe."

The antenna of the microgravimeter began to turn slowly on the bow, sending sound waves searching out into the black void around them. The returning pulses were interpreted by the computer and displayed like a radar image on the soft green screen before them. An instant later, a warning buzzer suddenly sounded from the console.

"There's an obstruction dead ahead," Heff said. "Descend fifty feet."

Lucia lowered the hoverjet, casting a worried look at the screen. A hundred yards ahead, a huge, rectangular shape jutted down into the sinkhole from the earth crust above.

"What is it?" Lucia asked.

"Building foundation," Heff said. "It's a big one; either the Dallas Convention Center or City Hall."

Lucia shuddered. Both those buildings were huge. They were about to pass directly beneath thousands of tons of concrete and steel.

The Gravprobe continued its circle, and the screen suddenly showed motion through the darkness to port. "What the hell is that?" Heff wondered out loud.

Lucia stared at the screen. "Whatever it is, it's swinging like a pendulum."

Heff flicked the bow light to long range and cast the spot toward the apparition in the distance. The light picked up the glint of metal, and a moment later they saw the macabre metronome.

Before them, a Dallas city transit bus swung slowly back and forth through the black void, its front wheels and axle entangled in a thick power line that stretched tautly up through a sinkhole that had suddenly opened in the street 160 feet above.

The wide emergency door at the rear had burst open as the bus plunged into the sinkhole and was suddenly yanked to a halt at the end of the line.

"The passengers never had a chance," Heff shook his

head. "The sudden drop and the violent swinging motion probably threw them all into the aisles, then out through that open door."

"It must have been horrible." Lucia shuddered as the Caverunner cruised past the twisting, lifeless hulk. "One moment they were riding through Dallas, the next they were falling through the dark under the earth. God have mercy on them."

Heff and Lucia continued on in silence through the cavernous depths, each absorbed in thought. Finally, the Gravprobe sound pulses found the range of the soaring southern wall of the huge sinkhole under Dallas. Moments later, almost two miles from the sinkhole entrance in Fair Park, a tracing of the mouth of the Ralt tunnel appeared on the console screen.

"There's the entrance, about five hundred yards ahead," Heff said, reaching across for her hand. "Ready, co-pilot?"

Lucia squeezed back. "I'm ready, Jedediah."

"Then take us in," Heff said. "We have a rendezvous with a river."

LATE AFTERNOON

The roads from Mexico City toward the U.S. border were clogged with vehicles of every description. Trucks, buses, cars, even farm tractors pulling wagons—everything with wheels had been commandeered by the religious throngs streaming north to rescue the Madonna of Dallas.

Overhead, CHICO watched. The National Reconnaissance Office surveillance satellite focused its television eye first on one road, then another, as the intelligence analysts two thousand miles away in Washington relayed orders to the orbiting probe.

Reconnaissance Office deputy director Joanne Hauser shook her head in disbelief as she stared at the screen. "Good God, there must be a million Mexicans on the move."

"A million armed Mexicans," engineer Mike Pennessi added, zeroing CHICO's camera in for a close-up of one of the truck transports. The focus was near enough to distinguish individual faces. "Some of those people must be in their seventies," Pennessi said sadly.

"Their weapons look as old," Hauser said, pointing at the ancient bolt-action rifles, rusty machetes, pitchforks, and makeshift clubs in the calloused brown hands of the ragged peasants.

"Their firepower may not present much of a threat, but their numbers do," Pennessi said. "There's no way our military can stop hundreds of thousands of them from surging across the border."

Hauser leaned back wearily in her chair. "They'll flood into Texas. God almighty, how do we keep them out? To use modern weapons on those people would be nothing short of genocide."

"Shall I transmit the tape to the Oval Office?" Pennessi asked.

"Yes, the President wants the latest pictures as they come in. I'll alert the White House that the tapes are on the way," Hauser said.

In the White House basement, Secretary of Defense Peter Beaudry took the call from Hauser. "Thank you, Joanne," he said when the deputy director had filled him in. "I'll inform the man."

Ten minutes later Beaudry sat with the President watching the CHICO tape on a television set.

"How long before they reach the border?" President Wilson asked quietly when the transmission ended.

"Our intelligence analysts estimate the first wave will cross into Texas some time early tomorrow morning, Mr. President. There's simply no way to stop them, not without committing ourselves to a massacre of civilians."

"After that fanatical harangue by Martí that the media reported from Mexico City, I doubt anything will stop them before they're kneeling in front of the Madonna of Dallas," the President said. "Any news from that Mexican missile base at Nueva Rosita?"

"Our agent on the ground there confirms that the radioactivity picked up from the base by surveillance satellite is being emitted by a nuclear warhead. It wasn't there yesterday. They apparently trucked it in during the night."

"What about those Mexican soldiers CHICO spotted trying to cut their way into the silo?" the President asked.

"They were political police, Mr. President. They breached the silo about an hour ago. Our agent reports they carried two men out on stretchers. One was General Hugo

Santamaría, commander of Mexico's northern missile defenses, and the other a Soviet missile programmer who just arrived from Moscow."

"Were they dead?"

"Our operative believes they were drugged, Mr. President."

"Drugged. Now all the Mexican political police have to do is ask that Soviet programmer the right questions and Martí has the codes to retarget his missiles for an offensive strike."

"We must assume that Prime Minister Martí can now launch at any time," Beaudry confirmed.

"What are the chances we can shoot down that missile from Nueva Rosita if it's launched against Dallas?"

Beaudry slowly shook his head. "That's the latest-generation Soviet cruise missile. Not only does it skim the ground, which makes it hard enough to shoot down, it also has its own onboard defensive radar hooked into the guidance system. That cruise can detect both incoming ground fire and attacking planes and maneuver itself out of the way. On the short flight from Nueva Rosita to Dallas, our chances of knocking down that Mexican missile are no better than one in five."

The Oval Office door opened and an aide hurried across and handed a note to the President. Wilson read the paper, then rose and gazed through the paned windows toward the floodlit White House grounds outside.

"It's from the Swiss Embassy in Mexico City. They've received a reply to our request for negotiations with Prime Minister Martí."

"His answer, Mr. President?"

Wilson turned slowly. "Martí refuses any talks. He insists the Mexican position is unequivocal. Unless the Rio Grande is returned to its course by dawn tomorrow, he will launch that nuclear warhead against Dallas."

Beaudry looked at his watch. "Twelve hours," he said, his face ashen.

"What's the latest report from Governor Duecker's headquarters?" the President asked. "Is there any chance those speleologists will be able to reverse the flow of the Rio Grande in time?"

"Jedediah Heffernan and his co-pilot are on their way through the tunnel complex. It's likely they'll face a fire fight with the Posse Comitatus. Their success is uncertain at best."

"We can't risk waiting to know the outcome," President Wilson said. "Put our military on alert worldwide, Peter. If that Mexican missile detonates over Dallas, we will have no choice. We will go to war."

EVENING

The twenty-eight-mile-long tunnel gorged out by the engineers of Otto Ralt's Colorado Mine and Mineral ran south from Dallas straight as an arrow toward the northern terminus of the Rio Bajo la Tierra.

In the Caverunner, Lucia Sanchez made occasional slight course corrections necessary every mile or so to keep the hoverjet centered in the bore.

"How much farther?" she asked Jedediah Heffernan beside her.

Heff calculated their speed and position with the onboard computer, then transposed the figures to the Ralt map.

"Three and a quarter miles to the pump station," he said. "We should be there in about half an hour."

At the main pump station six thousand yards ahead, Otto Ralt stared at his own computer monitor. The destruction of the subterranean dam near Rocksprings had set back his timetable several hours. The waters of the Rio Grande should have reached the pump by now and be on the way toward the bowels of Dallas.

Instead, the flow had had to be channeled through a parallel tunnel around the blown dike. The sensors set in the walls of the Rio Bajo signaled the computer that the headwaters were still sixty-four miles south of the pump station.

A pneumatic door opened in the station wall and Karl Stroesser walked in. "My men are all in position," the Posse Comitatus captain reported. "We're ready for them."

"Are all the feeder tunnels guarded?" Ralt asked.

"Every one that could possibly be reached from a sinkhole above. I have eighty men strung out between here and Rocksprings. If those intruders come back, we'll shoot the bastards to pieces."

At that moment, a low beeping sound pulsed from the monitoring equipment behind them. Ralt whirled around and stared at the computer screen. The radar warning system he'd placed in the passages around the station had picked up an approaching vehicle. Only the threat wasn't coming at them from the Rio Bajo where Stroesser's men waited in ambush. The intruders were three miles to the north.

"They're in the tunnel to Dallas," Ralt hissed, his voice a mix of disbelief and rage.

Stroesser gaped at the monitor. "How? How'd they find that entrance?"

The same question worked at Ralt. The discovery of the dam north of Rocksprings had obviously been pure chance. Jedediah Heffernan had entered the Rio Bajo on a search for a lost boy, and he'd come in through a sinkhole pocking the prairie in plain sight.

The approach through the tunnel from Dallas could be no accident. Finding the mouth of the passage in the huge, curving wall of the cavity under Dallas would have been the equivalent of spotting a pinhole in the bowl of a coffee cup.

Heffernan had to have a map. But where would he have gotten it? Was there a traitor among the Posse Comitatus? Sneed? Stroesser? Then it struck him. Rebecca. It could be no one else. That computer printout he'd flung at her in rage. She'd kept it. She'd used it against him.

Ralt shook with fury. Rebecca would join those five thousand dead Mexican soldiers drifting through the depths toward Dallas. Today. As soon as he'd dealt with the threat before him.

"I'll call my men back," Stroesser said, reaching for the radio phone on the control board.

"There's no time for that, you fool," Ralt snapped. "Break out two assault rifles. We'll have to stop them ourselves."

In the Caverunner, a small bell chimed and a warning suddenly appeared on the computer monitor before Heff and Lucia: INCOMING RADAR PULSE.

Heff came forward in his seat. "Damn, their radar defenses have picked us up." He punched a command into the computer and the Gravprobe antenna began to swing first right, then left, scanning the tunnel walls ahead.

"What are you doing?" Lucia asked.

"We're too easy a target in this tube," Heff said. "The map shows a series of small caves running behind the wall along here. We have to get into those passages where they can't get a clear shot at us."

The Gravprobe buzzed and they stared at the screen. The echo sounder had picked up a hollow finger behind six feet of tunnel wall to starboard.

"Dead stop," Heff said.

Lucia eased back on the thrust throttle.

Heff leaned forward and turned on the laser cannon. He reached for the manual control lever mounted on the instrument panel before him and swung the laser to the right. Then he aimed at a point midway up the tunnel wall and pulled the trigger.

A blinding shaft of dazzling white light shot from the barrel and burned into the soft limestone wall twenty yards ahead.

Lucia watched in fascination as the stone began to smoke, then crumble and fall away in great chunks. Even sixty-five feet away they could feel the intense heat from the disintegrating rock.

Ninety seconds later, the laser beam broke through to the

passage beyond, leaving a six- by six-foot corridor through the tunnel wall. Heff shut down the cannon.

"Slow forward," he said to Lucia.

"That's not much of an opening, Jedediah," Lucia said dubiously.

"You'll have about six inches' clearance on each side," Heff said.

"Great. If I dent this thing, don't blame me."

"Want me to take her through?"

"Hell, no," Lucia answered. She set her jaw and eased the nose of the Caverunner into the narrow channel. On each side, smoldering rocks still glowed faintly with heat, and the temperature shot up rapidly in the cabin. Then they were through, and Lucia guided the hoverjet down the low, narrow cave beyond.

Heff studied the Ralt map. "The passage we're in will squeeze down about a mile ahead," he said. "We'll have to leave the Caverunner there and go the rest of the way on foot."

In the pump station to the south, Ralt and Stroesser watched the hoverjet's image disappear from the radar screen.

"Where the hell did they go?" Stroesser asked in bewilderment.

Ralt keyed the computer, and a chart of the cave system around them appeared on the monitor. He jabbed a finger against the screen. "There. They're in that small run of caves parallel to the tunnel wall."

Stroesser stared at the irregular conflux of passages on the screen. "It's going to be hard to flush the bastards out of those caves, Mr. Ralt."

"I don't intend to go in there after them, Karl," Ralt said. "We'll let them come to us. The only passage out of those caves leads into the Rio Bajo about a hundred yards south of the pump station. We'll wait for them there."

Lucia slowed the hoverjet as the avenue before them began to pinch inward. She looked across uncertainly at Heff.

"This is as far as we can go in the Caverunner," he said. "Shut her down."

Heff popped the bubble and swung over the side. He opened the cargo hatch and took out the satchel of plastic explosive, along with lights and his crossbow and grappling iron.

"According to the map, there's a thirty- or forty-foot vertical cliff about halfway to the pump station," he said, strapping the bow to his pack. "We'll have to climb."

He shouldered the pack and handed a hat light to Lucia. "Ready?"

"No," she said. "But then I haven't been ready for anything that's happened in the last five days. Let's go."

Fifty yards from the Caverunner, the passage narrowed to a five-foot defile through the limestone. In several places, they had to squeeze through clefts where the walls were only fourteen to sixteen inches apart.

"Do you know where you're going to take me when we get the hell out of here, Jedediah?" Lucia said, her teeth clenched as she wiggled through a narrow neck.

Ahead, Heff grinned in the tight tunnel. "Where?"

"Dancing," she said. "Waltzing, to be more specific. Across an immensely wide dance floor out on the prairie under the sky."

Heff laughed. He'd had the same hunger for wide open spaces the first time he'd caved. "I'll have my suit pressed."

"Suit, nothing. I'm going to rent you a tie and tails. And a limousine. A big wide limo with a sunroof and room to stretch our legs out as far as we want."

Lucia kept up the banter, easing the oppressive air of the passage, and fifteen minutes later they reached the cliff Heff had spotted on the map.

Heff unfastened the crossbow and grappling iron. He looked up toward the top of the precipice, his hat light following his eyes to the jutting rock lip thirty-five feet above.

"Better throw your light up there, Lucia," he said, setting the shaft of the grappling iron into the bow and adjusting the bowstring tension. "If you recall the falls, I miss occasionally. Be ready to dive out of the way."

Heff aimed the crossbow and pulled the trigger. The bowstring snapped forward and the grappling hook flew upward, the attached cave rope uncoiling behind. The three-pronged iron disappeared over the lip of the cliff, and they could hear it clang against the rocks in the tunnel mouth above. Heff snagged the hook with a quick yank, and they started climbing.

After her experience at the stone waterfall, Lucia was no longer a novice at scaling a rock face, and it took them only five minutes to reach the top of the cliff. Before them, an oval-shaped tunnel eight feet high and almost thirty feet wide stretched away into the dark.

Heff strapped the crossbow and grappling iron back on his pack. "It should be an easy walk the rest of the way," he said, glancing at the map.

"Ralt knows we're here now," Lucia said. "You don't expect him to just let us stroll up and blow his pump station to smithereens, do you?"

"He'll be waiting for us, all right," Heff said. "But Otto Ralt has spent his life in boardrooms and mansions and private jetliners. Caves are an unknown dimension to a man like that. Sounds, perspective, reactions—everything's different beneath the earth. We're in our environment down here, Lucia, and we'll fight him on our terms."

"I'm glad you said 'our,' Jedediah," Lucia said.

"I meant it. We're in this together, win or lose."

"Any idea where he'll be waiting?" Lucia asked.

"Probably where this passage meets the main tunnel of the Rio Bajo. We should be there in a few minutes."

Five hundred yards ahead, Otto Ralt crouched at the entrance to the Rio Bajo. Across the tunnel, Karl Stroesser fingered the trigger of his AK-47 assault rifle. They waited in silence, their eyes probing the dark corridor before them. Then the first faint glow of the intruders' lights appeared from around a bend forty yards away.

"Here they come," Ralt said in a hoarse whisper.

A moment later, they could see the beams of two hat

lights turn the corner as Heff and Lucia emerged into the straight avenue leading toward the pump site.

"Now!" Ralt shouted, leaping out from the wall with his assault rifle barking. Had the billionaire waited, had he not mistaken shadow for substance in the distance, he could not have missed his targets only 120 feet away down the tube.

But the betrayal of his wife, and the penetration of his secret lair, had unnerved Otto Ralt, infuriated him to the point where his normal caution and control had dissipated in a flood of hate.

He was consumed with but one thought: to send death down the tunnel, to kill those who were coming to destroy his only chance to save Dallas and the empire he had worked all his life to build.

At the first flash from Ralt's rifle, Heff dove for Lucia, tackling her and pinning her to the sandy cave floor. Almost simultaneously, Stroesser opened fire, and a hail of bullets ricocheted off the walls around them.

A bullet found Heff's upper left arm, passing through the muscle and flesh near the bone. He grunted deep in his chest and rolled to the side.

"Kill those lights," Heff said through clenched teeth, crawling toward a low mound of debris against the cave wall.

In the moment before she dug the hat lights from the sand and flipped off the bulbs, Lucia saw the blood soaking Heff's shirt.

"You're hit," she said, finding Heff's body in the dark and scrambling next to him.

Another fusillade of submachine gun fire whistled overhead.

"I'll be all right," Heff said, the shock of the bullet through his arm beginning to subside to a dull ache.

Lucia's hands probed his wounded arm. "You're bleeding badly, Jedediah," she said, feeling his shirt sleeve sticky-wet from elbow to shoulder. "I'll need a light to bandage you."

Twin bursts from the guns of Ralt and Stroesser spattered the near walls of the cave.

"No lights," Heff said, slipping off his pack. He undid the straps and searched inside. He found the first-aid kit and brought it to Lucia's hand.

"Wrap a pressure bandage around it. That will have to do for now."

While Lucia bound his wound, Heff searched in his pack with his right hand for the cave knife he always carried. It was a duplicate of the knife he'd used to butcher Alex, and for a terrible instant it all came back: Alex's blood dripping down to soak his body, Alex's dead eyes staring at him through the dark.

He fought the terrible thought of what he now had to do. Once again he must sink the knife into a man, this time a man still alive. Could he do it? Even to save his own life and Lucia's, could he use the knife again?

Lucia felt him tense in the dark. "Am I hurting you?"

"No," Heff said, the sound of her voice wrenching him back from the paralyzing vision of Alex. "I'm going after them."

"Jedediah, no," Lucia pleaded. "They have guns. Let's go back and get the soldiers."

Again, the air over their heads was split by rifle fire from the sides of the tunnel ahead.

"There's no time, Lucia," he said as she tied off the gauze. "Besides, guns aren't that much of an advantage in the dark. I know how to move through black caves. And I know where they are now."

"Jedediah, please."

"Don't, Lucia. It's the only way, you know that. If we don't seal off the Rio Bajo soon, it could mean war. Nuclear war. Our lives don't mean much measured against that."

Lucia clutched his hand. "What can I do?"

"Give me a couple of minutes' head start, then follow with the plastic explosive. There are two low piles of rock debris between us and Ralt. Keep low against the cave wall, then wait behind the second pile until I knock out their guns." He slipped the cave knife into the top of his boot and squeezed Lucia's hand. "Remember, keep down," he whispered, then was gone down the dark passage on his stomach before Lucia could protest again.

Forty yards ahead, Karl Stroesser broke into a cold sweat at the silence down the dark tube. He had fought in the jungle and in the desert, but this blind battle under the earth was different—horrifyingly different—like being in a sack with a snake. The attack could come from anywhere.

"Do you think we got them?" he whispered to Ralt across the tunnel.

"I don't know," Ralt said. "We'll wait."

"How about throwing a light down there?"

"You're likely to get a bullet back, Karl. Wait."

Heff stayed close to the left wall as he crawled down the tube, the wound in his arm throbbing painfully. He counted in his head each body length forward, calculating the distance to the mouth of the tunnel where Ralt and his accomplice blocked the entrance to the Rio Bajo.

Behind him, Lucia began to squirm forward over the cave sand, her hand feeling her way along the side of the corridor.

Heff snaked over the first mound of debris and reached the sand floor on the other side. He'd only had a fleeting glimpse of the cave ahead before the guns erupted, but the picture his eyes had taken was sharp in his mind. The second pile of rocks was eight or ten yards ahead. After that it was another fifteen yards to Ralt's position.

Three minutes later he reached the last rock mound. As he started over, his boot kicked a stone loose and it clattered down the low hill.

Karl Stroesser tensed at the near sound. "What was that?"

"A stone falling," Ralt said. "Take it easy, Karl."

Heff slipped his cave knife from his boot and started forward again across the soft sand. He crawled slowly, one elbow and knee at a time, listening, feeling through the dark with every sense but his eyes. He heard a low metallic clink, the scrape of a gun barrel against rock. A yard farther and he could hear heavy breathing. He inched ahead now.

The smell of sweat wafted toward him, and he knew he was near enough.

Very slowly, his hand on the cave wall, Heff rose to a crouch and slid one foot forward. The rifleman could be no more than three feet away through the dark. He tensed, the knife tight in his hand, then hurled himself forward, turning his body to strike with the force of his shoulders. He felt a rifle barrel brush against his back as he hit and fell on the invisible body in the dark.

Stroesser screamed as he fell backward, his assault rifle clattering away against the wall as he fell. Heff landed on top, his hands flying to the mercenary's neck, then to his chin. In one move, Heff rolled to the side, jerked back Stroesser's head, and cut open his throat.

The Posse Comitatus killer gurgled as blood filled his windpipe, then jerked spasmodically and lay still.

Ten feet away, Otto Ralt half flattened himself against the cave wall at the sound of the near struggle. "Karl?" He probed the black. "Karl?"

Heff lifted himself off Stroesser's body and started toward Ralt's voice.

"Karl?" Ralt tried once more. When there was no answer, he yanked his flashlight from his pocket and turned it on. Six feet away, Heff froze in the sudden glare, a sick feeling in his gut as he stared at the barrel of Ralt's AK-47 pointing at him past the bright round face of the flashlight.

Behind the far mound of cave debris, Lucia sucked in a short sharp breath at the sight of Jedediah in the center of a pool of light. In the back glow she could see Otto Ralt with a submachine gun in his hands. She slid over the rocks and crawled forward to the second pile of stones forty feet from the men.

"Mr. Heffernan, I've been expecting you," Ralt said, hard triumph in his voice. "You have caused me a great deal of trouble."

Heff straightened. "There's a company of National Guard troops on the way down here, Ralt," he bluffed. "I suggest you hand me that rifle."

Ralt smiled thinly. "I think not. I watched your lights coming. There are only two of you.

"Keep your gun on him, Lucia," Heff tried another tack.

Ralt let out a hollow laugh. "I'll give you credit for trying, Mr. Heffernan, but the fact is you and your friend have no guns. If you did, you'd have returned our fire."

Heff turned toward the passage behind. "Lucia, go back. Take the Caverunner and get out."

Lucia peered anxiously over the mound, indecision tearing at her. If only she had a gun, a knife, anything.

"You in the tunnel," Ralt called. "If you don't come forward with your hands up in ten seconds, I'll kill Heffernan."

Lucia froze.

"Don't, Lucia, he'll just kill us both," Heff yelled. "Get back to the Caverunner."

"One," Ralt started.

Frantically, Lucia searched Heff's pack for a weapon. A steel piton? The scissors from the first-aid kit?

"Two."

Lucia rejected both the objects. She'd never get close enough to use them.

"Three."

"Go back, Lucia."

Her mind raced. A rock? Could she hit Ralt from this distance with a rock?

"Four."

She found a large stone, then looked back, her heart sinking. It was too far a throw.

"Five."

Suddenly, she remembered Heff's crossbow. Her hands went back to the pack, and she tore at the straps holding the bow and grappling iron.

"Six."

Lucia pulled the bow free and quickly drew the bowstring back toward the trigger catch. Halfway there, the string snapped back out of her fingers.

"Seven."

She tried again, pulling with all her strength now, and at last the string caught on the trigger release.

"Eight."

Her hands shaking, Lucia fitted the shaft of the grappling iron into the groove along the crossbow stock and slipped the projectile back against the taut string.

"Nine."

"Don't do it, Lucia," Heff called again.

Lucia took a deep breath, willing her hands to steady. "Ten."

Lucia sprang to her feet and aimed the bow at the light forty feet away down the tunnel. "Ralt!" she screamed at the top of her voice.

The billionaire swung his flashlight, searching for Lucia down the dark tunnel. He saw her and brought the sub-machine gun to his shoulder. At that instant, Lucia fired. The grappling hook shot down the tube and smashed into Ralt's chest, knocking him back in a heap against the cave wall.

Heff leapt forward and picked up Ralt's light, then whirled toward the stricken form in the sand. Otto Ralt's chest had been caved in by the force of the grappling iron and the blood of his heart sac was seeping out through the torn flesh and shattered ribs. The richest man in America lay dead on the floor of the Rio Bajo la Tierra.

Heff turned as Lucia ran toward him down the tunnel. A moment later she was in his arms and they were clinging to each other.

"We're almost there, Lucia," Heff said finally. "Let's finish the job we came to do and get out of here."

They clung to each other a moment longer, then went back and retrieved the pack of explosives. Five minutes later, their lights picked up the huge round metal face of the main pump set into the walls of the Rio Bajo.

Heff placed charges where the steel pump casing met the walls, then set the timers. "When the walls blow, the ceiling will come down on both sides of the pump," he said. "The Rio Bajo will be blocked with a plug a hundred yards thick."

"How much time did you give us?" Lucia asked.

"Fifteen minutes. We'll be far enough back down the tunnel by then to be safe from any secondary cave-ins. Let's go."

Heff and Lucia had just descended the cliff when the plastic explosive went off behind them. Even half a mile from the site of the explosion, the sound of tearing metal and falling rock rolled over them like a dull peal of thunder.

"That's it," Heff said. "As soon as the waters reach that plug, the river will begin backing up through the cave system to the south. The Rio Grande should be back in its bed along the border sometime early tomorrow morning."

Twenty minutes later, they reached the Caverunner. Lucia rebandaged Heff's arm, then they sped down the tunnel to Dallas and out into the huge sinkhole under the city. Two hours after they'd set the charges, the Caverunner nosed up through the earth of Fair Park into a starlit Texas night.

Lucia reached for a switch on the control panel, and the delta wings hummed out from the fuselage and locked into place on either side of the hoverjet. As they gained altitude over the dead city, both of them gulped down the fresh night air.

"What's our heading?" Lucia asked, angling the thrust nozzles back to the horizontal flight position.

"West, back to the governor's headquarters," Heff said, picking up the radiophone. "I'll let them know the Rio Bajo is plugged. They have to get the word to Prime Minister Martí fast, before he starts a war over the river."

"Do you think we were in time, Jedediah?"

Heff shook his head slowly. "I don't know, Lucia. I just don't know."

Lucia swung the Caverunner toward Mineral Wells while Heff waited for Governor Duecker to come on the phone.

Behind them, Parkland Memorial Hospital sank like a stone into the prairie. Elsewhere around the city, other buildings were being sucked into the earth, and everywhere large depressions were beginning to appear.

Dallas had only hours left.

11:30 P.M.

Ignacio Baptista rose from the silent knot of Chicano leaders before the television set in his small frame farmhouse and walked alone out onto his sagging front porch.

The TV news tape of Prime Minister Martí's harangue from the balcony of his presidential palace had sickened the fruit farmer, and the live coverage of President Wilson's response had left his stomach a tight steel ball of foreboding.

The cars and trucks of the faithful littered his farmyard and blocked the long drive bumper-to-bumper to the highway, where they lined the concrete for miles in each direction.

He took a deep breath of cool night air and looked toward the sinkhole in the trampled melon fields beyond his barn. The hand-held candles of nearly a quarter million worshipers shimmered from the shrine of the Madonna, and he could hear the distant murmur of a communal rosary being said.

Baptista struggled to understand what was happening to him and to his people. His was the worst nightmare of the immigrant: the country of his birth approaching war with the country that had adopted him forty-five years past.

The battle with the Texas Rangers had been the darkest

hour of the gentle farmer's life. So many dead, on both sides. And now the television was showing a million Mexicans surging north to battle with Americans over the Madonna out there in his field.

Baptista and his fellow Chicanos had sat stunned and ashamed as they watched the news tape of Prime Minister Martí lying to his people, exhorting them to violence from his palace balcony in Mexico City.

Martí had distorted everything. It was true the Madonna had been under siege for a time by the Rangers and the National Guard, but Baptista now understood it had all happened because individual men had failed to communicate with each other.

Governor Duecker had promised him that it was not the policy of Texas or the government of the United States to persecute religious expression. The shrine of the Madonna of Dallas would be left in peace.

Baptista believed the governor, just as he believed the words of President Wilson on television. The destruction of the Che Guevara Division and the diversion of the Rio Grande north into Texas had been the work of right-wing fanatics, the President had said. He had just received word from Texas that two American speleologists had penetrated the subterranean river system through which the Rio Grande flowed and dammed the main channel ahead. The Rio Grande would return to its bed along the border shortly after dawn this morning.

President Wilson's final words had stuck in Baptista's mind: "The United States does not wish war with Mexico. To Prime Minister Martí, we say, 'Stay your missiles, stop your people from crossing the border.' For the sake of untold thousands of innocent lives, let us reason together."

Baptista shifted his weight on his old rheumatic knees and stared toward the distant flickering candles. The millions advancing from Mexico City could not know of the President's words and would not believe the truth of them were they told. Theirs was a religious crusade, and only the physical presence, the sight of the Madonna of Dallas, would absorb the passions that drove them.

Father Timothy Quinn came out on the porch and put a
hand on Baptista's shoulder. For a time the two stood
quietly together, listening to the muffled litany of the rosary
drifting across the farmyard from the shrine.

"Tell me what is in your heart, Ignacio," the priest said
after a while.

"Death, Father." Baptista sighed. "My heart is full of the
death that will come with the sun."

"Do you know what tears at me, Ignacio?" Father Quinn
said. "Those many from both sides who are now doomed to
die at the border will fall for equally just and fervent causes.
The Mexicans are crusading north to defend Our Lady, and
the Americans who face them will be defending their
country. Whether they follow the cross or the flag, each
man's death will be glorious, sanctified by principle, and
utterly useless."

"I keep expecting Our Lady to provide a miracle,"
Baptista said quietly. "Perhaps, before the dawn, she will."

"It's a funny thing about miracles, Ignacio," the priest
said, the lilt of County Mayo in his soft voice. "Sometimes
we expect divine intervention, when God has put it in our
way to work the miracle ourselves."

"What are you getting at in your Irish way, Father?"

The priest smiled. "There is a pertinent saying among our
Muslim brothers: 'If Muhammad cannot go to the mountain, then the mountain must come to Muhammad.'"

Baptista stared toward the shrine. "You think we should
take the Madonna to Mexico?"

"To the border, perhaps to the United Nations post on
Santa Teresa Island between Eagle Pass and Piedras Negras.
The UN base is considered international territory. The
Madonna could be worshiped there in peace by both
Mexicans and Americans."

"If that is what you think best, Father."

"No, Ignacio, it is what *you* think that matters. Our Lady
first revealed herself to you. Her shrine is part of your land.
You must make the decision."

"I believe the decision has already been written, Father,"
Baptista said. "It is there to be seen in the face of the

Madonna. Our Lady has come to be the mother of our people, not their murderess. We will take the Madonna south. We will take her in peace."

"I'll make the arrangements," Father Quinn said, turning for the phone inside.

Within forty-five minutes, Governor Duecker had a flatbed truck and a crane at the side of the sinkhole. Baptista and the priest explained to the worshipers at the shrine what must be done, and then the fused stone figures of the Madonna and child were lifted carefully onto the truck bed. Thirty of the faithful took places as an escort around her.

Under orders from Duecker, the bus drivers who had just finished evacuating Dallas were recalled and the entire municipal fleet of 980 buses was dispatched to the Baptista farm. As many of the worshipers as possible crammed onto the dusty buses, while the rest dispersed to cars to follow in procession. With a phalanx of screaming police motorcycles leading the way, and the highways cleared by gubernatorial fiat, the procession sped south.

Overhead, TV helicopters tracked the convoy, and around the world people sat before their sets, watching the distant race against war.

DAY FIVE

APRIL 14, 1999

AN HOUR BEFORE DAWN

Teodoro Luis Martí was staring out the window of his office in the presidential palace, his gaze fixed on the eastern horizon, when he heard his aide open the door behind him and stride across the wide marble floor.

"Comrade Prime Minister, I am sorry to interrupt you," the aide said with trepidation. The normally fiery Martí had been volcanic of late.

"What is it?" Martí asked, continuing to stare out the window.

"As you know, sir, we have been monitoring the American television. All three of their major networks are now showing pictures of the Madonna arriving in Eagle Pass, Texas."

"Across the border from Piedras Negras?"

"Yes, Prime Minister. The television commentators are saying the Madonna will be brought to the United Nations post on Santa Teresa Island between the two cities."

"Santa Teresa Island. Of course." Martí turned. "The UN compound there is neutral territory. So, after centuries of abuse, the *yanquis* have suddenly turned altruistic toward Mexico. They are willing to relinquish the Madonna of Dallas to international hands so that our people may share in worshiping at the shrine. Is this what they would have us believe?"

"The newscasters say it was the decision of the Chicanos of Dallas to bring the Madonna to the border," the aide ventured timidly.

Martí scoffed. "Nonsense, they were coerced into it by those *yanqui* bastards in Washington. Now get out!"

The aide nodded and turned for the door.

"I want to be notified the moment those programmers at Nueva Rosita finish retargeting," the prime minister shouted after the retreating captain.

"Immediately, Prime Minister." The aide closed the door behind him.

Martí returned to his vigil of the eastern horizon. He had to admit it had been a brilliant tactical move, however they had persuaded the Chicanos in Texas to bring the Madonna to the UN post on the border. With that one stroke, the *yanquis* had neutralized Martí's million-strong army of civilian crusaders.

As soon as the fervent masses heading for Texas heard of the Madonna's presence on the border, the angry peasants would dissolve into so many docile worshipers at a shrine.

Could it be any coincidence that President Wilson promised the river would return "sometime in the morning," presumably hours after Martí's dawn ultimatum? Suppose he stayed the missile, then the *yanquis* announced a delay—the river would return by afternoon, or evening, or the next damn day?

Every hour gained would be that much more time for them to prepare their missile defenses around Dallas. Martí knew it wouldn't be long before the odds against his nuclear warhead getting through shifted in favor of the United States.

Slowly his face became a mask of resolution. If the dawn deadline passed, he would strike while he still had strength. He would not allow hours of indecision to whittle him down to a powerless puppet.

Behind him, the intercom buzzed and Martí strode to his large ornate mahogany desk. "Yes?"

"Colonel Vargas is calling from Nueva Rosita, Prime Minister."

"Put him through," Martí ordered. He picked up the phone, and a moment later the political police commander came on.

"Comrade Prime Minister, we have just finished running the last program here. We are ready to launch."

Martí looked at his watch. It was 5:45 A.M. The official sunrise this morning would come at 6:40 A.M. "Begin the countdown at launch minus fifty-five minutes, starting now, colonel," Martí ordered. "If the Bravo del Norte has not returned to its bed by dawn, we will send the warhead north against Dallas."

JUST BEFORE DAWN

Jedediah Heffernan strode into Governor Duecker's head-quarters outside Mineral Wells and plopped a tape from the Caverunner's Gravprobe on a desk before Lucia Sanchez.

Most of the headquarters staff had been evacuated in the face of the Mexican nuclear missile threat, and while Heff made a solo Gravprobe reconnaissance over Dallas in the hoverjet, Lucia had remained behind to monitor incoming Landsat data.

The satellite's Thermatic Mapper continued to scan the predawn prairie below, tracing the subterranean progress south of the now dammed Rio Grande River.

Lucia looked up and smiled. "How was your flight?"

"Lonely."

"Why, Jedediah, you missed me."

"Yes and no."

Lucia laughed, and Heff sank wearily into a chair beside her.

"That Gravprobe tape is pretty depressing," he said. "Do you know what the city reminded me of, Lucia? The burial site at a funeral, with the casket resting on boards across the open grave. Dallas is like that, a corpse over its own waiting grave."

"You look tired," Lucia said. "How's your arm?"

"Sore," Heff said. "I need a nurse near me. You were right, I missed you on that patrol."

Lucia leaned forward and kissed him, then brushed her lips against his ear. "Jedediah, I missed you too. I couldn't keep my mind on my work, thinking about you alone out there in the dark."

They held each other for a moment, then Heff kissed her softly and rose. "I've got to report to the governor."

"He wants the latest Landsat scans," Lucia said, hitting a button for a computer printout of the image on the monitor before her. "I'll go with you."

Lynn Duecker watched the Gravprobe tape, then sank back in his chair with a sigh. "There's not much holding the city up, is there?"

"Only scattered islands of columns and arches are supporting the crust now," Heff said. "And those are crumbling rapidly. Most of the cavern system under Dallas has collapsed into the main pit."

The governor turned to Lucia. "How far south has the Rio Grande returned?"

"The Landsat shows the waters now approximately twenty miles north of the border, governor," Lucia said. "The river should resurface about seven-oh-six A.M."

Duecker slowly shook his head. "Sunrise is at six forty. If Martí's ultimatum stands, we'll miss his deadline by twenty-six minutes."

Heff nodded toward the bank of television monitors showing the live broadcasts of the three major American TV networks from Santa Teresa Island. The Madonna of Dallas had been placed on a small knoll, and thousands of faithful were swarming over the island. Hundreds of thousands more lined the banks on both sides of the border.

"We'd better warn the United Nations people to keep those crowds out of the main river channel," Heff said. "In about forty minutes the Rio will surface upstream, and an hour later it will flood down past Saint Teresa Island bank to bank."

Duecker called an aide over and instructed him to contact the UN command on the island. As he turned back to the monitors, the screens flicked one after another to close-ups of Ignacio Baptista and Father Quinn welcoming Mexican worshipers to the shrine.

"That farmer and that priest ought to be nominated for the Nobel Peace Prize," Duecker said.

The three watched the scene of rejoicing silently for a moment; then the red videophone buzzed on the governor's desk. It was the direct line to the Oval Office, and Duecker reached forward quickly and turned on the transceiver.

"Governor Duecker," he said, instinctively straightening his wrinkled tie for his electronic appearance before the President.

"I'm afraid we've about run out of time, Lynn," President Wilson said from behind his large rosewood desk. "We've just received a reply through the Swiss Embassy in Mexico City to our last letter to Prime Minister Martí. He's rejected any negotiations."

Duecker sagged visibly at the President's words. "Then Martí's ultimatum remains in effect?"

President Wilson nodded gravely, his lips compressed in a hard line. "Martí's position hasn't changed. If the Rio Grande has not returned to its bed by sunrise, he will launch his nuclear warhead against Dallas."

"The latest Landsat scan shows the river still well north of the border, Mr. President," Duecker said. "We're going to miss Martí's deadline by almost half an hour."

"Then I advise you to evacuate everyone immediately, Lynn. Sunrise comes in about fifteen minutes down there. If Martí launches on schedule, my ballistics experts calculate that nuclear warhead will reach Dallas less than twenty minutes later."

"I'm going to need your help resettling the citizens of central Texas, Mr. President. To lose Dallas was terrible enough for my people. Now, with thousands of square miles around the city about to be poisoned by radioactive fallout, Texas will lie devastated."

"Don't abandon all hope yet, Lynn," the President said. "We've thrown up two lines of antiballistic missile batteries between Nueva Rosita and Dallas. In addition, our fighter pilots will be positioned to attack that Mexican missile as soon as it enters American airspace."

"I want you to be candid with me, sir," Duecker said. "What are the odds our defenses can stop that missile?"

"You have the right to know. Our chances are slim. That's a state-of-the-art Soviet cruise missile Martí plans to send against Dallas. My air force people tell me it has its own defensive radar system constantly feeding data to the onboard computer that guides it. The damn thing can 'see' our antiballistic stuff coming and maneuver itself out of the way."

Heff tapped Duecker on the shoulder. "May I address the President?"

Duecker turned back to the videophone. "Jedediah Heffernan and Lucia Sanchez are here with me, Mr. President. They're the speleologists who—"

"I know who they are, Lynn. I saw the network broadcast of them returning this morning from the Rio Bajo," the President said. "Mr. Heffernan, Miss Sanchez, I want to commend you personally for the skill and daring you showed in blocking that tunnel. You're two very brave people."

"For Lucia and myself, thank you, Mr. President," Heff said.

"You wanted to say something, Mr. Heffernan?"

"I'd like to volunteer my hoverjet for the defense of Dallas, Mr. President. She's armed with a laser cannon. What matters more, I believe I can evade that missile's radar defenses and get in much closer than our air force fighters."

"Is this hoverjet of yours so much faster than our attack planes?"

"On the contrary, sir, the Caverunner is far slower. That's the point. As you just told Governor Duecker, that cruise radar is programmed to pick up antiballistic missiles and enemy planes coming at it at great speed. The radar then orders the guidance system to take appropriate evasive action."

"Yes, but even at a lower speed, won't that cruise radar

still pick up your hoverjet approaching?" the President asked.

"I won't be moving at all, Mr. President. I intend to hover dead still along the glide path of the cruise and at the same low altitude, two hundred feet or so above the ground. The missile's radar will read the Caverunner as a water tower or a grain silo, perhaps the top of a small hill."

The President grinned in comprehension. "You mean to ambush it."

"Exactly, sir. When the missile gets close enough, I'll switch my engine thrust from vertical hover to horizontal propulsion and leap out on the tail of that missile. If I'm lucky, I should be able to get off a couple of blasts with my laser cannon before the cruise is out of range."

"If you believe you have a chance to bring down that Mexican missile, Mr. Heffernan, I must allow you to take it. I'll arrange to have your aircraft patched into our defense communications down there."

"Thank you, Mr. President."

"Good luck to all of you," the President said. "And may God save Texas."

The videophone went blank, and Heff and Lucia shook hands good-bye with the governor. Then Duecker and his staff jogged toward a waiting helicopter while Heff and Lucia hurried to the Caverunner.

"I didn't appreciate your volunteering me, Jedediah," Lucia said as they darted across the parking lot.

Heff threw up his hands as they ran. "If I live to be two hundred years old and acquire the wisdom of Job, I will never ever understand you, Lucia," he said. "For the past three days I haven't been able to start the Caverunner without you running up my chest to get in the co-pilot's seat. Now, the first time I accept your company as inevitable, you don't want to go."

"I didn't say I didn't want to go."

They reached the hoverjet. "Then what did you say?"

"I said I didn't appreciate you volunteering me. I make that sort of decision myself."

Heff plopped himself into the pilot's seat. "I thought we

were a team, and that's what I volunteered. Not you or me individually, but a team."

Lucia climbed into the cabin beside Heff. "Since you put it that way, I accept your explanation."

"That's damn decent of you. Now, if there's no further debate, perhaps we could get this thing into the air."

Heff eased the thrust throttle forward, and the Caverunner rose in a swirl of dust from the parking lot. The radio squawked to life as the hoverjet gained altitude.

"Texas Air Defense headquarters to civilian aircraft Caverunner."

Heff adjusted his throat mike. "Caverunner here, Air Defense."

"We've been ordered to patch you in to satellite and ground communications. Please stand by to receive the live television broadcast from CHICO first."

Heff punched a code into the communications computer, and the video monitor flickered on. The screen showed the shadowed Mexican missile pad at Nueva Rosita as it might look from the top of a nearby tall building.

"We have satellite video," Heff said, then quickly keyed the radio and radar relay settings that followed from Air Defense into the Caverunner's onboard computer.

"I don't want to fly into friendly fire, Air Defense," Heff said when he'd finished locking in communications. "Can you give me the deployment of our surface-to-air stuff below?"

"Affirmative. Our first Shield Line runs from San Antonio northwest to Sonora. Our antiballistic missile batteries down there are centered approximately ninety-five miles north of the border. Shield Line Two, our inner defenses, is eighty miles south of Dallas, running from Abilene down through Waco."

"We don't have time to fly very far south, Air Defense. If that Mexican missile gets through your lines, I'll attempt to intercept just north of Waco."

"I'll notify all our ground and air forces that you'll be operating in the area. Good luck, Caverunner."

Heff hit the wing extension switch, and the two delta

wings swung out and locked into position on each side of
the craft. Then he swiveled the jet nozzles to horizontal
thrust and the Caverunner shot forward over the prairie,
hurtling southwest at almost four hundred knots.

Suddenly Lucia shot forward in her seat, pointing at the
television picture from Nueva Rosita on the monitor. "The
silo doors are opening."

Heff and Lucia stared silently as the huge steel plates
capping the Mexican missile tube slid slowly apart. Inside,
the nose of the rocket was just visible, pointing up toward
the predawn gloom of northern Mexico.

Heff glanced at his watch. "It's six thirty-eight. We don't
have much time."

In Mexico City a thousand miles to the south, Teodoro
Luis Martí was also looking at his watch. Two minutes to
dawn. He leaned over his desk and pressed the intercom
button.

"Get me the commander of our observation team at the
Rio Bravo, then hold a line open to Colonel Vargas at
Nueva Rosita," Martí ordered his aide in the anteroom.

A moment later, the aide buzzed back. "I have Captain
Chavez at the river, Comrade Prime Minister."

Martí lifted the receiver. "What is the situation there,
captain?"

"Nothing has changed, Prime Minister. The Bravo del
Norte continues to empty into the earth. I am looking at the
waterfall as I speak to you."

"There is no sign that the pit is filling?"

"None, sir. The river is still plunging down far out of
sight below."

Line two lit up on Martí's phone and he slowly lowered
his hand, hesitated a moment, then stabbed the button.

"Colonel Vargas?"

"Yes, Comrade Prime Minister?"

"Start the one-minute countdown. My order is irrevoca-
ble, colonel. At six forty, you are to launch against Dallas."

In the cabin of the Caverunner, Lucia watched a sudden
flurry of activity at the Mexican missile installation. Tech-

nicians and ground crew were scurrying toward a nearby blockhouse, while fuel trucks and supply vehicles rolled off the pad and out of camera range.

"Something's happening at Nueva Rosita," she said.

Heff looked at the screen. "They're getting ready to launch."

"It will be dawn in thirty-eight seconds," Lucia said, staring at her watch face.

Heff glanced at the radar screen. "That string of pips from the prairie ahead is Shield Line Two," he said. "Each of those radar reflections is a mobile surface-to-air battery. Damn, there must be eighty or a hundred of them."

Lucia kept her eyes on the television monitor, her tongue flicking out every couple of seconds to lick her dry lips.

"Ten seconds," she said, darting a look at her watch.

Heff stared with Lucia at the monitor.

"Five seconds, four, three, two, one. It's dawn."

At Lucia's last word, a cloud of white vapor suddenly shot up out of the Mexican missile silo, and they could see heat waves spread across the pad from the mouth of the tube.

"Ignition," Heff said.

A moment later a tongue of flame licked up out of the tube, and the Mexican missile shot through the silo mouth.

The silver-skinned rocket rose rapidly above the scorched concrete pad, its forty-foot length shuddering slightly as the powerful jet-fueled engine thrust the missile ever faster into the dawn sky over Nueva Rosita.

Four hundred and eighty miles above northern Mexico, CHICO's computer brain flipped another lens over the satellite's television eye. The camera refocused itself and followed the missile as it gained altitude and headed north.

"Attention all batteries, attention all batteries!" The voice from Texas Air Defense headquarters in Waco came excitedly over the radio. "Hostile missile has been launched. Repeat, hostile launched. Line One, ready all surface-to-air batteries."

Heff punched a request into the computer for a navigational fix. "We're seventy miles from Waco," he told

Lucia. "We should be over Shield Line Two in about ten minutes."

"Hostile approaching border," Air Defense broke back in over the radio three minutes later. "Five miles out . . . three. . . . Hostile has entered U.S. airspace. Shield Line One, prepare to lock on radar."

The radio in the Caverunner was silent a moment, then a response came from Shield Line One headquarters on the prairie outside San Antonio.

"Texas Air Defense, this is Shield Line One command. We have hostile on radar. Distance, one hundred ten miles and closing; air-speed, fourteen hundred miles per hour; estimated arrival time over our defenses, four minutes, forty seconds."

"We copy, Shield Line One," Air Defense headquarters replied. "All units, stand by for radar relay."

Heff keyed a command into the computer, and the radar image from outside San Antonio appeared on the screen. "There it is," Heff said, jabbing a finger at the long thin white scar that the Mexican missile left behind as the radar's radius swept the screen.

The radio began to crackle with traflic from the American antiaircraft units spread across southern Texas. "Air Defense, this is Ground Observation Post Four at Elm Creek. That Mexican missile just passed over. Estimated altitude, two hundred feet."

"All batteries, please copy," Air Defense came back. "Hostile now flying at two hundred feet."

"I thought rockets flew through the upper atmosphere," Lucia said.

"Not cruise missiles," Heff said. "That's what makes them so hard to bring down. They hug the ground. One minute the missile is over a defensive position, the next it's twenty miles downrange behind a hill."

The first rays of the rising sun broke over the eastern horizon, flooding the hoverjet cabin with light and sending long shadow fingers across the deserted prairie below.

Heff looked at his watch. "We should be in position in about seven minutes."

"This is Shield Line One," they heard in their earphones. "Hostile now twenty-three point three miles out. Estimated time to our position, one minute."

"We copy, one minute," Air Defense headquarters answered. "All units, keep this radio frequency clear. Repeat, keep frequency clear."

The sun climbed as the seconds ticked by, and the shadows below the Caverunner began to flatten.

"Shield Line One. Hostile now thirty seconds out."

"Individual battery targeting, individual fire," came the command from Texas Air Defense.

In the Caverunner, Heff and Lucia stared at the radar image on the monitor as the Mexican missile approached the first American defenses west of San Antonio.

"Hostile ten seconds out," Shield One reported. "Nine, eight, seven . . ."

The thunderous sound of antiballistic missiles being fired erupted through the radio.

"Hawk missiles launched." The words came from San Antonio. "All batteries, report hit on hostile."

The request brought only silence from the U.S. batteries engaging the enemy in south Texas, and the radar monitor in the Caverunner showed why. The Mexican rocket had begun zigzagging across the screen as the white pips of American antiballistic missiles roared up from the defense line below.

"Its onboard radar has picked up our incoming Hawks," Heff said, pointing at the twisting course of the cruise missile coming at them. "Our surface-to-air stuff will be lucky to come near."

A full two minutes passed by with only the sound of missiles lifting off coming from the radio. Then the staccato bursts of rocket engines tailed off to a few last roars, and the radio fell quiet.

"Shield Line One command to Texas Air Defense." A dispirited voice came on. "No hits reported. Repeat, no hits. Hostile has penetrated our line."

"Air Force Intercept Squadron Three, stand by," Air

Defense ordered. "Hostile has entered your sector. Attack on own initiative. Acknowledge."

"Air Defense, this is Intercept Squadron leader," Heff and Lucia heard a jet fighter pilot answer from somewhere over south Texas. "We are commencing attack. Repeat, we are going in."

For the next several minutes, the radio was full of the sounds of screaming jet engines, the *whoosh* of rockets fired from beneath wings, and the curt and increasingly frustrated epithets of the American fighter pilots as their rocket and cannon fire repeatedly missed the evasive Mexican missile.

"There's Waco below," Lucia said, recognizing the central Texas city from the air.

Heff banked the Caverunner and headed toward their holding position ten miles north of the inner American defense line below.

The voice of the squadron leader came back on the radio. "Texas Air Defense, this is Intercept Squadron leader. My boys are out of rockets and cannon shells. We've shot everything we have to shoot, and we haven't even scratched the son of a bitch."

"Texas Air Defense to Shield Line Two. Hostile has now penetrated fighter defenses. Mexican missile is now one minute fifty seconds south of your positions."

"This is Shield Line Two command. We copy, Air Defense. We have radar contact. Confirm enemy missile is now forty miles south closing at fourteen hundred miles per hour."

Lucia stared at the radar screen in the Caverunner. "That rocket is less than fifty miles away from us now."

"Scared?" Heff asked.

She looked across at Jedediah. "Yes, but not for us, not even for Dallas. The city is doomed no matter what happens. But if that warhead detonates over the prairie down there, the very heart of Texas will be poisoned with radioactivity for thousands of years."

"It's not just Texas at stake, Lucia," he said. "If that nuclear missile gets through, President Wilson will have no choice but to declare war on Mexico. After that, if the

Soviets choose to honor their new mutual defense treaty with Mexico, we could be staring at a global conflagration."

Heff shook his head. "In another eight months, the second millennium will be here. The year two thousand. It seemed so far away when I was a boy, a time when I'd be someone else, a grown man, and the world would be a new and different place."

He bunched his fists against the controls. "Well, everything's changed, and nothing's changed. We've sent men to the moon, to Mars in '95, and last year to Venus. We've conquered most of the cancers, and the new gene-splicing technologies have given us food crops that can grow on subarctic tundra and Sahara sand. For the first time in man's entire damn history, an end to starvation is in sight."

Heff looked at Lucia, rage in his eyes. "And yet, no matter how far man's intellect expands, it seems, still there is the animal in us, the instinct to kill, to war. The only difference between men like Ralt and Martí and some ape-man murderer with a club is that finally the weapons have grown too big and the world too small."

"This is Shield Line Two command." The radio broke the silence in the Caverunner cabin. "Hostile is now fifteen seconds out. All batteries, fire at will."

Heff punched an order into the onboard computer, and the coordinates for the glide path of the cruise missile flashed on the cockpit screen. He brought the Caverunner's bow around and dove for the rendezvous position two hundred feet above the prairie below.

"Hostile ten seconds away . . . nine . . . eight . . . seven . . . ." The prairie before the hoverjet suddenly erupted with a fusillade of U.S. Hawk antiballistic missiles. Singly and in clusters, the dart-shaped rockets rose in a seemingly impenetrable curtain of fire.

The hoverjet reached the intercept point, and Heff quickly swiveled the turbojets to the vertical hover position. He grabbed a pair of binoculars from a compartment between the seats and swept the horizon to the south. The

Hawk missiles were spurting from the prairie like a fusillade of arrows from the bows of a thousand archers.

Then, low against the prairie between two U.S. ground batteries, the slanting sun glinted off the silver skin of the Mexican missile emerging through the shroud of dust and rocket exhaust over Shield Line Two.

"Here it comes," Heff said, tossing the binoculars aside. "Take the controls, Lucia. I'll operate the laser cannon. The moment I give the word, slam the thrusters into horizontal flight. It won't be easy, but keep as close to that cruise as you can."

"I'll do my best, Jedediah," Lucia said, her hands white-knuckled on the controls as Heff leaned forward and turned on the laser cannon. He went through a systems check, swinging the cannon barrel to port and starboard with the manual lever on the control panel before him.

Lucia suddenly grabbed Heff's arm, her eyes riveted on the silhouette of Dallas dead ahead on the horizon. "Jedediah, look. Look. The buildings on the west side of the city. They're shaking."

Heff followed Lucia's eyes toward the violently swaying glass and steel towers. "They're going down."

A moment later, one-third of the downtown section of Dallas, 150 square blocks of densely packed buildings, began suddenly to shudder; then, seconds later, they plunged from sight into the earth.

Heff brought his eyes back to the radar. The tubular shape of the Mexican missile was rapidly approaching the hover-jet's position on the screen.

"A thousand yards and closing," Heff read from the radar screen. "Five hundred yards. Get ready. Two hundred . . . one hundred . . . go!"

Lucia jammed the thrusters forward, and the Caverunner screamed down the glide path toward Dallas, the Mexican missile rocketing past only fifty feet above them.

Then the cruise was out in front, suddenly zigzagging violently as its defensive radar registered the alien aircraft now tight on its tail. Heff angled the barrel of the laser cannon up toward the fleeing missile and hit the fire button.

A pulse of intense white light split the dawn sky and stabbed toward the silvered rocket already a quarter mile away. At that instant, the missile's radar ordered the guidance system to make a turn, and the laser beam shot past twenty yards from the side of the cruise.

"Damn," Heff swore, as Lucia snapped the controls over and followed the turning missile. He lined the laser cannon barrel up again with the rocket, trying to anticipate the next turn. The missile was dead ahead, now, but leaving the Caverunner farther behind with each second.

Heffs finger hovered above the trigger button. This would be the last shot, he knew. If he missed, there was nothing left to stop the nuclear warhead from detonating over Dallas. He waited . . . waited . . . *now*. Heff stabbed the fire button and watched with Lucia as the laser ray slashed through the early morning sky and burned past the fleeing missile close enough to sear its silvered skin.

The Mexican rocket wobbled a moment, its port side blackened by the near heat of the laser, then retained its trajectory and sped off to the north.

Heff reached over and eased Lucia's hand back on the thrust throttle. "It's no use. The missile's out of range now."

Together they watched dejectedly as the nuclear-tipped Mexican rocket roared toward the shattered silhouette of Dallas, now only seventy miles away across the prairie.

"We'd better get the hell out of here," Heff said finally. "That warhead will detonate over Dallas in about three minutes."

Lucia brought the Caverunner around and they fled south, away from the nuclear firestorm that would soon consume Dallas and flail the prairie for miles around with poison winds.

"Bring her nose up," Heff said. "Let's climb."

"To watch the end, Jedediah?"

"That's right, Lucia," he said bitterly. "To watch the end from a damned grandstand seat at ten thousand feet. I've never seen a war start before. Have you? Don't you wonder what that moment looks like, feels like? That instant of crossover from sanity to madness, that vacuum between creation and death? I want to experience that moment, Lucia. I want to see the face of evil."

"I don't want to see the war start," Lucia said softly. "Perhaps I'm a coward, but I'm afraid that for the rest of my life that would be all I could see. I'm afraid it would close my eyes to the good that is also in the world."

They were both silent for almost two minutes as the hoverjet angled up and away from the doomed city behind them. At ten thousand feet, Lucia leveled off and the Caverunner began to circle eighty miles from Dallas.

The radio crackled alive again. "Texas Air Defense to all ground and air forces. Enemy missile is now thirty seconds from Dallas."

Heff suddenly came half up out of his seat. "Lucia, the city. Look at Dallas. Everything's moving."

Lucia's mouth parted at the sight of the forest of skyscrapers trembling on the horizon far below, like a city of toy blocks kicked by a kid. As they watched, half the buildings disappeared downward, leaving the surviving steel and glass towers crashing against each other.

Seconds later the remaining rock and dirt crust under Dallas collapsed en masse into the titanic black sinkhole below, taking the last of the broken, windowless buildings down with it. A huge, roiling cloud of dust and debris shot into the air over the yawning pit as the final 110 square blocks of Dallas disappeared into the earth.

"Enemy missile is ten seconds from Dallas," Air Defense reported over the radio. "All exposed personnel take cover. Repeat, take cover."

Heff grabbed the binoculars. Quickly he picked up the forty-foot-long silvered rocket against the background of thick brown dust. "The missile will reach the rim of the crater in a couple of seconds."

"Enemy missile is now five seconds from Dallas," Air Defense radioed. "Four seconds, three seconds . . ."

"It's over the sinkhole," Heff said, as the Mexican missile disappeared into the dust cloud.

". . . two seconds . . . one second. Enemy missile over Dallas."

Heff and Lucia froze in their seats, braced for the shock wave of the nuclear blast below. Their breaths tight in their chests, they waited suspended in time.

The seconds passed in excruciating silence. No mushroom cloud materialized on the prairie below. No white-hot blast wave tore out from behind the curtain of dust around the immense sinkhole.

"What's happening?" Lucia asked finally.

Heff caught the glint of sunlight off bright metal. The reflection was coming through the dust curtain along the western border of the sinkhole. As he watched, the silvered image followed the rim of the crater to the right, then curved around the eastern lip and disappeared again behind the dust.

"The missile looks like it's circling the sinkhole, Lucia," Heff said incredulously. "Almost as if it's searching . . ." He yanked the binoculars from his eyes. "That's it! The ground radar on that Mexican missile is searching for the city."

"I don't understand, Jedediah. The missile has arrived over Dallas. Why doesn't the warhead go off?"

"It can't go off, don't you see? A cruise missile is programmed to hug the ground in its flight path. The warhead it carries has to be set to detonate low over the target, maybe two or three hundred feet. The missile's flight recorder is telling the computer the warhead is over Dallas, but the downward radar pulses are bouncing off the bottom of the sinkhole and telling the computer the missile is still too high."

Lucia suddenly saw where Jedediah was leading. "How deep do you think the crater is?"

"Our Gravprobe readings last night showed the sinkhole floor almost two thousand feet below Dallas," Heff said. "That means that missile will have to circle down eighteen hundred feet into the crater before its radar reads solid stone and steel and triggers the warhead."

Heff hugged Lucia and grinned jubilantly.

"If the warhead goes off that low, it will bring the walls

of the sinkhole down on top. The radioactive fallout will be buried under billions of tons of rock and earth."

He released her and brought the binoculars up in time to see the Mexican missile circle past again through the thinning dust. It was much lower now, its silver fuselage almost level with the prairie surrounding the sinkhole.

"Its nose is down," Heff said. "It's diving, all right."

The missile had taken thirty or forty seconds to make its last sweep around the lip of the crater. Heff counted the seconds in his head. A minute passed, and the rocket failed to reappear. Heff kept the binoculars to his eyes for another thirty seconds, then slowly lowered the glasses and looked at Lucia.

"It's gone in," he said. "It's gone into the earth after Dallas."

Six hundred feet deep in the immense sinkhole, the Mexican missile continued to circle down relentlessly into the gloom, its radar scout searching for substance in the void below.

Fifteen hundred feet down, the radar in the spiraling rocket picked up the square steel corpses of Dallas's skyscrapers protruding from the rubble of the city on the sinkhole floor.

The radar passed the information to the missile's computer brain: Target five hundred feet below.

The nuclear rocket made one last spiral against the dark gray walls of the yawning crater, its nose angling ever lower. At four hundred feet, the triggering mechanism for the nuclear warhead clicked on, anticipating the detonation order that would come from the computer at two hundred feet.

Several acres of prairie overhanging the crater lip two thousand feet above suddenly gave way, and a deluge of huge dirt clods and full-grown trees rained down through the dusk around the lowering missile.

One hundred feet from detonation, eddies of wind washed back by the rocket's jet engine began to whistle through the steel skeletons of buildings on the sinkhole floor, and a low moaning rose from the broken body of Dallas.

A moment later the eerie lament vanished under a

thunderous, reverberating clap as the missile's nuclear warhead detonated in a white-hot blast of heat, sound, and shock waves. The confined power of the nuclear explosion concentrated incredible pressure against the sides of the sinkhole and forced the concave walls of the crater far back into the earth.

Shock waves hammered against the undermined ground above, and hundreds of square miles of overhanging rim began to plunge into the sinkhole, rapidly sealing the radioactive fallout in the depths of the huge pit.

Once started, the avalanche of earth around the borders of the crater fed on itself. The crater grew wider and wider as more and more of the prairie slid down into the funnel of the sinkhole.

Finally, minutes later, the huge avalanche slowed, then stopped. The surging earth had almost refilled the crater, leaving a gently sloping two-hundred-foot-deep depression that stretched for thirty miles across the prairie.

For the first time in five days, the ground of central Texas lay quiet in the early morning sun. Dallas had gone down, in death a sacrifice to life, and in Washington and Moscow and Mexico men pulled back from war, and peace gathered itself again.

DAY SIX

APRIL 15, 1999

AFTER DAWN

Lying on his army cot, weatherman Herb Mueller opened his eyes and listened. Still more asleep than awake, he slowly realized he was hearing the sound of drops pelting the canvas roof of the small tent he shared with his wife at the evacuation center at Fort Hood.

Then his senses focused and it hit him. Rain. God Almighty, rain! He leaped from his cot and charged through the tent flaps out into the storm. Laughing and crying at the same time, he stood for several minutes with his face lifted to the deluge, letting the water soak through his pajamas and run in rivulets down his chest and back.

Rain. It was all going to be all right now. The job. Janet. Life. It was all going to be all right.

Some said the fusillade of dust particles that shot into the atmosphere when Dallas went down had seeded the clouds. Whatever the reason, the day after the city disappeared, it rained heavily in central Texas for the first time in five years.

A hundred and twenty miles to the north, Jedediah Heffernan banked the Caverunner through the soaking sky and dove toward the shallow thirty-mile-wide bowl that now cupped the prairie over the grave of Dallas. The depression stretched from Arlington in the west to Mesquite in the east, from Richardson in the north to Lancaster in the south.

Beside him, Lucia Sanchez leaned forward in the co-pilot's seat. "Jedediah, look. The basin over the sinkhole. It's beginning to fill with water."

"Lake Dallas," Heff said. "I'll bet you a hundred bucks that when it's full they call it Lake Dallas."

Lucia sat back suddenly and shivered. "I just remembered what I felt like yesterday at this time. That missile was homing in on Dallas, and war looked certain."

"After those news reports from Mexico last night, I'd say war is very remote this morning, Lucia," Heff said.

The recklessness of the prime minister in almost bringing on an unwinnable nuclear war with the United States had terrified the more moderate members of the Politboro in Mexico City. Teodoro Luis Martí had been summarily sacked. An hour later, the Politboro had elevated General Hugo Santamaría to the nation's highest post. The wise old soldier who had fought to stop war would lead Mexico into the second millennium.

The nearness of nuclear war had also sobered the leaders of the Soviet Union. The mutual defense treaty with Mexico would go unsigned. The senior missile targeting officer was ordered home at once and promoted to colonel for his bravery in defending the missile silo with General Santamaría. Demyan Turgenev would return a hero.

Heff brought the Caverunner in low, skimming over the wet prairie, then angled the thrust ports and set the hoverjet down.

"C'mon," he said, popping the bubble.

"It's raining out there, you idiot!" Lucia shrieked, the deluge already stringing her hair.

Heff climbed down and walked back to the cargo compartment. "Are you coming or not?"

"All right, all right." Lucia slid down the slippery fuselage and stomped across the muddy ground to Heff's side. "What? What is so important you have to drag me out in a monsoon?"

He pulled a large flat box from the cargo compartment and handed it to her. "Your gown, my lady."

Lucia looked at him quizzically, then took the box and opened it. Inside was a long white ballroom dress.

She looked up from the dress to see Heff holding a formal-wear suit of tie and tails up before himself. "You remembered," she said softly, her eyes full.

"My lady, I shall never forget. If you wish, you have a date on this day for the rest of your life. A date to dance."

"I wish," Lucia said.

"Done. Now if my lady would care to change, we'll start the music."

Lucia laughed and tore off her shirt and jeans as Heff struggled with his wet tuxedo pants. She pulled the dress over her head and turned. "Zip me up."

Lucia tied Heff's bow tie, then he reached into the storage compartment and took out a tape cassette player.

"I hope my lady likes Strauss."

"Your lady loves Strauss."

Heff turned the cassette on and put the player on the wing of the Caverunner. The strains of the "Blue Danube" wafted around them.

Heff bowed formally to Lucia. "My lady, would you honor me with this waltz?"

"It would be my very great pleasure, sir."

Heff took Lucia in his arms and they began to dance, joined hands and eyes, twirling and dipping across the puddled prairie while around them the rains fell and fell and fell.